A. G. Riddle

The Tory's Daughter

A Romance of the North-West 1812-1813

A. G. Riddle

The Tory's Daughter
A Romance of the North-West 1812-1813

ISBN/EAN: 9783744676847

Printed in Europe, USA, Canada, Australia, Japan

Cover: Foto ©Andreas Hilbeck / pixelio.de

More available books at **www.hansebooks.com**

THE
TORY'S DAUGHTER

A Romance of the North-West

1812–1813

BY

A. G. RIDDLE.

AUTHOR OF "BART RIDGELEY."

———

NEW YORK & LONDON
G. P. PUTNAM'S SONS
The Knickerbocker Press
1888

Press of
G. P. Putnam's Sons
New York

CONTENTS.

ii
Contents.

PREFATORY NOTE.

In the following pages will be found a somewhat romantic story of the war of 1812–1813, on our northwestern border, written from the ground occupied by the refugees of the Revolution and their descendants in Canada.

The fortunes of my people are so interwoven with the incidents of the national struggle, that their history becomes largely a history of the war itself, and of some of the commanders on both sides.

A study has been made of many of the writers of that stirring but now obscure period, American, British, and Canadian, and an attempt made, subordinate to the main purpose, to place the leading incidents within easy apprehension of the reader. Misapprehensions and misstatements have not intentionally been repeated. Some popular stories and beliefs on one side as on the other, have been corrected. I may add that for all the statements in reference to the Shawanoe chief, save some of the incidents of his personal relations to my characters, there is ample authority, as the references will show.

The battle of Fort Stephenson, which so signally

marked the sharp change in the fortunes of the war, as also the great sea fight of Lake Erie, exercised such a controlling influence upon the destiny of my people, that they could not be wholly omitted from my narrative.

Whatever may be the fortunes of this work, it is believed that in its pages will be found something of the spirit and flavor of pioneer life in the West, of that time which sober history cannot embody, and which our literature has so slightly lent itself to preserve.

To the elder generation, the war of 1812 on the north-western frontier is already a legend; to the younger, the dimmest of traditions. Isolated as was its stage, small in actual event, yet most momentous in consequences, it has never received that attention and consideration which its intrinsic importance entitles it to. The war on that frontier began with the fall of Detroit, in mid August, 1812, and the events immediately preceding it; and ended on the fifth of October, 1813; and though it raged along the north-eastern and south-western borders until January, 1815, through all the Northwest, peace between the great parties was as assured as if secured by a treaty, and the interrupted tide of immigration at once resumed its westward flow.

The battle of the Thames put an end, substantially, to a chronic, and at times a most disastrous Indian war of more than sixty years duration, in the valley of the Ohio and basin of Lake Erie, and forever broke the power, the hearts and hopes of the immediate western tribes.

I have resisted the temptation to annoy a reader with long notes. For the curious, whose memory or means of information may not enable him to recall or trace them, I have subjoined some supplemental matter of the after fortunes of three or four men and events, mentioned in my pages.

I had a wish to tell a story which I hoped would interest some readers. As I made a study of the ground and material, there came a wish almost as strong, to awaken interest in the forgotten history of the Northwest.

THE AUTHOR.

THE TORY'S DAUGHTER.

CHAPTER I.

A MISTAKE AND AN ACCIDENT.

IT was a day of late October and past mid-afternoon; a day of squalls, rain, and flurries of snow on the stormy lake. A small craft had, with difficulty, been brought to near the mouth of a river, from which were landed her passengers. That accomplished, the boat pulled back and the vessel turned her course downward.

Seemingly, to the small party thus left, the place and surroundings were not what were expected.

"There is some mistake," said the elder of the two gentlemen, a grave, handsome man, well advanced in years, with the bearing of one accustomed to the world and affairs. "This is not a landing; there are no signs of the village; none of the presence of the natives; everything is wild, savage."

The river ran from the south, discharging its waters into the southern margin of Lake Erie, west of its middle. The ship was from Long Point, on the other side, and below. Its purpose was to land this party with their luggage, the means of a few days' subsistence, in the wild region of that side of the lake.

"The landing may be higher up," said the young man, of unmistakable military bearing, though in citizens' dress;

"they were in a deuced hurry to be rid of us, and get off this beastly coast," he added.

"There were good reasons for that. Can this be the Huron? You know there are several Huron rivers. Let us explore above," was the reply of the elder gentleman.

The two ascended the high bank, and looked about them. No signs of man or of human dwellings met their eager examination.

This was in the autumn of 1811, the period of exasperation between the owners of the opposite shores of the lake, and before the holders of the southern had more than nominal possession of much of their side.

From their fruitless examination the two turned silently back to their boxes, bales, and the subordinate males of the party by the river's margin, anxiety on the face of the elder, disgust in the look of the younger. "Coming to this nasty place on the word of an Indian. Was there ever anything so d—— absurd!" he exclaimed.

"You seemed very willing to come," said the other coolly. "As for the Indian, you'd better repeat that to Edith. She is apparently looking for chestnuts very unconcernedly, up there," with a motion of his hand in the direction.

The other men of the party were three soldiers, in laborers' apparel, and a servant of the elder gentleman. Two of the other sex completed it. When they landed, these, under the lead of her called Edith, took their way up to the higher land, looking about and searching for chestnuts. They were now seen taking their way down toward the group by the river's margin. Leisurely they moved. Their presence in that wild place entitles them to brief mention. Youthful, as their light, easy movements showed, both above medium height, with something in the air of each as if accustomed to care for herself, to whom the small attentions of male attendants might be but irksome. The face of Edith we see, when near enough, is beautiful; unmistakably virginal, fine eyes, with marked straight, heavy brows, noticeable at this distance. The upper person clad in a gayly-worked, close-fitting habit, from which descended a skirt, leaving the ankle free; the small feet daintily cased in bead-wrought moccasins, the head protected with a maroon-colored turban-like hat, with a small, white plume. A sash over the right shoulder, sustaining a small, fur-covered satchel against the left side, completed a figure which harmonized well with the idea of out-door adventure.

Her companion's appearance was more picturesque. Fully her height, her form had not yet received the magic of roundness it was destined to. A child of the native race, not so dark as the average, her face, longer favored and finely featured, bore indications of a fine strain of ancestors. Her dress, though of sober-colored fabrics, was half barbaric; head and feet clothed like the other, save her cap was scarlet, and ornamented with a war-eagle's feather, which few women were permitted to wear. Above her sash was seen the ivory hilt of a small dagger, which in the hand of a spirited woman, might prove something more than an ornament, for which it was worn. Her eyes, Oriental in shape and color, almost too large for the size of the finely-moulded face, were striking, and she moved with the light, sinuous grace of the young daughters of chiefs.

"We are on the wrong side," cried Edith, when within hearing. "The huts are over there," pointing to the west side; "you can see them from the top of the hill," she added.

"Oh, I knew there was some nasty blunder!" cried the young gentleman, his eyes resting on the face of the speaker, in a way indicating entire satisfaction with that, whatever other source of annoyance he might have.

The whole party made its way to the top of the bank, led by the girls, when after a little search the Indian maiden re-discovered the small opening through which their view had been obtained of the supposed cabin. Each of the gentlemen secured a sight of the top and outline of the body of a small building amid the trees, quite at the crest of the answering hill, on the other side, though the younger doubted its being one of the several huts they had expected to find on the east side.

"It would look differently if you had dined, Captain," said the young lady, with a little flash of sarcasm, turning to renew her suspended nutting, amid the newly-fallen leaves at her feet, the fragrance of which she inhaled with zest.

All the men of the party examined the supposed hut. One went so far as to distinguish a chimney and see smoke rising from it—as he said.

"You can always see smoke from a chimney," answered the chief of the party. "We are near enough to be heard there; let us give them a shout," he added. "Now, my men—all together!"

In response the three, with the leader, united their voices quite effectively.

"Bravo! Bravo!" cried Edith, clapping her hands. "Captain, I did not hear your mighty voice," she said.

"Once again!" from the chief, followed by a more decisive effort. "Still another!" The response made the near foliage quiver.

"Still the captain remained mute. In his present

frame of mind, his voice would raise the dead!" was the young lady's comment—resuming her labor.

No response from the opposite bank.

"Perhaps the men had better discharge their pieces," suggested the elder gentleman, to him called Captain.

"Well, let them fire," was the reply, with a look toward the three, which they understood.

The day was damp; the old flint locks hung fire, but finally roared out in the still wood with startling effect.

"They'll hear that, if they can hear anything. Reload," was the captain's comment and order.

With silent eagerness the whole party, including the girls, awaited the result. Two, three, five minutes, and the silence remained unbroken, the aspect on the other side unchanged. No man or thing appeared.

"Well," said Edith, the first to speak, "the invading army of British Tories and Indians will now proceed to assault the enemy's works, who fled at their approach."

"It may be well to remember where we are," said the elder gentleman to her, reprovingly.

"Certainly," she answered, laughing. "Pray tell me, and I will never forget it," vivaciously.

"And what we are," added the captain, dryly.

"As if the senior Captain of His Majesty's 41st of Foot, could ever forget what he is, or let us; and as if any disguise would hide him from Yankee eyes," she replied, with mock gravity.

"Who has talked of disguises," demanded the gentleman, possibly a little uncomfortable in his present costume, in a *quasi* enemy's country.

"Oh, there has been no declaration of war," said the teasing girl, assuringly. "For me, I would be very glad to see any of our cousins just now, in any guise."

"The place is deserted or not occupied," said the leader, who had been attentively observing the hut and locality. "Still it is our only chance for the night. What say you, Captain?"

"Nothing is easier than to cross and try it," replied the captain, arousing himself at the idea of action. He may have been held a little at disadvantage by Edith; if so its effect disappeared on this call.

"My men, we must cross this water—a raft will do it;" he called out to them. "Lively now!" leading the way rapidly down to their landing, followed by the whole party, Edith and her companion taking their way leisurely in the rear.

Among their effects were two or three axes, and within a short time there floated by the immediate shore, a raft, apparently buoyant and strong enough to pass the full banked stream, here some twenty or thirty yards wide.

When all was ready the captain approached the watchful and silent girls, hat in hand, and said, addressing Edith, "The ark waits, will my lady permit me to conduct her on board?"

"Certainly," she replied, "if the women are to-take the lead. Otherwise embark the army and baggage, and we will witness the voyage with composure, whatever the result."

"There is prudence in that; thanks," was his reply.

The traps were placed on board, the men, armed with long poles, under the captain's command, made the transit with little trouble, and returned for the more precious freight. The girls and the elder gentlemen took places on the raft, which was launched up-stream, caught and borne down by the current, which it traversed, was approaching some drift, formed by the bodies of two trees, the roots of which adhered to the opposite bank, against the upper side of which the float had rested on its former voyage. When the edge of the raft was now within a yard or two of this resting-place, in its downward trend, the bed pieces at one corner suddenly parted. Near this opening stood the elder man, and to avoid falling into the water, he made a sudden leap to the near drift. He failed to make his footing good, fell backward, his head striking with much force on a timber of the float, partially stunning him, and he went helplessly into the river, there of considerable depth, and having a current under the drift.

Edith and her companion, under the common impulse which induced her father to spring from the raft, also made a rush for the drift-wood, which they securely gained, and turning she saw the unfortunate man sinking in the black water. She uttered a loud cry of alarm— "My father! my father! help! help!" and would herself have leaped in had she not been restrained by the Indian girl.

The servant was on the west shore with the baggage. The first care of the captain and of his men was given to their own temporary safety, in the breaking up of the raft. In the emergency what might have been the fate of the fallen man cannot be known. Just at the instant unexpected aid intervened. With the attention of all upon the raft its progress and passengers, no one had seen the approach down the western bank of an active form, which reached the margin of the river as the float gave way. He saw the elder man fall and disappear. He sprang along the drift and leaped into the water a moment later and also disappeared. One of the men gained the place, and pushed aside the floating bits which formed the treacherous raft, now closing over the surface next the drift.

Edith held her breath in a spasm of suspense. It was no considerable part of a minute, though to her an age, when almost within reach of her hand the water parted, the head of the rescuer burst up through it, the face turned to her, almost laughing, with the water dripping from it.

"He is all right!" he cried, cheerily, to her, lifting her father's head and upper person above the river's surface, an arm around the intrepid rescuer's neck, now so near that Edith secured her father's hand and with the aid of the Indian girl and the man nearest, he was drawn upon the drift-wood, where the stranger, seen to be quite youthful, had already gained footing. The captain had been partly immersed and now with the two others gained that refuge.

Without waiting for words the stranger took up the form of the injured and unconscious man, and with little aid bore him to the near bank. His words as he lifted him, gayly spoken, were—"I shall not wet him much." The captain busied himself in offering aid to Edith to gain the land, which she did in advance of him and was by her father's side, as the young stranger and the servant placed him on the level land, on which his feet were permitted to rest. Feeling the earth under them the still dazed man, who had taken but little water, instinctively straightened up, with decided signs of returning consciousness, while his lungs made vigorous effort to expel the intruding liquid.

Pausing for a moment, while the party gathered around him, the stranger said—addressing the captain— "There are no inhabitants within miles of here. I am camping in an old hut up the hill. We can make him comfortable there. I fear it is your only chance." He looked and spoke very pleasantly.

"It seems so," said the Englishman, ruefully.

"We accept your offer with gratitude," cried Edith, effusively. Then turning to the still dazed man, she wiped the blood of a scalp wound from the face. He was now so far recovered as to nearly support his weight on his legs. He caught his daughter's voice and turned his eyes upon her, with a little smile hovering on his lips, which discovering, she kissed them tenderly.

With Edith's words the youth moved forward, still the chief support of the injured man. Just at the foot of the acclivity—the river's secondary bank—they met the tall, sinewy form of an old hunter, who came striding down toward them. At their approach he paused, and ran his observant eyes over the party; and then with them on the face of the young man, he awaited their approach.

" My old hunter—Carter," said the youth in explanation. And to the new-comer—"He got a dip in the river," he said. "We will give him our cabin. The other huts will serve the rest of his party."

" All right!" was the laconic reply.

" And he saved his life," said Edith to the hunter.

" Uv course," was the reply, and the old man turning, strode up the hill, followed by the slower party, for whom the young man selected an easier ascent.

At the summit was discovered three huts, standing near each other, around which had once been a small space of cleared land, now fast being reclaimed by the forest. The new growths had been cut away from the entrances of the huts, rendering them accessible. The larger was divided into two apartments, with a rude chimney and hearth, in the first of which Carter had already relit the fire. Near this he had also placed the younger hunter's pallet, upon which the injured man was extended, when the younger, referring the strangers to the other two as also at their disposal, said he would send them some roast venison for dinner, withdrew, leaving the now conscious man to the care of his party and their own resources. Their luggage was brought up, the huts taken possession of, and the strangers made their dispositions for the night, now closing down in the solemn old wood.

Ere his departure, the young man removed from the principal cabin his few effects, saying to the young lady, glancing about the rude, small apartments—"It is all I can offer you. Had you sent me word—" finishing with his pleasant laugh, leaving her to guess his meaning.

"And you?" she asked, a little anxiously.

"O, we—we have a charming place down by the spring; plenty of shelter and warmth." Then he bowed his adieu, saying he would venture to inquire after her father, later.

The injured man was placed in dry wraps, and the hurt of his head, found not to be great, was tenderly cared for. The girls were placed in possession of the inner apartment, and everything arranged for their comfort as far as the extemporized means permitted.

The contribution from the hunters was a well roasted, saddle of venison, which, with the sauce of keen appetites, was pronounced excellent. The elder hunter was an experienced cook and caterer of the resources of the woods, neat for his kind, and this was from his hand, and with the stores of the travellers, made their late repast a feast.

As the young hunter left the cabin for his near camp-fire, rekindled in the darkening wood, he was met by the captain.

"What may be the name of this river?" he asked.

"Black River."

"Black River? Oh! ah, this is the Black River—black enough. Is there a town—a place, on, or near it?"

"Cleveland is the nearest. No town west, save Indian towns, till you reach Detroit."

"Cleveland—ah! Cleveland is east—about how far?"

"Well, some thirty miles."

"Is there a Huron river on this side—where is that?'"

"That is to the west."

"And how far may it be to the Huron—about how far?"

"Carter!" called the young man to the hunter, "How far is it to the Huron?"

"Thirty-five miles, peraps;" was Carter's answer, repeated by the youth to the Englishman.

"And woods all the way?"

"All the way. No prairie, no clearings on the route, as I understand—is there, Carter?" who approached them when called to.

"Every mile on't woods"; in the sententious mode of speech which the forest imposes on its denizens.

"Any river to cross between this Black and the Huron?"

"The Vermillion, and several smaller streams," answered Carter.

Thanks were not a commodity with the stranger. Having received the required information, he turned away toward the brow of the high bank, not attempting to hide from himself the annoyance the position gave him.

"Black River! Damned black! Lucky Cleveland is no nearer. Forty miles to the Huron!" adding five by way of aggravation, and blowing out a long whistle. "Well, we are planted here for a week. What if the old fanatic had lost his life. He would have been drowned had it not been for this damned young prig, with his girl face and red lips. The old hunter eyes *us*, the young one will see nothing but— Has been in their army I'd bet a year's pay." A pause. "Well, I shall have things my own way till the old man is on his legs again, here in the woods. Damned little good it will do me though! Damn the woods anyway!" he added, peevishly, turning back to the huts.

Night was in the woods, and very soon its prowlers, the predacious, the hunters, were stealing from their hiding-places abroad. Notes and signs of their presence might have been detected by an expert in forestry, which none of the strangers were, save the Indian maiden, now housed with Edith, who was a lover of the woods.

A lovely spring made its way out of the side hill, a third of the way from the top, not far and up-stream from the larger hut, forming a dimple on the fair earth's cheek, whose limpid thread in several tiny cascades, found its way to the near river. Near this was the fire and cooking place of the hunters. An old sail, stretched from the northern lip of the dell formed by the spring, protected it from the wind; was ample shelter from rain also. Here they passed the night, leaving the huts to the strangers, so curiously thrown upon them, and who were now the subjects of their low voiced conversation. The taciturn Carter was the principal speaker, an indication that the theme was one of unusual interest for him.

"Ef ever I seen a British officer this man is rightly

called cap'en, and these three are solgers; their guns ˷ was inspected less'n a week ago. Appen 'roun there'n you'll find 'em stanin' guard there now. They cum in 'ere on that air sloop or sumthin. I seen 'er makin off fore I hearn their guns; an' them was a signal fer sumthin 'er ruther."

"That may all be true; what is the inference?"

"They cum frum Canady," was his summing up.

"Very likely; well?"

"Ye see, the las' we heern Guv'ner Harrison wus a marchin on the Prophit. They say there may be war enny day."

"What has all that to do with this party, Carter? You are shrewd."

"A man hez to be. Wal, they'r 'ere by mistake. This 'ere cap'en knows nuthin o' this side. They thought this wus the Huern ye see; an 'spected someone else to anser their guns, ye see."

"All very likely. The Huron is more than 200 miles from the Prophet's town."

"Yis, but its pesky near the Wyn'dots an Senicas and ole Round-head, Walk-in-the-Water an' them air though."

"They are fast friends of ours."

"An' that may be the reason for this 'ere jant. W'y don't they say 'oo an' wat they air?" spiritedly.

"Why should they? The woods are free to everybody. Were they on mischief they would have had a story for whoever they might meet. Why should the young lady be with them? And this Indian princess?"

"She's a lady, sartin; tho' I never seen menny."

"English?"

"Merakin born—I reckon."

"And this Indian girl,—an Indian princess?"

"Wal, there 'tis, ye see. These 'er spicious times. W'at is she 'ere fer, but to see 'er relations—some o' the chiefs? Wal, ef war cums, I'l take a'nuther crack at 'em —hanged ef I don't."

"They may be on their way to convert the Indians— who knows? Then the young ladies would be of the party."

"Yis, 'n the cap'en an solgers, uv course. They'd cunvart em."

"Well, they will be here two or three days, and we must do what we can for them," laughing.

"Sartin! Sartin! We'l give the young lady 'n 'er pa, 'n yer princess—aint she bright?—briled bass fer breck-fas, an' wunt grudge the cap'en a bite on't, nuther," responded the old hunter, cordially.

In the rude apartment, dimly lighted save where the brands on the hearth gave out light, were father and daughter, so strangely surrounded in the heart of the forest. The father, quite himself, propped on his rude couch, holding his child's hand as she sat by his side, her eyes on his face, which in the lamp's slender light looked wan. A glance would advise a stranger that these were more than even their relationship ordinarily implies to each other. The accident, the imminent peril and res-cue, the intrepidity of the young hunter, whose presence was not the least remarkable of the group of incidents, were the theme of their conversation. Tears were in the girl's eyes unwiped, in the silence which followed.

"When I left the land of which this wilderness is a part," said the man, in a sad voice, "in anger and bitter-ness I vowed when I revisited it—when I set foot on it again—I would come in judgment, in wrath, with sword, with fire. I am not an hour here—I fall, get a little rap on the head, plunge into one of its smallest rivers, am drawn under a log, pulled out limp and lifeless, like a soiled rag. There is no will or purpose left in me."

"You seem to me to be your dearest, truest self, papa, dear," said the child, laying her warm, tender cheek caressingly against his face. "The land you left was always dear to blessed mother's heart," she said, lifting her head.

"Yes; you women have power and strength for loves. Hatreds are necessary to steel a man's heart to the purposes of justice, retribution,"—turning away.

"Can hatreds be a part of justice?" asked the girl.

"Man's hatred is a part of God's justice," he said, with his eyes from her. "How dead and empty these things seem now—mere soulless sounds," added he, turning his eyes to hers, with their former tenderness.

Edith's face brightened as she received again their light. There was a minute's silence. The softness stole again into the man's face; with it came the expression of another thought.

"That face—does it come from an old-time dream, a picture, or is it a half-recalled memory; a face breaking on one in a crowd, which you are never to see again? Have you seen it before, Edith?"

"Never, I know, till it broke from the black water so near me. It laughed even then—I never shall forget it. I never should had I ever seen it before," she answered.

"It is a face to haunt one," he continued. "I caught it on the bank, coming from my daze I suppose, just as I felt my feet on the ground. My eyes were open, and the face turned to me. It was all as in a dream; I really saw nothing else. Have you seen him since?"

"Only a moment.   He lingered here a minute—he had to leave us to ourselves, you know."

"Yes; we will have him here in the morning.   I hope to be out to-morrow.   What can we say to him?"

"What we feel—only we cannot express it.   I am sure he will be more embarrassed than we."

"What is your impression of him?" asked the father.

"Oh, I can't tell—now.   He is the centre of light, strong, lovely; the only time I ever saw a man, except my father, so surrounded, so acting, that that word lovely could apply to him.   I fear he is but commonplace after all, and will look like all the rest in the morning;" plaintively the last words were uttered.

"How sad that would be!" almost laughing.   "Well, give me a good-night kiss, and call Peters," he said.

"It would be sad," she said, bending, her lips placed to his.   Then, calling the man from the outside, she lifted the blanket which served as a door, and passed to the inner room; a lamp was burning in this also, and she found the Indian girl by a small window, a mere opening which commanded a view of the lower part of the wood, made luminous by the camp-fire of the hunters already mentioned.

"What is it, Anita?" she asked, going to the girl's side.

"Him camp fire," in her imperfect English.

"Whose camp fire?"

"Young chief."

"So you call him a chief," she said, looking out. "What makes you think he is a chief?"

"Him chief!"—positively.

The view disclosed little save the light.

"I see nothing but the fire, and the trees," said Edith.

"Him there; hunter there."

"No matter; my sister must retire. We are not to look for young chiefs," she said, gayly, hanging a bit of drapery over the opening. "Now say your prayer, as I shall mine, and we will go to sleep like two good little girls in the wood," softly.

The Indian maiden approached her, smiling so as to disclose the gleam of her fine teeth, received and returned her kiss, knelt by her low couch, clasped her slim hands in silent devotion, and, already arrayed for rest, laid her slender form to repose.

The experience of the Caucasian had been wide and varied, from a king's palace to an Indian's wigwam. She readily adjusted herself to her present rude surroundings. A well arranged series of the spiney, small branches of the fragrant hemlock, formed the bulk of her bed, as that of her adopted sister's, and changing the garments of wakening life for the robes of slumber, she composed herself as well as she might, to await the change.

This was a new experience—fright, actual terror. Her fine nerves were greatly shaken. Her woman's tenderness, her sensibility, her imagination, had all, powerfully, suddenly, without warning, been appealed to. The scene of the river took possession of her. She did not know when the memory of it became a vision of sleep. She again came upon the raft, crossed, and found a drowned man—the young hunter—on the river bank; and was not greatly frightened by the spectacle as she thought. The scene changed with the facility of dream-power. There had been a great battle. The echoes of its guns, voices and cries were still in her ears. She was on the field where it was fought, strewn with its grim and ghastly sights. Some one she was looking for; whom, she could not at first tell.   She came upon the stark corpse of the young hunter.   It was him she sought as it then came to her.   Uttering a loud cry of pain and horror, she awoke. So vivid was the impression that the vision remained after she awoke.   As it faded, she found Anita, the Indian maiden, bending over her.

"Tell Nita," said the child, with tender solicitude.

"O Nita,"—greatly distressed—"I dreamed the young chief was killed in battle and I found him.   What can it mean?"

"My sister find him?"

"I was looking for him, and I found him."

"Happy girl! Look for chief, find him killed, him alway come back from war."   Very brightly this was said.

"O Anita, is that the real *Indian* of it?"

"All Indians say that," said the delighted child.

Edith arose, turned up the lamp, and looked out of the small window.   The camp-fire had burnt down, leaving a dull red glow on tree-trunks, limbs and foliage.   From a wide rift in the clouds the moon was looking into the old wood, where the wind, dying, was heard in little sighs and moans.   She again sought her couch, musing on Anita's rendering of her dreadful dream, and finally lapsed to restful slumber.

The young hunter's last act was to enquire of the condition of the injured man, where he found a guard as Carter predicted.

His manner of approach was reported to the captain the next morning, and confirmed his impression as to the young man's familiarity with military usages.

CHAPTER II.

A MEMORY.

THE storm disappeared, the clouds passed, the winds died, the waves of shallow Lake Erie subsided, and the sun of the next morning touched the colored foliage of the wood with warm splendor. The moisture in the atmosphere was changed to frost, aiding to detach the ripe leaves, which were here and there through the wood dropping to the ground, still pranked with perfect greenery.

The injured man resumed his garments, his head sore and shaken from the blow, a little languid from the nervous shock, yet rejoicing at his escape. He stepped out where the captain awaited him, and the two had an earnest, low-voiced discussion of their position and surroundings, the voice and manner of the elder showing that their effect on him was depressing.

With the light, the elder hunter from the high, cliffy shore of the lake carefully scanned its now serene surface. Not a sail was in sight. He turned back, gathering up his ample morning catch of the famous bass. One thing was settled : the strangers were not depending on aid from the lake,—not immediate aid. Peters and the men were busy about the morning meal, going and coming to and from the fire and spring of the hunters, where the cooking was done.

Edith slept well into the morning. Anita stole out and returned without waking her, and stood observing, when she came from her dreamless slumber.

"Oh—we are here, little sister," she exclaimed, as all the surrounding and late incidents flashed back upon her.

"All here," answered the bright child, showing her teeth, as she approached her adopted sister.

"How bright and lovely you look, Anita," she cried, as the girl came into the stronger light. "That ribbon lights up your glossy hair beautifully. Have you seen my father?"

"Him out, talk with captain."

"Oh, he is out! I am so glad; how does he look?"

"Him pale like, you call it; speaks well, call me and smile, only pale."

Anita was a close observer of Edith's toilet as it progressed, alert to assist, and quick to catch and treasure up all she saw. She noticed unusual care, much consulting of the hand-glass, and smiled, as with her woman's intuition she divined the cause. The captain was still a young and certainly not a plain man. It was not for him these maidens gave the touches to their dressing and its effects. There was a handsome young hunter, a hero, who did things as if born to them, in the near wood. One had seen him that morning, and the other expected to soon. When her array was complete, Edith went to meet her father. She verified Anita's words. He brightened at her approach, yet something peculiar she observed in the countenance so long and often studied; something like what she remembered long ago, in London, on the reception of papers from America, never explained to her, and which now came to her memory. The father smiled as if he divined her thought. Their meeting, undemonstrative, was tender and full of silent gratitude, which each understood. They clasped hands, the self-contained man bent and kissed the forehead of the daughter, and permitted her to receive and answer the greeting of the captain, to whom, in another way, her presence was as grateful.

A few bright words to her father, and she turned to the radiance and loveliness of the young day in the forest about her.

"O how exquisitely lovely! See, see, father, see, Anita, how gloriously the sun comes to us through the trees on the hill from that side. Was ever anything so rich and warm! And the fragrance of the fallen leaves,—only take it in,—rising to us like the perfume of rich wine with which the earth has been drenched. Oh the birds ought to sing, —hark! I do believe I can hear them—almost," laughing at her own exuberance.

"I heard an owl last night," said the captain, though exhilarated by Edith's presence, not at the time able to even seem to enter into the brightness of her spirits, set free by the removal of anxiety on account of her father. The speech was not a good one, as he saw himself.

"You never hear anything but owls, Captain. Of course you responded in their own grewsome way. They know you are here," was her mocking answer, gayly spoken, the sarcasm not wholly obscured by her manner.

An extemporized board with seats had been set up outside where the sun fell, and Peters announced breakfast, to which the little party at once made its way.

The woods and crisp air lent their united aid, and Carter's bass received full justice. Some ineffective efforts were made by Edith to light up the feast with conversation. But the gentlemen found their surroundings too depressing for even her influence, united with the flavor of the Ohio bass, and she soon permitted them to eat in silence. When they yielded to inability to partake further, Edith, who had carried on some talk with Anita, turned to her father.

"Have you met him this morning?" she asked. The officer did not like this word "*him*" for the young hunter.

"No," was the answer. "I waited for you; we will go to his camp together."

"Send Peters and ask him to step here," she said.

"That will be better. Peters, Dr. Gray's—*Dr. Gray's* compliments to the gentleman, and say to him he will oblige Dr. and Miss Gray, if he will call at his early leisure."

A smile on the captain's face was interpreted by Edith.

"The captain thinks that Peters may not know a *gentleman* when he sees one, like some others," she said to her father.

"He certainly showed a gentlemanly promptitude on a late emergency," replied her father, a little sharply.

"While others found it all they could do to care for themselves. I must bear witness to the fact, father, that the captain took his share of the river, and I think it was every drop *bona fide*, honest water;" laughing.

"Thanks," from the captain to the young lady. "Floating bits of disunited wood are not a good base for prompt action," he added.

"Well, Anita and I did not unite them, did we?" said the girl to her sister. "If we had, they would have been constant;" and the two laughed, and a little to the captain's discomfiture.

"I admit the great merit and great service of the *gentleman* referred to," said the officer. "I feel that my thanks are his due."

This was really well said, and met its instant reward.

"I know you speak that from your heart, bravely and loyally," said Edith to him, frankly.

. "Thanks! thanks!" said the pleased gentleman.

"'E will be 'ere himmediately," reported the prompt Peters, who had executed the mission.

"I will be excused from the interview," said the thoughtful captain; "but remain within call," he added, moving away among the trees. Anita arose, looking to Edith for direction.

"My sister will remain," said the young lady to the greatly pleased girl, passing an arm about her slender form.

They had not long to wait.

The young hunter came lightly up the steep, paused at the brow to determine the position of those who wished his presence. Discovering them, and not remote, he removed his foraging cap, and approached them a little rapidly. From the instant he stood fully in her sight in the strong light, the fear that he might be regarded as commonplace vanished from Edith's mind. A long drawn breath witnessed her relief.

He looked taller this morning, carrying his head well; not strictly handsome by rule, but much better, his face and eyes full of gay spirit, and ready to break into a laugh—alway ready to laugh. As he came forward, Dr. Gray and the girls advanced to meet him, the former resting his eyes intently on the youth's face.

"I am very, very glad," cried the young man, in a musical, ringing voice, "to see you so well this morning, Dr. Gray;" extending his hands to him.

"I owe it to you that I see this morning at all, my heroic preserver," said the deeply moved man, clasping the extended hands in his own.

"Oh, I had not thought that!" exclaimed the young hunter, a little startled; and turning to Edith, "I had not thought the danger great."

"To one so strong and brave, it may not have been. To him, to us—" she paused, much moved. "Under God, I owe it to you I am not an orphan. I—I cannot express my gratitude in words," she said, extending her hand, her voice breaking, and tears starting from her eyes.

"Indeed! indeed, Miss Gray!" said the young man, thoroughly surprised, taking the proffered hand. "Your —your emotion, your thanks oppress me. I must protest —as—as one not deserving;" now scarcely less moved himself.

"Her words are true," said the father, solemnly. "Before any of my party could have rendered aid, it would have been unavailing. This intrepid Indian girl, my daughter, unembarrassed by others, might possibly have helped me."

"I saw it quite all, and, fortunately, I was near. I may not have appreciated all the surroundings. What I did seems so little," replied the hunter, his face now breaking into a laugh.

"I really am glad you bear it so lightly. It seems to lighten the burden of obligation," said Edith, smiling, and lifting her frank eyes to his again.

"Oh, it was a little accident, in which we all bore our parts well—let us think," renewing his laugh. All this time he held the girl's hand, never so long a willing captive before. Their faces, each of such excellence, near each other ; a rare pair, standing in the glorious sunshine, in the perfumed wood. The loveliness, the perfection of the picture, it may have been, yet something indescribable; the father saw in it, as did the Indian girl, who felt it as well—something that caused the servant Peters to pause and look at them.

"You will not think us slow in making our acknowledgments," said Edith, who unconsciously felt the charm of the situation.

The youth laughed. "I never thought of it all. Had I an idea of your estimate of the incident, I fear I should have been slow to give you a chance," he answered, gayly.

"I do believe he would," said the now vivacious Edith to her father, laughing herself.

"Such an incident as last night makes life friends of the actors," said he, in reply. "But our friend will remember that we are yet to learn his name," he added.

"Oh—oh—oh, I thought of that as I came up the hill, but it went out of me;" laughing. "My name is Dudley," observing a sort of spasm as of pain, or of sudden strong emotion, which struck the face of Dr. Gray, and the meeting of the eyes of father and daughter as he paused at the name. "Dudley," he repeated ; "Cliffton— my mother's name—Cliffton Dudley ;" still noticing a changing expression on the father's face. "Perhaps I should say that was my Boston name. In New York, where I grew up with my mother's family, I am called Dudley Cliffton."

"Your father was of Boston ?" asked the gentleman. "What was his first name ? I've heard of the Boston Dudleys."

"Philip. I am one whose acquaintances shorten up

his name. I am often Cliff Dudley when not reduced to Cliff Dud."

"Or Dud Cliff," added Edith, catching his gay spirit, and feeling as if she had always known him. She went on, "coming up the hill you were trying to think which you were, Dud Cliff or Cliff Dud ; " laughing.

"Well I was one or the other and the difference was slight."

Mr. Gray turned away to beckon the captain forward. Edith still permitting her hand to be retained, turned the young hunter to Anita, a charmed spectator of the little scene between the three.

"My Indian princess, orphan daughter of a famous chief, and my adopted sister," she said to him. To her —"He is Mr. Dudley—a chief of the 'Long Knives,' and not a bit dangerous to young girls in the woods," laughing.

The young girl received him when now he turned fully to her, with a shy, very pretty native grace, peculiar to herself, presenting her small, slim brown hand, that had never known the toil of an Indian woman, her face more than comely, lighting up like a stained transparency from within.

"She insists you are a chief;" Edith added to the young man.

"Him be chief ; " said Anita sententiously.

"We are all chiefs on this side," said Dudley. "I am very glad to be presented to you, so I may claim your acquaintance, when I see you hereafter," he said, very pleasantly to her.

"Anita glad," she answered, withdrawing her hand which she placed behind her.

"At the river you held Miss Gray from leaping in

after her father;" he said, reminding her of the incident.

"I was an incumbrance. She can swim, and is absolutely fearless. She would have leaped in and tried to save him, had she been alone," said Edith, warmly.

"I have not the least doubt of it;" said Dudley with fervor. A little color struggled to the tawny cheek of the Indian girl, moved by the warmth of his manner.

"She has been with us five or six months. I hoped to meet some of her kindred when we landed here;" said Edith, in explanation to which the young man silently bowed.

"Mr. Dudley," said Dr. Gray, now approaching the group, with the captain. "My friend, Mr. Home."

"Of the army," added the young American, as if that but completed the proper designation; at the same time lifting his cap, which he still retained in his hand, now holding it in both against his breast; he bowed a little ceremoniously over it, repeating the name. "Mr. Home —it gives me great pleasure to be named to you;" he said gravely.

The Englishman observed him coolly an instant and said pleasantly: "The pleasure is mutual, *Mr.* Dudley," in the more youthful man's manner, when they both laughed. Then the Englishman advanced, cordially extending his hand said, "I wish to congratulate you for your intrepid conduct of yesterday. You may underestimate it; you may not know the value of the life you saved to—to us all; *my* thanks are due you also."

"Mr. Home—Mr. Home, I declare, I protest," exclaimed the American, stepping backward, throwing up his hands—laughing, the color deepening on his ruddy, sunburned cheek, ingenuously.

It was a manly face, to endure increase of color, and yet gain. He looked at Edith, at Dr. Gray, Anita, appealingly—the girls laughed in the pleasant way of girls. The Doctor smiled at his dismay and helplessness.

"Well, I don't care, it is a little discouraging;" he exclaimed, now laughing lugubriously, in which even Dr. Gray joined.

"It is really too bad, going round jumping into rivers, and things, getting your clothes all wet, pulling out folk you don't know, getting thanked, and yourself talked about as a hero. Oh, it is too funny for anything in this world;" cried Edith, now going off into peals of merry laughter.

It must be admitted that Home did not join in it very cordially. Over his ears in love with this very young lady, and still in the gravest doubt after two years, and here this *prig*, by some lucky accident, had fallen into the depths of her grace, yet too stupid to be aware of his luck—the only tolerable feature of the affair, to him.

A word of Dudley's lingered in the mind of Dr. Gray, who, as the mirth of the young people subsided, said to him, "Mr. Home is *late* of the army, and we have two or three, recently discharged soldiers. We address him by his title still."

"We may both have served," said the claimed *late* soldier. This he directed to the American.

"We hardly have an army; my father served through the old war," was Dudley's evasive and modest answer.

Edith did not like this grave turn. "There is another important cause for our gratitude—we might as well finish you—the wonderful bass; with the loveliest brown;" she cried.

"Ah—your thanks are due to Carter for them. May I be present when you render them!"

"And the venison," suggested Anita, thinking *that* must have come by the younger hunter's hand.

"Oh, well, Carter roasted that. It was a small affair. Anyone can shoot a deer. Anything further?" he asked, laughing.

"You surrendered your house to us," added Dr. Gray.

"All the. huts, for that matter," said Home, trying to be gracious, and succeeding in being grim.

"When you see my camp by the spring, gentlemen, you will not wonder at my readiness to do that," he answered. "These huts, as the woods, were open to any who cared to occupy them. They were deserted about the time Carter's brother settled at Cleveland twelve or thirteen years ago,—he says."

"They are wattled, you see, Edith," said Dr. Gray to the young lady. "That is an old German method of fastening the logs together in a wall, by green withs. We notch them together in this country. They have kept their places well indeed. Who were they built by, Mr. Dudley?"

"Said to be by the Moravians. They undertook to establish a town here, long ago."

"I never heard of that," said Gray. "They built quite a town on the Huron."

"Yes, so I've been told. They began here; a hostile Delaware chief compelled them to leave this place, and they removed to the Huron. I heard it talked of at Cleveland last year."

"Have you heard of the Huron Moravians recently?" asked Dr. Gray.

"Oh no, there are none there now; at least it was said they left that region some years ago."

"You must be misinformed. They are certainly there now," said Home, very decisively, turning away.

"Oh, very possibly. My informants had no personal knowledge of them." Dudley answered.

"You may have heard," said Home, now coming forward for the first time, as spokesman, "that much interest is felt on the other side in the Moravians and their missions. There was a considerable mission on the Huron, and also on the Sandusky Bay and river; we are really on a mission from the Anglo-Canadian leaders, to these Huron Moravians, and their native friends. We were to have been, and supposed we were, landed on the right bank of the Huron. A nasty mistake dropped us in these beastly woods "—these adjectives would drop out. "We are of course provided with papers, which we will cheerfully submit, if our presence is questioned here."

He paused, and Dr. Gray said—"You may see, Mr. Dudley, that Home's statement is also preliminary to the important and apparently difficult matter—means to pursue our journey to the Huron.

"I have a stanch boat, carrying a sail, just up in a creek here, safe and ample, in which I will carry you gentlemen and the young ladies, with your traps to the Huron. Your men can easily make the march," said Dudley, frankly. A moment's consultation in which Edith took part, and this was declined with thanks.

There followed much talk. Dudley said horses could be procured at Cleveland, of Carter's brother, or through him; and he was asked about Carter.

"He was a native of New Hampshire, grew up a hunter, a scout of the border, a sharpshooter, an honest, tender hearted, intrepid man, silent and simple ; not without prejudices against his enemies of the old war, of both races," was Dudley's account of him.

Then a further consultation between Gray and Home, when the captain went with Dudley to find Carter.

As they moved away, Edith ran up to her father, placed her hands on his shoulders, saying—"Oh, father! can this be a son of *that* Dudley?" in a plaintive, anxious voice.

"His only son—my child. My brain worked that out while I slept."

"Was he like this young man, born of sunshine and happy spirits?"

"Very like him, at the same age."

"Oh, there must have been some awful—awful mistake some—"

"Hush! hush! child. There was. That all came to me ten years ago."

"Oh, father! and you never told me."

"No, no, I have always felt guilty toward you, and this has come upon me to crush me," placing his hand to his head.

"Oh, this is not punishment! it is a reward, it brings joy," cried she.

"God grant it. It is very dark to me."

"Dark? the world is full of sunshine ; full of God."

" Yes, you and this youth can yet see God in this sunshine. I must shut that out, and seek the inner light; " sadly he said this.

" He was like this Cliffton, and my mother preferred you, loved you instead, bless her dear girl heart ! How beautiful you must have been—are still. You blessed papa," caressing him.

"There, my children, run round here in the woods. Light will come to me. God's way will be made clear, if not his purpose. I am glad that you can regard this as reward," he said sadly. "I hope nothing but joy will spring from joy. There—I will go and shut out this light, for the truer." He made his way toward the cabin, leaving the light-hearted girls to their devices in the woods, their thoughts and words tracing airy embroideries about the name and form of the young American.

The two gentlemen found Carter at the camp by the spring. Dudley told him Captain Home wished to secure him as a guide to Cleveland; which he readily undertook, and the Englishman returned to the hut for slight preparation. He would start at once.

"No harm can come on't; and I'de like to let 'em know enny way;" Carter said to Dudley. "Mebby 'ees playin' off to sort o' spy out the place tho'," he added.

"Spy out the place? Good Lord! what have we there that anyone can care to see? If they want to, anyone can go there any time, by land or lake."

"That's so. Per'aps 'twould do 'em no good to see thare want nothin' there;" was the thoughtful answer.

Home had the spirit and pluck of an Englishman. His only regret for the journey to Cleveland, was the two days absence from Edith; not lessened by the fact that she would be left quite dependent on Dudley. He lingered near her as long as excuse could be found, as she saw. It is not in woman's nature to deplore the reluctance a brave man might feel at leaving her.

He said few words to her, several on her account to the corporal left in charge during his absence. He would be back toward evening the next day. Then he took leave, though the girls went to see him off, with his guide, of whom they had but a passing glimpse. Edith felt a special interest in him, and in return he was a shy admirer of hers at long range. They found him armed with his rifle, awaiting their approach, near the camp, a place of profound interest to the girls. Without a word the old hunter led the way along the brow of the hill, a hundred yards up stream to a point where it was broken down for the passage of a small confluent of the river, in which, near its mouth, lay Dudley's boat, by the low immediate bank, her spar with the sail neatly furled and corded leaning against a tree. Here with the oars they found the young hunter, awaiting to set them across the river.

"It is a lovely boat! I should feel safe in her—with a good sailor;" said Edith laughing, her appreciative eyes taking in the little craft's just proportions, and turning to the boatman.

"You would be absolutely safe; she would carry you to the Huron," said he. "If you had a good sailor," laughing in turn.

"She'd want good weather;" muttered Carter, not intimating which she he meant, taking a standing place in the bow of the craft.

"A good many goods would have to concur;" answered the young lady, carelessly.

Home stepped on board. Edith noticed still abundant space in the boat, and cast her eyes to the east bank of the narrow river, as if estimating the voyage. They then fell to the eyes of the boatman fixed on her own face. She construed the smile that lit them up as an invitation to make it; the boat still motionless.

"Anita, we will see Captain Home start from the other

3

side, " she said, accepting Dudley's hand, and stepping into the boat, as did the Indian girl, unaided.

Had Edith consulted the eyes of Captain Home, she might have doubted whether a more speedy parting on the west bank would not be as grateful to his feelings. Dudley pushed the boat from the bank, turned her bow down stream, and a sweep or two sent her into the dark water of the full banked river. As they gained the open of its now sunlit tide, Edith exclaimed—" Oh! if we had known, we should have come up to this little creek, and seen this lovely boat and then—" finishing with a look, as if all had then been well.

" If we'd known we would not have come up this river of beastly omen at all; and then—" responded Home.

" Well, then what? It is of such moment to speculate of what might be, if that which is were not. I am so happy to-day at our escape from yesterday that I am almost glad we did come," was Edith's response; answering Dudley's eyes also, whom she sat facing. " I wonder what will happen from this—this—" finishing with a little laugh this time, turning her eyes into the grand, sunlit wood, from which they fell to the surface of the shining river, which bore many colored leaves downward.

" O the lovely lost things ! " she said, skimming three or four out with her ungloved hand, from the water. " I wonder if the mother trees are sad at parting with them ! " her face and voice now pensive with the thought.

" They take it about as most people do ; " replied Home, with grim irony.

" You remember, Anita, he heard an owl sing last night." She responded in answer—

"Me remember," said the child with a gleam of her teeth.

The boat touched the other bank, the guant old hunter stepped upon it, pulled the bow up a little, straightened himself up with his head still bent, his back to the boat, he called out—"Wal, look out!" and strode a few yards up the bank, where he paused for his companion.

"His leave taking," said Dudley laughing.

"Which means?" from the young lady.

"Oh, everything—all last words. 'Good-by,' 'take care of yourself '—' of all the things;' 'everybody, I leave behind.' It was addressed specially to me," was Dudley's explanation.

As the captain now followed Carter from the boat—"Wal, look out," called Edith to him; in the manner and voice so like the hunter, as to produce a laugh. "I spoke it in its narrowest sense, and as purely supplemental—Captain;" she added.

"Oh, well, I re-echo it to Dudley," replied the Englishman pleasantly, moving to join the waiting guide.

"Look out," responded Dudley, to him, cordially in reply.

Home faced about at Carter's side, lifted his hat, placed the tips of his fingers to his lips, and waved the hand-back, his eyes on Edith, and turning again the two were soon lost amid the trees.

"O Anita!" cried the girl, with a sigh of relief, as the two disappeared, her face lighting with a happy smile. "Oh, my precious little sister! not *much* taller than am I, what a time we will have! Two full days all to ourselves, in these loveliest old woods! We will run in them, hide in them, rustle the new fallen leaves; we will go chestnutting too."

"Me saw lovely ones," said the pleased Indian child.

"You would not care to see the river from the boat?" asked Dudley, a little hesitatingly, addressing Edith.

"Well, not now—my father—" She checked herself, and remained silent.

"I beg pardon," his face falling. "I forget I am such a stranger, and no one to vouch for me," he replied.

"You need no one to vouch for you, and you are not a stranger, Mr. Dudley. What if you had waited for an introduction last night?" with frank seriousness.

"Thank you—many thanks," he replied warmly.

"My father is alone, and well—a good deal shaken—a little mentally, by what has happened. I must now return to him," she said in explanation.

"How exceedingly well she says things," was the young man's mental comment.

"Perhaps you will permit me to land you near the camp?" he said, fully restored by her words and manner.

"Where—where you found us last night?"

"You might not wish to see that place?" he asked by way of suggestion.

"I very much wish to see it," she answered.

The boat was put about, and a few strokes sent her around the bend of the river, when a broad straight sweep, now dimpling in the sun, the stained shores aflame with gorgeous color, opened to view.

"Oh, how exquisitely lovely!" cried the girl, clasping her hands. "O Anita, it is cruel to take you from the woods! We will come and set up our wigwam by this river. It is not of evil omen, as Mr. Home declared."

Down the shining blue black water, from bank to bank,

up to the high tree tops, went the girl's eyes, to fall to the face and eyes of the rower, and always to smile when they rested there, as if after all the splendor of the wood, these were more excellent, while his eyes were ever on her countenance. Few faces were more deserving, so young, so fresh, so satisfying ; the high set-apart expression, usual to it, had vanished. That which at times indicated long pursued thought, and purpose, of experience of twice her years, given to contemplation, yielded to the warmth of moved pulse, with a liquid light in her eyes.

Her words of her father returned to Dudley.

"It might do Dr. Gray good to make a little excursion on the river ; " he suggested.

Her eyes came back, a little as uncomprehending—" Oh, my father ! I am sure it would, and Anita and I will gladly be of the party ; " now coloring very prettily. The youth noticed it. He did not care why it came. They approached the place of the yesterday's adventure, then so dark and repulsive, now innocent in the warm light. "Is this the place ? " cried Edith, not at first recognizing it in the changing effect of the light.—" So bright, with the laughing water running in little swirls and gurgles, and yesterday so black and hungry? As I live it is ! and there are some of the very woods of our treacherous raft *bobbleing* round in the eddy now. Oh, you bad things ; I'll not trust you again ; " shaking her finger in mock reproof at the wobbling floats.

They landed. As the girl gained the bank—" You stay here and watch him, Anita. Somehow this is like a lovely dream this morning ; I am afraid it will all vanish, and he and his boat with it ; " laughing gayly. "Now, don't you let him persuade you to get into his magic bark while I'm gone ; " she said to the girl.

"Me not 'fraid," said the girl showing her lovely teeth.

"' *Wal, look out,*' I'm afraid ; girls never are afraid, when danger comes in this form ; " she replied, laughing, and shaking her finger at the youth, who stood by the boat's prow.

It seemed to Edith as if she floated up the hill, wafted by an unbreathed wish, a thing of light, warm color, and fragrance. Her thought was of those she left. She turned for one glance of a face now toward her, the eyes lost in the distance. She knew they were on her. Anita stood by the boat as if regarding its owner as enjoined.

CHAPTER III.

THE year was at its complete ripeness, ere decay began. The foliage fell from its perfected state, and the forest was filled with its fruity flavor, as of incense from unseen censers. The atmosphere was ripe and full, stimulating and satisfying. One felt embraced and sustained by it, could lean upon and trust it. A day on which life was its own justification—sufficient for itself, leaving no wish for a morrow. Beyond its sun, its vigor, its sensuous fulness, there was no need.

Edith hastened to the cabin, and found her father shut in, buried in a profound, depressing study, in which no light had yet sprung to cheer his perplexity, a thing for feeling, emotion, prayer, as well as study.

"What does it mean! that by a sailor's blunder, we should come here to find *him*, for whom I once made diligent and vain search," he said.

"Oh, I never knew that."

"There is much you never knew, but which I must impart. So much is clear to me now. God has a purpose in it. Maybe my mission, to the Prince Regent so important, was really subsidiary to God's greater business."

"Well, papa, are you not glad? Surely no ill can come to him. If what you said an hour ago be true, he has had hurt enough from us."

"How can we know? It is many sided. See this people, drunk with their seeming success, are ripe for punishment. Unprepared, a peaceful, unarmed people rush on a powerful, warlike, armed Nation, trained by endless wars. How must they fare?"

"Well, father—please hurry the argument, and go out with me, that's a dear papa."

"What can the result be? God's arm will be bared, devastation, desolation, blood, death, in all their borders. It will be a girdle of war and woe."

"Oh, father, you have dwelt on this until—"

"I am an instrument; you are one, set apart, by the laying of royal hands on your young head," solemnly.

" Father, will you never forget your personal wrongs?"

"Oh, that is all lost in the wrong to the Sovereign, driven mad by the rebellion of this people—the very land itself. This young Dudley, so gay, brave and noble, the spirit which sent him to our aid, will send him to this war."

"He takes his chance as all brave men must, father."

"Knowing him now— are we to arm his murderers? We—you would never have met him, my child, but for this."

"Can I bring him harm? It will be but for a day, our seeing him."

"A day is sufficient for God's purpose."

"If it be God's purpose, let us leave it to him. It is idle to try to evade or avoid."

"I would have light to walk by, so I might not seem to evade."

"The light is outside, my dear father. You know you are my all. Go with me out into it. Forget all the past, the Dudleys—we will call him Cliffton. Come."

She pulled him to his feet, brought his cloak and threw it over his shoulders, placed his hat on his head, his cane in his hand, and drew him into the warm sunshine. She was irresistible.

"You were dreadfully shaken up by your fall, and are not the least yourself. We have put off the mopes, megrims, and here we are again. You shall not go back to them." They gained the open, sunlit wood. "Now look about you! see the splendor of these untouched woods. What stained windows equal the openings through which the blessed light streams down these cathedral domes? Take in the bouquet of the fallen leaves," drawing in long full breaths herself. "Take the elixir of the atmosphere, full deep lungfuls of it," again drawing her chest full to its utmost capacity.

He obeyed her, looked about, drew in the spiced air, again and again, did his best to abandon himself to her control, imbibe her gay, bright spirits. His blood began to move and life to stir anew.

"Oh, we will fill you, saturate you, lungs, chest, soul and spirit; surround you, immerse you, bathe you in sunlight. This is God's day; we will give in to Him and it. To give ourselves to it, is to give to Him," she cried.

No voice like her's had power to charm. No presence could so inspire. All her faculties were in full play to draw his better self from the darker and lower abyss, into which his worse self sometimes plunged him.

"It is God's day assuredly", he said; "I will do my best to draw near Him in its glory, and in your way, with you. My precious child, what do darkened old men do in the presence of youth and light?

"Share them, my own dear father; with you to bless

me, all others are as nothing to me," said Edith, conducting him toward the river.

"May I remind my child of these light words, hereafter?"

"When you please papa—but they are not light words, save as coming from a light heart."

Just below the brow of the hill, stood Anita, her face glowing with pleasure, awaiting their approach.

"What is it?" asked Edith, running forward to her. "Has he got away— really from you?"

"Him up there;" with a gesture up the river, now showing her teeth, so pleased was she at Edith's return. "Him thought down there," pointing to last night's landing; "not good for my sister's father," was the answer.

They changed the direction of their walk, and Edith told her father the cause, and Dudley's reason for the new place of taking the boat.

"Indeed! Indeed! How very thoughtful;" he cried, touched by the young man's consideration for his nerves.

As they approached the boatman at his chosen place of receiving his guests, Edith called out to him, "Oh, here you are, Mr. Cliffton; I really began to fear my dream would prove to be a dream."

"Oh, I'm not the stuff a lady's dreams are made of," he answered in her vein, handing her to a seat in the boat's stern, to which he also aided her father; the agile Anita meantime found her own place; imitating the usual course of Edith, in avoiding the minor services of gentlemen. She was the first to detect the change of her sister's usual manner toward this young hunter, which she entirely approved.

Laying his cap on the seat by his side, the youth, with

the easy mastery of the long ashen oars, which was noticed by Home and at once won the confidence of Dr. Gray, sent the boat up the river.

"Mr. Cliffton says he is not the stuff ladies' dreams are made of," said the exhilarated girl to her father.

"Ah! a rash speech—a very rash speech," said the quickening man, looking into the animated face and laughing eyes of the youth.

"Do you know what such dreams are made of, Mr. Cliffton," she asked, with seeming seriousness.

"Haven't the slightest notion. Possibly they come ready made," he answered.

"This one did to me," she said, casting her eyes over the sunlit banks, the shining river, and letting them come back to the young man so near. "This one came ready made and you are in it—you see."

"And dreaming also"; he added, and the two laughed a musical light hearted laugh in unison.

"A dream that an old man may wake up to and join in"; said the elder man, his face quite lighting from the face and eyes before him, and the kindling, almost radiant face by his side.

"Oh! and you are to wake up to this—wide awake," cried the child, passing her hand within his arm. "See how gay·and bright Anita's face is," she said, looking past the oarsman to the dark glowing face of the Indian girl in the bow. "She dreams. Don't you suppose two may dream the same dream at the same time?" she asked.

"And each conscious that the other dreams the same dream?" Dudley asked.

"Well, yes, of course; or there would be no special fun in it,' she answered.

"Two may perhaps. I doubt a whole boat load performing such a concensuous dream," said Gray, smiling now as near at one with them, as his years permitted.

> "Dream, dream, may we ever dream;
>> The real after all may be seeming;
> Let it fade with the mist of the sunlit stream,
>> And our world be the world of dreaming."

he added.

"O papa! where did you get that? It is pretty."

"Nowhere."

"Is there any more there?"

"Not a line."

"Well, it is a little sad—so I don't care."

"All poetry is steeped in sadness, tells of pleasures past, with regretful memories, when it does not cheat with delusions. Why may we not somewhere, for a little space, find a shore where Time stops; and we left to float —come and go, and not have the hours counted against us," said the elder man.

"But see! see! papa; we are going against the tide! Turning time backward;" dipping her fingers in the passing water, which rippled between them.

"Yes, but we must turn my child; when we do the tide will bear us down all the faster."

"Oh, you are pensive; the sun and wine of this wondrous day have not yet worked their charm. We will not linger in the shade to-day, will we Nita? Will we, Mr. Cliffton? We will defy time to-day. The night shall not come till we will it "—a little plaintively.

"I never remain in the shadow when I can escape it. If I cannot, I stand still, and it floats off over the trees. The sun always comes chasing after," the young oarsman answered, untouched by the girl's pathos of voice.

"Let that be our gospel, our philosophy, only let us drop those goblin names. The sunshine always chases the shadows "—a half minute's silence, then—"Do you notice I call you Mr. Cliffton ? " she asked of him.

" I really had not noticed it."

" Well, you have few old acquaintances here, and may prefer a change," she said.

" I really think I do ; " gayly.

" Which name do you like best ? " she asked.

" Well, I don't know. Do you think anyone likes the sound of their own name ? "

" Or the look of their own face ? " she added.

" Well, a face is inevitable ; one gets accustomed to that. A name may be changed," he answered.

" Yes ; " said Edith, her eyes falling.

"Time changes the face—sculptures all manner of lines and expressions on it ; " said Dr. Gray.

" You evaded my question, sir ; " said Edith chidingly to the boatman.

" I try to wear my father's name—well, not badly, but I think I fancy my mother's family name more."

" And her first name ?" she asked.

" Maud."

" Maud Cliffton—what a pretty name ! I know she was beautiful and lovely. One's mother always is, though."

" I have but the faintest glimmer of a memory of her," he said.

" Shall we call him Cliffton ?" said Gray to Edith. " I have a fancy for that. He will permit it for the little time."

" Oh, anything, Cliffton or Cliff, not minding the Mister," said the young man—gayly.

"O dear! this dream is slipping from us. Let us not talk of names. Pretty ones are *poky*. Mr. Cliffton—no Cliff,—tell us something bright. I know you can, something to make us laugh. It won't take much," she said.

"I can't say even that little;" he replied, laughing in his bright way. "I never said a funny thing in my life. You see we are in real shadow," looking up at the high bank above them that made the water black, and bending with might to the oars.

"Oh, it was that! How glad I am!"

The boat shot into a broad space of radiance from the sun, now nearing the meridian.

"Oh, here comes the dear blessed sun again!" cried Edith, lifting her face up to it, and laughing with glad hearted mirth. In the world is there anything so sweet and musical as a light-hearted girl's laugh—a laugh wholly feminine, as was that of Edith, gushing from the depths of a virginal heart.

Reaching the sun-kissed space, the boat was permitted to slow, and Edith, with her ungloved hand dashed the water in a fine spray playfully over the boatman.

"Oh!" exclaimed the father in reproof of the childish act.

"I wanted you should see him as I did yesterday. He looks best in water," she cried mirthfully.

There was no space for a game of romps between the light, gay-hearted girl and boy. Their mood could find expression only in laughter. That was its proper form in the absence of action. Thought—mind, save in the most transient sparkles, were out of place, words of any meaning were to be gayly scoffed. The only thing they could do they did. There could be no impropriety in the presence of the father, though the proprieties born of society were out of place, in the free wild wood. Men and women there are remitted to primitive expressions of thought, feeling, emotion. So these bright children laughed as children do—peal on peal. Whatever Edith said, they laughed at as the wittiest, brightest thing ever uttered. Their laughter nursed mirth, which broke forth afresh. Anita went off spontaneously with them. Dr. Gray became infected and finally inspired, and soon added his hearty chest cachinations to the concert of the young people, which sent its tide up and down the surface of the shining river, rising and overtopping the banks, ran pealing off under the forest arches and through the glades. Is there anything which so makes men one, as hearty laughter?

Left to itself, the boat drifted into still water, under the western bank, opposite the high shelf of a wooded cliff, with shallow cave openings in its face, which catch-ing threw back in weird perfection the mirthful notes, words and tones of the gay joyance.

The ear of the Indian girl first caught the mocking voice, than which in nature, nothing is more weird, nor so sad, as its dying cadence, bringing to the inner vision the idea of vanishing form—melting away in a sigh.

Cliff took it almost as soon. Edith saw them listening and soon heard it, as finally did her father.

As it threw back to them the voices of their mirth, it became a provocative to laughter, and very soon regu-ated their vocal manifestations of it, so as to secure the most effective return. By concert they simultaneously and suddenly suspended their open-mouthed notes so as to receive the fullest effect; again and again repeated, till the impulse and power of yielding to it were ex-hausted. Then words and short sentences were addressed to the hidden mocker of the cliff, reflected back faithfully, tone, voice and emphasis, the last syllable vanishing seemingly from sight as from hearing, phantomlike, with a sigh, repeating the native words of Anita, with, as was declared, more fidelity than the accents of England.

"Oh, *Indian* is its native tongue—as I live!" cried Edith, clapping her hands, only to have her applause repeated to her.

"Of course it is aboriginal, its native tongue," assented Cliffton, with perfect gravity.

"Its native tongue," came back to them ending in a sigh.

"Oh, so pathetic!" exclaimed Edith, yielding to the influence.

"—so pathetic," faintly and dying away, it replied.

"Why—I shall cry," she said, almost overcome.

"I shall cry," in a despairing tone, exaggerating the sadness of her accents.

"Let us go, Cliffton," said the girl in a lower voice, now really moved.

"Go Cliffton," very faintly it said, back to him.

"Cliff is going," said the youth addressing it in a saddened voice.

"Cliff is going—" the last word in unmistakable sorrow.

"Good-by, Cliff," he said, his voice influenced by the growing sadness.

"Good-by, Cliff," sadder yet it repeated.

"Till we hear you again," cried Edith cheerily, to dispel the depression resting upon them all.

"Hear you again," gayly repeated the cheered sprite.

Dudley swept the boat away, and Edith drew a long

breath of relief.' "I was really oppressed," she said. "I am glad the spell was dissolved," looking back at the grim cliff. "Poor spirit—to think it must forever remain captive there," she added.

The boat gained the downward drift of the current, and was again lit up with the warm noon sun.

Cliffton had an opportunity to observe the head and features of Dr. Gray. He had not reached a time of life when men study the heads and faces of men for character, or signs of intellect. Certainly few men of any age could do that in this instance, with the face of his daughter so near his. For the hour the cloud upon his spirit had passed; care had left his brow, and his face and eyes lit up pleasantly. The head was fine, the forehead high but narrow—a striking, distinguished looking man, and he might be called handsome. So much Dudley carried away from the interview, quite unconsciously, for he could not remember thinking of him at all—indeed he was not called upon to think during the little excursion. None of its experiences were intellectual.

If for any reason Gray could have wished the young people should not meet, or had regretted their meeting, that regret changed apparently to satisfaction, his brooding thought yielding to enjoyment due entirely to their inspiriting presence, which if strong enough to thus effect him, must have been much more potent upon each other. This was very apparent to him, accustomed to study others. Edith, in the new light which surrounded, exhilarated her, was never so interesting, while Dudley had a fascination for him. He could but wonder, as he observed them. They seemed like life-long companions, meeting after an hour's separation, in which nothing had happened to either to be told the other. There was no need to talk

4

of their past. They said no word of any future. The present was rich and ample for them. They seemed all sufficient for each other. Never had the presence of any person, man or woman, so inspired the self-contained Edith. She had never before met such a man, nor any man under such exceptional conditions. As they now drifted away from the mocking river cliff, Gray noticed that the gay, bubble-like spirits of the two had effervesced.

Some words were spoken by Edith, having some passing meaning, Dudley seeming content to hear them. Possibly to him but melodious sounds, beyond which they signified little. Dr. Gray thought he had never met one so entirely unconscious of himself, as this young man. Not in the least bringing himself forward, or asserting himself. The girl's words really had very little meaning, had no special relevancy, were not many, and brokenly spoken, yet after a little, as he thought, they seemed to be full of significance to Dudley, though they were not to him. The young man now appeared to answer once in a while, with a word, a tone, a smile, or a laugh. Clearly something was passing between them, some sort of converse, full of pith to them, of which they seemed aware. Once or twice he tried to catch the thought, translate it to his own apprehension. Beyond the pleasure of the presence of each to the other, it was all unintelligible to him. Possibly there was nothing more between them. If there was, it was too elusive for the acute man, who set himself to study them. Apparently they took no note of time, which Edith had banished for the day. He had quite become one with their light mood, and for him her decree for the hour was effective, and to himself later he seemed to awake to find the boat lying by the low moss-grown bank, where he first saw it, now hours ago. Was it all an unconscious reverie? The awakening like coming from light slumber, where actual and seeming things had been pleasantly blended? The party stepped from the boat to find themselves in the shadow of the high western bank, so often mentioned.

"Ah, what did I tell you, my child?" said Dr. Gray, lifting his hand to indicate the lapse of the hours.

"Oh, the west has become east. The day is lengthening," with a laugh that had lost none of its music. "To-day is not to be counted with the common days, is it, Anita?"

"Him begin new time." She answered, showing her exquisite teeth, meaning the present day, and not the young American, by her pronoun.

Dr. Gray and the girls took their way leisurely through the woods to the main cabin, where they were joined by Dudley. The faithful Peters soon brought them face to face with a mid-day dinner.

"This is the stuff most dreams are made of, Mr. Cliffton; let us play we are hungry," said Edith gayly.

"Quite too serious for play with me, I fear," he replied, in his bright way.

For a play the parts were really well taken, as were the viands, and Peters was left to ring down the curtain.

Anita produced a small, beautiful basket of native workmanship, and the three young people strolled again away in the surrounding forest. There really was little else to do. They thought it was the charm of the wood which led them into its depths.

"What a paradise of trees!" cried the fair girl, pausing and looking round her. "So wide, so endless; trees everywhere; one must not be afraid of getting out of the woods, and see them fade off. To be in the woods, live in the woods, in the heart of an endless forest; wake in the morning, and find ourselves there—it was not a dream; not have to go over stumpy fields, over the wreck and ruin of prostrate kings, wearying and disgusting one's self to get into the woods, but wake and find one's self among tall, healthy, untouched old monarchs, and move over their falling crowns and robes, strewing the fragrant pure earth." She moved along while speaking, and now on a small summit paused again. "Was there ever such a wonder? See, see, Cliff! see, Anita! That long avenue, overlaid with shafts and pencils of sunbeams, great sheaves of gold and soft brown shadows, lying across it; gold on a field of brown, pricked with every hue of green. Oh, the forest is full of these arched, overhung ways." Looking upward, following up the huge, straight shafts, up and through the openings to the soft blue beyond—"How high up, and far away the sky is. These tall trees help to measure the distance," and her eyes came down to the smiling face of Dudley, from which her own caught the smile. Wondrous as were the trees, the earth, the sun and sky, this almost radiant face was sure to catch her eyes, when they came back from an excursion. Anita, quick to see, noted whenever her eyes traced up the grand trunk of a tree they invariably came back to and rested an instant on his, and always lit up with a smile, or broke into a laugh. To the Indian girl, it seemed the most natural place in the world for Edith's eyes to land. She now also noticed that when her sister's eyes flashed upward to the tinted and now torn canopy of foliage, Dudley's eyes invariably were upon her face, waiting with exemplary patience to receive them, and seldom waiting long, or if he threw a glance upward it was only when she called him to look up, and that he wasted little time on trees or sky.

So they went sauntering about, the girls in their gay moccasins, rustling the painted leaves, the young man with his light elastic step, having one of those well-made, well-knit, long-limbed forms, supple, strong, and full of flexile, unconscious grace alike in action and repose, Edith pausing to look up and wonder at the trees, Dudley to look at Edith, and Anita to look in ecstasy at the two, especially when they happened to pause in the sun's rays. Occasionally she picked up a chestnut, as did Dudley.

" Do you know the soul of the woods—their spirits? The forest has many," Edith said. " They are with you, possess you ; you see them, hear them, feel their presence. You turn for a better view; the forms change to shadows or sunbeams, the voices to wind voices, sighs and moans, and like the dying cadence of our echo become the rustle or waft of leaves. You hear their mocking laugh, like that of the loon, and it turns to the groan of a huge arm of a tree creaking on the body of another, moved by the wind. The woods are full of spirits," she said, musingly.

" The soul of wildness," said Dudley.

" We call it wild for want of a better word, or appreciation. How this flavor is given to everything the wood harbors or hides ; all of its own. Trees, plants, leaves, flowers, fruits, all roots, barks, perfumes, all have the flavors of the forest. All living things : birds, animals, insects, all *wild* —we call it. It is in all their motions, cries, notes ; all their ways, all alike in this—all are of their mother, the woods. Men slay her children, because of this flavor of their flesh."

"Roasted venison and wild plum sauce;" said Dudley laughing. "Game dinners."

"Yes, roasted venison, and wild plum sauce. I accept the illustration. I never regret my father's daughter is not a son, only as I think how much easier *he* could run wild in the woods. But he would want to murder her innocents."

"Would you live with the natives?" asked Cliff, glancing at Anita.

"The spirit of the woods is her soul. Its life her life; its voices and ways are hers. She has its subtle, elusive flavor. They are very exquisite in her. Of course you like them in her—very much. But the Indian embodies the ravin of the woods, as you find it in wolves; all the predaceous, all the hunters, warriors, are alike. They are all taught by the same hand and voice—are all alike, cruel—we call it."

"Do you suppose those of the highest civilization are most appreciative of this elusive spirit of the woods, as you call it?"

"Well, yes, perhaps so. He, the cultured, sees it, feels it, appreciates it, as no barbarian can. He knows all the contrasts. An Indian is at the head of the predaceous children of the woods, developed only in that line. I know one—a family, Anita is of it, on a more elevated plain. To the average Indian, all things are alike. He does not appreciate the difference. He regards the wonders of art with the same indifference that he sees a tree, a rock—all are alike to him. Poor, dear child," turning to Anita. "She has not the faintest idea of the charm, the flavor of her wildness, so exquisite in her rich and really gifted nature. Oh, let us get away from this! we are in deep shadow; get into the sunshine, into our bright dream land. We are still in the woods," she cried, catching inspiration from the eyes so near hers, and laughing in her old way of the morning.

" Why do you call the forest woods instead of wood or forest ? "

" Well, in childhood, I called small bodies of trees woods, as they were. I liked that name, that form, the best. To me it meant more. Woods,—the woods— endless hills, wild, lovely slopes with streams, great, far-reaching plains, covered with lovely trees, like these." Then catching the laughing expression of his eyes and face : " Do you always laugh ? " her face lighting up under his eyes.

" Well, when I am not laughing, I am ready to, I fancy. I really never thought of it before."

" Yes, so I see, and I like it."

" I think you have a charming aptitude for musical laughter," he said in reply.

Spontaneously these things were said, with no thought of compliment, nor did either feel complimented.

Dudley meantime had purposely conducted the girls to a south-westerly slope of a noble chestnut ridge, where the declining sun sent his now yellow rays with warm effulgence, which lay like a gilding on everything it touched. Here the great, newly-coined chestnuts, in their satin coats, were found in profusion. A few min-utes' attention to the nominal purpose of their ramble filled Anita's basket, and the pocket room of the party.

The sun was withdrawing his rays, and the forest trees and colors were growing cold. Dudley now turned their footsteps toward the river. Edith was surprised when he told her the camp was a full third of a mile distant.

Dudley spent the evening with the Grays. Probably

in the long and very animated conversation between the two gentlemen, to which Edith was content to be a listener, the elder had no purpose to draw out the younger, yet the extent and variety of topics he dwelt upon or touched, served admirably to test the reach and versatility of the young man's studies, which proved to be respectable, while his reading of the English classics was exceptional. His remarks upon men and current events showed him a man of action, with a very quick mind, inventive and fertile. To Edith the hours passed with something more than pleasure. She had rarely seen and heard her father at better advantage. The ready and suggestive mind of the youth, fresh and original, was very inspiriting to him. His face was animated, while his mind fully awake, worked with force and vigor. Contemplative, reflective, he was something of a thinker, and if he produced no things new, he put old things in new lights. She regretted to have this young man go—return to his solitary camp. In their room after his departure, she stood with her arm round her sister's waist, her cheek by hers as together they looked out of the small window, and caught the glow of his re-kindled camp fire. She said nothing, and the Indian girl only speculated of her thoughts. To her the last twenty-four hours had made a revelation of the unsuspected nature and character of her fair sister. Bright-spirited, light-hearted, she had uniformly been grave, reserved to others, as if dwelling apart. A cold, beautiful white vase, with scarcely perceptible characters traced upon it, save in the most delicate lines, seemingly indicating that it was consecrated and only to be used in the worship and service of the gods. It had suddenly lit up from within, bringing out the loveliest colors, with warmth and unsuspected beauty

The scarcely perceptible characters were in relief, revealing the strength and excellence of their design. Not in this form did the thought of the Indian flow, nor did she give it form to herself. It was more impression and feeling than thought. She felt that her sister was waking to a new life.

The following day, like its predecessors, was rich with sun, painted leaves and fruity aroma. The young folk made it an idyl, all too short, though they permitted the sun to get a little the start of them. As soon as he had the wood well alight they were there. The river excursion was to the lake, when Dr. Gray was of the party, now well restored. For the rest they were left to themselves, following the suggestions of Edith. The doctor saw that they two were in spirits less exuberant than on the day before. Their intercourse had the frank unreserve of two half-grown children, between whom an intimacy might ripen in an hour. Theirs seemed as innocent and unconscious. It would end with the day, or at farthest the next morning. The frankness with which the girl met the youth's eyes, without increase of color, or a coy turning from them, was to him, if he thought at all of it, proof of its harmlessness. Truth to say, he was preoccupied, and gave up the day to the consideration of grave and perplexing matters, to which, as we have seen, this meeting brought new and unexpected lights. His first inclination was to turn back from his mission, accepting this incident as a sign from heaven that it was displeasing to God. This he pondered prayerfully, in the spirit of his puritan ancestors. His impressions instead of ripening to convictions, faded, and the will of the Most High was still to be groped for, waited for. His original purpose would for the time remain.

Home and his guide were expected, certainly by the close of the day. Home came, and on his arrival the Englishman thought he surprised Edith and Dudley at the camp by the spring. He made his presence known by a loud *guffaw* of laughter, at what he supposed must be their confusion, on being thus taken. To Edith his mirth seemed forced and not shared by his face. It half frightened the Indian girl, whom he had not seen and whose appearance changed for him the aspect of things, and he went forward to meet them with a really smiling face.

"Where *did* you get that horrid laugh?" were Edith's first words to him, frankly extending her hand which he took with a pleased manner.

"Caught it on that horrid Cuy-hoggy—is that the right name, Dudley?" turning to the young man pleasantly.

"It is very *Englishy*," answered Dudley smiling.

"Well, you take that laugh right straight back where you got it and leave it there; I don't like it," said the girl.

"I presume you would like to have me," he answered.

In reply to Dudley, who asked for Carter, Home said, he accompanied by two young lads, were with the horses, secured for the journey west. They followed the trail to a ford three or four miles above. He would find them on the high ground; when with a word, the young man hurried away to look after their disposition for the night.

"I expect you'd like to have me go back," repeated the still not wholly placated Englishman.

"That is very *Englishy* also, as Cliff would say," she replied.

"Ah! so he is promoted to Cliff?" sarcastically.

"When he is not Dud," gayly, turning toward the cabin.

"You are not a bit glad to have me back;" lugubriously.

"You have'nt eaten since you left us," laughing. "Not glad to have you back? Well, let me see. Yes—no. You see, it is about balanced;" laughing again gleefully. "O Captain Home!"

"The no is the last, and more emphatic, I do believe;" he said, his face taking light from hers however.

"It should have been plain no, to such an insinuation. You see, there never were two such days as these—were there, Nita? where are you?" she was moving a little apart, with the fine instinct of a true woman.

"Oh, your unsupported word will do for that," was his dry assent.

"Well, it is all over. You've come back with horses, and we shall leave this lovely place in the morning," she added pensively.

"Well, don't despair. I had to agree to take *him*—this Cliff, when he isn't Dud, or whatever his name is—with us, if he'll go," a little sharply.

"Oh, goody good! Do you hear, Anita? The young chief is going with us;" she cried a little mockingly.

"If he will;" added Home, a trifle disgusted.

"Of course he will, what else did we come here for, I'd like to know?"

"Sure enough!" growled the Briton.

"But why does he have to go?" she asked.

"It had to be him or this old scout. Dudley is the least dangerous."

"Do you think so?" laughing gayly.

"Well, we are going into the enemy's country—to them. Some one must see to the return of the horses. I think

the old hunter don't care to go among the Wyandots,
any way."

"Will Mr. Dudley be safe?" a little anxiously.

"Safe enough from the *Indians*;" laughing in a meaning way.

"Oh!" prolonged, and standing silent an instant. "Oh,
I never thought of that;" her face coloring, which the
shadow of coming night hid from the Englishman's
eyes.

In an interview later it was arranged that Dudley should
accompany the party to the Huron. All the preparations
were made for an early start the next morning.

Among the things mentioned by Home as picked up at
Cleveland, he was told that Dudley was regarded as a
very promising officer, and had been stationed there—a
wretched little place, he called it. That the young man
had been educated at the Military School, of which he had
never before heard. His manner and words did not
greatly flatter the Americans.

Gray said a school had been established on the Hudson
he thought nine or ten years, by the American Congress.

Edith warned the Englishman that she was of full
American blood.

CHAPTER IV.

"WAL, look out! ole feller;" were the old hunter's parting words to Dudley. He conducted the party by a short cut to the trail west. When reached, he stepped aside for it to pass into the not very plain track. The young man called the words gayly back to him, as did Edith, with the hope of seeing him again. Dr. Gray and Home had pleasant words for him, and Anita asked him specially to care for the young chief thereafter, with a glance at Edith.

To Gray was assigned the best horse. Edith's, the only one that had ever worn a lady's saddle, was a very spirited mare, a little wayward. The girl was a fairly good horsewoman, absolutely fearless, and looked well in the saddle. Anita, mounted in the fashion of her race, was perfect mistress of herself and horse. Master would perhaps be the better word, as she used two stirrups. Home was an indifferent horseman, unused to mounted parties in the woods and rough ways, where care of himself was all he could achieve. From leader or guide, Dudley at once became the commander of the party. He soon yielded his horse to carry a portion of the baggage, a necessity, unless it was abandoned. Hardy and lithe, his short heavy rifle in hand, to march in advance of the horsemen, was no tax upon his travelling power. The three men of Home were also on foot, as were the young men sent to care for the horses.

Edith's mare was restive and over spirited, with ideas of her own at times differing from her rider, and there were several encounters, in one of which, the ready aid of the alert Dudley saved her from a fall. To render this in time required a feat of agility and strength on his part, not lost on the appreciative young lady or her thoroughly alarmed father. It is possible Home saw less merit in it.

The hope was to reach the Huron that evening. There was a delay in starting, several stops and hindrances on the way, and the Vermillion was not reached till mid-afternoon. The late rains had effaced the ford. Obviously means must be found for passing it. The horses could be made to take water and swim. The ladies and baggage must be taken over by other means. The mishap of Black river was fresh in their memories.

Dudley and the young men gained the bank in advance of the party. At a glance he saw the condition of the stream and grasped the means of its passage. On the approach of Home, he briefly stated what he had decided upon, the preliminaries of which the stalwart ready handed youths, armed with the axes of Gray's party, were already about. The sensible Home called up his own men and told them to aid, really placing them under Dudley's orders. His directions were few and easily understood, and he put his own skilled hands and ready strength to forward his design.

"He works like an engineer," said Dr. Gray much interested.

"And gives orders like an officer;" said the admiring Edith.

"He is both, as I told you," said Home. "I learned at Cleveland that he was a captain in their 2d Cavalry or had served in it, and that he planned the slight works there. He certainly knows how to take a party across a river. I suppose their few officers learn all arms."

"And how to handle horses;" added Gray. ' I saw him picketing these last night, on the hill."

"Him a chief!" was the sententious comment of the Indian girl.

"That was her declaration when she saw him first," said Edith.

Ere an hour the entire party, horses and *impedimenta*, were on the west bank, dry and in good order.

To reach the Huron that day was out of the question. Dudley's dispositions for the night were soon made. His consultation with Home was perfunctory merely.

"A purely military encampment in an enemy's country, with our rear protected by a river, as in no event can we retreat," was Home's comment to Dr. Gray. "Of course it is well enough to humor him," he added.

In a way thrown into a novel position, with unexpected emergencies arising, Home had been at disadvantage, ever since the landing at the Black river. To-day was for him more unfortunate than its predecessors. The place of leader which was his, was usurped by another. Another had taken his place at Edith's side. He had ceased to command his own men, in her presence. She, who had always evaded the attentions of himself, of all gentlemen, evidently received them from this American with pleasure. Seemed in no way to regret the occasions which might excuse them. It was his arms that received her, when unseated from her horse, and restored her. Home was himself much nearer her when the trouble with the restive mare began, but this Dudley rushed in, caught the flying rein, the falling form. He reached the west side of the Vermillion in a very ungracious mood. Indeed, so far off his balance as to have words with the young lady herself. The opportunity was an excursion from the one tent pitched, down to the river, in the twilight, where he managed to detain her alone. He began by saying—"I really feel as if I was freed from my *parole.*" This was in a tone of affected bandinage.

It did not impose on her. "Freed from your *parole?* Very well. What would you have?"

"Well, it seems to me if I am not to speak of a certain matter—and I can think of nothing else; do you really feel that you should be—be—well—, so approachable to this Dudley Cliffton—*Cliff,* as you call him—on a *very* short acquaintance?"

"What can you mean?"

"Even Anita notices it, and is on the grin half the time."

"*Approachable!* Who are you, that I am to answer to your absurd words?"

"A man you and your father have authorized to approach you as a suitor."

"You find me *approachable*—do you?" laughing gayly.

"Why should I not be approachable to this young man, if I choose? Do you forget how we met? We, my father and myself, were thrown on him for help, for service—attentions you were privileged to render, and which we should with gratitude accept from any man."

"You assuredly have never shown the same *pleasure* for attentions from any other"—still trying to laugh.

"She would be no woman who would not accept attentions from him with a lively pleasure. I shall not in the least regret any occasion in the future for his attentions. He renders them as my due, without a flourish, or as expecting—reward." Then her face grew grave, a little severe. "Now I will not be questioned. You were— had some recognition as a suitor. You promised me on the honor of a man, if permitted to be of this mission, not to remind me of your position. Well, you feel released from your word. What will you have? I am quite ready at this instant to give you a final answer."

"Edith! Miss Grayson! I protest! I implore!" with energy throwing up his hands in alarm. "I—I— well, I was not serious."

"Well, I am. I will not permit you to treat me otherwise than with the utmost sincerity—and as the freest of women."

"If—If I loved—"

"Beware!" interrupting him with added severity of manner.

"You will at least consider the unusual, the unexpected things which in a way have rendered me powerless," he ventured to suggest, quite reduced.

"It is the unexpected things which try—test a man—as they do a woman. I may deplore, excuse, but really it is not my fault if things arise not of my invoking, to which you may at the instant, have been unequal, nor withhold my gratitude, my admiration, from another more fortunate."

"You seriously pronounce against me."

"I do not. I have thought well of you, how well is shown by your being able to remind me of your position toward me at home. I thought you brave, manly, loyal, generous. I hope you will permit me to so regard you

5

ever. We must be true to our common service, whatever happens," she added.

"I have been gravely in fault. I am grateful for your generous words. I will merit them." This was spoken in a very manly way.

"I do believe you will." She said in her fine manner, frankly extending her hand.

"Thanks, thanks!" receiving it effusively, and bending to kiss it, when it was withdrawn, ere his lips paid full homage.

He was much elated, and could not wholly retain his satisfaction within the safe limits of silence. "One thing I've gained—I never before knew you had so high an estimate of me," he said.

"That is what I did think," coldly. "What I may think hereafter, will depend wholly on yourself." This quite cancelled her words.

The party moved early the next morning. The road struck the Huron some miles above the deserted Moravian village, which the travellers reached in mid-afternoon. The little town stood on the eastern bank of the river, consisting of eight or ten small hut-like structures, built of small trunks of the abundant trees, wattled, as their mode was. A few acres had been cleared, now overgrown by the reconquering forest. The Moravians abandoned the place five or six years before the arrival of the Canadian embassy. On the side opposite was a temporary camp of Wyandots, Senecas, and their friends, from the Sandusky, some of whom were permanent residents, assembled to meet the English emissaries. After the manner of Indians, they had placed three or four of the cabins in condition to receive their intended occupants, whose arrival was expected from the lake, where a lookout had been kept for four or five days. Save a few women, children, and warriors of small note, Dr. Gray found nobody to receive him. The warriors discharged their guns, and very soon the seemingly deserted Huron bore the forest sovereigns over to meet the agent of the Prince Regent. George III. was then in eclipse.

To the travellers, the vicissitudes of the day's journey were duplicates of the day before. Dr. Gray was an adventurous man, and saw the approaching end of the ill-starred expedition with satisfaction. Home set forward with high spirits. He had many reasons for satisfaction. This was the last day of an intruding presence, more than distasteful to him. His spirits effervesced by the way, and he reached the lovely Huron, with lowering brow. More than one sinister glance had been cast from under it at the youth, who maintained his position at the head of the party, when not at Edith's bridle rein.

When the blue dimpling Huron met their sight, Home saw these two turn their eyes to each other, a way of theirs as he had observed, and now as he was certain with regret. This was the end for them. Their countenances fell—he thought, as the folk of that day would say. The young lady did not turn her eyes to him—never had that way with him. His heart, though near its hour of relief, was full of bitterness, and in a mood to entertain black thoughts and unpleasant guests.

The last two or three miles down the river were passed in silence. The English officer specially noted, while Dudley was alert and cheerful, his words were few, his light laugh which he had come to hate, was no longer heard ; while Edith was grave and silent, not in her old lofty way, a being apart, but drooping and sad, as a woman might be.

The party alighted in front of the principal building in silence. Anita springing from her horse, as would a gay and gallant cavalier, went to the side of Edith. Dr. Gray's horse had taken sudden fright, and Dudley felt obliged to turn his attention to him.

The Indian women approached the young ladies with respectful wonder and curiosity. Anita addressed them in their own language. They were greatly pleased; the oldest answered her, then they gathered about the two girls, and led them to a small building connected with the larger, which they had decorated and set apart for their special use.

Dudley's first care was for the two young men and the horses for the night. This accomplished, he turned to the main building, in front of which he now found twenty or thirty fine athletic warriors, standing about a group of three or four chiefs, of the highest rank, with whom Dr. Gray and Home, with the aid of an interpreter, were in conversation. Gray turned, met and led Dudley forward, and presented him to the famous Round-head, a fine-looking old chief, in festive array, and a reputed friend of the Americans.

"Me Round-head," said the old barbarian, with dignity. "Wyandots grandfathers of the Nations;" waving his hand with a comprehensive sweep westward. Dudley knew that to his tribe had been committed the great belt of the Indian league, dissolved by Wayne at the Battle of the Fallen Timber. He remembered the suspicions of Carter, and he noted the peaceful aspect of the natives before him. He knew he was expected to say something in reply to the chief.

"My people have all heard of Round-head," he said

gravely. "They respect him in war. They are glad .to be the friends of the Wyandots."

The young man's person and bearing evidently were much in his favor, with men accustomed to note and read quickly and accurately all that meets the senses.

His words, rendered by the half-blood, were received with satisfaction.

"My son speaks good words," answered the chief graciously. He was then presented to Walk-in-the-Water, a saturnine, ill-favored chief, of whom he had also heard, and with whom he also exchanged compliments. He was less favorably impressed by him. He had once seen Black-Hoof, the most famous of the Wyandots. His quick glance discovered his absence. He noted, however, the presence of one who held himself aloof—king-born, if men ever are, not taller than were three or four before him, to whom his glances would stray before formally presented to him. He now came a step forward, and Dr. Gray, taking the youth by the hand, conducted him to the stranger, and left them to stand five or six seconds confronting each other. Lighter of complexion than the northern natives, light, graceful, yet powerfully made, a noble head, finely featured, aquiline, carriage erect, dignified, wearing the simple deerskin hunting shirt, leggins and moccasins, red cap and eagle's feather, without other ornament or a tint of paint, he stood the finest specimen of native manhood the American had ever seen.

"The Shawanoe," said Dr. Gray, naming the native gentleman ; such he certainly was ; and turning to the youth, "the Americans call him Cliffton. Shawanoe has been told what his brother owes him," he added.

"My English father's friend is very welcome," he said with natural grace, in a voice singularly musical.

"The Great Spirit made Shawanoe a chief," said Dudley, impressively. "He has looked on many things. His enemies have never seen his back." He thought he was of one of the fine South-western strains of men.

When these words were rendered, many tokens and signs of assent and pleasure were given by the Indians.

"The braves will follow the young chief. Shawanoe trusts his young brother," was the reply. The chief gave him his hand, followed by the other chiefs and warriors present.

"Well, by Jove, my boy," said Home in recovered spirits. "You've exchanged speeches with the natives before. That speech to the Shawnee took them."

"The one to Round-head was more politic," added Dr. Gray.

"I was out with a mission to the Creeks and Cherokees last season;" said Dudley, "and heard a good deal of Indian speech making. One catches the phrases easily. Who is this Shawnee, I wonder?"

"Never saw him before;" said Home.

"I have heard of him," said Gray evasively.

"He must be from the South-west. He looks like the fine men of that region. He is lighter, with the bearing of a prince."

"He is Shawnee or Shawanoese, and goes by the name of his nation, I believe," said Gray.

"Well, he came from the South then—or the tribe did, I am sure," said Dudley. "They are on our Sciota I believe now."

"Maybe," said Gray. "He has a sister at Brownstown or Detroit. Edith knows her well. Anita is the sole child of an elder brother, an Indian hero." He spoke hesitatingly, as if uncertain of his data, or the expediency of giving it.

Dudley went out in a thoughtful mood. " What does it mean ? The Moravian Mission was their pretence to impose on him. This was a mission from the English government of Canada. It had a special purpose. These men had asked him nothing of himself. They might feel called to say something of themselves. The Shawanoe was a man of the greatest importance. It was a thing of note and report," were his mental reflections.

Edith was not at supper, nor was the Indian girl. Cliff did not inquire why. He ventured, however, to hope she was not overcome by her journey, and heard from her father that she was much fatigued. The young man remembered that she took her way from her horse to the group of women, without a look or word to him. That could not be her leave taking, yet why not ? It would be characteristic of this strange adventure. The manner of the father was now cold and constrained. Nothing was said of Cliffton's return. He was there voluntarily, purely to oblige these strangers, was his own master, would go when he pleased. He would like to see a little more of this mission. He wanted very much to see Edith ; yet to what purpose ? why should he care ? In all human probability they would never meet again. He felt that this would be a great misfortune.

He went out to find young Carter and his companion uneasy in their quarters. They fancied something sinister was hovering about. The presence of the Indians accounted for this. He made a little scout around, and then returned in good spirits. He would pass the night near them. They had a borderer's dislike and suspicion of Indians, and knew of the old hunter's suspicions of the Canadians.

On his final outing Dudley found the night chilly. He made his way towards the river which was silent, and deserted. From the high ground, he saw the Indian camp fires ; and heard occasional sounds, nothing unusual. While he stood on the river's margin, a light canoe passed from the other side, toward the huts. It landed in the shadow, and Anita stepped from it alone and glided noislessly up the bank. He completed his observations and returned to his quarters. Had he remained by the river thirty minutes later, he might have seen Home enter the canoe, and row to the other side.

The night passed peacefully, and the three gentlemen sat down to breakfast the next morning, the young ladies still absent. Dr. Gray told Dudley he was entrusted with an invitation to him to be present at a council, near the camp, in the afternoon of that day.

Home said if he wished the horses started on the return that morning, one or more of his men should go on with them. Dudley would be well mounted, and could easily gain their camp for the night. There were many concurring reasons why he should remain, and he felt like being at the council. When Dr. Gray told him that Edith had gone to the other side for the day, he decided to go. Her conduct seemed strange. He did not know the native usage with women guests. Perhaps the young lady placed herself voluntarily beyond the chance of his meeting her again. He could think of no reason for such a course ; but that he should think of it, made it seem probable. He would cross the river, but the young lady should find no difficulty in avoiding him. He directed the boys to complete the arrangements for the departure, and await orders. As he went out again he saw Anita hurrying from the landing to Dr. Gray's quarters. On his return Dudley found him much disturbed.

"Mr. Dudley," he said directly, "I received a message from the other side. I must ask you at once to mount your horse, and set out on your return. Some bad influence is at work, to cause you the greatest personal ill. It comes from a source not to be disregarded. In no event are you to cross the river."

"Oh, my absence is wished from this council then?

"You were invited in good faith, I know."

"I would not go unbidden, I will not stay away under the threat of danger," showing spirit. "If I am the guest of Round-head, who will dare menace me?"

A light hand was laid on his arm. He turned and was confronted by the Shawanoe, whose entrance was unheard by him.

"Bad men," he said in English with a gesture toward the other side, "Round-head not control. My American brother will go."

"Into an ambush, if what you say is true, Shawanoe," replied Dudley.

"Shawanoe guards his brother's trail;" was the reply.

"A great chief invites me to his council, a girl sings of danger in my ears; shall I run like a frightened woman? Does my great brother so counsel?"

"Shawanoe says go. He knows his words." His utterance and manner were very impressive.

"I implore!" cried Dr. Gray. "Don't for heaven's sake let your serving me involve you in peril."

"As you please, gentlemen, I go.

A word to the young men and all was ready.   Dudley, chafed and hurt, turned back for leave taking,

" Mr. Dudley," said Dr. Gray, clasping his hands, " Nothing has so moved me as the painful way of this parting.   You will certainly see or hear from me again."

" Oh, it is to be, my dear sir.   Don't let it disturb you. I don't see Home," he added.

" This evil word took him away. I will say your adieux to him."

" Thanks !   Any terms you choose." He looked about and lingered.

" My daughter is—"   Dr. Gray hesitated.

" Is also on the other side ; " supplied Dudley, smiling pleasantly, though there was sarcasm in his voice.

" I greatly regret her absence—as will she.   You can certainly trust me with any word or message to her, Mr. Dudley."

" It is no matter, she knew I must go soon.   She sends me word to go sooner.   Tell her from me that I ran at once," laughing in quite his old unconcerned way.

" Is that all you would say, Mr. Dudley ? "

" That is all, Dr. Gray ; " quite decisively, turning away.

Dr. Gray was sorely hurt.   He was in no position to take exception to anything the youth might say, or do.

" Mr. Dudley, even in this hour I may ask, has my child deserved this at your hands ? "

" Dr. Gray, I beg your pardon.   I will see the young lady herself if she permits.   I will attend this council." Haughtily, with something like a flash of his eyes, this was said.

" Go, go, Mr. Dudley, go at once, God will grant another time.   May he ever bless and keep you," with fervor."

In the outer room the young man met Anita, weeping bitterly. "My poor, poor child;" he said tenderly, taking one of her slim, brown hands in both his own. "Don't cry; you break my heart."

"Me so sorry," plaintively she said.

"Why should you weep? your friends and relatives are here, your sister, all you love;" very brightly. He took from his vest pocket an old fashioned jewel for a woman's ear, curiously wrought of gold and silver threads, containing a topaz, which he placed in her hand. "This to remember Cliff by. It came from my dead mother," he said.

"Oh!" prolonged in a little **ecstasy** of delight. "Edith? my sister Edith?" asking if it was for her.

"Is it for Edith? No, for you, for Anita."

"Edith?" again asking what he had for her.

"Did she know her sister Anita was coming across the river?" he asked.

"Edith a girl," was the pathetic answer. Being a girl she could send no word or message which the sorrowing Indian maiden would regard as fitting, on this occasion.

"No matter;" was the curt reply; the youth, man-like, in his anger not catching the girl's subtle meaning. "Good-by, my little sister. May the Great Spirit keep you ever." With fervor the words were spoken.

The poor child heard and understood what passed between Edith's father and Dudley. She still hoped to secure from him some tender message—a word for her sister. Failing, she cast her face into her hands, and abandoned herself to a paroxysm of grief. Had she received it, her plan was to fly across the river and return with some responsive message from Edith.

Everything outside was ready and awaited Dudley's approach. On his appearance, "Shawanoe will show his young brother the trail;" said that chief. They mounted, entered the wood, and were soon lost to the sad-eyed Anita, who was too heavy hearted to fly across the river in her light birch canoe as she had intended. As they disappeared, with her now uncared for trinket in her hand, she moved slowly to the river shore, and stood by her waiting boat, unwilling to seek the presence of her sister.

A few yards over the decaying trunks of fallen trees and through thick second growths, brought the cavalcade to the well defined bed of an ancient trail, running south-easterly, an old Indian road leading to the far interior, and which intercepted the trail of the returning travellers, several miles from the river, thus shortening the distance considerably. When this opened to the party, a gesture of the guide induced Dudley to direct the young men to pass in advance, which they did, each leading a horse.

The mare ridden by Edith, wearing her unburdened saddle, was in Dudley's care as he paused by the side of Shawanoe, who observed her, and knew something of the chivalrous regard in which the white gentleman held the woman of his race, he said as if to himself, " Her horse."

" She rode her," was Dudley's response.

" It is well;" replied the chief approvingly.

As they moved forward now in the rear, in fair English he said. " The heart of Shawanoe is under the eyes of his young brother, will he open his ears ? "

"Gladly, to the words of a chief."

" Shawanoe is at peace with all the Americans. He would not have war. The Seventeen fires* have land enough. Let them keep it, let them not drive my people farther west, and Shawanoe is their strongest friend.

---

* 17 fires—17 states of the U. S.

Listen. My brother should know, the land was the land of all the red men, not this the land of the Wyandot; that the land of the Delaware ; and beyond the land of the Cherokee, the Choctaw. Each owns everywhere. All and each own, nations live here, there on the land of all. Does my brother understand ? "

" Shawanoe means that each nation is an equal owner with every other nation of all the land ? "

" Dudley understands. *Listen !* All the nations must sell all our lands, much or little."

" The Wyandots cannot sell the land called theirs, set off, reserved to them by the Seventeen fires, unless all join in the treaty—is that it ? " asked the youth.

" That is Shawanoe's mind ; " said the chief. " The past was the work of our fathers. Shawanoe leaves it in their graves. He has seen the nations. His mind is the mind of all. Not a hill, plain, stream ; not a tree or stone more, shall the Seventeen fires, or their great father, the President, gain, until all the nations unite in the sale. Shawanoe builds a wall ; all his people stand on the other side of that wall."

The voice was full, sonorous, yet musical, the hand moved in graceful gesture ; the whole man, face and eyes, spoke with energy.

" My older brother's ideas of the red man's ownership of land are new to Dudley. Do the Seventeen fires and their great fathers know the mind of my brother ? "

" They do."

" My brother knows of the gathering of his people, beyond the Wabash ? "

" Has my young brother heard that the great American father is now preparing to survey the land beyond the Wabash ? He knows it is ours."

"Does the Prophet mean war?" Not answering the chief's question.

"He means peace. There will be no war, unless you take the land from under our feet. Then war," his eyes flashing.

"Should the Americans have war with the English, what will my brother do?"

"My people are poor, they do not want war; leave them their land and I am a friend of the Americans."

Dudley could hardly turn his eye from the fine, lithe, elegant form, the noble head and face of the barbarian, still quite young in looks. Who could he be, who spoke for all the tribes?

"I am glad to hear my older brother;" he said. "His words will keep place in my mind."

"My young brother's words are good. His acts are good. Shawanoe will always be his friend, though war comes."

"Dudley will be true to his brother;" he said warmly in reply.

"It is good;" said the chief. They moved on a little distance in silence. Finally the chief said, "The English Home—does my brother know him well?"

"Captain Home? Dudley never saw him till four days ago."

"When war comes between the Americans and the English, my brother will meet the English chief in battle, and strike him;" said the chief, with energy.

"Is he an enemy, more than other Englishmen?"

"Speaks foolish words. Bad men hear them. They go out. He cannot gather them back in his hands."

Dudley breathed out a long drawn, low whistle and then laughed a light hearted laugh.

" My young brother's heart is good. He laughs, and has no fear ; " said the chief, a plesant smile on his lips.

" Did my brother hear the bad words ? " asked Dudley.

" They reached Shawanoe's little sister."

" Anita ? "

A look of assent.

" So I am running away from Home," laughing. " Chief, I will go back ; " turning his horse back.

" My brother will go east," said the chief, catching the chief's rein and arresting the movement.

" Shawanoe is right. There is no time or room for a quarrel," said Dudley, much vexed and chagrined. Yet to save him he could not help laughing at the position he occupied in his own eyes with this half light on the cause of his flight. He asked many questions. The chief could not or would not answer them. Some miles they went, and struck the trail of the day before. Here Shawanoe dismounted. He had ridden the horse of Home on the journey west, and would walk back. Standing, he took from the breast inside his hunting shirt a deer skin parcel, from which he drew a small, quaintly fashioned, well-worn medal—it may have been wrought of gold, to which was attached a fresh scarlet ribbon. This he handed to the surprised Dudley, saying—" My young brother will wear this in battle."

" In battle ? Why ? "

" My warriors will know it."

Dudley holding it in his hand, still had his eyes on the chief's face, as if he would know more.

" It came to Shawanoe from his sister · " added the chief.

"Anita?"

"From his English sister."

"Oh!" prolonged. "And—and for me?" eagerly.

"If that pleases the heart of my young brother."

"More than he dare say."

"When Dudley again meets Shawanoe's English sister he will show her that;" pointing to the decoration. "She will understand. Shawanoe leaves his young brother." Extending his hand, his face showing sadness, Dudley grasped and pressed it warmly. Just then not able to command his voice, their hands unclasped. The Indian turned and walked back along the old trail, moving with the light, firm step of Dudley, rather than with the shambling gait of his race.

The young men as they entered the known trail, seeing Dudley and the chief stop, halted also, and witnessed the parting.

"Boys," said the youth, approaching them, "There goes the finest form and the noblest soul that ever appeared in the woods of America."

"Yis. 'E's a good looken enuff Ingin;" said the old hunter, showing from behind a tree, as if all the time of the party.

"Hullo! Carter—what's up? what sent you here?" called the surprised yet pleased Dudley to him, cheerily.

"Wal, nuthin purty much. I'se kind a lonesome like, 'n I thought I'de foller on an see 'ow ye cum on, " he answered. "'E's a good looken Ingin, an' gon right back— mebby. You go on, and I'le kinder purtect the rare."

"Well, I'm glad to see you, anyway," said the now laughing young man. "Go on, boys," who obeyed with alacrity.

"Wal, ye see, I didn't know w'at might 'appen," said Carter, thinking his presence needed an excuse.

"All right. Boys, we'll camp on Black River to-night," called Dudley cheerily to them.

How bright the world was to him with his toy! He had flashed to the conclusion, that it was from the hand of Edith to *him*, direct. So he managed to press it many times furtively, to his lips. It did not occur to him that Anita would be the bearer, instead of an Indian chief. If it had, who would expect a young lady to give such a thing to an Indian for himself, and why should he bestow her gift on a stranger? He for the time forgot what Anita said of her sister. "She was a girl," and so could send him nothing. No matter—as he said to the weeping child, who besought him for one poor word to the absent one. He had his toy, it was from her, perhaps not a token of love : of course it was not, but of kind remembrance and favor, so he kissed it again. How cruel his unkind words of her now seemed! He was very young. He may learn more of the magnanimity of Shawanoe. Lessons, however learned of the exceptional nature and character of women of Edith's quality, will harm him none, unappreciative of himself and pure of heart as he was.

It is probable the young woman was induced to pass to the west side of the Huron and remain there, till the departure of Dudley, and I am quite certain both she and her father were not then informed of any supposed connection between Home, and the suspected design against the young man.

The twilight of that day was deepening in the room occupied by Edith and Anita. Weary from her journey, depressed with sadness, Edith reclined on a low couch,

6

her head in the tender Indian girl's lap. She had given way to tears; though now composed, she was, perhaps for the first time, oppressed with that sense of helplessness, which comes many times upon women by reason of their womanhood, under some conditions in which one of the other sex is involved. They are to be and remain silent, passive, because they are women, girls. Let what will happen, they cannot seek or offer explanations.

"O Anita! we are two helpless, motherless girls, with no one to say a word for us, or do a kind act, or tell us what we may do or say ourselves," she said, in a sad voice.

"Edith father," suggested the Indian girl.

"He is a man. A father hides his daughter. Cliffton asked if I knew you were to come here; your answer admitted I did know it, though I did not know why. Your answer—'Edith a girl,' merely a helpless mute woman, that told all to a woman. It said nothing to a man. What poor creatures they are, when proved. A poor little good-bye, would have contented him, had I known. How did he look, Anita? Tell me all about it."

"What call sad face—white; then proud to father, say 'no matter' twice. It hurt him."

"'No matter!' 'No matter!' They were the best words. Oh, I know how he felt! a good-bye word across the river to me, were nothing. His words here, his look, his being hurt, are much more, much better. You don't understand my words, do you?"

"My sister's heart good!" answered Anita, lifting her head and touching the red mouth with her lips.

"These four days and then this bitter fifth—Oh, so bitter! Was this a plan to hurry him away, prevent a leave-taking? I wish I knew!"

"Chief—Uncle go with him—Home, English Home," sharply.

"What of him?" eagerly.

"Say bad words—very bad."

"What do you mean?"

"Hate young chief."

"Anita is to think nothing but good of Captain Home."

"Anita think nothing. Edith ask Uncle—ask Shawanoe." Then came two or three minutes' silence.

"Where do you suppose he is now?" asked Edith.

"My sister's heart is with the young chief?"

"Why not? I've nothing else pleasant to think about. Where does Anita think the young chief is now?"

"In camp, by black shining water. All still. He close his eyes and listen. He hear Edith laugh, he start up to look for her; all still, night come down in woods. Him very sad, very lonesome."

"You blessed child," caressing her. "Will Edith ever see him again?"

"Will sun rise? Anita meet young chief in woods. She bring him to Edith. Anita bring him?"

"Shall you bring him? If you find him."

"Anita find him, bring him," confidently.

CHAPTER V.

I812–1813, characters of fire on the brow of the western province of the Crown, then called Upper Canada or Canada West. An episode which gave her name and place in English and American history, to which her children turn with pride. It was then largely the home of the English inhabitants; had become the place of refuge of most who fled from the States, when self-constituted law gave form to their appeal to arms, against the common sovereign.

These adherents to the cherished loyalty of Englishmen became the objects of hatred and persecution, that in our traditions and literature, took the most odious forms, and still endure. Their sole offence, their sharing largely the once universal sentiment of devotion to the sovereign, taught in all the colonies as a primal virtue, a part of religious faith essential to private worth, and the crown of civic and public service. In the breaking up, as it seemed to them, of the foundations of society, incidental to an impious rebellion, they stood firm in old faiths and devotions, took no new ideas, entered upon no new action, were guilty of no crime, shared in no apostacy of faith, or deviation in conduct from established standards. In their devotion to principle, honor, education, tradition, and what for them was duty—they took up arms, went to battle, to prison, confiscation, exile, death. Men capable of such devotion were men of high natures and inflexible character, which in any other cause would have won from their countrymen the most exalted respect and the warmest admiration. Between the revolted colonies and the loyal provinces lay vast stretches of stormy sea, and wide regions of dreary wilderness, to be traversed by the exiles for conscience's sake. The Crown received and sheltered it, in the scantiest way, indemnified its subjects, who renounced all for it. These expected, hoped, prayed, fought, for the triumph of the royal arms. They looked forward to a return, a realization of what men in their position might expect from victory. They reciprocated the hatred of their new enemies with the added sense of personal wrong. When their hopes perished, impoverished, heart-sick, doubting the justice of God, or seeing it deferred to a day of later retribution, they rebuilt their lives as they might, and awaited its coming in the ripening time.

Remote in the distance and late to be informed, they watched with the restiveness of men personally interested, through the years of renewed quarrel between the two nations, knowing it was but a continuous burning of the old, smothered, not extinguished animosity. That the Americans should take advantage of the perilous condition of England to strike her, they expected. Still when Congress declared war, so confident were they that to them it seemed the madness preceding destruction. They knew the aroused bitterness of their enemies. They did not anticipate a renewal of Arnold's expedition. The lower province was protected by the same sea, the same wilderness, traversed by no road. The western, where they mostly lived, was behind the lakes, which Great Britain ruled. The tribes of numerous and powerful Indians were their allies, eager for the word to leap upon a wide exposed frontier; fit instruments in the hand of God to work his long delayed vengeance. They felt little apprehension of invasion from the western border. Michigan was an unbroken wilderness, as was all northern Indiana. There were feeble settlements at Cleveland and eastward. The inhabitants of Ohio must traverse two hundred miles of savage wilds, and the people of Kentucky nearly twice that distance to reach them. They felt safe.

Not long did this sense of security continue. Suddenly, with but a day's notice, an American general at the head of an American army, crossed the Detroit river, issued a stirring proclamation, and was in possession of everything but the feeble fort at Malden. Consternation, a sense of utter helplessness, paralyzed the Canadians. They were capable of being aroused and taking arms effectively. There was a man at the head of civil and military government, equal to any demand. Creative, masterful, confident, the ablest English commander ever appearing on the continent, not excepting Wolf or Cornwallis. His voice called into action the latent courage and energy of the people of his province. They only needed to hear the trumpet call, and find a leader.

The refugees, old and young, all of English, Scotch and Irish blood, arose at the call, nor did the French linger long. The Robinsons, Coffins, Sheaffes, New Englanders; the McDonalds and Evanses, men of high courage; the McNabs, and others first planted in Canada, at once responded. With these and a small body of his old regiment, with him under Nelson at Copenhagen, Brock flew to meet the invader of his western border. He reached it to find that his enemy, thinking better or worse of his enterprise, had returned to the American shore, sheltered in a strong, well-armed fort, whose guns did not command the river (it was built to protect from Indians); but he was amply prepared to erect powerful shore batteries which would annoy him on his own side. The American had a spirited, well-armed body of troops, which in efficient hands might set him at defiance, and who evidently desired nothing so much as his approach. Brock also found awaiting his arrival an ally worthy to share his counsel and confidence, undoubtedly the ablest leader of native warriors ever met by soldiers of European origin on this continent.

The Shawanoe returned from his meeting with the English emissaries on the Huron, to find that, in violation of his explicit commands, his brother, Tensk-wau-tawa, the famous prophet, had with all his bands attacked Governor Harrison in his camp on the Tippecanoe, and been utterly defeated. Many of his bravest chiefs and warriors were slain, and the survivors, depressed and sullen, escaped to their villages or were dispersed in the forest. Thus in an hour the well wrought fabric of years was dissipated. The wall along the border of the Indian lands, behind which at his call the embattled nations would stand, vanished like a mist. The surveyors resumed their work beyond the Wabash.

Embittered, enraged, the great leader repaired to Malden and accepted the terms offered him on the Huron. These bound him not to strike, save in concert with the British, who were to subsist his warriors and their families. There assembled under his standard a thousand or twelve hundred warriors, the flower of the immediate Western nations, who, commanded by him, were more than equal to the same number of soldiers however commanded, in forest warfare. Encouraged by this English ally, he now entertained the idea of driving the settlers south of the Ohio. Pontiac's plan was to sweep them east of the Alleghanies.

These remarkable men, Brock and Tecumseh, first met on the arrival of the Englishman at Malden, where they stood a moment confronting each other. Mutual surprise, admiration, with the untaught etiquette which is observed by many barbarians, kept them silent. Nearly of the same age, and of equal stature, what the Englishman gained in breadth and massiveness, was more than compensated by grace and symmetry in the Indian.

Harrison was the finest looking Anglo-American Tecumseh had met till now. He had come to hate while he still admired and respected his foe. For the average American he cherished contempt. With the person and bearing of Brock, he was more than satisfied. With his aid he would avenge Tippecanoe. He would recover the lost lands. Harrison was in his mind; by him he estimated Brock. Brock was his superior, he thought.

" My brother is welcome," at length said the general, as he stepped forward, his hand extended.

"Tecumseh is glad," responded the chief, taking the offered hand.

Like is gifted to recognize its own in others. Brock did not see an Indian, a savage, a barbarian; he recognized a broadly, highly endowed man, limited by his birth and surroundings, which in many ways he had overleaped. He found him a master of forest strategy, capable of bold and striking designs, with the audacity which he intended should mark this campaign. His time there must be short. His Niagara frontier would soon reclaim him. The American here must be effaced. Then a

lieutenant, with Tecumseh's aid, must not only hold this
border, but sweep the southern shore of Lake Erie. He
found the chief well advised of the strength and weakness of their enemy, and they concurred that it was fortunate Harrison was not opposed to them. Both expected
to meet him later. Their plans very nearly coincided,
which gave each confidence in the other. The points of
difference were soon arranged. Tecumseh would command the Indians, under the orders of the British general. Brock did not contemplate a reconquest of the
North-west. He did not discourage the chief's broader
scheme.

"I ask two things more of my brother," said Brock.
"Will your warriors refuse fire-water?"

"Till they recross the Wabash. Tecumseh requires
that."

"It is well. Our great English Father, the Prince
Regent, requires that all prisoners and wounded shall be
well treated; and women and children of the enemy, and
their dwellings, be everywhere protected."

"Tecumseh has promised all this to his English
sister."

"Ah, the lovely Edith," the general's face lighting
warmly. "All men keep their promises to her. Now we
go to meet Colonel Proctor and his officers, and review
the soldiers; and then we will meet your chiefs and warriors. My brother will learn to like the colonel. He
will probably be left in command here."

They found him and his officers awaiting the general's
approach. Proctor was still young, a stout, person-
able, handsome man, of the average height of Englisha-
men; his face indicative of good-nature and good cheer.
A coarse-fibred man, as we shall abundantly see. The

officers saluted; the colonel came forward to receive the commander, well known to all. Brock's manners were of the frankest, and by the small circle of the army he was warmly loved.

Tecumseh knew Proctor and most of the gentlemen present, and the general detected coldness and distance in his manner, not only toward Proctor, but some of his officers. Brock knew of the adventures of his agent in Ohio, knew that the chief met Home there, whom he thought well of, and was inclined to attribute his manner as due to the reticence of a native in the presence of Europeans, whose language he was not master of, nor was he familiar with their customs.

The available force of English were under arms. Of the very respectable body which wore the prescribed livery of the Prince Regent, Tecumseh at once detected a difference in the precision of action of a portion, from the larger part. The most were automatic, these seemed to move individually. The general was pleased with his accuracy of perception, and explained that some three hundred were really militia, now in scarlet, for the eye of the American general, which might not be so quick as that of his brother. Tecumseh appreciated the strategy, the pleasantry, and the compliment.

"Well," said Proctor, who studied the effects, "they wear their clothes well, d—d if they don't now."

"Yes, they wear their clothes a d—d sight better than they *dress*," was Home's response.

Home was the wit of the western contingent, an article never in excess in the British army, and estimated accordingly. Brock smiled dubiously at the compliment to his show, which was greeted with as much laughter as his presence and the gravity of the occasion permitted.

" Devilish good," said the more appreciative Proctor. " Deserves honorable mention. Do you good at the Horse Guards." His want of appreciation of militia marked his lack as a commander in dealing with a mixed force.

The pageant over, Tecumseh in turn became host, and led the general, Proctor, and their officers to his camp, a cantonment of the wild soldiery of the forest. There were Wyandots, Senecas of the Sandusky, Miamis, Kickapoos, Pottawattamies, Delawares, Shawanoese, Ottawas, men of many nations. Here the general and his officers held a reception. Colonels Elliott and McKee, names of dread and hate in all the western American border, presented the chiefs—Round-head, Walk-in-the-Water, Blackfish, Young Little-Turtle, Jim Blue-Jacket ; but the great old chiefs, Black-hoof, The Crane, Turkey's tracks, Blue-Jacket, Little-Turtle, some were dead, all were absent. Still the array of fine athletic well made men, good heads and gallant bearing, showed no falling off in the manhood of the woods, and the leaders displayed a brave following of warriors, most satisfactory to the eye of the appreciative Brock. The-camp, its plan, arrangement and rude police showed the presence of a careful, exacting hand, a ruler, as well as a chieftain in war.

Brock had hastily convened the upper Canadian Parliament at Little York, awoke the members with an electric flash, secured its sanction of his measure, called about him the chivalry of the lower section of his province, hurried to Long Point, a large point of the war, where he rendezvoused his force. Some three hundred embarked in open boats, and made the voyage along the northern coast.

He reached Malden the night of August 13. Undis-

turbed by his enemy he planted his guns, opened on the
fort and palisaded town, had his interview with Tecumseh, reviewed the Malden force and met the chiefs on the
fourteenth. The fifteenth was devoted to final preparation for the invasion of the enemies' territory in turn.
He grasped the situation. His plan was audacious. In
other hands it would have been criticised. None thought
of aught but the promptest obedience to his orders.

One there was, his chief of civil government, privy
councillor, cabinet minister, man of all work, to whom
he opened himself, for his own relief.

Perhaps talking over his plan, giving himself the ben-
efit of his own voice, placed it in clearer light. It also
occurred to him, that it might be well to place with
another, not only what he would do, but the reasons
which induced him to do it. It was Saturday night.
The week had proved too short by a day. He must
borrow Sunday and find what he seldom sought, a day of
rest later. He dismissed his aids and secretaries from
the room, and began :

"You look anxious, but remain discreetly silent, O
councillor, minister, grand chamberlain mine. I can't be
detained here. I improve the Macbethian rule : the
quicker it were done the more certain it will be to be
well done.

"The American General Dearborn, commanding below, entered into an armistice with my chief, the good
Prevost, tying his own hand and liberating me—as I may
do anything beyond his department. It can't last long,
when it reaches *his* chief at Washington. When ended,
his six thousand soldiers may cross the Niagara. To my
officers I give orders. They might not like my reasons.
I never offer any," laughing. "A general who calls a

council of war, and speaks himself, unless to mislead, is gone. So if he only knows the numbers, arms and disposition of his enemy, even if he knows his plans, he is but half informed. He must know—*know him* well—the man who commands against him, the counsels and men back of him.

" Here is a nation, several nations of farmers, artisans, shop-keepers, with a rabbly government of demagogues, unwarlike, no army, no navy, who after thirty years of peace, rush into war with a powerful nation, armed at all points,—never at peace. Mr. Madison, a timid man, his councils divided; the strongest states in opposition. Intending to declare war, they send an old man, who has seen no active service since his youth, two hundred miles from their Urbanna, through the swampy woods with two thousand men, four-fifths of whom are the rawest militia. He is wholly unsupported. It would take half his troops to keep his communications open. Michigan has three or four thousand hunters and fishermen. He cannot subsist his army two days, on all he can draw from them. An advance with supplies, has been for near two weeks on the river Raisin, forty miles away, and he has made two vain attempts to communicate with, and bring him into Detroit. See how the Washington men managed. Ignorant that war was declared when he struck the lake, he placed his baggage and papers, as those of his officers, on the unarmed Cuyahoga. They have not a gun on the lake, where I have the Queen, Charlotte, Hunter, Lady Prevost—forty guns! Well, we, better informed, captured his baggage and papers. I know the inside weakness and mutinous spirit of his militia officers and men.

" When he reached Detroit what did he do, and what

will he now do?   He landed on our side July 12 ; thinking better of it, he returned Aug. 8.   Why he came or why he left, will be a question for Yankee historians ; perhaps for a court martial.   He struck no blow, offered to strike none.   He issued a proclamation—"

"Colonel Cass wrote that, " said his companion.

"The hero of the Tarantee?" laughingly.

"So it is said."

"Well, we laugh at these raw young men.   They mean mischief.   I am glad Cass is not in command over there with Colonel Miller, and what he has of his 4th to second him.   *They* mean fight.   They believe war is to get at the enemy, and open at once.   I expect these youths worried the old man into coming over.   He would naturally expect Dearborn would demonstrate in his favor —would at least detain *me* on the Niagara.   Well, while here, he did not even reconnoitre our feeble works at Malden.   Miller and his four hundred regulars, supported by Cass, would have carried the fort in twenty minutes. They fought the battle of Tippecanoe—they and the Kentuckians."

"Very well, Miller is over there now, is he not—with him?"

"Of course, but *he* commands Miller—the best of his volunteers, with Colonels McArthur and Cass, are now absent on the third effort to reach the Raisin.   Why did he permit me to plant my batteries?   You hear them now," and they did.

"He refused your demand for a surrender yesterday, General."

"Yes, after detaining my officers two hours.   Then he sent to me by them, what really was an apology for his invasion.   My war will differ from his.   Then he has heard of the fall of Mackinaw; and to-day, he intercepted Proctor's letter to Captain Roberts, now in possession there, announcing that *five thousand Indian warriors are on the way to attack him at Detroit!*"

"Why, don't he understand that was intended for him?"

"Not a glimmer of it! Why, who would practise on him?"

"Poor old man!" exclaimed the listener.

"The poorest of old men. I pity him. How the demagogues will rend him! He thinks Tecumseh has twenty-five hundred warriors. You know they crossed over to-day. He has but little over a thousand of all arms in and about the fort. It is weak on the land side. We built it, and just why we constructed it weak on that side and unable to command the river, is not apparent, unless it was anticipated that I would have to capture it to-morrow. Now I shall cross at daylight, and land at Spring Wells. The Queen Charlotte will cover my landing. If I am not met at the landing, *as I shall not be*, the fort is mine without a blow. If attacked at the landing, I will carry the fort by assault. Have it I will. Audacity, if you will—the apprehensions of my enemy will make a short and bloodless campaign—an expedition rather."

"God grant it;" fervently.

"Now, my dear Grayson, you know all about it. I will not trouble you for an opinion. You are only asked to clear that clouded face, and look and feel cheerful."

"I confess, General, your face, voice and manner are very inspiring."

"Why should they not be? I am thoroughly awake. At the bottom there is always a reserve of good spirits."

"You'll need the reserve to-morrow, General."

"They'll respond.   I am never so light as on the eve, except in the fray."

"I am glad to find the war so popular with the army," said Grayson, with a look as if he would hear from the general on the matter.

"Very, very."

"All war is, I suppose."

"Oh, that is a mistake.   There is more in this."

"Well—yes?" finishing with a look.

"Now, *you* wish to punish a wicked though an old rebellion.   The army wants to wipe out an *old* disgrace. We exchange buffets with the French, Austrians, Germans, Dutch, Spanish; lick and get licked; give and take.   They are soldiers, trained to war, our equals. The Americans were *militia;* we laid down our arms, surrendered our swords to *militia generals.*   Oh-h!   I know—I know.   The French were with them finally; but the end would have been the same.   Who was Washington, Green, Starke, Morgan—Oh, lots of them," shaking his head.

"Well, we shall find lots more like them," said Grayson.

"Of course—*if the war lasts.*   We must strike quick, decisive blows.   Your New England may rebel—only it will not.   No, we'll strike hard, ringing blows, knock them on to their knees—that is our way—my way."

Grayson arose to go.   "I am glad to have heard you, General, on all these things.   I wish to-morrow was over," he added.

"Don't go.   There are two or three things—How is the lovely Edith?   She is a true heroine.   Makes heroes of us common men."

"She is high hearted and full of hope, a little nervous. She believes in the general, you know," laughing.

"God bless her! what a man she gave me in Tecumseh!"

"You don't know him yet, General."

"How did she make his acquaintance, get her influence over him? and she a woman—though that may be it;" laughing. "She does about as she pleases with the rest of us. Certain things are more potent with us in women, than the same things are in men."

"Well, five or six years ago—Oh, longer than that; over the other side, we were there one winter. Tecumseh had a sister there, Tecumapease, as remarkable in her poor Indian woman way as he is. Edith was teaching Indians to read—when she was fourteen or fifteen, it was a great thing with her. Tecumseh was there, and she taught him, Tecumapease and Wasegoboah, her husband. Both the men were then, like all the natives, given to drink, and they came in one day half drunk. The women were frightened—all but Edith. She managed to control Tecumseh; when he was sober she got him to promise to never drink again. He never has. He attributes his present position to this reformation which was wholly her work. Though free from superstition he regards her as specially gifted from heaven."

"What became of Tecumapease and her husband?"

"They are there in the Indian camp—or were, as is Tecumseh's wife and son."

"And this Anita—who is with you—is she their daughter?"

"She is the sole child of the elder brother, Cheeseekau, a very famous chief, slain in battle at the south-west, when young. They lost their father while Tecumseh was

7

a lad, and Cheeseekau had the care of him, trained him and formed his character. Several things he dwelt upon, until they made parts of the boy's nature. He was always to tell the truth. Be brave and fearless under all possible conditions. Always protect a prisoner, always care for the aged, for helpless women and children.* These are cardinal points, and so far as we have ever heard, he has strictly conformed to them."

"Really! I am very glad to hear this. Tecumseh and his niece are very light; is there white blood in their veins?"

"Tecumseh says not a touch—they are pure Indians. He is the soul of honor, his word given, is kept in letter and spirit. One thing; he don't at heart like us much better than he does the Americans. He thinks we are more honorable, and are useful to him; but he is an Indian of very exceptional endowments."

"I fancied as much. Well, we will be true to him, serve him in good faith, win his gratitude, and through these his love. They are a remarkable family. The younger, the Prophet, must be a remarkable man."

"Very, very. He is under a cloud now."

"Well," said the general, "my regards to Miss Grayson. I intended to call upon her,—can hardly do so this evening. I wanted to ask her of my gallant friend Home. There is something in him that might enlist a girl's fancy, though after all he is commonplace, is'nt just—well— Is there a man deserving her? That is not the way to put it. Of course there is not; but a man fit to mate with her? O dear! Tecumseh is married, and I am rough and old;" laughing. "Your rescuer of the Ohio

---

* Drake's "Life of Tecumseh."

woods may prove to be the man; who knows? Some of them are fine fellows."

"I suspect he is over the other side now," said Grayson.

"Ah! well, that would be interesting. You may have an opportunity of serving him; who can tell!" laughing.

"I hope he is not there. Of course we have never heard a whisper of him since our strange parting, on their Huron."

"Well now, Grayson, you and the girls will see us move in the morning; and hold yourselves ready to cross over." "If I win without blood, you will want to go. If we assault, your Indians may need looking to. You are all powerful with them. Not for Canada, would I have a prisoner harmed."

"Only win, General; only win and we will be with you. Tecumseh will control his warriors; don't fear on that score."

Then they parted for the night.

CHAPTER VI.

MISSING.

T HAT Saturday saw the end of two busy days of intense planning and preparations on the English bank of the Detroit. The end of another week of waiting, vacillation, of anxiety that became agony, on the American side. Its chief renounced all effort to regrasp the conditions of his own fate, and abandoned himself to what might happen. Miller with the 4th regulars were in the fort. Colonel Findlay and his militia, the 3d Ohio, with those of Michigan, were outside. Late Friday afternoon, Colonels McArthur and Cass, with three hundred picked men of the 1st and 2d Ohio, were hurried off for a third attempt to meet and escort Captain Brush, his command, cattle and stores, from Frenchtown to Detroit, where were still ample supplies. They were started without rations, which were to follow them. None were sent. Instead of which, the next morning, an express rider was hurried after them, with orders to·return. He found them weary and hungry, bivouacked in a wide swamp, where darkness overtook them, when at the call of their officers they arose and turned cheerily back.

At Detroit the shore batteries were replying to the British, and two 24-pounders placed to sweep the approach to the fort. Major Jessup divined Brock's landing-place, Spring Wells, four miles below the fort, and asked permission to plant guns there and oppose him. This was refused.

Later he asked for 150 men, then for 100, to cross over and spike the enemy's guns. The general would think of it, but came to no conclusion, and such of them as his own did not dismount boomed the short night through. Under its cover, Tecumseh placed his Indians in the shelter of the forest, from the landing to the rear of the town, to cut off a possible retreat. And so the August night wore on. The next day was not to be a day of rest, a Sabbath of any kind.

In the vanishing twilight of that dawn, the English crossed. Brock standing erect, conspicuous, in full dress, in the bow of the leading boat, the most exposed man of the expedition; a third of his soldiers were militia. He knew what eyes would be upon him from the wooded bank. His chivalrous bearing was appreciated by Tecumseh.

"See! see!" exclaimed the emulous chief. "A warrior in his canoe, erect, leading the way to battle!"*

As the general anticipated, he found the landing unguarded, and no enemy even to witness his debarkation. Leisurely his troops breakfasted on the enemy's ground, were formed for the advance, the commander conspicuously alone, many yards in lead, with his right on the river, his left protected by Tecumseh. Thus the high hearted column moved to the attack. It was a gallant show, those eight hundred soldiers in scarlet, in the morning sun, with banners and shining arms,—the men of the 41st in front.

---

* Chron. of Canada.

Findlay informed his commander of the advance of his enemy, and asked permission to attack with his regiment and the Michigan militia, which was refused. Instead, he and all the troops outside were ordered within the already crowded fort.

On came the red column with gleaming arms, the veterans as if under the eye of the Regent in Hyde Park. On and on, till they were almost within range of the 24's. The gunners lit their linstocks. They were within range. The gunners became restive, eager. The alert young officer in command, his trained eye measuring the lessening distance, restraining the soldiers with brandished saber, saw his foe almost within his predetermined range for the deadliest effect, turning his eye to the fort for any signal. Already the returning McArthur and Cass had gained a distant view, made their disposition for attack, and a vain effort to communicate with the fort. They noted the ominous silence of the fort. To them the British army seemed delivered into their hands. The first gun would be their signal to advance. *It was never fired.* Instead of the thunder of the 24's a *white flag* was displayed on the fort. Had the earth opened they would have been no more amazed. Had it swallowed them it would have been a welcome refuge.

All night, all the morning and forenoon, the miserable man called general at the fort, gave signs of sore distress. Away from possible succor, disappointed by Dearborn, the woods teeming with Indians, thousands more of whom were hurrying from the North, fierce Ojibways, Chippewas and Tawas. Among the women in the fort were his own daughter and her children; the fort must fall after maddening battle, so he reasoned, or rather these were the spectres of his imagination, in his inability to reason. He sought no counsel, spoke no word, sat on the ground, with his back to the wall, a pitiable spectacle of distracted weakness. Finally the one gun of the enemy, which his own battery left uncrippled to them, sent a solid shot, which came bounding over the fort's wall, dashed into the officer's house, and into a group of men and women, killing two or three, followed by the shrieks of the surviving women, his only casualty. This brought the end. The white cloth was at once displayed, and the unhappy man's own son was hurried forth with an offer of surrender.

The young officer in command of the 24's uttered a cry of anguish and dashed his sword upon the ground. The advancing column halted in amazement. The terms of surrender, including the territory of Michigan, were soon arranged, and at twelve meridian the column advanced to its formal conquest ; the solemnity of investiture with parade and circumstance to be celebrated at noon of the next day.

The conception and execution of his conquest was a brilliant and important stroke of generalship by the British commander, and the honors becomingly worn by him. He appreciated the part borne by his ally, which he evinced in a striking manner when they met at the noon of this day in front of the fort, in presence of victors and vanquished.

Advancing to the chief, extending his hand, he said :

" The general commanding congratulates his brother, General Tecumseh, of the British army, on the success of the allies. To mark my appreciation of his character and conduct, I ask him to accept and wear this from me." Speaking these words he untied the splendid scarlet silk sash from his own person, and deftly invested the slender waist of the noble figure of Shawanoe with it. The chief gracefully yielded his person to the gaudy decoration, in dignified silence. When adjusted, he drew his form up, wearing his crimson cap with its war eagle's feather, showing the prized cincture to advantage, and said with simple grace, his voice betraying slight signs of emotion:

"My great brother makes glad the heart of Tecumseh." Then turning to the Wyandot chief, Round-head, he undid the sash from his own form, saying: "Here is one older and more deserving; Round-head should wear this:" which he placed about the robust loins of the delighted chief. The act was greeted with applause, led by the admiring Brock.

One thing further. The politic general proclaimed a bestowal, so far as the power rested with him, of the territory of Michigan upon his allies. He retained the prisoners. Public property was subject to division. The rights of personal property to remain inviolate. The inhabitants and all non-combatants, to be protected with care.

So fell Detroit, the American army and flag.

The American people were never able to account for this amazing result, even by supposing the twin crimes of treason and cowardice. There must be a third—bargain and sale for gold. A wave of consternation, mingled with shame and wrath, swept around the southern border of Lake Erie, southerly, startling the men of Ohio, Kentucky, Pennsylvania, Indiana, and reaching the Capital. Mr. Madison's government revenged its own weakness and want of care upon the head of its officer, whose imbecility only equalled its own. Another commander had to be named. The eyes of the nation were upon one not yet discernible by Mr. Madison and his secretary of war

(Dr. Eustis), who were to look for yet another elderly fossil, that other battles and forts and armies might be lost on Michigan soil; while the peers of him who surrendered Detroit should be left to meander on their ways, after their kind.

One, the youth in command of the 24's, did not answer the roll-call of prisoners. He was reported missing. One of the best known of the young officers of the expeditionary force, there was special inquiry for him, and some talk of his disappearance. Generally it was supposed he had escaped, and unless cut off by the Indians, would reach Captain Brush at Frenchtown. The last certainly known of him, he was noticed at his post near the guns, apparently greatly dejected.

"He was certainly included in the surrender," said an English officer, who seemed to know something of him, and interested in his fate.

The cross of St. George floated peacefully over the fort as in the day of rightful dominion, won from St. Louis. Tecumseh remained with a strong force of warriors on their recovered soil, knowing as well as the royal giver the vicissitudes of his title. Scarlet guards succeeded the blue, in larger numbers; otherwise Detroit appeared much as on the day before. The warm August night, darkened the not remote forest; the tender moon hung its thin crescent near the western horizon, the stars were taking their sentinel places in the sky, and innumerable crickets and katy-dids were piping their shrill notes in the meadows.

Several of the British officers, and men of the civil service, were permitted to return to their quarters. Of these were Mr. Grayson, Edith, Anita, and two or three ladies, wives of the officers, of the 41st. Mr. Grayson had, during the day, experienced every emotion of anxiety, triumph, exultation, and supreme satisfaction. This bloodless victory, won in the face of odds and difficulties, that no other leader would have dared to brave, was to him a heaven-sent omen of the war. There had been an awful decline in American manhood in a single generation, a little humiliating to him, of the same strain. His emotions had been fully shared by Edith, as women share in feelings common to the sexes. Both were now under the influence of the reaction certain to be experienced by persons of fine organizations. Neither said much on the way down the river. Both had a peculiar cause for concern, which to Edith was a source of depression. Anita, her constant companion, fell into her sister's mood, and like her was grave and silent also.

At the late supper of the returned party, where Edith was conspicuous, she was at her best. If less joyous and gay of spirit than in the idyl days of the southern woods, thoughtfulness now imparted the charm of character to her face, which had rather gained than lost in maiden purity and beauty. Something of appealingness was in her eyes, which many felt, though they could not describe. The gentlemen—all friends, admirers, and some of them beside Home, lovers of hers,—were in rollicking spirits, as loud and reckless of voice, words, and manner, as the presence of three or four women of position and refinement permitted. Drunk with the exhilaration of success, and two or three of them half drunk in the usual way, there was boastful, gratulatory talk of the incidents of the day, the prospect of the war, with depressing comments upon the character and conduct of the enemy.

"Well," said Robinson (son of a refugee) to Mr. Grayson, "our countrymen persuaded the royal negotiators that lakes and rivers were preferable boundaries, and the general has corrected their blunder of yielding Michigan."

"It was a blunder, our ever giving up the posts," added Glegg. "Now we'll man Fort Miami. We built that, did we not, Mr. Grayson?"

"*Dr. Gray, of Ohio,*—permit me to correct you, Glegg," said McDonald, which produced a laugh, in which the subject of the pleasantry slightly participated.

"Governor Simcoe built it in '93, mainly to defend against the north-western tribes, old allies of the French who had a post there," he replied to Glegg. "Later we used it to countenance them," he added.

"Or if Mr. Grayson will permit, to discountenance them," added Home. "When they were defeated and pursued by the Americans at the Rapids, they found the fort shut in their faces, with the words from the commandant, 'Go away, my children, you got so much paint on your faces,' as Little Turtle rendered it," followed by another laugh.

"It's a wonder old Wayne didn't storm it," said Robinson.

"He would, had the Indians been admitted," added Muir.

"*Our* countrymen, as you call them, Mr. Robinson, were content with a line south of the St. Lawrence; we will give them one from the south end of Lake Michigan to the Maumee. They may be glad to take it now," said Grayson. "Tecumseh may insist on the Ohio though. How he does despise the Americans!" he added.

"No wonder he despises 'em! As we have already taken so much, why not claim the Ohio? They'll consent," said Home.

"If they don't, by Jove, the general will take the whole an' give 'er to old Round-head," piped in a clerk.

"Yes, and then clean out old granny Dearborn, and hand New York over to young Brant and the Mohawks," added another.

"All in good time, boys," said Evans. "I presume this little matter—which took him three days—off his hands, the general will return, leaving Proctor in command here. He'll be a general soon—eh, Home?"

"He and General Tecumseh. Won't the Indian show off a laced coat, epaulets, and plumed *chapeau?* What do you say to that, Miss Grayson?" to Edith.

"They will not disguise him, Captain Home. What an act his giving the sash to Round-head was! That was a stroke of genius," she replied.

"Not another man in the world would have thought of it; not even Bonaparte," said her father.

"No one who knew Round-head,—would they, Anita?" said Edith, turning to her sister.

"If saw him in his camp—as we did," replied the girl now improved in her English, knitting her dark brow.

"The young ladies have suspicions still I see," said Home, with affected sarcasm, to Mr. Grayson.

"And memories," added the Saxon maiden.

"By the way, that reminds me—who do you suppose I saw over there to-day?" said the doomed Home to Edith. "The fellow in command of the guns you know;" to McDonald. Home as some of the others drank recklessly.

"Which he didn't fire," added a lieutenant of militia.

"Which he didn't fire," repeated Home.

"For which thank God and his general," said Muir, with real fervor.

"For once they concurred," observed Glegg.

"A really brave man—one thirsting for gore—might have said the word, notwithstanding the flutter of an old table-cloth, and that none of the cleanest," added Home.

"That speech from a British officer, would cause surprise on any other occasion," said Grayson, gravely.

"Had you sent him word he might have run, as you said he did once," said Edith to the captain playfully.

"Ah! you have heard of Captain Dudley, of the American army," he said, recklessly.

"I saw him to-day," she answered.

"Indeed! You may know where he is," said Home.

"I greatly wish I did," was her emphatic answer.

"If you'd seen him as we did, while at ease, you would have seen the funniest specimen of a cock with his comb cut and feathers down, that even *his* country ever produced," said her chief admirer.

"How was it, Captain?" asked the officer of militia.

"Captain Home will do it justice. I trust he will spare us now," said Edith, with quiet dignity, while Anita sat, her wide eyes under her brows of jet flashing on Home.

"Was this Captain Dudley the man you met on the river, in Ohio, at the time—the time you know?" asked a lady friend of Edith.

"He is the gentleman."

"You came near—near—I've understood—excuse me," said McDonald to Grayson, wishing to guide the talk away from this incident of the day.

"This is the young man who rescued me from drowning under circumstances showing he possessed very heroic qualities," said the gentleman, a tremor in his voice, moved by recalling the incident.

"This occurred in the presence and under the eyes of the senior captain of the 41st, of foot," added Edith, in her serene way.

Home, if not sobered by these speeches, was brought to an apprehension of his present position. His suit to Edith had for months been the theme of conversation in army circles and of society at York. He now arose from his seat and approached the perfectly composed young lady with an air of humility.

"Captain Home, before you say what you are about to, I will add one thing. On the occasion of last autumn, without fault of yours, you were compelled to appear at disadvantage almost as great as you do now. This American gentleman relinquished his quarters to us, slept on the ground, distinguished us with care and attentions, conducted us to the Huron, and you will bear him witness, that by no word, act, or manner, did he seem aware that you had not shown the utmost heroism. Is not this strictly true?"

"It is," he replied, in an abject voice.

"Father, have I not spoken truly?"

"Truly, my child," moved to tears.

"Anita, my sister, you know more of this than do I. Does Edith speak truly?"

The Indian girl started from her seat, ran to Edith, clasped her neck with an arm.

"Truly! truly! My uncle Tecumseh guarded the young chief, himself from river Huron," she said, her eyes flashing scorn on the humiliated officer. Her words of Tecumseh made a sensation. Nothing had ever been heard of the matter underlying this statement, though the main incidents of the mission had been told and talked of.

"Captain Home," said the young lady, extending her hand to him, "I forgive you."

"Miss Grayson, I shall ever deplore my forgetfulness. Your gracious pardon is a punishment," he said, and said it well. Raising the hand and bending low, he was permitted to touch it with his lips.

The scene caused some sensation; two or three of the company, with tact, led away from it. Not wholly from the missing American officer, who for the time, and was long to remain an object of interest, with many of the present enemies of his country. Some discussion was had as to his present fortune. Muir thought if he had attempted an escape he would fall into the hands of the Indians. Grayson said if they brought him in, Tecumseh would at once liberate him.

The officers thought if he escaped after the surrender and before rendering himself a prisoner, he was guilty of a grave military offence. Doubtless Brock would overlook it. Some would regret to see him fall into Proctor's hands. He had declared his purpose of dealing severely with all the Yankees who fell into his hands, till they paid some observance to the rule of civilized warfare.

"Gentlemen," said Mr. Grayson, "you surprise me. When was it a crime for a prisoner of war to escape? He may even slay his guards to effect it. These are the incidents of war. In what worse position can this officer be who after his general has relinquished his command of him, and before ours has reduced him to custody, if he walks himself off? My only regret at his escape is, that he will notify the American advance on the Raisin."

"Young Elliott will look out for that," replied Muir.

He then went on to discuss the laws of honor, which bind an officer to render himself a true prisoner, after which he may escape if he can.

Grayson ridiculed this, unless he was to be tried in a court of honor, unknown to law.

"You may say he was guilty of disobedience to his general's orders, who surrendered him. Proctor will hardly try him for that. He will be safe with the Americans," he said.

Home would be sorry to see him in Proctor's hands, and looked up to meet the large eyes of Anita on him.

Then they separated for the night. Later, father and daughter had a conversation, in which Edith related the incident of seeing Dudley during the day. Her party was opposite the fort at the time the English column appeared on its advance. At the showing of the white flag, they took a boat and pushed across. Grayson and two or three gentlemen went on toward the fort. Edith, Anita, and two or three ladies remained near the river below the fort; not far from the guns, Edith observed the young officer without recognizing him, walking backward and forward restively. He finally approached near where Anita and herself were standing, unconscious of their presence.

"When near us," she said, "Anita pressed my hand, whispering 'Dudley, young chief!' I never was so startled—never can be again. He saw us, lifted his cap to us, but said nothing. His face was pale and rigid. He stood irresolutely; then as if a new thought struck him he turned and walked away. This was before the ceremony, for Anita managed to tell or get to her uncle, that Dudley was here.

"Why did not you go to him, and take him in your charge?"

"Oh, I could not move; all he did for us, our practices on him, were on me. Before I was myself he disappeared. He could not approach me; all he had to do at that moment was to walk away—as it seems to me."

"I deplore his going."

"What had he before him but long captivity here?"

"Why, I should have managed that."

"How could he know who and what we are but enemies? Liberty, duty, called him away. I am glad he has gone—for gone he has."

"Well, it is the one thing that mars the otherwise perfect day. We shall hear something more of this to-morrow noon, over there," added the father.

"Oh, I don't want to be there!" said the girl, sadly. "I can't bear to see their humiliation."

"Oh, dear! What must Philip Dudley think if he can see the strait to which his rebellion has reduced his son?" cried the father.

"His son? Do you know, father, this thing begins to look to me like an epoch in human history, which had to be, and your rebels were the heroes or victims of it, and not the responsible doers of crime."

"Well, well, my child," a little impatiently, "heroes or victims, their doings bore to them the bitter fruit of this day—to them and their children—the first of unnumbered similar days. I would save this child, God knows."

"I know you would, and I shall fervently pray that all may be ruled for his true best good, as I believe it will be."

Then with a silent kiss she withdrew.

8

At the ceremony of the next noon, Captain Dudley was not present, nor did anything transpire of his whereabouts or fortune. If any of the red allies had information of him it did not reach the public.

CHAPTER VII.

DUDLEY when ordered to the expedition into Canada, was assigned to command the small body of dragoons, a part of it. On the return to the American side of the Detroit, his horses were idle, and he had a position in charge of the guns placed in the shore battery. His familiarity with all arms made him available for any duty. Naturally his association was with Miller and his officers. He was well liked by McArthur, Cass and Findlay, to whom he was of much use in their new duties. He was aware of the dissensions between them and the general in command. He could not long remain blind to the unfortunate man's faults. He early saw that failure would attend the enterprise. Gay, light-hearted, alert, showing high qualities, he was esteemed by the men of both branches of the little army.

That the fort could be successfully defended, that Brock could be met in the field, he had every confidence. That his commander would surrender without a battle, a siege, when .he finally huddled his men into the fort, had not entered his head. When restraining his eager soldiers at the 24's his eye caught the ghostly gleam of white, on the wall of the fort; it was an illusion of vision, and a second look was necessary. The apprehension of its purpose struck him like a blow. The act of dashing down his emblem of command was instinctive. For an instant it was a horrid dream, in which everything waveringly floated. The advancing red column flared and reeled, then halted. The world grew steady, and his alert mind noted and knew the significance of things. He saw the young aid leave the fort, pass not far from him, and the aids of the British general go forward to meet him, and then they retired to arrange, write out, and sign the terms.

This was a new position for him; he had no experience, knew of no rule for subordinates, when his chief had abandoned the command of his own army, and the general of the enemy had not taken it up. He was in the transition period. His first distinct thought of himself was one of almost agonizing regret that he had not opened fire on his enemy; a battle would then have been inevitable. His better instinct arose against this. It would have been a useless destruction. Surrender by the fatuous commander was inevitable. What was he to do? He thought of his poor men, to whom he now turned,— young, fresh, bright, nervous, athletic fellows; men to follow an officer to an assault with cheers, or stand and fight steadily and coolly, and die by their guns. He saw they now stood ghastly and silent, several with indignant tears in their eyes. Some of them turned to him.

"My brave boys, you see it is all over," he said. "The enemy commands us now. Stand at ease and wait till they come for you." Then he turned back, picked up his sword, replaced it; unbuckling his belt he removed it and placed it under his left arm, walking away some yards that the soldiers might not see in his face signs of the distress he felt.

He took a rapid survey of the immediate situation.

He knew messengers had been sent to recall McArthur and Cass, who would return, and turning to the line of their approach he thought he saw signs of their presence. They had not then reached Brush at Frenchtown. Means must be found to save him.

The column of the enemy advanced. He estimated their numbers. Terms had been adjusted. Walking, studying, lost in thought, he moved toward the fort, saw near him a group of three or four women. He changed his course a little to avoid them, drew nearer, looked.— There stood Edith Gray and Anita! Still he was not greatly surprised. The power of being surprised was not yet fully restored. He lifted his hat. Edith was there. She was of the enemy, was there to see the humiliation of the Americans. A light flashed back on the events of the Ohio woods and rivers. He noticed that she saw him—made no note or sign of recognition, save a look of surprise. He would not meet her. She was some yards distant. *He would escape.* The thought and the certainty of doing it came together. He turned away. The column had passed; all the stragglers hurried forward. The river came into his mind. Some one would guard the boats. The armed ships would have to be passed. He dismissed it. Meantime he moved south-westerly across the open. No one called to him or interrupted him. Why not keep on? The ground was nearly level. He passed behind a breadth of growing corn, which covered him from eyes near the fort, or in that direction. He had his watch, a small compass, a pair of pocket pistols and sword, and wore undress cavalry uniform. Why not walk on? If seen he was not remote. So far as the British soldiers were concerned he was safe. The trouble was the Indians. They must be in force in the wood he was approaching; at least if they kept pace with the column, he should pass near their rear. Of course they must by this time know of the surrender, but doubtless Brock would permit only a few of the chiefs to enter the fort. He knew his old friends Round-head and Walk-in-the-Water were with them, who would remember him. He thought it inevitable that he would be seen by some of the Indians.

As he moved now, seemingly uncertain, he came upon a sink of land, thickly grown with tall ferns, from which the summer sun had drawn the water. He might have avoided it : he did not choose to; nor did he linger in it. When he emerged from the other side, an acquaintance would not have known him without study, and would then have said he was daft. He went out astride his sheathed sword, like a small boy, carrying his plume in his hand, wearing his cap awry, the frond of a fern in the place of the plume, his coat fantastically buttoned, and wearing a woe-begone expression of face. From this point he moved to reach the not remote wood, in a very indirect way. Had he seemed to want cover, he had but to remain in the swamp, or follow it to the forest within an edge of which much of its body was a part. Various impulses seemed momentarily to control him. A stranger by his arms and dress would know his calling; from his striking pantomime, he might have supposed the disaster to the American arms had stricken him with madness. Finally he gained the wood, and seemed distressed by it; ran out and looked up at the trees in amazement, grew reconciled, and calmy re-entered the shade, finding it grateful, as it certainly was. After some solemn and effective pantomine, consisting in part of a reverent appeal to Heaven, he entered the wood, and walked some distance directly forward, until he came upon the thread of a small run from a spring. From this he recoiled as if in fear, walked up and down its tiny course, made many ineffective attempts to leap it; finally, with a bound five feet high, he gained the other bank, where he stood a moment with uncovered head, and returned thanks as for a wonderful escape. A new impulse seized him, under which he laid down on the little brook's margin, permitting his feet to dangle over the low bank and bathed his boots in its tide.

Whatever may be said of his acting, alive to impressions and refraining from all examination of signs or indications, he was strongly impressed as by assured human presence, and remembered that by experiment he had more than once been awakened by a person noiselessly entering his room, their mere presence acting on his sleeping senses. He was under this impression, and labored the subtle problem. He had mentally peopled the wood with Indians. This idea may in turn have acted upon his fancy, rather than the mere atmosphere. However he turned it, the impression deepened. Eyes of men were on him. This was strengthened by the air of the wood itself. Not a bird or squirrel in sight. Though ripe summer, not a chipmunk sent his metallic chirp, however subdued, through the forest. He might as well await things here. He would gladly have drunk of the limpid water, literally at his feet. Its coolness to them did in a way refresh him. He could not go on safely if permitted till nightfall. He might as well play quiescence for the time, and await events. Already the shadows pointed north-easterly, nearly eastward. Some degrees more southwardly must they incline, ere they would melt into the shadow of the earth itself. He was certain more than one pair of eyes were on him, and did his best to realize the character of one made sacred by the touching finger of the Great Spirit. Visions come to the thus favored in sleep. As he lay thinking, the drowsy hum of flies in the sun, the tinkle of the rivulet, induced drowsiness, and he did sleep, really. His last conscious thought was of Edith. Then came visions of the Indians, as he passed the margin of dreamland.

He awoke—was it a fading form of a vanishing dream, or a vanishing Indian of his awakening? Whichever it was, it disappeared, yet brought the useful consciousness of his position. He drew his well washed boots to dry land and looked about, thinking that looking round would now be in order, as a visited intellect. The woods were full of the cool shadow in which the charm of approaching night was being wrought.

Once or twice he heard a shrill note, like the peep of a hylode, answered apparently by one or two fainter, from different points and more distant. It was not the unseasonableness of the notes which suggested they were signals. He supposed he was in an Indian haunted forest, and so interpreted these. He arose, turned a little toward the near clearing, from which came the broad sharp shafts of outer day, where his eyes fell upon the stately figure of a warrior chief, in battle costume, not a dozen yards distant. Light was still strong under the trees. Though a warrior, his aspect was pacific. The war paint had been washed from his fine face and shaved head; though armed, tomahawk and knife were in his belt. When the eye of Dudley met his, he raised his hands to show they were empty and passing half the distance between them he paused.

"Dudley?" he said as asking the name.

"I am Dudley," answered the youth, smiling.

The chief advanced to within two yards, saying—

"Brooch—medal?" as if asking.

"My brother means the brooch, given by Shawanoe?"

The answer was a nod, and extending a hand for it.

Dudley removed it from his neck, drew it from its case, and handed it to the chief. The instant it met his eye he ejaculated, "Good! Good!"

"Dudley no crazy! Dudley no crazy. Him make crazy," he said, almost laughing at the idea.

The young man's answer was a gay, light-hearted laugh.

"Dudley big chief, very big chief," as if this flight of strategy was a master stroke of genius.

At this point, two fine Indian youths, in the panoply of war, drew near, each from points whence came the answering signal. They paused within two or three yards, were approached by the chief and shown the decoration. He also said something to them in their dialect, and from their manner Dudley supposed he gave them to understand the character he had assumed. They stepped a little nearer, passed around him in different directions to take in the full measure of a man equal to such a stroke.

At a signal from the chief they then withdrew out of hearing, when he approached, and with his hand on his bosom, said with gravity—

"Wa-se-go-bo-ah—Shaw-an-oe brother."

"You are Shawanoe's brother?" A nod. "Your name is Wasegoboah?"

"Good! English—'Stand-Firm.'"

"Your name means stand firm?"

"My brother says true."

"My brother glads Dudley's heart. He trusts Stand-Firm," extending his hand, which the chief cordially took; as he did so he returned the medal.

"My brother go Frenchtown?" waving his hand to the south.

"Dudley would go to Frenchtown," he answered.

"Wasegoboah go with Dudley. Nothing hurt Dudley."

"Stand-Firm go with Dudley?" showing his pleasure.

"When night come. Tecumseh send Wasegoboah."

"Tecumseh sent you to go with Dudley?"

"Good. Anita tell Tecumseh."

"Anita told Tecumseh of Dudley?"

"Um," with a nod. "Go by river. Canoe. There, sun-rise."

"Will reach there at sunrise?"

"Um," with a nod.

The chief beckoned the young men to him, and had words in their tongue with them, when they immediately started together, and moved away noiselessly toward the river. The chief made a motion of his hand toward the deeper wood, and Dudley readjusted his dress, save replacing the plume in his hat, belted his waist, and with his sheathed sword in his hand, the two passed 300 or 400 yards into the forest where they came upon the basin of a spring, about which were signs of the recent presence of men, where they halted till night became confirmed in the wood. Here the chief produced from an opening into the hollow of a tree, a calabash shell, with which Dudley supplied himself with water; also a liberal parcel of roasted venison and bread, when for the first time he learned how very hungry and thirsty he was. Refreshed he now arose to commence the journey.

Evidently the guide intended to avoid observation,

using the cover of the wood where practicable. They moved south-easterly, and when they emerged into the open, Dudley saw by the line of mist that the river was near. They crossed the road leading south, and approached it above the landing-place of the invaders of the morning. At the wooded margin of the Detroit, Wasegoboah sounded the note which first attracted Dudley in the forest, and was answered from just below. Here they found the young warriors of that adventure standing by a small canoe, which was at once placed in the slow moving water of the shore. Dudley bent over to examine the craft. It was what he supposed, one of the famous birch barks, and daylight showed it to be of rare workmanship, beaded at the gunwale and otherwise ornamented; a shallop fit for a forest princess. The young man silently took his place in it, showing in this the purpose of his inspection. His friends saw that he was familiar with their craft. His position was such, that with the chief in the stern the bubble-like shell would be best freighted for its voyage. He beckoned the youths to his side and placed in the hand of each an equal portion of the silver coin on his person, the chief took his place with his paddle, and the canoe was sent from the shore. The little thing held her way till the middle of the river was gained, when its prow was turned southward, and the strong current bore it like a boat of condensed foam toward Lake Erie. Not far, and they swept past the frowning battery of the grim looking Queen Charlotte, and a little lower the taut Lady Prevost was passed. If seen in turn the boat was not hailed. Had it been, there was the smallest danger of its being hit by shot and none of its capture.

Passing these and gaining the solitude of the lower

reaches of the river, the hitherto silent Wasegoboah said in the way of the natives—"My brother sleep." Dudley found a blanket for his use. He stretched himself as well as the dimensions of the boat permitted and resigned himself to sleep.

There came through his brain a rapid survey of the two last months, the events of which now took their proper places in perspective, of which the deed of this last day was the fitting end. His mind lost its grasp. Edith, with the startled expression worn at their meeting of the forenoon, was present with him, bringing thoughts of the Huron and her father's mission there. He would banish it. He looked up to the far off stars of the warm night sky. The swirl of the water from the canoe's prow sent its low monotone to his ear, and there were the notes and calls of the nocturnal aquatic birds and animals from the marshes and reedy margins of the river, under the shadow of the forest. These grew indistinct in his be-numbed senses and he slept.

When they reached the lake, he awoke and used the the second paddle until the boat was hidden under the bank of the Raisin. In the light of the morning, Dudley amused himself with making inscriptions with a pencil on the bark inside the boat. At the point of concealment he parted with his faithful guide, who carried with him full evidence of the youth's gratitude, as well as messages of thanks to Shawanoe and Tecumseh; also specially to the Indian maiden, Anita. He reached Brush's quarters an hour in advance of Captain Elliott, the half-blood son of Colonel Elliott, Indian superintendent. Brush, with a company of militia cavalry had everything in readiness for departure, if approached by a superior force, or for fight if the numbers made it prudent. His cattle were soon on the way toward distant Urbanna, across the swampy divide between the basin of the lakes and the valley of the Ohio. The British officer came, with merely a guard, to receive the submission of Brush, and conduct him, his stores and party, to Detroit. Brush laughed at him. Learning that the pleasant looking young officer with Brush was his informant of the surrender and the leading conditions, he knew he must be the missing Captain Dudley, now a personage of interest in both armies. He claimed him as a prisoner, and was laughed at again. He then delivered the letter he bore from McArthur and Cass, and truculently threatening Dudley if he ever fell into British hands, he turned back from his "sleeveless errand."

The escape of Dudley remained one of the mysteries of the British army in Canada. The exploit and the service it enabled him to perform, gained for him a credit which he felt was not his due. Light of heart and gay of spirit, he was nevertheless introspective. His modesty, his sense of justice, made him exacting of himself, and nothing was more distasteful to him than praise undeserved.

Brush escaped with the public property. Brock and Tecumseh knew the uselessness of pursuit, with many hours and forty miles the start, and commanded as the enemy would now be. Unquestionably Brush's force never having become a part of the army at Detroit, were justly held by Dudley not within the terms of the capitulation. A few of his men were sick and unequal to the march, and these Elliott conducted to Detroit as prisoners of war.

With no superior officer, Dudley reported directly to the war office, and meanwhile offered his services to

Harrison, who gladly accepted and placed him upon his staff, of which he soon became the chief, a name then unknown, with the rank of major. His first service was in the expedition for the relief of Fort Harrison, of mounted militia from Kentucky. He commanded the advance on the last day's march. The Indians did not risk a battle with him. His arrival was opportune. The palisades and block houses were burnt away on one side, the garrison at the last gasp, worn and exhausted by their persistent and desperate defence.

Harrison, meantime, had been appointed a brigadier-general of the regular service, but limited to a field of command that made him hesitate to accept it. He followed the relieving expedition of Ohio troops, which raised the siege of Fort Wayne, where he was joined by Dudley.

The new general of the north-western army, which the genius of Harrison called into existence, made his appearance at Fort Wayne soon after the arrival of Harrison, who turned the command over to him. Winchester was a brave man, a soldier of the old army, a gentleman of the old school. His manners and bearing were unendurable to the hunter and pioneer volunteers, who expected to serve under Harrison, and who now peremptorily refused to be led by Winchester. They mutinied, in fact, and it was only after an effective speech from the victor of Tippecanoe, a master of popular oratory, as of the popular heart, that they consented to recognize him as their general. Winchester offered Dudley the first position on his staff. He felt free to choose, and remained with Harrison.

As he anticipated, the cabinet at Washington, better advised, superceded Winchester with the Kentucky general of militia, who now accepted his national appointment. The confidence now reposed in him seemed boundless, and he was formally invested with discretionary powers in his department, only second to those of Washington in the war of independence.

Winchester was soured by the treatment he received. He had no knowledge of the kind of war now being waged ; he soon became a sharp critic of his commander, and never gave him cordial support or effective aid.

For more than organization and preparation, power came to the new general too late for a campaign to recapture Detroit and humble Malden, the present season.

The department of the North-west was the limitless region from the west line of New York, westward. In the main, a level, swampy, roadless, bridgeless wilderness. Under the Autumn rains the streams were swollen and the spongy soil ceased to have a practicable bottom for transportation purposes. Not a man or horse, not a gun or pound of stores, could be used at the point of impact, that did not have to make the transit of this wide expanse. The lake, as will be remembered, was closed to the Americans.

Once the new commander saw a gleam of chance to recapture Detroit. The means of approach—the frozen river—were too precarious, the men for the assault too remote, and Dudley saw it vanish as impracticable.

General Brock confirmed his promise of protection to the people of Detroit and Michigan, turned the command over to Proctor with instructions, and with a few of his personal staff sailed on the " Hunter " for his threatened Niagara border the 22d of August. Nine days were sufficient to destroy an army more numerous than his own, swallow up a large province, and paralyze the national power of his enemy in the North-west, till winter should intervene.

He returned with plans of sweeping the American border from lake to lake, to find the armistice which set him free still continued by the American general, *spite of the orders of his Government annulling it.*

The famous British " Orders in Council " were the final cause of the American declaration of war, and though revoked two months before the date of that Act, slow winged news of it did not reach America until a month after its passage; whereupon Prevost and Dearborn, whose war hardly arose to a breach of the peace, sus· pended the declaration of the war. Dearborn entered into this convention, in face of his orders, to demonstrate against his enemy in aid of his Western colleague, and excused himself later on the ground that he *did not know* the Niagara frontier was a part of his department.

Brock, with his Western laurels fresh and bloodless, met the American army of invasion, and fell on Queens-town Heights, leading a charge, where he encountered the younger Scott, two months from the day of his landing at Malden. His enemy paid his entire army of invasion for this life, and gained in the bad exchange of war. Yet Brock's fall was deplored by his slayers as a common loss.

Brock required that Mr. Grayson and Edith should remain at Malden. He desired their influence with Proctor and Tecumseh. He knew an early and decided effort would be made to recover Detroit and capture Malden. He could spare no soldiers. They must re-cruit from the Indian tribes. Pressed in its awful life struggle with Napoleon, England could not send a man to America. With Tecumseh to command them, he employed the savages with less reluctance. He knew Proctor's character, but choice of a commander was not his.

Canada West was a remote region, and when winter closed Lake Erie, entirely isolated. Its only connection then with its capital, York (Toronto), was by a road from the Thames mouth, two hundred miles through a gloomy forest, striking the head of Lake Ontario at Burlington Heights.

Save Muir's ineffective demonstrations against the American posts, an Indian incursion at Sandusky, another into Kentucky, the arming and organization of the hunters and pioneers, the season closed without real war in the North-west.

In January, Dr. Eustis made way for Major Armstrong (author of the Newburg letters) in the war office, and the Americans resolved to capture Lake Erie.

9

CHAPTER VIII.

EDITH hoped that Malden and Windsor would be enlivened with the presence of Mrs. Proctor, and two or three ladies who would accompany her. In this she was disappointed. For her the winter closed in with unrelieved gloom.

She had been educated, had taught herself to regard the unfortunate king with the self-denying devotion of Flora McIvor for the young Pretender. To her the loyalty of those who bore the livery of the crown seemed cold and uncertain, merely a professed sentiment loosely worn for personal ends. Not the *one*, as with her, or the strongest of many incentives to action. With clever intellect and strong lines of character her vision had been narrow. She saw everything through the atmosphere of her education and self-dedication, not without much refracting power upon such rays of light as surrounded most objects brought within reach of her vision. If she had beauty, attraction, intellect, she set no woman's value on them as means of winning admiration, even love, for herself. That they might serve such a purpose had not occurred to her.

For the five or six years of her maturing life, the growing differences between the kindred nations, in the father's judgment, were the means in the hands of Heaven of conducting to inevitable war. Their duty was to strengthen the hand of the king.

In his heart still rankled the unmitigable sense of personal wrong. The heart of the girl, however mistaken, was influenced by lofty and pure sentiment. That, as she supposed, could be only won by loyalty as unselfish as her own, illustrated by great service and gallant exploit. She had seen but one man she could love. She never thought of him as a possible lover. She had in no way tested her power to love. This hero' was the general who almost commanded her to remain in Canada West. She did not like Proctor; he was coarse fibred, loud voiced, boastful, might be brutal, even cowardly. She once tried to look kindly on Home. She felt she could never love him. Recently she regarded him with increasing indifference— more than indifference. Something had happened in the Ohio woods, now a year ago, very strange it seemed, revealing unsuspected secrets of her own nature, showing that whatever she was she had the common and cherished qualities of her sex. This woman side of herself, or this side of this woman, stood to her inner view in Rembrandt light and shadow, a little startling. She also found that the old cherished objects of reverênce, devotion, and labor had received a strange new light, which not only diminished their importance, but showed them in changed aspects.

Her father suddenly disappeared in the black water, drawn under the drift. She realized she might never even see his form again, when a face broke from the drowning flood and laughed in hers, and strong arms bore up to her the lost.

The rescuer did not ask her love, confront her as seeking it. He set no value on his service, and seemingly little on himself. One to do things naturally, as belonging to him to do,—not for reward; they were his work, and so there was nothing to be said. She was very sure were she a man she would do things this way; that she would never approach a woman as demanding her love. He was in her heart from that, first as something precious, like the dearest girl—no, not a girl, but like a girl. He was a virile, heroic man; more than any possible girl a thing to love, to be near, yet to be coyly shy of; to be afraid of with that tremulous fear which was not fear at all. She could not describe it. It was very sweet to have. She wondered if he had something of this same feeling toward her? Of course he had, because it was hers toward him. Of course one could not have this alone,—what precious logic.

For some time her thought was,—this is not love: love blinds, fascinates, intoxicates, has the uncanny thing of magic. This was inspiring, lifting one's soul into purest white light, where God dwelt; not selfish, not akin to that passion of the senses called love. When her mind saw it clearly, she had no doubt of what it was,—a pure and exalted love. Of course nothing as common lovers could ever come of it. They were enemies—might never see, or even hear of each other. Mountains, seas, continents, divided them. No matter, she was glad— glad they had met; glad of her own love. It was its own priceless recompense, bringing her nothing but good.

Then came the war with some rekindling of the Joan of Arc. Brock came with that day of glory and triumph. It brought that vision of *him*, looking as she would have him look, bringing all the recalling and introspection with which she had grown familiar.

She was glad of his escape for many reasons. Largely that he was free, was with his friends, had gained much, as she thought, deserved credit. Certainly his reputation should not suffer in the British army. One thing had been settled by the Ohio mission; she should never wed. She now knew there could be but one man in the world to whom she could ever be wife and that could never be.

The thing that in any way reconciled her to remain at Malden, beyond her diminished sense of duty, was the presence of Tecumseh, and possibly an unconscious sense of the nearness of this other, which she never grasped or made mental note of.

The fall of Brock, Edith's one hero of the British army in America, greater than Wolf,—as she regarded him,—was to her an irreparable blow. On his fate, as she supposed, the war on the northern frontier of the States must depend in large measure. The news benumbed her. She had fancied his was a charmed life. The hail of battle was to leave him untouched. He was stricken, and Canada was helpless. Nobody was left but a herd of ignoble men, with no mastering hand to wield and make them heroic. The drums were muffled, the banners draped; the old soldiers wept. The swaggering Proctor, grim old Colonel St. George, the colonels, the majors, and captains were ghastly and silent. When Harrison came, as come he would, who would lead the soldiers to meet him?

There was but one now, king born of the woods, whose ability as a leader the English were yet to learn, and learning were yet to contemn, because a barbarian, and born out of England. If incapable of profiting by his genius, he regarded them with a lofty scorn. He did full justice to the fighting qualities of the British soldier. He held the tactics of civilized war in slight esteem, and he despised Proctor nearly as much as he did the Americans.

War was now supposed to be postponed until spring. It was understood at Malden that the Americans would attempt to dispute the supremacy of the lake, the next campaign, and yet in the frozen heart of the winter was to occur an incident of the war, itself very war, that was to startle the heart and nerves, and darken the life of Edith, more than anything within the circle of her years— except the death of Brock—and although it was to gild the royal arms with triumph, and win a general's epaulets for Proctor, it would bring into relief, painfully, some of the defects of his character and generalship.

CHAPTER IX.

VERY-WAR.

THE oft mentioned river Raisin, then a beautiful forest stream, runs into the west side of Lake Erie, near its head. On this, built both sides of it and two miles from its mouth, was the pretty village of Frenchtown, composed of thirty dwellings ; it was forty miles southerly from Detroit and eighteen miles south-westerly from Malden. It was well built for the pioneers' time. Its people were thrifty, had small, well-cleared, and cultivated farms and gardens, fruitful orchards, and ornamental shrubbery. It was on the road of approach from Sandusky as from the forts of the upper Maumee to Detroit, and had, as will be remembered, a small stockade constructed of palisades or pickets, round sections of tree trunks, set firmly in the ground, and rising twelve or fifteen feet above its surface, pointed at the tops. This was the general character of a stockade. A larger, stronger fortification had well constructed block houses, at least at the angles—this was of the simplest form, with one small block house.

Upon the fall of Detroit, although within the territory of Michigan, Captain Elliott received the submission of the inhabitants and promised them protection,—a promise never kept.

It was the southern outpost of the British ; Major Reynolds, of the provincial militia, was in command, with two companies, and 400 Indians, mostly Wyandots, under Round-head and Walk-in-the-Water; and, as the British and Canadians say, there were also in the neighborhood about 200 of the great Indian trader Dickson's Indians from the upper lakes, for whom the British were not responsible. However this may have been, the people of Frenchtown suffered greatly from hostile invasions; Reynolds could not or would not protect them. Repeated applications to Proctor were ineffective, and in their despair they sent two deputations in the dead of winter, in quick succession, to the nearest American post, appealing for aid and defence against the outrages to which they were subject.

At the junction of the Auglaze with the Maumee was then situated Fort Defiance. The old fort was built by Wayne; General Harrison built a new and stronger work, the past Autumn. Here General Winchester, who changed its name to his own, was spending the winter with 800 young Kentuckians, in some respects the flower of the State. He was able to maintain hardly a semblance of discipline over these chivalrous young men, with whom he lived or spent his time, rather than commanded. It was to these the Frenchtown deputations appealed. Winchester referred them to the Kentuckians in mass meeting, who unanimously resolved to chastise their oppressors and protect them, notwithstanding the distance and season, and the nearness of Frenchtown to Malden. A detachment was hurried to the Raisin, which fell upon the enemy, and after a sharp battle forced them and their Indians two miles into the woods. The Canadians tenaciously contested every tree and rood of ground. So near the enemy the Americans knew they would be speedily assaulted by Proctor with an overwhelming force, unless they retreated. They came to protect; they must remain. The battle over they retired to Frenchtown, took possession of the stockade, and hurried messengers to Winchester for reinforcements. The general, with nearly the residue of the Kentucky contingent, hastened to their aid. He reached the exposed point just at nightfall of the day after the battle. The stockade was on the north side of the river, a little distance from it. It was not large enough to accommodate all his force.

The residue encamped near in the rear of it. Having seen to the disposition of the troops, Winchester returned with his staff across the river half a mile or more, to a house for the night. This was against the remonstrance of his officers, who earnestly requested him to remain with them. He was a good deal annoyed in the evening by the report of the scouts, who announced the enemy in the neighborhood in force. He laughed in their faces, and with his aids betook himself to serene slumber. Ere daybreak he was wakened by his own reveille which was immediately lost in the thunder of Proctor's artillery, the volleys of his musketry, and the war-whoop of Roundhead's warriors. On his way to the battle-field, that chief met and made him a prisoner, and despoiling him of his coat and boots, he conducted the late commander of the north-western army to Proctor.

The day of the first battle was the anniversary of good Queen Charlotte's birth; the English officers and the elite of Canada West celebrated the occasion at Mrs. Draper's tavern.*

---

* Chronicles of Canada.

Early in the evening, as the gayety of the occasion began to sparkle, in strode grim old St. George, sent over to educate the militia, equipped for the field, looking like a belated martial Santa-Claus out of place, and announced that the officers were to be ready for march at four the next morning. Wild rumor found itself on the wing. Harrison was advancing on Detroit. Antitype of Napoleon's approach, three years after, upon the Belgian capital. The enemy were to be met on his own soil.

Edith felt constrained to be present at the ball, in honor of her royal mistress, a reluctant spectator of a joyance she could not share. She witnessed the departure of the expedition, knew that Proctor took nearly his available force, and was not a little anxious. Tecumseh was absent on a mission West ; not only would he be absent from the expected battle, and victory, but his restraint over his heated warriors would be lacking. She heard the loud voice of Proctor, and shuddered as she thought of the American wounded, or prisoners, who might fall into his hands. All the next day she was nervous and anxious, more so than when Brock moved to attack Detroit. In the morning of the second, the day of the second battle of Frenchtown, she induced her father to cross to the American side with herself and Anita. She had a fine pair of horses with a sleigh and robes. The Detroit had been frozen six weeks, and the snow was deep. She persisted in going on the southern road to the native Brownstown. There about noon the victors came hurrying back, more like fugitives, than conquerors from a field of triumph. Everything indicated they had been roughly met, though Winchester was a prisoner and accompanied the loud-voiced Proctor in a sleigh. Then came a considerable body of prisoners, dejected, silent, the British wounded, even the bodies of their slain. Where were the American wounded? above all where were their own red allies, a considerable body of whom made a part of the expeditionary force? and why was there such haste as if pursued by a superior enemy?

It did not at the first all come to Edith. Later she came to know more than enough, much more than should have been. Proctor attacked at daybreak. The Americans outside the pickets were finally overpowered, and retreating to the woods were surrounded by the Indians and slain to a man; not one escaped. Not a prisoner was made.

The fire from the stockade, by the Kentucky rifles, was so hot and well directed that Proctor was compelled to draw off. He finally bullied the captured General Winchester to send an order to the gallant defender of the stockade to surrender. This was refused. The officer in command would not recognize the authority of a superior in the hands of the enemy. Finally, on a pledge personally given by Proctor, of protection to prisoners and care of the wounded, the Americans grounded arms. The Indians at once, in Proctor's presence, began an attack on them. Their American commander ordered them to resume their weapons, when the British officers interfered effectively.

Then came the senseless rumor, no one ever knew on what authority, *that Harrison was at hand*, and Proctor almost in a panic, withdrew, fancying himself pursued, though as English Reynolds, the royal commissary, naïvely said—"The enemy never came in sight."

Finally Reynolds returned with his sleighs, and a flag for his own protection, for the enemy's wounded. Edith would follow the procession on the hard beaten road.

As they approached the battle-field, signs of its neighborhood, as of the haste of Proctor's retreat, increased.
Near the town Reynolds, who had mastered the ghastly
problem, hurried back to her, and succeeded in having
her driver turn her horses' heads northward again.

Not an American was alive.

Edith was told that this nameless deed, the dreadful
finish, was the work of Dickson's Lake Indians. This is
still asserted. To her it made no difference whether
the allies of the British did it, or savages not allies, who
were permitted to do it.

When it was reported to Proctor his only remark
"Indians are good Doctors," was significant of the
man's nature as of his methods of warfare.

· Though Edith turned back, knowing only the general
fact, she was sick and depressed beyond what she had
supposed was in her power to suffer. All the way back,
as night deepened in the wood through which the glid-
ing sleigh sped its noiseless way, muffled, with her head
bowed, one lovely pale dead face was present within her,
lying in the snow reddened with blood.

This was war, stripped of its trappings and reduced
to its simples.

She could not rest on her return, till her father, in an
interview with one of the captured officers, learned that
Dudley was not at Fort Winchester, but with General
Harrison, and promoted. It was a great relief to her.
She was glad on the whole that he was attached to the
American general's staff; he was comparatively safe.
She would know where he was when told where the head-
quarters of the enemy's army were. She thought his
preference would be for a position in the line. She knew
that the personal wish of an officer was seldom consulted.

He would certainly do his duty wherever he was. Her heart went out to him in a gush of relieved emotion.

Soon the wretched condition of the people of Frenchtown came to her remembrance, now in the heart of winter, unprotected by their countrymen, plundered and annoyed by their enemies, with the ghastly scenes of battle and blood about them ; and she shuddered as she remembered that her woman's hand had helped to bring this upon them. She talked with her father, who, while he regarded these calamities as a just visitation of Providence, still illogically esteemed it his duty as a Christian to do what he might to mitigate its severity, and he went with her to Proctor, and procured from him an order for their removal to Detroit. She then busied herself in securing comfortable abodes for them in the town. The kind-hearted Reynolds furnished means of transportation, and in a week under her supervision they were for the time housed from the winter and Indians. It was from these objects of her care that she learned the details of the scenes following the surrender of the Americans. She had a discussion of the matter with Home, who came to have a very clear understanding of her estimate of it, and an apprehension that his position toward her was not largely improved.

That Proctor left Frenchtown after the battle under the influence of an honest fear of Harrison's approach, can hardly be doubted. He even left the gallant St. George bleeding from three severe wounds, freezing in the snow where he fell, and who would have perished but for the care of others. His victory was hailed with plaudits throughout Canada, and in England. The Prince Regent promoted him, the Canadian parliaments gave

him votes of thanks. He was yet to hear the cry of
"*Frenchtown!*"

The winter wore on, Edith finding ample employment
in the care of her protegees, the exiles of Frenchtown,
who would require aid for the indefinite time until they
could return in safety to their abandoned homes. The
employment was grateful to her feelings in every way; at
first undertaken largely from a sense of duty, its continu-
ance became a source of exquisite satisfaction, filling her
heart with gratitude that she was enabled to render the
homeless ones this service.

Toward March, her "Knight of the Forest," as she
called the Shawanoe, returned. His mission extended to
the Sacs, Foxes and even the more distant Sioux. He
was shocked at the report of the slaughter of the
wounded prisoners. His honor was involved, and he
made enquiries into the horrible excesses at Frenchtown,
the result of which in no way relieved his own subordinates, or the British commander. He censured his
chiefs in the strongest terms—declared he would sum-
marily punish any repetition of it in the future. Proctor
and his officers were surprised, that "Now the thing was
over, he should make such a — of a fuss about it;" were
the general's words. Tecumseh retorted with scorn, not
depending on Elliott to render his meaning.* So that
matter stood to a day in the near future.

"You conquer to murder, I conquer to save," were his reported
words.—*Anthony Shane—Drake's Tecumseh.*

CHAPTER X.

THE FIRST GUN.

THE Northern winter held the rivers and lakes, the wide level sweeps of land, under its ices and snows, till after mid-March. Tecumseh had returned, with him came his brother, and as spring came with its warmth, and lent its tint of color to wood, hill-side and plain, he mustered his warriors from all Michigan and beyond the Wabash.

The American general was glad to have all the hostile bands in his front. His flank, the distant cabins, were for the time safe. He meant the campaign of 1813 should make this last forever assured. Harassed by the short terms of the militia, tied by the orders of the secretary of war, soon to become his enemy, the opening season, earlier by many days on his side of the lake, found his preparations well in hand.

In that day of primitive arms, the rapids of the Maumee were a strategic point of forest warfare, held so by the commanders of both races. Little-Turtle, Blue-Jacket, Black-Hoof and Turkey-Tracks, awaited Wayne there. There the French built a fort, and the British, Fort Miami. The Maumee—the Miami of the lakes—runs north-easterly. After the expulsion of the French, Fort Miami side, the left bank was called the British side, while the easterly or southern was known as the American.   Old Fort Miami was now a ruin.   Two miles above, on the American side, and twelve miles from the lake, was the site of the to become famous Camp Meigs. The banks of the river there, are about one hundred feet high, from the top of which, save where cut down by small confluents, the table-land stretches back in level sweeps, then heavily wooded. On the easterly side, a stream made a deep ravine in its course to the river. Just above this, Harrison's engineer, Captain Wood, planted the camp, the ravine becoming a natural defence. The front of the camp was some three hundred yards from the river, and the works consisted of a wall of heavy palisades, of 2500 yards in extent, enclosing eight acres of ground, many sided, with numerous angles and strong block-houses. The whole was surrounded by a ditch and abatis ; the timber for a sufficient breadth had been removed from about it, and a battery commanded the river.   The Americans were deficient in artillery, and ammunition for it, in the war. To man the works required 2500 men. Here at mid-March Harrison made his headquarters, with less than half that force. Ohio and Kentucky were to furnish the needed reinforcements. The Black swamp lay between him and Sandusky. The breadth of Ohio between him and Kentucky. Franklinton, on the west bank of the Scioto, opposite Columbus, was then Governor Meigs' capital, and the headquarters of the General.

He had many famous scouts and runners. On Dudley's arrival with his chief in March, he found Carter there, and he attached him to himself as an outside aid, under his immediate orders. As to others Carter's position was wholly independent. He had been at Detroit, Malden and Windsor. In the guise of an old Canadian of ill fortunes, he lingered about these places, observing and picking up much useful information. He was a scout for Wayne and knew the neighborhood well. He discovered the approach of the British army in latest April, and hastened back to camp with the information. Then there was a great running of messengers from the American camp towards Sandusky and Fort Winchester, to Governor Meigs and Kentucky.

With his scouts and runners, Tecumseh was advised of the movements of his enemy. He did not admire his methods of fortifying a camp. It would be an admirable cover to assemble his forces under, and a secure place to retreat to, if repulsed. If permitted, he would assemble and organize a force which would recapture Detroit and endanger Malden. Tecumseh would assail the place over the ice and snow, ere its growth to formidable proportions. Proctor and his council decided it must be crushed. It could not be done until the river and lake admitted of transportation. The chief was impatient; he was ready long before the tardy sun performed its part of the enterprise. The tardier Proctor was not then ready.

With the rekindling warmth of the sun, the flutter of banners, the gleam of scarlet, of buttons and arms, the high spirits and confidence, the expectations of officers and soldiers, by which she was surrounded as part of her daily life, Edith felt the reawakening of her own heroic spirit. The bitterness and pain of mid-winter passed with its snows. Her interest in the river, the cause of the crown, revived; the voice of the boastful Proctor was less offensive. He had shown enterprise in the river Raisin expedition. His fault was his haste and want of care in leaving the well fought field. He now had a thousand trained soldiers ; Tecumseh would lead 2000 warriors, would command them in person, and another effective blow would be struck for the Prince Regent and the homes of his red allies. Her father was eager and confident. It was hoped another campaign would sufficiently humble the Yankees. True an amazing series of naval victories of the enemy had balanced the moral effect of his reverses by land. These were in the now past. He would by autumn sue for peace, with an amended boundary. Mr. Grayson, a man of fortune, owned a small sloop bearing Edith's name; in this, with his daughter and a small party of ladies, he would accompany the expedition against Harrison, the new general. The voyage would be a short one, the danger to them none. The scenes of Frenchtown must not be repeated. Edith was more than willing. The officers were anxious she should go. They would carry large and commodious tents, and camp-equipage. She would be quartered and sheltered in the lovely woods, mid spring flowers and notes of song birds. The Miami of the lakes was said to be the most beautiful, as the most considerable of the rivers, emptying into the lake on that side.

Anita was in an ecstasy of delight from the day of her sister's determination to go. Naturally she resolved to bring about a meeting between her and the young chief. She observed the prudence of silence as to her purpose. She was now too mature a woman not to know that a maiden's words were not infallible interpreters of her feelings and wishes.

The English squadron of all vessels, freighted with Proctor, his army, and fortunes, made a gay show down the Detroit ; winging out in the broad lake, and floating away to the mouth of the not distant Maumee. It was a lovely day of softened air, and the sun came back from the water blindingly, in the eyes of the confident throngs on board. The course up the full banked river was more laborious.

Just below the old fort on the British side, the bank bends away from the river, leaving a bit of interval large enough for the British encampment, safe from the enemy, and which was selected for that purpose. The Indians were on the American side, and there made their camp. Their business was to infest the woods, so as to invest the works of the enemy completely.

The royal engineers were on the ground in advance and selected the site for the batteries of the 24-pounders and cohorns. On the morning after the landing, the two generals rode up to examine the ground, and inspect their enemy's works. Tecumseh, a noble horseman, was mounted on a powerful charger, and in his uniform coat, golden epaulets, scarlet cap and eagle's feather, was a warrior to be seen. Short, pudgy Proctor, sashed and gorgeous, an indifferent rider, appeared at disadvantage by his side. Everything from sky to sunlit earth, was gay and glorious. The Maumee had never seen a more gallant spectacle. The morning parade on the old grounds of Fort Miami, the gleam of arms, the scarlet uniforms, the generals and aids, with a troop of provincial cavalry, who rode well, galloped up to see the mounting of the heavy guns, which were to demolish the wooden walls, behind which Harrison and his soldiers hoped to find shelter.

Eyes from Camp Meigs had detected signs of a presence not healthful in the wood on the British shore, a gleam of red, a flash of bullion, and plumes, and an 18-

pounder sent a round shot, with precision, into the group about the guns, fatal to two or three, and the boom of the gun rolled down the high walled valley, rolling through the old wood, startling the bronzed warriors on the east side, who never could hear the thunder of ordnance with indifference. There was a vein of superstition in Proctor, and the result of the first shot was an omen of ill. Tecumseh laughed at the influence which it had on the feelings of his commander, not advancing him in the chief's estimation. The engineers changed the position of the battery, and the light of the next morning saw the woody curtain which hid their labors pushed by, revealing their heavy guns in position. When the artillerists were ready to open, upon turning to the wooden wall, lo! a change there. The white field of tents that the day before filled the foreground of the camp, and gleamed a wavering line of white through the early night, had vanished, and their expectant eyes met a dull line of yellow earth along the whole extent,—a *grand traverse*, on an ample base, rising twenty feet from the surface, behind which stood the white town of tents in absolute security.

Chagrined and angered, Proctor roared and thundered out his stupid rage from all his wide throated guns, sending harmless iron to strengthen the wall of senseless earth, or bore and splinter the now useless palisades easily renewed from within. He was but sparingly replied to by his provident enemy, whose limited supply of food for his small and few guns restrained his impulse to prodigality in its use.

The warriors streamed through the forest in the rear of the camp, weaving an impenetrable net-work of invisible links which could only be broken by a determined charge of a body of well handled soldiers. They stole up to the margin of the wood near the fort. Here and there a bronzed face in paint, a shaved head with the scalp lock challenging the scalping knife of an enemy, flashed from behind a protecting tree, to disappear ere the alert riflemen of the fort could sight the deadly weapon. There were useless exchanges of shots at a range too great for the arms of that day. Some of the adventurous warriors ascended trees and fired into the camp. Some of the Ohio men, who garrisoned the fortress, carried with them a heavy rifle which discharged a four ounce ball, effective at a half mile, which was used fatally more than once on the aspiring braves, and came to be called "Old Meigs."

Something occurred the evening following the appearance of the grand traverse of the Americans, near and within the British camp, of much interest, and influencing the fortunes of those whose history I recount.

CHAPTER XI.

SQUAW-BLOW.

THE " Edith " on landing the Grayson party, found a pleasant place below the craft of the expedition, where she was tied to trees on the shore, under which, on the leaf-strewn earth, their double-walled tents were set up, and the ground covered with mattings, carpets, and rugs. Here, protected by the wood crowned bank, where the warm sunbeams came in, the early spring was perceptibly working its charm; her earliest flowers were in bloom, her birds in song. It was below the camp, between the limit of which and the group of the Grayson tents was a tiny spring run, which cleft the high bank, making for itself a ravine seemingly disproportionately large.

Edith would be beyond sentinels and pass words. A standing order admitted all of the party to the camp in which were the quarters of the husbands of two of the ladies. They were accustomed to the boom of heavy guns, and were little disturbed by the cannonade.

The day of the inspection by Proctor, the ladies were abroad in the warm sun, and they found several of the alway out of place hangers-about Malden, who came, as was inevitable. The nondescripts had two crafts in the river below, one of which belonged to a well-known sutler; useless everywhere, they were familiar figures, their names known to but few.

The opening of the heavy guns and feeble response that second morning, were the absorbing theme of conversation. An assault was expected. The boats were ready and the soldiers under arms should the wall be broached. As the sun warmed up the small plat and sloping bank, the girls and their friends were on the alert, making excursions along the now deserted river, and climbing the secondary hill-like bank to the wooded land above for better observation.

On their way up this ascent one of the oldest of the worn fort haunters of Malden, whom Edith saw the day before, was reclining on the northern bank of the ravine, in a position to take the full warmth of the sun. Evidently his companions had left him for the more attractive scene of the cannonade.

The Indian girl lingered a little and passed nearest the old man. To her he showed a lovely "*squaw-blow*," removing from it for the purpose a bit of light tracing paper, then used by engineers. She was attracted by it, and went to him, when he gave the flower to her. She remained a moment by him, and tripped along to gain Edith's side, holding out her present gleefully to her. Edith took and greatly admired it ; its three lily white petals, and golden anthers make it one of the most striking of the earlier flowers, and was the first the girl had seen that spring.

"Old man gave it me," were the words of the girl, in her improved English, as she received it back. "I promised him some bread and meat—poor old man," pityingly.

Edith turned to look back at him compassionately, touched by the gentleness of a nature that prompted such an offering. She said some word of approval, and

Anita ran back to execute her promise to the old man, and examined with more care the paper which she received with the flower. She found a pencil inscription on it, which deeply engaged the attention of the curious young woman. Twenty minutes later she joined her sister on the plain above. On their return the meek old man was finishing his repast with apparent satisfaction, bestowing the surplus of Anita's bounty in a capacious pocket of a loose outside garment. Then he arose, went down to the spring brook, extended himself on the ground and took a seemingly copious draught from it, in that primitive mode. Apparently refreshed, he arose seeming to listen a moment to the sound of the guns, turned and moved slowly in the direction of the lower craft, and past from the eyes of the girls as from the mind of one of them. He carried with him a scrap of paper on which were two words written by the Indian girl.

On their return, Edith found the flower in a small china pitcher filled with water, to which her sister went at once and hung over it with the liveliest interest.

"What is it, Anita?" she asked.

"*Squaw-blow,*" she answered, showing her teeth in her delight. A little later she said, "Young chief over there;" throwing a slender brown hand toward the American camp.

"Who told you?" Edith may have supposed this as probable, the color deepening in her face, on hearing it asserted.

"*Squaw-blow,*" replied the child, now breaking into a peal of girl laughter. "Edith remember that night on the Huron, after the young chief went?"

"Well, Anita?"

"I told her I bring him back."

"Oh, I remember."

"Edith said,—'Bring him.' "

"Oh, I did?" now laughing in turn. "Well, you never brought him—naughty girl," with playful reproach.

"He come to-night," still laughing.

"Who told you?" startled by the thought.

"*Squaw-blow*," with increasing mirth.

"What a wonderful flower! Did it say when he would arrive?"

"When the moon is in the tree tops over the river; Anita bring him. She keep others from sister;" relapsing into her earlier form of speech. Then she ran away laughing, avoiding her sister.

What did the child mean? At the first her words startled and impressed Edith. She was full of elfin pranks. Edith supposed Dudley was near, and the wonder was, Anita had not teased her in this way before. The impression passed from her mind, though the child's words lingered in her memory. When she next met her, the girl's face was unusually grave, contrite, her sister thought, for what she had said.

The day wore away, the river ran sombre in the deepening shade of its high bank. The sunlight faded from the trees on the eastern shore, lingered on the American flag-staff and disappeared. Mr. Grayson had been summoned to meet the general. Edith's lady friends were on a visit to their husbands in the camp. As daylight yielded to confirmed night, she saw Anita on the river's immediate bank, watching the moon rising through the eastern tree tops, and then she flitted away. What did it mean? A sudden tremulous sensation, as if caused by a strange presence, thrilled her, like a chill. She turned, walked over the heavy rugs to a charcoal burner, as　for warmth. Two lamps shed a soft light through the canvas apartment.　She heard a little rustle outside the folds of the opening canvas entrance.　The eyes and dark face of Anita showed an instant.　She drew the heavy folds aside, and Dudley's self entered! He took a step forward, and halted, as if at the word of command.　He held his cap in his hand, and stood an instant spell-bound.

"Cliffton!. Gracious Father! what madness is this?" she exclaimed, recoiling a little from him.

"Madness to meet your wish?"

"My wish? *My wish?* What can you mean?"

"Lightly, idly spoken, it may be.　It was of my seeking.　Anita met and guided me here."

"Oh! the silly, idle child! Surely she did not—you do not mean to say—" .Unable to finish, the hot blood surging into her face, still showing distress.

. "I sent Carter to her.　He brought me this," producing Anita's script.

The girl took it and read— "Edith Gray."

"And you chose to regard her as my emissary?" The color deepening with something of scorn also in her face, as she remembered her thoughtless words to the girl.

"She was *my* emissary," he said quietly.　"I may have been mistaken when I received this," he said, untying and withdrawing from his neck, the trinket given him by the Shawanoe.

"Was that given you *as from me?*" in amazement.

His answer was a look of surprise.

"As an avowal, a pledge, unsought, unasked, sent by an Indian chief?" Her eyes now flashing with indignant scorn. . "Oh, Dudley! and you thought this of me?"

"I did not think it an avowal—a pledge. I did think it was a permission to remember you. I was mistaken. It was not to say these things I came. Some words I will say, the words I came to say, scornfully as you meet me."

He took a single step nearer her, touched the ground with his knee, raised his eyes, clasped his hands, and said with passionate fervor,

" Edith Gray—with every fibre of my heart and soul, I love, I reverence you. You are my ideal of womanly perfection." There could be no danger that his sincerity would be questioned.

Not at the instant did even these words allay the tempest of her bosom. She turned from him in the pride and anger, which still ruled her, and murmured as to herself, her mind dwelling on his first misapprehension, " Oh, the cruel vanity of a man ! "

As she turned again to him, he had risen, and stood with a proud abjectness, waiting the return of her eyes, that he might take silent leave. She may have divined his intention. Whatever may have been her purpose, she would not thus have him part from her.

" Mr. Dudley, you are under a mistake ; you do not know me, even my name," her face softening.

" Love knows that it loves. It knows when it is scorned. It seeks no further knowledge," he said, his pride and spirit mounting.

She would not thus be silenced.

" Did you ever hear the name—Grayson—Edward Grayson ? "

" Something of it. He adhered to the king. I know nothing of him," coldly.

" A Tory ! ay, *a Tory !* Condemned to death, his prop-

erty confiscated, he escaped to devote himself to retribution." She paused. As he made no reply she went on.
"Him you met in Ohio. I am *the Tory's daughter.*
Surely you understand now. It was to the Tory's child
you proffered love but now;" and she laughed a bitter
scornful laugh. "It was to gain the Shawanoe, Round-
head, and the Wyandots to this alliance that *Dr. Gray*
made that mission to the Huron, which had failed, were
it not for Captain Dudley of the American army.

"You assaulted the nation of your father and mother,
when in dire extremity. You made the necessity which
drove us to this alliance. The work was more yours than
mine. Why do you reproach us? You fight by the side
of the savage—*when you do fight.* The Shawanoe long
had that trinket. I renewed the ribbon that day. It
was *his* gift to you ; not—not— " *mine* was on her tongue,
she could not say it. "I heard something of the supposed conspiracy against you. I never knew the truth of
it. Shawanoe took it upon himself to care for you."

"Shawanoe! Who and what is he?"

"Is it possible you do not know? Tecumseh—who
could he be?" Dudley started at this. "I was thought
to have influence over him, and through him gained
Round-head and the Wyandots."

"So that was your work?"

"Our work."

"And Frenchtown! Great God!"

"I am the Tory's daughter—" yet wincing under
this.

"Return your gift to your chief, or give it to Round-
head," said the youth, with answering scorn of voice and
manner, tossing the bauble upon the ground at her
feet.

"You had better keep it," she said, bending and pick-ing it up, touching her lips with it, and drawing his rib-bon through her fingers. "It did you good service once. There are men in power here who think your escape from Detroit merits death. They would not hesitate to enforce it against you," she said, showing real concern in her voice and manner, and continuing to caress the ribbon, upon which her eyes fell several times.

"Let them. The man who endures your scorn has little to fear," he answered. The step of trained men, at that instant caught his ear. "Your friends come," he said with a smile, unmoved. "You saw me in their hands once before, Miss Gray—I beg your pardon—Miss Grayson. That pleasure is to be yours again."

Her less accustomed ear now also caught the sound. "Oh! Cliffton! you do not—you cannot suppose I would betray you!" clasping her hands in an agony.

"Why not? You boast of being the Tory's daughter," laughing with something of his old gayety.

There came a sharp but low word of command, followed by a *thud* of musket butts upon the earth, with a rattle of arms and trappings.

"Oh!" was Edith's unconscious exclamation. She clapped her hands, and Dudley replacing his foraging cap turned to face what might await him, and the distressed girl escaped from the room unseen.

A moment later, and a youthful, slightly formed officer entered, cast his eyes about, as if he expected to find others present.

"You are alone!" said the intruder, his eyes coming back to Dudley as if surprised.

"As you say," was the answer, confirmed by his cov-ered head.

"Dudley?" asking his name, in a suggestive form.

"Dudley," was the laconic reply.

"Ah! you see—I am not aware of your rank," again glancing around the spacious apartment, as if the man before him was not what he expected to find.

"My title is of no consequence," was the good-natured reply.

"I am ordered to arrest Captain or Major Dudley, and conduct him to headquarters," he said, evincing by voice and manner that the service was distasteful.

"*Arrest?* Ah! *Capture* would not answer, I suppose?" quite in his old laughing way. "I am entirely at you disposal, Lieutenant," he added.

They stepped out to find a squad of twelve soldiers, six facing the entrance, and three each side of it. Dudley laughed at the formidable array, and the evident place intended for him. "I am honored," he said.

"Well, you see, Dudley," said the officer, laughing in turn, the frank pleasant way of the American putting him at once on the best terms with him—"You see, you have such a deuced reputation with us, of disappearing you know."

"Ah, yes. I appeared to disappear. I remember something of it. Things will happen you know—Lieutenant—"

"Gordon," said the Briton.

"Thanks, Lieutenant Gordon. I am glad to know you," extending his hand, which was cordially taken, and the two walked off arm in arm, preceded and followed by a platoon of six soldiers.

A lantern borne by the sergeant lit the way, under the trees. As they went out—"May I know the cause of my *arrest?*" asked the American. "A capture in this neighborhood, I could better comprehend," laughing.

"I am not advised," was the reply. "Perhaps something of your departure on an occasion before referred to."

"Ah, yes. The fact is, Gordon, I had not the honor of your attentions then, and really felt neglected," he replied, laughing gayly.

"I should regret any unpleasant thing here, Dudley, and I do regret that this duty fell to me. You have been talked about some among us boys, and I wish to say, you have friends among us."

"Thanks, thanks. Your words are very pleasant, very grateful. Those who happen to think well of me, I hope will have no occasion to change their minds." He spoke warmly, and while he could think his position no more than unpleasant, unfortunate in his detention, he gathered himself up to face things as they might arise.

The interview with Edith had stirred his nature to its depths. There was no sediment there. His faculties, his intellect were aroused, and would work clearly. His feelings were a chaos. That he had been victimized was clear. Whether by himself or the conspiracy of circumstances, was not so clear. Edith was a consummate actress. Her surprise, amazement, were certainly genuine, as was the scorn, the contempt, alike of words and voice, look and manner. He would not think she was a party to his capture. If it was planned, Carter would be made prisoner also. If not, Anita would notify him. His confidence was unshaken in her. Carter would learn he was a prisoner. Shawanoe was Tecumseh. Wasegoboah told him this in his Indian way, but he missed his meaning. He ought to have thought this out for himself.

He was glad to know it. Anita was Tecumseh's niece
then.   He dismissed the chief from his mind.   To build
on him now would be delusive.   He remembered Edith's
clapping her hands.   It was in his ears constantly, with
her exclamation.   He would not think it was a signal to
Gordon to advance.   That gentleman used no stealth in
his approach.   He might have escaped, but he never
thought of it.   It was not a place to run from, nor he
a man to run from any place.

CHAPTER XII.

THAT had been something more than an unsatisfactory day for Proctor. The ominous shock of that 18-pounder of the enemy's battery was slow to dissipate. There were deeper, older causes of disquiet: smothered differences between himself and officers of detachments under his command; a lack of harmony between himself and the officers of his own regiment, so fatal to the efficiency of an organization nice and even delicate in some lines, and in the cement of association and confidence found in the best of the British service of that day. Reynolds and his militia, who rendered such gallant service at Frenchtown, capable of good, of excellent work when well used and commanded, he held in almost open contempt. Stout old St. George had not yet recovered from his wounds. Proctor had been very accurately advised of Harrison's force. His day's bombardment must advise him of the strength of his works. He knew there was a strong body of men at Fort Winchester, to which messengers had been despatched, as also to Sandusky. He was advised to send his gun boats up the river to intercept and demolish any flotilla that might seek to reinforce the enemy from the upper forts. He derided the idea.

"Let them come to us here, the more the better.

Tecumseh's Indians will have the hair of every devil of them before they get in. And what if they do? the old trap is ready. I'll blow their d—d old *puncheons* out of the ground in an hour," and so he went on.

Well, he opened the next morning, and now after twenty-four hours of bellowing and thunder, the wall was as strong as ever.

"No matter," he now said, "a heavy battery would open at daylight from the lower rear."

"To find another mud bank to fire into," replied the irritating Colonel Elliott.

This enraged him. He would let them know. He drank all day. Drank brandy after dinner. Its exhilaration had passed, and he was very irritable. The enemy's expected re-enforcements again came up. Well, they must land somewhere. It was Tecumseh's plan to fall on them, and enter the old pen with such of the survivors as reached it—if it still stood, was his reply.

Then came the report of Dudley's capture. He heard it with great satisfaction, relief in fact. He had been bated a good deal. Here was a man whom he had never seen, yet toward whom he felt a strong grudge, delivered into his hands, and who would not dare answer back.

"Ah, ha! So we have him, have we? The great American walking gentleman. Keep your places, gentlemen," to those present, who showed signs of dissolving informally. "We'll make short work of him. What in —— could have sent him round here?"

"He may be backed," suggested Warburton.

"He's certain to be damned—eh, Home?" casting his eyes toward the officer, was Proctor's reply, coarsely laughing.

Glances passed between Elliott and Grayson, the last

changing his seat to one more obscure. They had not to wait.

There came a signal from the main entrance. " Bring him in," called the loud voice of the general.

The escort marched in. The front rank opened, the officer and prisoner advanced two or three steps. The officer saluted, wheeled and took his place in front of his men, in a single rank across the entrance, yet out of hearing, leaving Dudley alone, standing immediately in front of Proctor, three or four yards distant.

When the rank in front opened, he lifted his cap with a graceful inclination to the general, advanced a step and halted, as much with the manner of the drawing-room as the parade ground. A fine figure, appearing tall in a closely fitting undress of blue, which never looked better then when worn by him ; a frank, handsome, spirited face ; a good head, well and modestly borne, he stood the centre of the eyes of men of wide knowledge, at least of soldiers. His very striking personal advantages, his easy, modest bearing, were not lost on them. Proctor was himself im-pressed, and for a little time silent. It incensed him.

" So, so, young man," he said at length, "who are you ? You have a tongue I s'pose, can't you speak ? " as if it was his duty to open a conference.

" Dudley—my name is Dudley," in an ordinary tone, in no way moved by the general's manner.

" Dudley—yes—Dudley. You have another haven't you ? "

" Cliffton."

" Dudley Cliffton ? "

" I have been called Dudley Cliffton."

" Oh, you have been called Dudley Cliffton, have you ?

Take notice, gentlemen;" looking about as if a strong point was gained.

"On the roll I am written Cliffton Dudley."

"The deuce you are! Ah, yes, I see. You are Cliffton Dudley on the roll; when you roll off, you are Dudley Cliffton," laughing coarsely at his own wit. "Well, on or off, you have some rank over there," with a nod of the head toward the American side—"you did not give it to the officer who arrested you, I've been informed."

"He did not ask it."

"Not ask it? Tell Gordon to step forward," which he did.

"Now repeat what you said, *Mr.* Dudley Cliffton."

"He knew my name. Excused himself, as I took it, for not giving me a rank title, saying he did not know what it was."

"Well—your answer to that?"

"I replied it was no matter."

"Oh, ah, very well. Now, Mr. No-Matter Dudley, you have some rank?"

"I rightfully wear this," laying a finger on the sign of rank, modestly.

"You should bear in mind that we so seldom see your regulation coat that we are to be excused for not knowing its quarterings," said Home, with the ease of one privileged.

The sally was received with a loud laugh by the general, and echoed by Colonel Short and one or two more.

"Right—right, Home. We've seen it on some of my Indians though," responded Proctor, with another laugh.

"Your Indians have the reputation of taking the hair also," said the prisoner with a smile.

Absolute silence followed this speech, and then—

"How! How!" roared Proctor. "This to my face? By —— young man! do you know where you are? Answer; do you know where you are and who you are?"

"I heard the order to conduct me to the general's *marquee.* I presume I am before the Prince Regent's general commanding his forces now investing Camp Meigs, and a board of British officers. *I am a prisoner.*" This was very well said. The pathos of his position was expressed with a force that reached many present. An officer arose. Ere he could speak—

"Take your seat, Colonel Elliott. There is no occasion for interference. What is your rank, Mr. Dudley? come, that is a square question."

"I am a major of the regular service."

"So, so, we have a major. Why could you not tell me that before?"

"I am not a volunteer," with his eyes in the distance.

"Well, who in —— said you were? I won't be trifled with," frowning.

"He means," said a quiet voice from the shadow, "that he cannot *volunteer* a statement. That question had not been asked him."

"Who is conducting this examination?" sharply, with a flash in the direction of the voice. "So you were caught sneaking through my camp?" to his prisoner.

"I was honored with an armed escort when I entered your camp."

"Well, you'll be honored in the same way when you leave it," (acknowledged by a bow from the prisoner;) "if you ever do," was added.

"Well, skulking outside my camp—then?"

"Your officer can inform you where I was found, possibly."

"Possibly! young man, I'll have no trifling—answer."

"Your question asserts what was not true. Choosing to take the risk, I had a perfect right everywhere outside your lines. I approached a tent occupied by persons of the civil service, outside your camp."

"Ah, you did. Come now—that is something like. Go on—go on—can't you? Of course you were expected there?"

"Very clearly I was *not*," with modest emphasis.

"Oh, indeed! not expected—you took somebody by surprise?"

"I may have surprised some one; I think I did very much. I was myself *taken*. If my opinion is of value, I was not only not expected, I was not wished."

"Not wished—no, I should think not. Well, sir?"

"I should have gone as I came but for the polite attentions of Lieutenant Gordon—quite gratuitous."

"You had a purpose in your visit."

"I had."

"State it."

"Purely personal. It had no reference to the public service."

"You decline to state it?"

"Most decidedly," smiling pleasantly.

"Oh, decidedly you will not. Well, Major—we will see, we will see. In your fort, camp, yard, pen—the place where you stay when not out on a private lark, what are your duties?"

"Well, just now, keeping the British and Indian generals out of it," laughing in his old way.

"And a d—d troublesome job you find it, young man."

"Pure idleness, or you would not have found me here."

"You find this very funny—very funny, no doubt, no doubt. You are on the staff of General Harry—Harryson, are you?"

"Yes."

"Quite in his confidence—so sprightly an officer, out on a lark. You know his plans—his expectations?"

"In a general way—yes. He plans to defend his position. He expects to do it."

"Good God, young man! You forget who I am. Do you know General Harrison's plans?."

"General Harrison communicates so much of his mind as secures an intelligent execution of his orders; no more. There is no *babble* about his headquarters. No one divides responsibility with him."

"Ah! a very Marlborough, no doubt. He may wish there was. You know his present force?"

"I knew what it was at sundown. I do not know what it may be."

"Well, what was it at sundown? I'll answer for the increase—I say I'll answer for the increase! Mind now —I know his exact force, to a man."

"Ah! that relieves me from telling you.—Thanks."

"It does, does it? We'll see."

"One does not like to have his word doubted even by those he is compelled to hold his enemies. Were I to tell you the exact truth, you would believe I intended to deceive you."

"Ah, ha! Ah, ha! Here is a model young man for you, gentlemen. I suppose you have no objection to telling me what they were up to, when you left?"

"None in the least.   Getting ready for the battery you are now kindly planting below the ravine," carelessly.

Proctor glared around, but said nothing.

"You expect reinforcements?"

"We've room and rations for a few more," looking as if in the distance.

There were those present who enjoyed this examination.

Home said in an aside—"Damned clever way of putting things."

"Yes," answered Warburton.   "If he was dangling after *my* girl, I'd shoot 'im myself, or *get it done.*"

Home glanced up at him, but said nothing.

Proctor had another—his sole purpose.   What it really was there is nothing to show, and it was always a matter of dispute among his officers.

"Major Dudley, you were of the army of invasion, retreat, and surrender?"

"I was."

"You commanded the cavalry?"

"I did."

"You are charged with this—that on the 16th day of August last, at Detroit, after the surrender, and before rendering yourself a prisoner of war, as was your duty, you escaped, and without exchange are now captured in arms, and thereby have incurred the just penalty of death.   To this what say you?"

"That you have no authority of any law to thus arraign me.   As a *prisoner* charged, I say nothing."   A moment's silence.   "As a gentleman I am very willing to satisfy a laudable curiosity.   I was aware of the surrender.   I saw your column advance, pursuant to terms, I presume.   I walked away in presence of your whole army, in broad day—through your curtain of Indians, all seemingly willing I should go. I reached Frenchtown quite early, reported at once for duty. I am captured in the military service of the United States. I have violated no law, betrayed no confidence, incurred no penalty." Modestly, yet spiritedly this was said.

"The prisoner confesses the charge and specifications," said Proctor.

"He denies your pretence of law, and defies your authority," was the reply, taking a step forward, with an energetic downward sweep of his closed right hand, his manner proud, scornful, and defiant.

"As Commander-in-Chief, in presence of the enemy, I assume the entire responsibility. The prisoner, Major Dudley, will be shot to death at sunrise," — truculently. "Major Muir will see this order executed."

Every man in the *marquee* sprang to his feet, with various exclamations.

"Remove the prisoner;" who stood, the only composed person present, his face breaking into its old-time laughing expression.

As Gordon conducted him out, Mr. Grayson hurriedly passed them.

The party halted at a camp-fire, now quite deserted, where Home, very much agitated, joined it.

"My dear fellow," he exclaimed to Dudley, seemingly much distressed, "was there ever anything so deuced beastly?"

"Outside the British camp, I should say no," was the laughing answer.

"Such a h—— of a—"

"Don't break your heart over it," said Dudley, ironically.

"My dear Major, you carry it off d——d splendidly—but don't deceive yourself. You don't know Proctor."

"Well, I must be stupid, then. He'll have no idea of shooting a man on such an order, made in such a farce."

Home solemnly shook his head.

"All right," said Dudley, examining his watch. "It's some time to sunrise. Your camp may be stormed before that time," laughing carelessly.

"Oh, we'll look to that," said Home, with a start, spite of himself. "Is there anything I can say or do?" He seemed nervous and anxious. "Any message?"

"You are very kind, Captain—nothing occurs to me," turning away, a feeling of repugnance to the Englishman arising in his bosom.

"Well, I shall do all I can," he persisted in saying.

"Thanks."

Home had a few words with Gordon, aside, and walked rapidly away. As he did so, Gordon muttered something, which, to Dudley, sounded like—"insufferable puppy."

Gordon stood in thought an instant, and turning to Dudley, said : "What do you suppose Home said to me?"

"I have not the slightest idea."

"He would not have said it now, had he not wanted you should hear of it—or hear it, I presume."

"Well, I'm not greatly interested in anything he may say about any earthly thing. I know him pretty well."

"Well, I'm to be relieved here, and while waiting, may as well mention it. Well, 'had a certain American officer known a certain young lady was engaged—you know '— Oh, the d——d puppy ! "

"Well, there are puppies and d——d puppies, and a

choice lot beyond," added Dudley, laughing. "When the thing you intimate occurs, I'll send congratulations."

An officer approached and saluted. Gordon turned to Dudley. "My dear Dudley, I am sure we shall meet again; until then, good-bye, luck go with you," extending his hand.

"We shall meet, my dear boy, and I shall remember you as long as I live." They shook hands, and Gordon, dismissing his soldiers to their quarters, turned to his own.

The relieving officer touched his plumeless hat to the prisoner, saying in a business way, "I am to show you quarters for the night; not all I could wish, Major Dudley."

"I am quite at your service. You'll find me not difficult to please." He saw nothing to indicate the rank though the bearing of the stranger was distinguished.

"The place is a little distant; you will find some *conveniences* there, to compensate—may make something out of them." The tone of this speech—the latter part, was peculiar.

The two officers, preceded by two soldiers and a sergeant, and followed by two more, lighted now by a torch, moved past the tents, the last sentinel, past some trees, struck a well-beaten, though now little used, path, which led along the slope of the second bank in a way to ascend considerably and among trees. They passed a dark structure, and reached a second, which they approached. The torch disclosed a door-way, now open. Here they entered. The sergeant produced and lit two small metal lamps which he placed on a table within. By their light the room looked large and cheerless. Two or three blankets were lying near the table, on which was a refection of bread, cold meat, and a bottle of wine, or spirits, with a tin cup. Dudley's idea was that the apartment was new and unfinished, or old and dilapidated, though the air was fresh.

"I hope you will find things to suit you. I commend the *prog;* you may *need* it. The wine is specially good. I will close the door as I go out. The guards will not trouble you. Good night."

He turned and drew the door to behind him, gave his orders to the guards left in charge, and Dudley heard his footsteps an instant, as he moved away. Apparently, sentinels were placed, one in front and one on each side of the building.

Dudley glanced around him. The room was large, without windows, of much depth, and had several angles. His mind was active, at first summarizing the happenings of the evening, and after this fashion—"Well, Cliff my boy—this is an experience for one evening. A declaration, a rejection of course, a capture, trial, found guilty, sentenced to be shot, and "—consulting his watch—"not yet eleven o'clock—and here I am. I wonder how I should have got out of it, had it not been for Gordon— *Little* Gordon, the boys all call him. Pure gold, he couldn't be large. It was a deuced awkward place, reject a man and not let him go. On the whole Gordon inter- vened in my favor. This "—looking around—"is pref- erable to that." Then his mind jumped to the present conditions. "If Carter was captured, it would be kept from me. He is not. He could not be. No one could find him but Anita. She told Tecumseh of my getting away from Detroit—from the fort; she'll tell of this. This is some of Home's work. Well I don't wish Miss Grayson such a fate. Oh, dear! Oh, dear! and oh dear again. Cliff old boy—if I catch you whining—self-pity-ng—if I *do* catch you—mind! Well, *he* hoped I'd find conveniences—compensating conveniences for the *long* walk—so I am remote and am to find *conveniences.* Make something *out* of them—*out.*" He breathed a low whistle. "The guards not to be troublesome. I would like the prog; the wine good. I'll try 'em and then look a little into these same *conveniences*—Thanks," uncovering a savory joint of cold meat, which he ate of with relish. Then he tried the bottle, in which the cork had been started. On removing it, and lifting to test by its fra-grance—"Brandy, for the world! well there is meaning in that. I'd better take some—the bottle, if the conveni-ences to compensate—" a slight sound had once or twice reached his ear. "A rat? and 'dead for ducket.' It's not that—sounds more as if something or somebody wanted my attention. I really have little else to do. Eleven," examining and returning his watch. Then his mind took another freak. "Grayson! How I was sold! one of the Boston Tory Graysons. Was that his voice? and I thought he brushed past me. 'Shot to death at sunrise?' what a truculent old *duffer*. '*Duffer*, a dealer in contraband'—Eh! Not rats certainly," as something like drawing a stick along a wall or hard sur-face, in the dim back distance, beyond the light of his lamps reached his ear. He took a slight sip of the generous liquor, whose bouquet imparted its fruity flavor to the atmosphere about him. Some of it he turned upon his bread, and then listened for a time to the faint tread of the sentinel, pacing slowly forward and back-ward in front of the door, apparently making a beat of thirty or forty feet; the only steps he could hear. Then he turned back, leaving the lamps—outside eyes might be on him. He would not aid them by lighting his way.

He passed back to an angle where he fancied was a door, whence came the sounds he had heard. It was an open passage way, and dark. There as he looked steadily into it he saw the shadowy outline of a man. A hand seemed to beckon him. He stepped boldly forward and clasped the extended member, which drew him willingly forward. As they moved along the totally dark way he heard a volley of five or six guns outside, immediately followed by shots from the sentinels. Soon a ladder was reached, up which went the silent form of mystery, and Dudley followed. Very many rounds were ascended and an upper floor gained, over which he was led to an outside opening. Dudley had entered at the east end. This was in the west. From this, the guide stepped out, followed by the American, who found himself on the edge of the high table-land, sweeping indefinitely away, from the bluff. The firing was from the river side. The alarm reached the camp, whence came sounds of men getting under arms. The guide stood still and silent the fourth of a minute.

"My young brother is safe," then he said, in a low, musical voice which the American knew.

"Shawanoe!—Tecumseh!" breathed Dudley in wonder and delight. "Next the Great Spirit, Dudley thanks his elder brother!" with fervor these words were spoken.

"My brother trusts Tecumseh?"

"As he would God."

The chief led him westward a few yards, moving noiselessly and then turned northward. The drums beat in the camp and the commotion increased.

"My English Father, General Proctor, is disturbed in

his sleep," said the chief contemptuously. "His sentinels will hear nothing but his drums now." Some distance was gained, and in the darkness of the wood, safety. They reached the little ravine in the rear of the Grayson tents, and paused,

"Shawanoe does not take back a gift," he said a little sadly, placing a small parcel, containing the decoration of the German Princess, in Dudley's hand.

"General," said the greatly moved youth, receiving it and grasping the chief's hand, "for this, for your most generous aid last summer, how can I ever thank you—repay you?"

"When not in battle, be kind to my poor Indians."

"As the Great Spirit aids me, so will I ever."

"My English brother, Mr. Grayson, told me. My brother owes him thanks."

"I am very, very glad. Tell him how glad I am to thank him."

"And my little sister?"

"Dudley is very grateful to her; loves her as a true sister. I owe her many thanks."

"My brother glads Tecumseh's heart. My English sister?"

He paused for an answer. None came. "My young brother's soul is dark toward her. Tecumseh can now walk this wood as in the sunshine. He does not know the way of a woman's heart. My young brother is very brave, is very comely in men's and women's eyes. No woman in her heart scorns him. His scout waits. He may sound his signal."

Dudley placed a small instrument to his lips, and produced a good imitation of the peculiar whistle of the small brown owl, heard usually only in the early part of the evening.

"Good!" said the chief. "Late in the night for that call."

Dudley repeated it, and received it back as an echo, from the upper part of the ravine. The chief passed noiselessly toward the river, where a canoe with a single rower, received and passed him to the east side. Dudley could see the ghostly sheen of the Grayson tents, through the trees, not fifty yards distant, and heard the mingled notes of the frogs, the croakers and hylodes, from the river's margin. It seemed a month, a year—an age, since he had passed down this glen conducted by the Indian maiden, toward these tents that then seemed to glow and invite—so cold and repellant now. A change of the world, of life and hope had come upon him since then. He turned from the pale uncertain shimmer, to Carter, moving down to him at the trysting tree. They met and stole away in silence.

Ere they gained a distance which made oral confidence prudent, the acute perception of the scout received the impression that the usually light, elastic youth, from whom he parted so fresh and buoyant, and now found in a drooping, languid form, must have received a hurt. At length, when he felt secure—

"Wounded?"

"No. Why?"

"I never seen ye so pimpin like."

To this no answer. The old hunter with the young man whom he loved as the pet youngest of the family— the crown of human perfection—now certainly safe, felt like giving an Indian whoop. Something had gone wrong. He would liven him up with cheerful talk.

"Pears to me, Major, like 'twas a darned *close shave.*"

"Well, interesting—rather."

"How'd ye spose they found it out enny way?"

"By one of the girls—possibly."

"No, no, Major. Wimin is safe—purty ginerly. That Ingin gal—wal a feller couldn't do better—ef he could git 'er—if 'e wanted 'er—that is."

"She is for no *feller*," said the major, quickened with the idea that a *feller* could aspire to this splendid dark princess of the forest. "Why she is the niece of Tecumseh!"

"Du tell! wal I never!"

"Who do you suppose Shawanoe is? Did you ever think of that?"

"Wal, I've spicioned, then agin I dunno."

"He is Tecumseh himself."

"Wal, I'd kinder thought mebby," showing less surprise than Dudley expected.

"He told me so. Called himself Tecumseh to me."

"O–h! So that's his work—is it?"—referring to the alarm. "So that's Tecumsey! Wal! Wal! Wal!" as if to himself.

"Now, Carter—see here. Neither you or I can kill or capture Tecumseh—no matter what the chance is."

"All right. It seems only fair. They do say though, Major, he an' *ole Proc.* has agreed, when they take Gineral Harrisin, the Ingins shall burn 'im."

"I know it; and men who know better, believe it. Why should he rescue me?"

"Wal, I has my notion o' that. Why'd 'e take ye away frum the Huern?"

This touched a hurt, and Dudley made no answer.

"How did you know what happened to me to-night?"

"The Ingin gal tole me."

"Oh, she did! Bless her heart! I thought so. How did she suppose the British found out I was there?"

"Hadn't no idee. She thinks Capen Home some way—"

"Ah! Tecumseh warned me of him on the Huron."

"Home? Wal, 'e ain't to be spaired is 'e?" with a laugh.

"He is to marry our Miss Gray—so they say. So *he* says."

"Bah! a hundred times to that— Ye seen 'er uv course?"

"She was utterly surprised at seeing me. She had no way of letting my presence be known, if she had wanted to."

"I guess she didn't! Wy, Majer—bless 'er eyes, she'd give one on 'em fer ye enny time, only y'ed ruther have it w'ere it is. Don't tell me!"

"Well, Carter, I wouldn't risk an empty egg-shell that she cares for me." The poor young man could not help saying so much.

"Oh, pshaw! fellers an gals—gals speshaly—has ter hev a time o' playin off like a fox savin 'er pups, an' she draws ye off an' on. Mebby ye sed suthin, or ye didn't, 'er done suthin, or let it alone; 'er 'twant the right way, ye took 'er wrong—a feller never knows they say. I'll bet a dozzen bear skins to a musquash tail, she'd jump to have ye the fust chance—now."

Dudley heard Carter's analysis of a young lady's nature with amazement. He always gave him credit for large acquired practical wisdom. This must be intuitive; the unused wisdom stored in men's natures. What he said was—

"All right. I will take that bet. Just now, I don't care whether I win or lose."

"Oh, that's where ye'r hurt! Wal, I'll make anuther bet. Fifty deer skins ye'll ask 'er,—if the ole gent don't gin 'er to ye fust."

"I'll take that too," laughing now at Carter's grotesque absurdities.

"Oh, I know now jes how 'twas. Ye's havin one o' them air times, an' the British cum an kerried ye off fore 'twas through—that's jest it now, want it, Majer?" laughing heartily.

"Well, something like, I do believe;" a good deal brightened by Carter's conversation, and wondering what had come over the old man.

They now approached the river above the camp, where was hidden their birch canoe, and much caution was necessary. They traversed the Maumee and the camp was gained in safety.

It was late, or, accurately, early; when they gained entrance. Dudley had much information for his general.

He opened the parcel given him by the chief. It contained the German decoration, with a change of the suspending ribbon, not then observed. Edith and the thought of her love were now to be put by for all time.

CHAPTER XIII.

DAY OF BATTLES—THE MEETING.

BRIGHTLY broke the third morning of the siege on forest, river, plain and the hostile camps. In the British there was the flavor of the last night's racket, the cause of which was a mystery to man and officer. The soldiers saw by the camp fires, a gay young officer in closely fitting blue, marched to and from the general's *marquee.* The higher officers knew something more. As stated, the real purpose of the general was matter of speculation, and various comments and asides were indulged in. It was known the prisoner had escaped, and generally supposed to have been by an attack of his own party. Proctor so far as known, beyond setting on foot a perfunctory inquiry, never spoke of the fate of his prisoner. Certainly his papers and despatches contain no reference to him.

Some supposed the disturbance was a wholly independent thing. "Some of Dickson's Indians came upon an out-picket, and were fired on." "Dickson's Indians" were usually responsible for the awkward things which no one would father.

Proctor was in good temper that morning and merely remarked, "D——n 'em, I'll show 'em. When they surrender this time there'll be no *leaking* out, I'll bet," which may have referred to the adventure of the night before.

With daylight the batteries on the eastern side opened on palisades and another grand traverse of earth. It was annoying as well as baffling. The cannonade from all the siege guns, mortars and cohorns was loud and furious all day and all night, pounding and resounding in senseless rage and noise, the American replying from his lighter guns as occasion presented the chance of an effective shot, showing that had they been well armed and supplied, their enemy would have suffered severely in his exposed batteries.

All day and all night, and all the morning of the fourth day, when a flag of truce showed from the heavy battery, and all the guns, mortars and cohorns were silent.

"Ah!" said the American general, ordering an answering flag. "So having demonstrated his inability to harm me, I am to be now, politely—after the manner of an Englishman, asked to submit. Such a demand two days ago would have been more logical. Well, Dudley, they are old friends of yours. You shall do the honors. They must be anxious for your health, and will be very glad to see you," he said, laughing pleasantly.

A boat with a flag approached in line of the enemy's eastern battery, and in due time the insignia appeared at the margin of the forest, 300 yards away. There it was met by Dudley with an escort. Warburton and Home bore Proctor's message.

The Ohio men who manned the fort, the young Kentucky officers of Harrison's family, to whom formal war and its usages were new, with eager eyes followed the form of his officer as he moved over the ground, blackened from the late burning of the trees which recently covered it. Many thought it a lure to regain possession of his person, having heard some rumors of his night's adventure. Very many expected to see him fall under the guns of the Indians. Hundreds of savage eyes flashed from the forest, on the little party as it passed.

The officers exchanged the formal salutations of flags, and moved toward the fort, the English guard remaining at the forest's edge.

Home's face was a study that morning to some of the juniors in camp. It was schooled very well, and he may have anticipated who would meet him. Dudley received him with the gay frankness of the Ohio days. Warburton scanned him many times and saw small signs of the rejected lover, the condemned, twice-sentenced, of the late adventure. Home also, as opportunity occurred, studied his face and manner with a wondering curiosity.

As they approached the gate to which they were conducted, Warburton lingered for the expected bandage.

"Oh, it is not necessary," said the American. "It is your one chance," laughing.

Thought may have been taken for the appearance inside to be seen by the Englishmen; while everything was in its usual form the men nevertheless grouped and conducted themselves, so as to do no discredit to their officers.

An arch led through the eastern grand traverse and up the wide avenue to the general's *marquee*, the entrance of which was broadly open, showing the chief, and a glittering staff, ready to receive the enemy's summons.

The embassy advanced with a grave dignity. Warburton, whose rank by blood entitled him to be received by his prince, himself a superior man, took a rapid survey of the American general, and carried away a satisfactory impression. Above the ordinary height, broad browed, fine head carried well, handsome features, large, dark, lustrous eyes, which notwithstanding their size flashed with the quick, assured glance of one accustomed to observe everything and note for himself, and which matched well with his dark, clear complexion; broad shouldered, yet light and active, he would be a marked figure anywhere.

The Englishmen halted at the prescribed point. Dudley, plumed chapeau in hand, stepped forward, with a graceful inclination to his chief, turned to the Britons, announced them by their titles, names and present office, and moved aside.

The English officers bowed with the dignity of their mission, and Colonel Warburton said :

"General Proctor, commanding the British forces now investing this place, requires that it be unconditionally surrendered to him. I am instructed to make this demand of General Harrison, here commanding."

This was well and impressively delivered.

"Your general doubtless feels warranted in making this demand," replied Harrison, in a cool, sonorous voice, with a slight smile playing around the large bland mouth. "I feel warranted in declining to entertain it for one moment."

"General Proctor has a large, well appointed force, and ample material," urged the Englishman.

"His entire available means are immediately before me. He has a low estimate of my intelligence, if he supposes I have now to learn their extent, and from himself. He certainly has afforded me ample opportunity to judge his power of annoying me." Almost playfully this was said, a smile lighting up the fine face now decidedly.

"General Harrison is too good a soldier not to know

that General Proctor as yet has employed but one of several means of annoyance," added the Englishman a little sarcastically.

"I shall await his change of tactics with composure. Say to your general if he ever acquires this place, it will be by means infinitely more creditable to him than a thousand surrenders. His demand is unqualifiedly refused."

"I regret to bear this answer to my general," with a leave-taking inclination of the head.

"I should be unhappy were I compelled to send him any other," with a courteous wave of the plumed chapeau.

Dudley returned the British officers to their guard. They were on the whole favorably impressed by the American and his surroundings. Obviously his camp would be won by the hardest. The general, as Warburton saw, had the qualities to make a successful commander of irregular troops. Spirited, fearless, popular, a born orator, though he heard none of the free forms of speech that startled some of the Western Reserve Puritans, and which seemed graceful from his lips even to them.

Silently the embassadors, attended by Dudley, moved back to the point of meeting. A few words only were spoken between Home and the American as they approached the English guard, not of the slightest significance. The leave-taking would have been silent, but as the Englishmen turned away, Dudley laughingly called out to Home—"*Wal, look out!*"

"Oh!" he exclaimed, called back by the remembered words. "I see old Carter is with you."

"Of course he is."

"Ah!" reflectively. "I might have known. I echo—

'wal, look out.' " With this reminiscence, the younger officers parted. The flags of truce were struck, and the artillery re-awakened the echoes.

There had been much running through the woods by Harrison's scouts and runners, as up and down the Maumee, by Captain Oliver, young Combs, and others. Some got through Tecumseh's net-work of Indians, some failed, some fell.

General Green Clay was at Winchester (Defiance) with 1200 Kentuckians. Proctor's guns were heard there, and he prepared to sweep down the river to Harrison's aid. He had eighteen scow-boats, the sides of which were built high enough, with thick wooden shields, to protect from Indian gunnery. In these he embarked his entire force, and reached the upper end of the Rapids at the close of this day of the siege, which was the fourth of the young May, also. The intention was to resume the voyage so as to reach the landing at the fort, at daylight of the fifth, eighteen or twenty miles below. During that night he communicated with Harrison, and received an answer and orders. These required him to land 800 men a half mile above the fort on the British side under the senior colonel, attack, carry the batteries, spike and dismount the guns, return to their boats, cross over and fight their way into the fort. The terms were direct and clear, admitting of no discretion. The residue, 400, were to land on the fort side and at once push for the camp. The forces in camp would be held in hand, to aid the admission of the Kentuckians. This accomplished, a sortie of the regulars, under Miller, was to carry the batteries on that side, and disable the guns. The plan was bold and skilful. Its execution dependent on raw troops so far as Clay was concerned, of unquestioned fighting qualities, the kindred of those who fell at French-town, and with them represented the best blood of Kentucky.

Care will be necessary to a clear apprehension of the events of the day, happening on both sides of the river, at the same time, and for which a map and diagram are necessary.

Tecumseh was not apprised of the approach of the Kentuckians, but he will be found ready. If they reach the fort, numbers would be equalized with the advantage of artillery and discipline on one side, more than balanced by position on the other.

Five miles above Camp Meigs, the programme, with full instructions, was placed in Clay's hands. His boats advanced in the order of intended action. The twelve first carried the men who were to storm and disable the batteries on the British side, situated the best part of two miles above Proctor's camp, the approaches to which were covered by the heavy forest of the region.

The senior colonel of Clay, save in personal courage, was unequal to an enterprise so simple as this, unfortunately committed to his hand. He landed, formed in three columns, with Combs' company of spies and Logan's Indians, armed with rifles, in advance. Beyond the order to carry the guns, wherever found, he gave no directions or instructions to his officers in command, but pushed forward. It seems that Combs and the left column passed the batteries in their rear. When the colonel's immediate command discovered the enemy, the Kentuckians raised the Indian war whoop, and made a rush. Lightly supported, taken by surprise, the gunners were slain and scattered in a breath. The colonel should then have disabled the guns, recalled his men, hurried to his boats, and hastened to the camp. The woods on that side were full of Indians, with over a thousand soldiers just out of rifle shot below. What he did was to pull down the British flag, and give three cheers, which were answered by three from Camp Meigs, when his men, curious, broke and scattered about, examining things, careless of their exposed position and duty.

Harrison from the platform of his main battery, saw everything, and signalled the captors to hurry toward his camp, in vain. Already he heard the notes of getting under arms, in the British camp, and the position of the Kentuckians was critical in the extreme. They would neither see, hear, or know. Major Dudley was at his general's side, sharing his anxiety. He volunteered to cross and personally recall the incapable colonel, and summoning Carter, hurried to execute his purpose. Events on the British side were rapidly reaching a bloody climax in advance of him.

The whoop of the Kentuckians went with startling effect through the woods, reached the English camp and the ear of every Indian within miles of them. Each warrior sprang to his weapons. Every soldier at the instant drum beat, was in place to meet whatever menanced them. Tecumseh thought it a signal not only of an assault of their batteries, instantly silenced, but an attack upon Proctor's camp by a force which warranted it.

Then came the cheers and answering cheers of the Americans. Combs came upon the nearest Indians, and rushed to attack them, as a Kentuckian would. His enemy gave way, he pursued, and was surrounded. His countrymen flew to his aid and beat the enemy ·back.

Their blood was now heated. No thought of turning back occurred to them. The slight tie of discipline was dissolved. They were in the woods, which soon resounded with shots and yells, and answering shots and yells, which for a time beat downward toward the British camp, and the whole wood became a wild scene of conflict, between many hundreds fighting as individuals.

Here for the time we leave the British side of the river. The alarm of the British camp, as stated, reached Tecumseh and his warriors on the American shore. He called a few chiefs and warriors, rushed to the river below the fort, and pushed across, passed over the island in the middle of the river, and gained the British shore below the battery, taking the wildly fighting Kentuckians in the flank and rear.

Thus the remaining of Clay's command would land in the absence of the great chief, whose war cry was as potent as the bugle blast of Roderick Dhu :—

> " One blast upon his bugle horn,
> Was worth a thousand men."

The bank on that side was precipitous, the current rapid, even near the shore, and two of the remaining boats failed to make the intended landing, a half mile above the fort, and could not securely strike the shore until opposite the upper angles of the camp, thus dividing the party. Both parties were sharply assailed by Indians. Both were armed with the effective musket and bayonet of that day, were fresh, spirited, and well handled. Each of the thus separated parties formed and charged up, gaining the table land. Indians have never been known to meet and successfully resist a body of determined men, in this formation, too numerous to be successfully flanked. There really was great peril to the soldiers of both parties. Hesitation or confusion would have been fatal to either. Each heard the war of the other. The Indians had to divide their force to meet both. Clay's party was not distant when the smaller gained the plain, and they were soon reunited under their general, when they turned against the fierce, determined foe, on their own ground, under cover of the forest. The Kentuckians bore their assailants steadily backward for more than half a mile, with small loss on either side.

The watchful Harrison from his elevated position, commanding the widely separated scenes of conflict, discovered a body of British soldiers and warriors, advancing under the bank of the river from below, to cut off the access of the Kentuckians to the fort, by gaining their rear, when he ordered a recall of the pursuing soldiers, and his sortie to be made by Miller and the regulars of the 4th.

On the west side it will be remembered that the Kentuckians, with barely thirty days in camp, at sight of the Indians, attacked furiously, and very soon their slight formation disappeared. The Indians were driven back upon the Canadian Infantry, Proctor's first line, who fought at river Raisin. At sight of them the maddened Kentuckians raised the cry " Frenchtown ! " " Frenchtown ! " Their wild, headlong rush was too much for Reynolds' men, who were thrown back upon the two thin, red lines of the regulars, who permitted the militia to pass through their ranks, and reform in their rear, while the scattered Indians on their flanks were bloodily troublesome to the broken assailants. The moment their front was clear of friends, the British delivered two volleys with not the fourth of a minute interval, at short

range, into the on-rushing multitude, followed by a charge
of bayonets. As the red coats advanced, the war cry of
Tecumseh rang in the rear of the shattered and scattering Kentuckians. Every warrior heard and responded.
Two thirds of the Americans thus surrounded, surrendered to the .British ; the residue, more determined,
rushed back, and the most of them dashed through
Tecumseh's warriors, just taking form under the skilled
leader in person.

The Kentucky colonel had early paid the penalty of
his incompetency, and has ever been spared the criticism
of his countrymen. Brave to a fault, he was heavy and
incapable of continued rapid marching. Wounded, he
died sword in hand, defending himself against a rush of
warriors attracted by his size, sash and apparent rank.
He too was a Dudley.

We left Harrison's aid in a canoe, in the hands of
Carter. He lent his own strength to drive the little bub-
ble to the other side, and gained the site of the battery,
about the time that Tecumseh made his presence known,
the best of a half mile or more below that point.

Here were thirty or forty soldiers, well-armed, who had
been shaken out of the fight, fortunately for themselves
and some of their fellows. There was no officer with
them. They had no idea of retiring, and did not know
what to do when Dudley appeared. He announced his
name and rank which at once took their hearts. He
was a born leader, and was a Dudley, a name of potency
with them. There was yet another with General Clay.

Cheerily he called to them, and as if by magic, they
were soon in line, facing the now lessening roar of battle.
They could never tell how, but they found themselves
with loaded muskets, rekindled confidence, following this

glowing-faced, flashing-eyed, laughing young man, whose ringing voice went through them, as he turned. back to them, or ran along their front to give a personal direction, speak a word for care and coolness, and hold them in hand. The recovered men looked at their young leader with admiring wonder. They had never before seen anything like him, a sort of superior being, armed, dressed, and gifted,—given to restore order and confidence, perhaps win a lost battle.

Then came the fugitives. At first singly, then in twos and threes, in groups of a dozen, then a cloud, they rallied, or passed his line and rallied in his rear. Not panicy, not scared, defeated and fleeing, when defence was impossible. Scarcely were they in effective position when on came the pursuing warriors, a hundred or more, an irregular line, with others in their immediate rear, and were upon him, when Dudley gave the word, and a wide, close volley from a hundred and fifty muskets—a long line in open order, to prevent flanking—flashed scorchingly in their faces. The warriors had dropped their guns, and with brandished knives and tomahawks, had made the headlong rush for the bloody finish.. As an American fell they stopped for the reeking trophy, and thus disordered they reached Dudley's fence of steel. His volley was fatal to many; the rest recoiled from the line of levelled bayonets, turned, sought cover, and hurried back to their abandoned guns, not confident and reckless enough to impale themselves on the gleaming steel for the chance of reaching an assailant with hatchet and knife. All found cover save the intrepid leader: wearing the uniform coat of a British general, scarlet cap with eagle plume, brandished sword, face and eyes aflame, on he came, as if followed by his warriors.

Carter, ever near Dudley, confronted him with levelled rifle, which gave forth its contents almost in the face of the daring chief, only distant enough to leave his sword ineffective. The great leader would never have seen the Thames, had not the alert Dudley with a stroke of his sabre, as the trigger was touched, thrown the rifle out of fatal range. As it was, a slight wound of the sword arm compelled the chief to lower his weapon. For an instant Shawanoe and the young American confronted each other, Dudley's face lighting with almost a laugh. The frown and flash of battle dissolved in the regal face of the chief, and softened to a look of recognition, almost a smile. Each turned to his duties as leader. It passed in an instant. Carter only comprehended it, as in cover of a tree he grimly reloaded his rifle, as did the Kentuckians.

Tecumseh turned to find himself alone, and glided from tree to tree until he could rally his repulsed followers, momentarily increasing in number.

The distant fire in Dudley's front had ceased, the battle was over. He had received, as he judged, all the surviving fugitives. He had recovered two subaltern officers, of the grade of second lieutenant, whom he placed on either flank, and commenced his movement toward the boats, his men making the march, orderly, and with care, in two ranks or lines. He, with Carter, marched in the rear. Two or three times he ordered a halt and right-about-face, and was charmed with the prompt obedience of his soldiers. As they approached the river, the Indians, still half-armed, pursued in large numbers. His prompt right-about kept them at a prudent distance, and he did not apprehend an attack under Tecumseh. He held a third of his force on the upper bank, while his officers led the main body to the boats, and saw they were in order. When this was accomplished, he marched down, observing the care of a skilled officer in the presence of a superior force—if the British were taken into account. He was permitted to embark, taking all the boats to the American side.

13

CHAPTER XIV.

AS Tecumseh turned back, gathering up his bands, many signs of the method of dealing with the enemy by his warriors met his eye. He had suggested to Proctor an order allowing his warriors twice as much for a prisoner as the usual trophy of an enemy slain, yet on this day of blood they took no prisoners. On landing he had despatched a youth for his horse, which he now found under the bank, awaiting his use. He had a clear idea of the events on the British side of the river. The fighting on the American side was over, apparently, and he took his way to the old fort. Ere he passed a third of the distance, ominous sounds reached him from that direction. He increased his speed and finally put his mettled charger to his best, yet to the impatient chief he seemed to bear him tardily.

The American prisoners were crowded into the old fort, and Combs, though wounded, and his riflemen, Captain Logan, the famous half-blood Shawanoe, who commanded the Indians, were compelled to run the gauntlet between two rows of grim and painted warriors, aflame from the battle. Permitted this luxury, they were not slow to engage in pleasures more exciting and exquisite. They gathered about the unarmed Kentuckians, and selecting such as pleased their individual fancy, shot them down in the presence of Proctor himself, and his officers. Combs appealed to Proctor, who truculently refused to interfere. Emboldened, the Indians began to select victims, and drag them out for more space and freer sport. Thinking they were to have their way with the 300 prisoners, the chiefs hastily assembled to decide their fate, when a voice of thunder arrested hands and thought of British soldier and Indian warrior. It was Tecumseh, calling to his countrymen in their own tongue, commanding them to stay their hands. An instant later, and he sprang from his horse, in their startled midst, scattering them like frightened sparrows. He alit where a powerful American was struggling in the hands of two or three warriors, who were at preliminary torture. One the chief struck down, another he grasped and hurled to a distance from his victim, the third escaped.*

Disdaining the sword, he flourished the native weapons, tomahawk and scalping knife, and with his magnificent form at its greatest height, every muscle at tension, quivering with energy and rage, his eyes flashing, he denounced the chiefs as dogs, and dared a man of them so much as to point a finger at a prisoner. For a half minute he towered—Tecumseh the avenger, from whose eye they shrank coweringly away.

"Where is Proctor?" he now demanded in a thunderous voice. His glance caught the pudgy form at no great distance. He strode toward him.

"How is this?" he haughtily demanded in English.

"Sir, your Indians cannot be commanded," the general replied sullenly.

"Begone!" thundered Tecumseh in contemptuous dis-

---

* Drake's "Tecumseh."

dain. "You are unfit to command! Go put on your *petticoats*," stabbing his finger scornfully at his face.

He turned from the Englishman to his cowed warriors and their ghastly victims, when the horror and full significance of the spectacle smote the apprehension of the high-souled chief.

"Oh, my poor Indians!" he cried in anguish, dropping his weapons, and clasping his hands above his upturned face, as in appeal to the Great Spirit. "My poor Indians! what will become of them!"

Colonel Elliott reached the ground at this instant, rode into the old fort, and in a ringing voice bade the Indians withdraw, which they instantly did, when by the orders of Tecumseh they departed for their camps.*

On the American side of the river, we left Clay pursuing and punishing the retiring Indians, with a message of recall from General Harrison on its way to him, a party of the enemy stealing up under the river bank to intercept him on his approach to the fort. Miller was marching out to assault the batteries on the lower bank of the ravine. To these we turn attention for a minute to note the close of the actions of the day.

Miller's attention was called to the advance of the mixed party of British and Indians. On his approach the Indians did not care to meet him in the open, and the regulars alone were too small a body, and withdrew, leaving him to advance against the batteries whose support these soldiers were. Crossing the stream that formed the ravine above, Miller took the batteries in flank. The infantry support had returned, but the guns were carried, spiked dismounted, and as a battery the

---

* Drake's "Life of Tecumseh."

slight works demolished. Colonel Miller's return to the fort was simultaneous with the landing of Dudley with the remnant of his namesake's command.

The persistent Indians, only beaten back by Clay, who entered the fort, had returned to their position, and sharply resisted Dudley's landing. He leaped ashore, formed his now fully recovered men, who had exhausted their ammunition, yet who now under their intrepid leader dashed forward with shouts and bayonets. Among the many objects of interest demanding the attention of the American commander, he did not lose sight of his aid. He heard his volley, saw him emerge with a considerable body of the Kentuckians, and he now hurried the returning Miller to clear his way into camp. Their bayonets, with Dudley's own, dispersed the stinging Indians, and very soon his general welcomed and congratulated him on his success.

Of the 1200 men under Clay, about half reached Camp Meigs. Of the residue, a third had fallen, killed and wounded in battle. More than a score perished at the old fort, prisoners of the British.

As stated, Proctor supposed his position was the real object of attack. He never gave up that idea. He claimed to have destroyed, killed and captured a force of the enemy, superior in numbers to his own. For this victory he demanded credit, as for the defeat of Colonel Miller's sortie. Substantially this vaunted victory of Proctor's ended the siege of Camp Meigs, though his guns again feebly opened.

CHAPTER XV.

IT will be remembered that our last sight of Edith was at the instant of the entrance of Gordon upon her interview with Dudley, from whom she vanished.

Anita had hovered near them, so near as to hear their words, in which she became absorbed and forgot her office as picket. No thought of military interruption crossed her mind. Her first notice of Gordon's presence was a flash of him through the parted curtains as Edith rushed to their common room, wildly exclaiming in smothered accents to herself,—

"Oh! Oh! Oh! my wicked, cruel pride! So false to myself—so—so utterly false"! She cast herself upon the rugs and gave way in anguish to self-reproaches,—conduct so strange as to greatly surprise the Indian girl. Anita knew that she had long cherished the purpose, if she ever again met Dudley, to at once make known to him who she was, and her share in the Ohio mission. That ruling intention she accomplished under the influence of anger and shame, at the implied accusation of his unguarded words, so misconstrued. As the new and strange excess of emotion subsided under the caresses and soothing care of Anita, came the conviction to the overcome girl, that no man's love—one of the sensitive, heroic nature of Dudley, could survive such an assault—a fitting but awful retribution to her. Anita assured her that the dear Saviour would forgive her, and could but see that her sister was more unhappy over the offence given her earthly lover.

It was long a mystery how Dudley's presence was betrayed to his enemies. Anita had taken no account of the presence of Peters, nor could she have known that so far as Dudley was concerned, he was the spy of Home. Many things were to happen ere she came to know of his agency in the transactions of that night.

Anita had certain native-taught, inherited notions of her own of the rights of lovers, supreme over the stupid laws of war. To her the fittest thing in the world was for a young chief of one nation to fall in love with the daughter of the chief of another, with which his tribe was at war. This furnished conditions more romantic, and in a certain way more favorable to the lovers than could otherwise exist. The heroine and her women friends, would, of course, conspire to advance the wishes of the lover. Maiden diffidence and reserve were to throw as few obstacles in his way as the laws of war. His main advantage was the divine right of capture. She hated Home ever since the Huron days, and was certain he there set on foot a plot against the life of the young chief, which Edith would never believe. That he brought about his capture now, she had no doubt. She fervently hoped to see the day when Dudley should take full vengeance on him, though it involved the discomfiture of Proctor. All the day following the eventful night, the Indian girl devoted to consoling her sister. The fault was with the wholly unwarrantable intrusion of Lieutenant Gordon. It would all have been right but for him. Edith need not be so disturbed. Her chief would always love her. It was the right of a chief's daughter to be asked many times. The Indian girl's talk was not without its comfort, though Edith was shocked by her aboriginal notions, and was at pains to show that the rules of forest courtship, could hardly govern in cases of those reared in Anglo-American ways. That the daughters of the proud Shawanoe, had privileges and advantages denied to maidens of the pale faces.

On the day of the battles, the girls were out on the wooded plain. They were accustomed to the roar of the cannon at Detroit, and now scarcely minded it. The Indian yell raised by the Kentuckians startled them. That was war, battle, an attack of the enemy. They would fight after all. The ears of their own warriors detected it, as the product of amateurs, although Logan, the famous half-blood, and his Shawanoes, soon gave voice with their allies. This was war brought by the enemy, and on *their* side of the river. The girls turned back. The drums beat to arms; in the camp, to their ears, everything was noise and confusion. To all, that wide reaching yell was a call to arms, a challenge, a defiance to battle, immediate. The voices of the officers, quick, sharp, and not loud, scarcely articulate sounds to untrained ears, sent the 41st's men, as all the regulars, forth in rapidly moving red files, as if by magic. Reynolds' men made a little more noise. Warburton was in the saddle as were Proctor, Elliott, Short, Muir ; and the whole force soon in rapid motion, to meet the enemy. Scouts and Indians in advance.

Then fell the ominous silence of the guns of the heavy battery on their side of the river, followed by the cheers of the victorious enemy, and the answering cheers from Camp Meigs. Scarcely had these ceased when nearer came the war whoop of their own warriors, who engaged Combs and the Kentuckians generally. The sound swelled in volume, grew louder and seemingly nearer as the first tide of war rolled toward the camp. Then came the sharp roll of the provincial militia, followed by the heavy explosive volleys of the regulars, and the British cheers as they swept forward with the bayonet, and the enemy's war was broken and beaten back, scattered.

The spirits of the girls arose and their veins quickened in the presence of the battle. Through it all the great guns preserved an ominous silence. Nor yet when the sounds of war no longer beat the air, did they begin again on the west side. The notes of Dudley's defence, feebler and more remote, reached them, and then all was still, and remained so, on their side, and they knew they were the victors. Soon was this confirmed by messengers, sent with the tidings. They had met the American army, defeated it, and nearly all unslain were captured. For the wounded they should take thought. Rumor was that the fort had surrendered also, though, as they could see, its flag still waved, and would until formally delivered. Then came the rattling fights from the easterly side.

Ere these were over the young girls had returned down the glen, Anita showing Edith where she met Dudley and Carter. Also telling her how, by an accident, she met her uncle on his way to the youth's rescue, as she was on her way to notify the chief of his capture. Some of the soldiers had now already returned, and the girls approached to inquire of the battle. Edith knew a grim old sergeant, who gave her some of the details. A soldier seldom knows more than he sees of a battle, which is little, and may fight and retire, not clear as to the general result.

Just then the batteries on the easterly side ceased also and the soldier was sure the fort had surrendered. The girls turned away, Anita deploring the fortune of Dudley in being again captured. The soldier caught the name "Dudley" on her lips and said :—"*Dudley was killed*—as them said as knows it."

"Major Dudley!" cried Edith, with pale face, and almost rigid form.

"Some calls 'im major an' some colonel," replied the sergeant, carelessly.—"Enny ways 'e's killed—airly this mornin'."

Edith was not one to lose self-control, faint, or cry out at anything. A *rigor* made her shiver for an instant. They knew of but one Dudley. This must be him. For her the world had a changed aspect. Slain up there in the woods, where she heard the yells of warriors, the volleys and shouts of the soldiers. She was back in her own tent ere quite herself. She knew Anita had murmured words in her ears, and had an arm about her waist. What she said she did not comprehend, nor did she make reply or ask a question.

In the tent she met her father, just returned after meeting some of the officers. His face confirmed what she was told by the old soldier. He saw she was in possession of what he was spared the pain of telling her.

"Two Dudleys," suggested Anita. "Cliffton Dudley *cannot* be killed."

"There may be," said Grayson, brightening ; "Philip had a cousin in Virginia."

"Make sure. If—if—well," said Edith, pathetically, yet relieved by the suggestions of both, so that now tears came to comfort her. She could not finish the sentence, even mentally, but she could weep.

The smoke of the battle rolled away and dissipated. The waters swept on, still touched by the sun, whose early May rays filled the now serene and lovely valley. A bluebird flew up from below, dropping little trills of joy, and such joy! A robin recovered his voice in the unwonted stillness and sent his tide of song down from his perch on an old maple by the river's margin. They fell on Edith's ears unheeded, save as discordant sounds, as she went forth again, unable to remain inside.

Oh, what was the victory worth at such purchase! Why was war? He may have been met by their *allies*. What a horror was that thought! She would not think, she could not, nor yet avoid the distraction which came as the conclusion of thought. Mingled thought and feeling, the exquisite of anguish.

"Oh—Oh! When he knelt in his loveliness, his beautiful manliness, with his love lighting his eyes, his face, why did I not kneel by him in God's presence, place my lips to his, so our souls should have been wedded!" Her mother's spirit, his father's, would have hovered near and blessed them. God would have blessed the dedication, the union.

An hour elapsed and she knew how much anguish sixty minutes could contain. Then came this note from her father.

" *My dearest child:*

"Praise and thank God! Cliffton Dudley is unharmed. ('O, praise and thank God!' clasping her hands with fervor. Reads.) Anita was right. The slain Dudley was Colonel William Dudley, of Kentucky. I have seen Captain Combs, who commanded their spies; he says Colonel Dudley was killed.

"Major Dudley was on this side; came over alone

and rallied the fugitives, two or three hundred, and made
a very determined stand.　Tecumseh also came over with
a few warriors, and *they met in battle*, face to face, hand to
hand.- ('O, he met Tecumseh ! I never thought of that ; '
looking away, the color leaving her face, crushing the
paper unconsciously in her hands.　Her eyes returned to
it, she smoothed it.　Reads.)　Tecumseh's warriors were
beaten back ! and he was compelled to retire. _ ('Tecumseh beaten back.'　Reads.)　He was slightly wounded.
('Merciful Father !　Tecumseh wounded !'　Reads.)　He
says Dudley saved his life.　('O, joy, joy ! Dudley saved
Tecumseh's life !　Of course he would !　How these noble
men help each other.　Glorious Dudley !'　Reads.)　His
force was too small to do more than retire, which he did
without loss in the face of the chief and his warriors.
('Good, good !　I am glad of it.'　Reads).　He crossed
the river, and is supposed to have reached the American
camp in safety.　(Here she expressed fervid thanks,
kissing the paper, which she resumed.)　The chief is
greatly distressed at occurrences after the battle at the
old fort, on the arrival there of the prisoners.　Proctor
was there ; Tecumseh came.　It would have been better
had he reached the fort sooner.　Of course he put an
end to it.　It was bad.　You would hear of it.　Let us
not think of it."

"The enemy's dead will be honorably interred, especially Colonel Dudley.

"His wounded will be cared for.

"Be with you in an hour.

"Your father,

"E. G."

Edith had to go again into the outer day with this
almost celestial missive.　What a divine radiance was
shed abroad by the dying light upon the now laughing,
lovely earth—battle strewn though it was.　She was even
glad that the flag of the enemy still floated over the head
of the young hero.　Then she thought of his wounded

countrymen, passed by for the wounded British soldiers, and left to the hands of those who had failed to destroy their lives on the field. She went away to enquire into their condition, which she found sad enough. They with the English, less in number, would be sent to Malden the next morning, with the whole body of the American prisoners. She did what she could, and promised herself to see them when they embarked. She resolutely put from her all thought of the possible occurrence at the old fort, yet its shadow was on her.

In the roseate twilight, Anita launched her bark shell, of which she was mistress, and sent it across the river to the landing near the Indian camp. A group of young natives, youths and maidens, gathered there as she approached.

Two boys ran forward to hold it for her to land from, took the light shell from the water as she stepped from it, and remained near to guard it, proud to render the service for one whom they remembered as the daughter of lost Cheeseekau, the niece of Tecumseh and Tecumapease, and worshipped as the Indian youth's ideal of a born princess. As she moved lightly through the group, speaking laughingly to those she knew, they formed an irregular procession, and followed as she passed along the way winding up the bank. There she found many women who came to look at and catch a word from her. The young warriors drew near with respectful admiration, as did many a grim participant in the battle. In some lodges was darkness and weeping; in more were heard notes of triumph. Note of her presence ran through the camp. The young chiefs, Jim Blue-Jacket, young Little-Turtle, Anita's cousin, young Tecumseh, met her; and the last named attended her to his father's

quarters, a little apart from the irregular village of wig-
wams, huts and lodges, forming the temporary camp.

On the other side Anita was the gay, light-hearted,
laughing, pliant shadow, or sheaf of sun-rays, playing
about Edith whom she worshipped, whose ways she
studied and made their spirit hers. Here she was the
Indian princess; wild, arch, sparkling, but never less
than princess, taking the love of children, the love of
women, the worship of the young warriors, and the admiration of the older braves and chiefs as things of course,
to be glad for, to be proud of, yet to seem unconscious
of. It was much to be the daughter of the great Indian
house; it was more to be the lovely, winsome Indian
maiden, and receive the admiration which was to her the
atmosphere surrounding her.

The leaders of untaught races are necessarily austere
of manner: much unbending would be loss of power.
Tecumseh was alone, brooding over the events of the day,
moody, and aware of the hurt to his arm. He submitted
it to Proctor's surgeon. Had himself applied a native
salve, but it was sore, becoming stiff from the hurt to an
important muscle.

Anita entered his presence silently, and stood in the
bending attitude of the Indian woman in the presence of
her lord. He was soon aware of her presence, and his
face relaxed and lit up with a tender smile. He extended
his hand to her and she moved to his side placing her
hand in it, murmuring words of affection, and was re-
warded with an unwonted caress.

Her visit was wholly on Edith's account.

"My sister," she said, "they told her the young
American chief was slain in the battle. Has my uncle
seen him? Does he know?"

He turned his eyes, no longer cold or austere, upon her.

"Why does my English sister hide her heart when the young chief seeks her in his enemy's camp? Should a Choctaw seek my little sister thus, she would at least hear his words!"

"The high-born English maiden must be asked many times. She is not bought with horses. The young chief must prove himself," she answered naïvely.

"Tecumseh has proved him in battle this day. He leads his braves to war laughing, like a young chief when the girls see him in the dance, at the feast of *succotash*," he said.

"We were in swift pursuit of running deer. My warriors dropped their guns. There came a flash of fire in their faces, and then a gleam of the stabbing knives on the muzzles of their guns. My warriors turned back. Tecumseh was alone. The scout of the Huron aimed his rifle at his breast. I looked in at its muzzle. Tecumseh could not fly. The young chief, laughing, struck the gun aside. Tecumseh lived with but this," touching the wound. "The young chief and Tecumseh looked into each other's eyes and smiled. Tell my young sister in her own tongue, till she sees and knows. A leader of warriors knows when to retire. My warriors were gathering up their guns. Warburton and Short with the soldiers were near. The running deer, when he called them turned to fierce wolves, and slowly they backed through the trees, their teeth to us, the young chief between them and us, calling to them in laughing words. I followed him, but forbade my warriors the use of their guns. Tell this to my English sister. The young chief is safe in his camp."

Much more was said, and finally, with a kiss upon her uncle's hand, Anita turned to go, the blaze of the fire showing her form and face half in shadow, to the best advantage. Tecumseh for the first time seemed aware of the excellence, the almost perfection, of her person.

"My daughter is a woman; more comely than her mother or Tecumapease, when a girl. She will have to consider what answer we shall make to the young chiefs," he said, a smile now lighting his handsome face.

The pleased child dropped her head, her eyes flashing from their sides, while her hand toyed with the hilt of her dagger, her parted lips showing the gleam of her teeth.

"Came you alone?" he asked.

"Many came from the river with me," evasively.

"Call my son!"

The young man was at the opening, heard the order and stepped in.

"Look on your cousin," said the chief, which the youth, her junior by a year, was very willing to do,—had already done much looking on her. She certainly was never so lovely as now, as she stood, one hand still on her dagger, her face warm with her uncle's praise.

"See, it is not mete that she go about unattended, like the child of a hunter of rabbits. Call your cousin, Jim Blue-Jacket, Young Little-Turtle, and see her returned in honor."

Anita was in no way displeased at this mark of consideration. Her presence had drawn the young men, the two chiefs by inheritance, and others, near their general's quarters. Upon the appearance of Anita and her cousin, they were joined by the son of Tecumapease who like his cousin had not yet gained a name of his own. The two by right of blood walked on each side of the maiden, while the others, walking behind, attended her to the river.

Her boat was launched, and young Tecumseh paddled it across, attended by the others named, in canoes. So she had a guard of honor back to her residence for the time, where she dismissed her escort with thanks, her manner dignified but very gracious.

It took her till a late hour in her very pretty, yet still imperfect English, to render the chief's account of his meeting with Dudley, which she did in a picturesque way, dwelling much on Tecumseh's chiding. It must be said, that Edith listened with exemplary patience to her extended version, in fact showing many signs of interest in it.

It was late when the girls retired. Anita, with no troubles but those of her sister on her heart, bore them lightly to the land of dreams, as doth the young maiden still "fancy free."

.The next morning was chill and raw. When the wretched prisoners embarked, they became aware that a gentle influence had mollified the rigor of their position, alway, in all war, the extreme of human ill. Something had been done for the wounded, a slight atonement, thought the American, for the atrocities of yesterday. They had been taught to expect treatment little short of death when they fell into the hands of the British and their red allies. We judge enemies by their failures, ignoring the good they do.

At the place of embarkation, each wounded man received a cup of hot tea, broth, and refreshment suited to him, and was gladdened with the face and form of a lovely girl, attended by a lithe, winsome Indian maiden,

14

who glided among them tenderly, and smiling, though
tears were in their eyes, ministering to them. To them
these were as if from heaven direct. A few words the
English girl spoke to each. They should soon see her
again. So she won their blessings. More amazed were
they when she told them that her sister was a niece of
the dreaded Tecumseh. She thought they should know
that.

It was unavoidable that the English attendants should
first think of their own wounded. Edith showed an
equal, and in her anxiety, more care for her conventional
enemies.

CHAPTER XVI.

SHAWANOE IN COUNCIL.

BY the utmost exertion the artillerists got many of
their guns into position during the night of the
fifth, and there was a great bellowing up in the woods on
both sides of the Maumee that morning. After an hour
or two of idle practice, Colonel Short was sent to repeat
the summons of two days before. The American could
hardly conceal his astonishment at this demand. He
told the Briton to look through his camp if he wished,
make sure of the effect of his bombardment, ascertain the
number and condition of the defenders, and report to his
chief, who he trusted would make no more requisitions of
this sort.

This was doubtless to test the temper and position of
his enemy. Proctor knew the American was now too
strong to assault, and a further pounding of his oaken
and hickory palisades was a stupid waste of means. He
resolved in his own time and way to retire to Malden.

General Harrison supposed, as have the American historians, that Proctor's abandonment of the siege was compelled by the withdrawal of his allies and the inefficiency
of the Canadian militia. To them it always seemed that
no other causes could be of sufficient gravity—a military
necessity in fact. In this they under-estimated the effect
of their own war upon him personally.

So it was supposed, later, that Tecumseh more than

once was on the point of abandoning his ally and that nothing but his pay as a British general retained him. These suppositions are an entire mistake of the facts and the character of the chief.

The Indian warriors served without pay. They had a share in the plunder—*loot.* In addition they received a premium for each enemy slain in battle, or taken prisoner, with a difference in favor of the live soldier. The main inducement, was the subsistence of the warriors, and the maintenance of their families. Like all barbarians, the Indians went to war, taking their women, children, old men, and dependents. To secure the warriors of a tribe for war, was for the time to sustain the nation, a thing the Americans never allowed for in estimating the resources of the English in this war. The Indian camp was a group of Indian villages.

There was not the least warrant for the generally believed compact, charged to Proctor and Tecumseh, that upon the fall of Camp Meigs Harrison was to be delivered to the Indians and burnt.

The result of the fifth day's battle, and accessions to the Americans, disheartened Proctor and his inner circle of officers, notwithstanding the heavy punishment of their enemy. He must retire or hazard an assault. Tecumseh discovered at the close of this sixth day that the heavy guns had been dismounted, and slid on skids down to the river margin. He demanded a council of war. Its session was stormy and all the officers of note made speeches. Proctor admitted his purpose of returning immediately to Malden.

Tecumseh spoke at length, in his own tongue, as usual. Elliott translated him into English. Bold and impressive as alway, among other things he said,—"Our father brought us here to take the fort; then why don't we take it ? If his children can't do it, give us spades, we will dig into it—eat a way into it for him." Harsher words followed. When he finished, he filled the bowl in the head of his inlaid tomahawk with tobacco, reclined on the earth and began to smoke. When Elliott came to these bitter words, Proctor fancied he was taking liberties with the orator's text. At one sentence he turned angrily to Elliott and exclaimed :—

" Sir, you are a traitor ! "

" Sir, *you lie !* " was Elliott's fierce retort, drawing his sword.

" What does he say ? " demanded Tecumseh of Elliott, springing to his feet, and brandishing his tomahawk.

The officers intervened, and for the time the tempest subsided to break out in a challenge at Malden.*

When news of the incident of the guns reached them, the militia respectfully asked to be permitted to return to their farms and plant their summer crops. The general thereupon denounced them, and on their return to Malden he contemptuously disarmed them, and for the time dismissed them in dishonor.

Proctor retired to Malden, leaving Tecumseh with bands of his chosen warriors in the woods, to observe the American and annoy him if opportunity presented.

Secretary Armstrong determined to no longer depend upon militia. He had authority to raise a large number of new regiments of regulars. The Ohioans and Kentuckians to a man, would follow Harrison ; scarce a man enlisted in the new regiments. The entire force of the New England colony of North-eastern Ohio were now

---

* " Chronicles of Canada."

on the way to raise the siege of Fort Meigs, as also volunteers from the southern part of the state. Their purpose was to push Proctor back, capture Detroit and Malden, and secure peace for themselves. With the aid of Kentucky, Harrison felt confident of doing that ere midsummer. He was not permitted to attempt it. He met and thanked the Ohio men, and returned them for the time to their homes.

With the opening season the Americans were pushing with vigor the building of a fleet at Erie, to secure the dominion of the lake. The deep and safe harbor of Presque Isle Bay gave shelter for this enterprise. Here Perry, worn and chafed by delay and lack of men, material and armament, was exerting himself to the utmost. The department had promised he should be able to sail forth by the 10th of July.

Meantime, fully advised of the intended weight and strength of the embryo fleet the veteran Barclay, in the sheltered water behind *Bois Blanc* Island, was pushing the new ship "Detroit" to completion, and fitting his squadron for the decisive contest. With his new, heavy flagship, he was confident.

Harrison would invade, capture Malden, seize the navy yard, and make prize of this dangerous naval creation. Restrained from Washington he fortified a camp on the Sandusky River at the Indian Seneca town, nine miles above Fort Stephenson, at the present town of Fremont. This was his headquarters. His left extended to Camp Meigs, with the intervening Black Swamp; his right to Cleveland; with this two hundred miles of lake frontier accessible to Proctor, with his transports and armed ships, who might any day or night land at any of the exposed points, he was compelled to wait.

Stephenson was now a well-built stockade, under the command of Major Croghan, with 160 regulars, having one gun, a six-pounder, and was the most exposed point accessible from Sandusky Bay, and in Harrison's judgment indefensible against heavy ordnance. Thus stationed, building, arming, training, waiting, watching, to the American passed the early summer months of 1813.

Proctor expected to be attacked. He could expect no aid from Prevost. His resource for soldiers were the wilder and more remote tribes beyond Lake Michigan, the Sacs, Foxes, Chippewas and still more remote Sioux.

Dickson had visited them all. Tecumseh met and secured their chiefs. They came on with their warriors in early June, and Tecumseh was at the head of the largest body of native warriors known to our history. Of course they brought their women and children. The warriors were to be armed with muskets, and all to be quartered on the British commissariat.

Many famous chiefs came, as their immediate leaders: Osh-aw-ah-nah, head of the Chippewas, and Black-Hawk, then about the age of Tecumseh, of the Sacs, and their kindred the Foxes, accompanied by his gallant nephew Red-Wing, the son of a sister, wife of a Sioux chief.

In the rivalry of ship building, while Perry was nearer his supplies, Barclay, with his command of the lake, had constant access to the British depot at Long Point, and was confident of having the Detroit in readiness ere Perry could gain the open lake. In the face of Barclay's ships this would be a very hazardous thing in itself to accomplish.

CHAPTER XVII.

EDITH was conscious of a reluctance to leave the valley of the Maumee, place of battle, blood, and murder though it was, and she was well aware of its cause. She steeled her heart, closed her eyes, and turned bravely from the chance of accident, by which she might possibly feel the presence of one whose image would be her mental companion. She intended to follow the vessels that bore the wounded, the same day. She was detained till the next morning.

Anita felt no wish to hurry away. She would not by a minute cut short the chance for something to happen. On the deck of the " Edith," both turned a little wistfully for a glance at the empty place under the distant trees, where their tents so lately stood, thence to the British camp, from that up to the American side, where floated the hostile banner over the palisaded hold, seeming to flaunt them in the face.

" Dudley on bank below, with big guns," said Anita, her eyes and teeth gleaming with mischief. " He take our ship, and carry sister and Anita to his camp," laughing at her conceit.

" They never make captives of women," replied Edith.

" Anita tell him, then he come carry her off. Two or three days he come, find us in the woods, my cousin with us, then he take us all," laughing.

"You bad girl, I do believe you would try it," said her sister, laughing.

"Certain. Tecumapease, young warrior, help me."

The conception of this *coup*, possible only to an Indian girl, was very attractive to her, and she went on recounting the details, in which occurred the names of Jim Blue-Jacket, and young Little-Turtle, when Edith playfully accused her of a secret personal interest in the adventure, at which she laughed a good deal, neither admitting or denying the impeachment; but her account of it was arrested and never resumed.

It was a crisp May forenoon, of that voyage down the Maumee. The girls were quick to note the advance of spring in the ten or twelve days of their sylvan sojourn. Along the banks were many signs of kindling warmth and color. Not with a gush does spring come upon that clime of snow and late sharp air, though near the lake and protected by the dense forest, as it then was. There were under the river's banks, in many deep thickets, favored nooks, dells, and parterres, fastnesses of fatty swamps, where life throbbed the long winter through; but these were the favored haunts of nature; even there the pulse was faint and the breath often congealed to frost, and everything but the bubbling streams wore the rime of winter. To eyes less observant, the forest appeared naked and empty, a region of merely suspended winter. To theirs it was full of life and signs of waking.

Edith found the wounded doing very well, and learnt that the slightly injured, with the rest of the prisoners, would soon be sent below.

Her Frenchtown exiles in the lovely May, were pining for their homes on the lonely river Raisin. The thought of returning them under the protection of Tecumseh,

"King of the Woods," the one apt thing said by Proctor, came to her. She proposed it to them; they were eager to accept it. The chief returned about that time, and gladly undertook at Edith's request to guarantee them from molestation by the natives. At her father's request, Proctor made a formal order for their return, requiring a pledge of neutrality from the males and matrons.

Tecumseh was a born ruler. He went on the late expedition with a certainty of success. He returned with a chagrin little short of mortification veiled under an impenetrable austerity of manner. He was realizing the futility of his first hopes of reclaiming the lost lands. Tecumapease went with Edith to him, on behalf of her proteges. Of all their sex, these were the two women whom he most loved and respected, for the qualities which made them the equals of men, and fit to share their counsels. It was an unusual position for women to attain. Now and then one was known to. Among some of the nations, as with the Iroquois—the title to their lands was held to vest in their women, and could only be alienated by their consent formally given.

Their appeal was not only to his humanity, it was an appeal to his sense of dominion, to his notions of policy. He may have had no very accurate notion of the real causes of the war, nor of its magnitude as a whole; nor what would induce the two nations to make peace. He doubtless over-estimated the importance of the theatre of hostilities, where he was one of the most conspicuous actors. His view was limited to the head of Lake Erie, and the territory immediately north and west of it. Here, up to this last measuring of arms, the Americans had decidedly the worst of it. Notwithstanding their losses, they stoutly maintained themselves. He had never visited Washington or the Eastern cities. A barbarian's only means of forming an estimate of a people's power is by personal inspection of their numbers, the extent of their territory, and the material signs of wealth. At this last meeting of these enemies the British had turned back. The capture of Camp Meigs would practically have ended the war. He now found the Americans were building gigantic ships to try the fortune of battle on the water, a useless waste of means and time, and seemingly decisive of nothing, as the armies would then have to settle it in a great battle. A series of battles between the same enemies lay out of the usual experience of the natives, whose principal business was war. True, the Americans had not dared come out and fight him in the woods, and when they assaulted the soldiers they had been nearly all killed and captured; but the fact remained, Proctor turned away and left them, and the remote Sioux and Sacs were called in. Here was this people of Frenchtown, a large number of mouths to be fed. There were their farms and houses. He never intended to despoil them. The Americans would drive his people off. He would not so treat these. It was better every way to return and protect them, and let them care for themselves for the time.

When they were in possession he promised to visit their town, and place his sign manual on all their dwellings, and woe betide the man, red or white, who should violate his pledge. He made no account of Proctor in this case; had more than once openly compelled him to liberate a prisoner, to whom he felt under a personal obligation.* Wasegoboah and a few warriors should

---

* "Drake's Life."

attend Edith, and Tecumapease, when they went to restore this people, as an escort. It would be understood as under his, Tecumseh's sanction, and he did not over-estimate his own power and reputation, when he supposed this would assure the safety of this abused people.

Edith and her wards hurried their preparations, a party went in advance to open and repair the houses, and remove or bury any unseemly remains of the battle-fields. Good commissary Reynolds furnished stores, the quarter-master means of transportation ; and one morning of the warming May, they started on their return. Edith, Tecumapease and her husband, with Anita, and half a dozen of the youths and young chiefs in festive paint and feathers, attended them as an escort. The road was now hard and good, all the people were in high spirits, and the considerable procession was a gay progress. Out through, now over peopled Maguaga, the native Brownstown, both of which swarmed with the Indians, back from the investment of Camp Meigs. The lovely river, running and dimpling in the sun, murmured a wel-come to the returned, and the courting birds piped glad notes of rejoicing. *They* had been long in possession. Fires were rekindled on the deserted hearths, smoke arose cheerily from the unused chimneys, and as the gathering twilight deepened into night, the windows were again reddened with the cheery fires from within.

These were eventful days in the life of Edith. Every minute had its labor, its hope, and its anxiety. It also had its pleasure, wholly from the consciousness that she was contributing to the happiness of others, enhanced by the presence of the kindling season. What was most sat-isfying was the sense of security with which the restored inhabitants took possession of their houses and farms.

Stand-Firm had never recovered the boat with which he carried Dudley from Detroit. He hid it, as may be remembered, and returned thither by land. It was a mile below Frenchtown, and in the afternoon of the second day, he, Edith, and Anita went in search of it. An old oak tree marked the place of deposit, and he had no trouble in finding it, and in the same condition it was when placed there, and with it the Indian paddles.

Removing it from the little cave under the roots of the oak, the chief placed it on the river strand, and examined the inner surface, near the bow where he saw Dudley make an inscription. He found the marks strong and fresh as when made. Placing the tip of a finger upon it, he gave Edith a significant look. She approached and discovered two or three lines, written with a red pencil in a firm hand upon the smooth surface of the bark. The words were as follows:

"Black River, October 9 and 10, 1811. On the 12th and 13th, journeyed through the wood; 14th, turned back without a word. She who would know the significance of these words will never see them, nor know or care how those days live in memory.

Monday morning, Aug. 17, 1812.   C. D."

"Her eyes do see them, and she knows it all," was her mental comment.

"Wasegoboah, I want this boat—will you give it to me?" she said to the chief.

"It belongs to my sister," he said, graciously.

She beckoned Anita and read the lines. "Yes, another knows," said the Indian girl. "Anita will yet see him in this boat with her sister," she added, confidently. "He will come."

"When he comes, everything will come; all the loved and lost," said Edith, sadly.

"When the battle is ended, then will he come," said the dark maiden, with gay assurance. "And Anita will paddle this canoe for them."

Wasegoboah stood gravely observing the girls. Anita read the inscription audibly. Some of the words he knew the meaning of, as he knew there was something of tender interest between the fair girl before him and the young American chief, whose exploits on the Maumee he was familiar with. It was something after the fashion of their race, which he did not fully appreciate. He said some words to Anita in their tongue, with a gesture toward the southern forest, and a glance at Edith. Anita laughed and replied to him. He received it with a grim smile, and spoke back to her.

"What does he say?" asked Edith.

"That the American chief could come here, and carry you to his own village," laughing.

"Oh! And what did you say to him?"

"That *he* thinks you would not go with him; and his smile meant that a young Indian chief *very much* in earnest, would not mind that;" and the girls laughed very pleasantly together.

"You said something further," declared the fair girl.

"I told him a young white chief did not win a wife that way; and English maidens would not be so gained. He thinks your ways are very funny."

"No doubt. Your Indian way, Anita, would be a simple way of removing many difficulties."

The answer was a significant look and a sheen of white teeth.

"You bad, Anita. I shall have to look out for my sister on her own account, I fear; she is so tall, so much more than comely, and has become so much a woman," now laughing in turn. "I wonder which I am to look out for? Jim Blue-Jacket, or young Little-Turtle?"

Anita laughed her most musical laughter, saying, "We English, oldest sister married first."

"Oh, that is why you are so anxious to have me disposed of." Had she ever witnessed the sensation produced by Anita's presence in the Indian camp, she might have feared for consequences to the child herself, whose interest in her affair made her liable to the suspicion of overmuch susceptibility.

The next morning the two girls took leave of the restored villagers, and returned to Malden, carrying Edith's prize with them. On closer inspection, Edith's name was found written in many different places, showing how constantly, even in that time of peril and flight, she was in the young man's thoughts. It was grateful to her maidenly pride, that her heart had not gone out to one who did not prize it above all things; and she had a right to wear his retained ribbon.

These hidden and now revealed treasures, coming so soon after he sought her to tell his love, were very precious. Surely such love would survive the assault it had sustained at her hand, and seen by the providence which had caused their meeting, would at the least give her an opportunity to show how entirely she appreciated and reciprocated it. For the present it must be put by. She must call up her old spirit, closing her eyes to this thing, and go forward. As she reached this inevitable conclusion, she drew herself up, withdrew her hand from the little birch, carried behind her seat, and turned her fair young face forward with a very determined air.

Seemingly, Anita's mind had followed the mental process of the heroic girl. She burst into a peal of light-hearted laughter.

"My English sister is very brave," she said. "She is a woman."

Mrs. Proctor, with her three children, the wife and family of the general, arrived at Malden, in the absence of Edith on this memorable excursion to the river Raisin, a handsome, charming woman, of gracious manners, and elevated character. Her coming was a social event at Malden and Windsor, and not without influence on that theatre of the war, supplying stimulus and strength to the infirm purpose and character of the British commander, who had been advanced to the rank of major-general.

With her came Edith's childhood and girlhood friend, Mary Coffin, a grand-daughter of the refugee Coffin, and niece of Lady Sheaffe, whom she had not seen since her excursion to the south side of Lake Erie. She was a charming, high-spirited girl, not so beautiful but that she could sincerely admire her friend. What a night for the restored associates was that! Anita was banished to her own apartment. They shared Edith's, and had one good unrestrained, all night's, universal, never-ending, all-embracing girls' talk, amazing and incomprehensible to men.

Mary had an affianced lover in the Canada West contingent, the gallant Lieutenant Gordon. The nuptials had been postponed by the war for a year. The year had elapsed, time called, and the faithful maiden came in prompt response. All this had sprung up and matured since the girls last met.

Edith, in her heart, though she greatly admired Gordon, had never forgiven him for his untimely intervention

and arrest of Dudley. He had partly redeemed himself
by the testimony he bore of Dudley's conduct before
Proctor; but why need he come on such an errand, his
men throwing the butts of their old muskets down with
such a startling sound? True enough, it gave her lover
notice and time enough to retreat, but that was the last
thing on earth she then desired, as he might have known.
Very well, he was Mary's lover. That added a needed
inch to his height, and surrounded him with a halo of
romance which transformed him to a hero. Their love
history had its incidents, its episodes. Edith was always
sympathetic in the affairs of her friend, of all women.
Now Mary found her an apt, appreciative listener. Her
story does not belong to this history, which is obliged to
await the inefficiency of the American navy department,
in equipping and manning Perry's fleet.

During the lulls, brakes, and questioning times of Edith
in this true story of her love, Mary had time to study the
face and form of her friend. An elusive something
arrested her attention and puzzled her. Edith discovered that Mary detected or fancied she did, something curious in herself, and was about to ask what it was.
Mary anticipated her.

"Turn a little, Edith. I saw it yesterday. Let me
have a better look at you. What under the moon is it?"
she said. This was after her history and its discussion
had subsided.

"What is what?"

"That is the puzzling thing. In some way my Joan of
Arc has disappeared, and I find a very lovely, soft, sweet
girl, with heart, tears, and sympathies for love and
lovers."

15

"Well, upon my word!" laughing and coloring with consciousness.

"'How very prettily you color!   Who can he be?"

"Who can who be?" now coloring more.

"Your lover.   I've heard all about Home—he's not the man."

"Will you explain yourself?   What is the elusive something you fancy in me?   Then we can talk of the man."

"Well, you were perfect before.   Yet, you are a trifle rounded.   It is not that, but a wistful sweetness—I can't describe it—in your eyes, face, as if something had come, or was looked for; some new thing in you, asking for something or somebody."

"Oh!   Something you can't see, nor hear, nor think," laughing, her color deepening.   "Well?"

"Well," dropping her eyes from her vain study, " I had a wise old grandmother, a bit of a philosopher in her old woman's way," pausing.

"Oh, we've all heard of her."

"Yes.   They say no woman understands herself.   She seems to have had notions of women.   Let me tell you. It was her notion that when a girl, any maiden you know, met the one, the predestined one, and became very, very much interested, our dear *old mother*, who always knows what is going on, and what is for the best of all, silently, in her own way, prepares her for what awaits her."

"Why, Mary, how absurd!   Do you believe any such thing?"

"How should I know?" laughing and coloring in turn.

"Why should you?   You are soon to be a bride." Then they both laughed.

"Well, you see, the girl herself would never know."

"Well, let me look at you," said Edith, in turn, looking

her friend over—of slightly more fully developed form
than herself. "Mother nature did her work for you so
well,"—she said, laughing again, "Certainly Ed has the
best reason to think so."

"Oh, Ed was not hard to please, fortunately."

Then more teasing from Mary, as to a possible lover.
The hour of confidence for Edith had not come.

"I shall ask this princess of the woods—what a dark,
arch thing she is," said Mary.

"Yes," said Edith, with assumed carelessness. "She
will know all about it."

"Oh, I'll ask her. She looks so cunning, and full of
something too good to keep. Were there any handsome
prisoners? Say what you will, we Americans can give
odds to the average Englishman."

"Ed of course is above the average?"

"No woman marries an average man," was the answer.

Nor did she. The wedding was what we should call
swell.

May ran into June, and June swelled and waned to
hot, voluptuous July, when came the trumpet call to
battle, and the bride must be left wholly to the sympathy
of her appreciative friend.

CHAPTER XVIII.

SANDUSKY.

TECUMSEH chafed under idleness. Here was his host of thriftless warriors. There was Camp Meigs, and sixty miles below, Camp Seneca, with exposed Fort Stephenson, approachable from the lake. He required action. If Proctor would retain his allies he had no choice. Tecumseh planned the capture of Meigs. To Proctor it seemed admirable. The whole force, white and red, streamed forth—the British and many Indians on shipboard, the rest through the woods to capture Meigs. It involved a mock-battle. The soldiers, on their way as if from Camp Seneca to their friends at Camp Meigs, were to fall into an Indian ambush so near the camp that when the deceived garrison should sally out to the rescue, both combatants would turn upon and overwhelm them.

The firing in the mock-battle died away; the Indian yells dwindled to echoes; the enemy silently withdrew—the British to their ships to sail for Sandusky Bay, and Tecumseh's warriors to swarm across the Black Swamp to cut off isolated Stephenson—the second objective point of attack.

With nightfall, there dawned upon the startled garrison of Meigs, the real character of the peril and the narrow escape from it.   Days elapsed ere they ceased to shudder at the strait through which that escape was made.

Fort Stephenson stood on the west side of the beautiful Sandusky, many yards from the bank, there not high, and near the western margin of a small prairie, the river being near the eastern-most line of the treeless plains.   Harrison deemed the stockade indefensible against heavy guns, and left a standing order to Major Croghan, that if approached by a force thus armed, to remove the public property betimes, and rejoin him at Camp Seneca, where he then had about 800 raw troops.

Proctor, with the 41st and other regulars, his heavy guns and 500 Indians, made his appearance at the head of the bay on the last day of July.   Meantime, Tecumseh occupied the woods between the fort and Camp Seneca, with two thousand warriors, the élite of the Indian army, deemed ample to hold Harrison in check, or destroy him if he should come forth to aid leaguered Stephenson, while the British disposed of the little fort.

On the report of this force, Harrison sent a peremptory order to Croghan to withdraw.   The gallant major, then fully twenty-one years of age, returned a peremptory refusal.   "I can defend the fort and by heavens I will," were the concluding words of the curt reply.   Harrison dispatched Major Mills to relieve him, and ordered ·him to headquarters.   The youth explained.   He expected his reply would fall into the enemy's hands.   The woods were full of Indians, and while a few men could elude them, his force could not.   He was permitted to return and resume the command.   Dudley asked permission to accompany him, and share his fortunes.   Harrison had great confidence in the skill and coolness of his chief, and readily consented. The young men reached the imperilled fort in safety. The well-known form of Dudley was a shield. Tecumseh had ordered that if met alone, or with a small party, he should neither be killed or captured.

Proctor placed his guns in position, and in a hurried, half prepared way, commenced his assault. The secret of his haste was long a mystery to his enemy. The eastern bank of the river, opposite the fort, was left unoccupied. The unexpected appearance of a small party of citizens on this bank, wholly fortuitous as is now known, induced a supposition that it was the advance of a force from Cleveland. The party discovered the presence of the British and Indians in time to turn back and escape. Proctor was alarmed and determined to open, if on summons the fort was not surrendered. He and his officers believed it would be given up on demand, and hence he cared less about being in perfect readiness for an effective bombardment.

The first duty of the returned commander was to receive and reply to this summons. Proctor's embassy was composed of, Colonel Elliott, Captain Chambers, Captain Dickinson, and Lieutenant Gordon. Croghan was represented by Lieutenant Shipp, accompanied by Dudley, who as a volunteer was without command or rank. These met the British outside the fort near a small ravine. Dudley was recognized by the Englishmen who greeted him pleasantly. He explained his position and referred them to Lieutenant Shipp.

Colonel Elliott.—General Proctor desires to spare a useless effusion of blood. His guns, now all in position, will destroy your works in half an hour. The woods about you are filled with savages, who cannot be restrained if we are obliged to reduce your works.

Lieutenant Shipp.—The fort will be defended to the last extremity.   My commander is resolved on that.   The demand is refused.

Colonel Elliott.—I pray you consider, be advised; I am sure Major Dudley must see the uselessness of resistance.

Dudley (with a little flash).—I am here for the express purpose of seeing you do your worst, Colonel Elliott.

Captain Chambers (imperiously).—Your commander will certainly regret his rashness.   When we are in possession of your works, no power on earth can restrain the Indians.   The last man will be massacred.

Lieutenant Shipp (haughtily).—There will then be no man to massacre; you and your allies may do what you will with the dead.

Captain Dickinson (pathetically).—I shall alway deplore the fate of such fine young men.

Dudley (with a touch of gay irony).—Thanks, my dear Captain.   We will do what we may in our own way to save your tears.

The parting was in silence.   Two or three Indians had drawn near, under cover of a clump of bushes.   As the Americans turned back they sprang toward them, and one attempted to snatch Shipp's sword from its scabbard. Dudley dashed him aside.   The Americans drew their swords and confronted the warriors, who with brandished tomahawks stood on the defensive.

The British turned back, and Elliott shouted in an angry voice to the Indians,—" Begone, dogs! " and they went cowering away.

" Poor devils! they knew it was their only chance," called out Dudley to the Englishmen gayly.

At that instant Croghan showed on the parapet.

"Come in, boys," he shouted, "and I'll blow them to h—— in half a minute."

The great guns opened one after another as at Meigs. The wide throated howitzers and cohorns sent shot and shells.   The deep intonations set the summer leaves in a tremor, rolled up the bright Sandusky, warning Harrison of the peril of his devoted officers and soldiers—all the livelong night, the next morning, all day, till five of the afternoon ; then the final effort came.

Through these thunderous hours there was little the defenders could do.   Croghan had ten or twelve trained gunners ; these, with his one six-pounder, he placed under the command of Dudley.   As usual, food for this one gun was scant.   Dudley moved it from one block-house to another to produce the impression on the enemy of many pieces.   A few shots were exchanged between prudent Indians and cautious sharpshooters.   The dreaded "old Meigs," the Ohio gun, was there, and used effectively more than once.   The British fire was concentrated on the north-west angle, and though strengthened with bags of sand and flour, here the assault would be made.   The columns would sweep forward, dash over the glacis, leap into the ditch, cut through what the 24-pounders should leave, and fight their way in.   Five hundred trained soldiers with bayonets, and 500 Indian warriors, once an opening was made, would make quick work of the 160 Americans, though led by Croghan and Dudley, and six or eight more equally brave and trained officers.   The skilled instincts of the young men knew when the decisive hour would come, as their training and experience taught them just how the attempt would be made.

Dudley placed his gun in position to sweep the ditch to be crossed by the assailants, charged with a half allowance of powder and a thribble grist of musket-balls, slugs, scraps of iron, and grape, and masked from the assailants. There were some hundreds of new muskets on deposit in the fort, in excess of those used by the infantry. These were inspected, their flints fixed, loaded, and placed in convenient reach of the soldiers.

There was a half hour's increase in the rapidity of the firing. The assaulting columns were formed and the nude and painted warriors, with their knives and hatchets, gathered in the wooded margins near. The confident defenders braced themselves for the inevitable struggle. At the signal, Colonel Warburton, with 200 grenadiers, swept around to assail the south side. The men of the 41st were to do the real work. The fated hour, five P. M., of the hot August Sunday, came with a massive thunder cloud blackening the west, its peals now alone heard. Two minutes after, silence fell upon the guns, whose smoke like a white cloud shrouded the near space, when suddenly came the steely gleam of bayonets of the assaulting columns stabbing through it, toward the weakened angle. They emerged upon the vision of the defenders thirty yards distant, one led by Colonel Short, the other by the gallant Gordon. From the first smiting hail of American lead the men recoiled. At the call of their officers they steadied, and pushed across the narrow space, scorched by the blasting fire, withering, blinding, maddening. On they came, on over the glacis, leaping into the ditch below.

"Cheerily, cheerily, boys, Fall to! fall to! my men," called their fearless colonel, and maddened by his loss, and what to him was a criminally useless defence, he added, turning to the now waiting soldiers : "Give the damned Yankees no quarter !"

At the instant a sound drew his attention to the right. The masque fell from the gorged six-pounder, a blazing match lit up the flashing face of Dudley, then a wide belch of fire and death, as from the nether world.

Gordon's column in like manner, scorched and smitten, had also leaped in. A second rending discharge of the six-pounder, and Frenchtown and old Fort Miami were avenged. Whatever had life and limbs dropped unused axe and useless musket, and scrambled out of the reeking ditch, hot with gushing blood, and scampered, panic-stricken beings, to the nearest cover, and the battle was over on that side.

Short and Gordon fell. The last act of the furious colonel was to twist a white handkerchief on his sword point, a mute appeal for the mercy to his brave wounded he had forbidden them to extend to their slayers. Over a half hundred were left in that reeking trench. Five minutes more and the ground on that side was clear of the foe. The catastrophe had overtaken Short and Gordon ere Warburton and his tall grenadiers reached their point of attack. The fire that greeted them was too hot and fatal. They also broke under it and fled for cover to the not remote forest. No Indians were in the assault.

Beaten, stung with the loss of a fourth of his soldiers, after nightfall Proctor sent his stealthy Indians to gather up such of his dead and wounded as they could come at, and before three o'clock of the next morning, with his hurriedly embarked soldiers, he was on his way down the bay, leaving a vessel with valuable clothing and supplies to his enemy.

As the day closed on the Americans, the shifting wind

sent the black thunder clouds northward over the lake,
which was to bear the burden of the next battle, and the
last rays of the now Sabbath sun lit up their flag still
floating over their battle battered walls. The tide of war
had turned. No hostile foot was again to press that
northern border of the young Ohio,—save as prisoners in
the last and greatest war.

The fatally repulsed expeditionary force came back to
Malden, with its humiliation heightened by the fact that
it was inflicted on them by 160 Americans under a mere
boy, in a pen of logs, and one six-pounder.

Gordon came not with it. The last his countrymen
saw of him, was when with branished sabre he called to
his soldiers and leaped into the trench. It was said that
he was slain. The sky turned dark and the earth faded
from the vision of his swooning, expectant bride. When
she returned to consciousness Edith was with her. She
came back to realize the certainty of her loss.

" No, no, Mary, do not utterly despair of his life. I was
told that the most beautiful, and the bravest of men, the
beginning and end of love for me, had fallen in battle. I
saw him in vision, mangled by the warriors I had armed,
yet within an hour came the tidings that he lived."

Mary heard the words as a kindly figure of speech,
bringing small hope, and she saw not their pertinence to
the experience of her friend, who yet could so entirely
enter into her feelings. Edith, on the strength of her own
history, felt a strong assurance that they would certainly
soon hear that Gordon was with the Americans, a prisoner. To her repetition of this, her friend came to listen
finally with something of rekindling hope. At near nightfall of the day following the return of the British, came
an Indian runner from Brownstown bringing an open let-

ter to General Proctor, under the care of Mr. Grayson. It came to Edith's hand and she read it.

"FORT STEPHENSON, *August* 4, 1813.

" *General,—*

"Lieutenant Gordon was severely wounded, and suffered most from loss of blood. Is in good hands —will assuredly recover. A flag bearing this note will admit Mrs. Gordon and attendants—any friends of his. He will be paroled when wished. All wounded doing well.

"C. D.,
"Chief of Staff N. W. Army, U. S."

She knew the hand, and had familiarized herself to the significance of the initial signature. In the impulse of grateful emotion she knelt, and with the missive to her lips thanked God for herself, as for her stricken friend. She then ran with it to her, to whom it was as the voice of Him who called back the dead. Then Edith sought her father, who carried the missive to Proctor.

A verbal message came with it faithfully delivered, as the trained native bearers transmit and deliver messages. A Shawanoe serving with the Americans, carried Dudley's note to Tecumseh as he was gathering his force to return to Malden, who sent it forward by a fast runner.

Gordon was a favorite, and the word that he was safe soon made the circuit of the little circle of officers. It also transpired from whom the joy bearing note came. Edith was almost as happy as was the young bride. Her father so managed that the letter came back to her hand, where it remained.

Early the next morning the little " Edith " with her one tall mast ran down the river with Mary, bearing a letter commending her to General Harrison, with thanks; also an experienced nurse. Edith and Anita saw her off. Five days, and a letter came to Edith from Mary, covering twenty-three pages closely written. She was hopeful and happy. There had come to her a wonderful revelation, an account of which occupied most of her paper.

She found her husband in a hopeful way. Dudley rescued him from the gory trench, where life was fast ebbing way. The now happy youth told his wife what he knew of his friend's luckless love. This then was the suspected lover. Of course she met Dudley, and found opportunity to verify Gordon's statement. The young American said little to her and she saw that he accepted the tent scene and Edith's words as final of their relations and rendering his love hopeless.

Five days later the " Edith " bore the wedded lovers back to Malden.

Perry was abroad with his armed ships seeking his foe,

THE native warriors returned from Sandusky disappointed, discontented, sullen. Many whose villages were nearest stole away with their women and children,—as the way of the uncertain Indian is.

Tecumseh had now no confidence in Proctor as a general, no trust in his honor as a man. He constantly compared him with Brock, which was unfortunate. While they held the lake undisputed, he would have swept all the settlements on its southern border. Because the enemy sheltered himself behind palisades, he could see no reason why Proctor should butt his stupid head against them. Pontiac failed to take Detroit. They failed to take Fort Harrison, Fort Wayne, Meigs and Stephenson. The Americans would never fight unless in a log pen, with a ditch around it. Let him stick to his coop if he wanted to. He would leave him there, go by him, and sweep everything from around him. He would lay waste all his plantations, make desert the settlements, cut off all supplies—that was his plan.

Now what? Suppose Barclay took the new ships, what then? They would be just where they were before. Harrison in his forts, Proctor withdrawing his sore head from them ; and so it would go, till the warriors deserted, then Harrison would come and Proctor would run away.

If his one armed father failed—if Perry took *his* ships,

Harrison would come in all the ships. He saw no preparation to fight him at his landing. The guns had gone from the forts, all the warriors saw that. No wonder they were discouraged. The Sacs, the Foxes, the Chippewas, and Sioux could not go so easily. Tecumseh had lost the heart and hope which enabled him to hold, govern, and lead them. He put on added austerity at times; at times more address. His personal resources though remarkable were fully taxed. He was in constant association with the chiefs of the remote tribes, was their sole hope and stay. He knew their defection would ruin all. Walk-in-the-Water had shown signs of walking away on land. All would go but those of his immediate personal following. For himself to withdraw would be to return to the intolerable condition of things which drove them to war, aggravated by a virtual defeat. The Americans had lost many men, and their numbers in no way seemed to diminish.

The Indians had many causes of complaint, and the chief approached the general with a freedom none other dared assume.

The militia though dismissed with contempt were soon called to resume their arms which they were prompt to do; little was grown for subsistence, and now Perry was abroad. The question of food soon became pressing. The subjects of the "King of the Woods" were served with horse-flesh, while the soldiers had beef. At his demand this had to be set right.

He was on Bois Blanc Island when Perry first approached Malden. He was pleased that he came. He assured his warriors that the British would go forth and destroy his ships. He believed they would. The Indians hastened down to the shore to see the battle. The chief

saw no signs that their ships were even going out. He
launched his canoe and hastened to Proctor.

"You boasted a few days since that you commanded
the lake. Why don't you go out and fight the Americans?
See, see them yonder—they have come for you! They
dare you! You shall go and fight them." *

There seemed to him no excuse. None why the new
ship was not ready. The Americans had built ten in the
meantime.

When the new ship was done, and Barclay refused
Perry's more formal challenge, Tecumseh was certain
that something beside material was wanting. He dis-
trusted Barclay, and began to have misgivings of the
result when the fleets should join battle. Barclay was
reluctant. The fleet in his hand was what he had asked
for, when he knew to a gun the proposed force of the
American.

The matter of supplies became imperious. The men,
the sailors were on short rations. The fleet *must* go to
Long Point. On the way it *must* meet and fight the
American.

The morning of September 10 was the beginning of
a ripe summer day, and the six royal ships in the glory of
fresh paint, white canvas, and flags, went forth to battle
and assured victory. There was a great waving of hand-
kerchiefs from dock yards and points of observation, and
a dipping of flags from fort and standard bearers. The
ladies of Windsor and Malden were there, with the scarlet plumed officers, gay and high-hearted, to see them
sail to the conquest of green, dimpling Erie.

In a group conspicuously apart, stood Mrs. Proctor,

* Drake's "Tecumseh."

Edith Grayson, Mary Gordon, and Anita. How glad and proud the brave show made them! Britain sending forth her ships and sailors to chastise an insolent foe on her chosen field. Undoubtedly they would be gallantly met. Mrs. Gordon brought back a great deal of American gossip of young Perry. They knew the English officers spoke respectfully of him. They knew he would fight heroically, persistently. Since the older Hollanders, the English had met no such foes on the sea as these young, lithe Americans. Many brave men would fall. All three ladies were each devoutly thankful that the one dearest was not on those low, unguarded decks. Neither they nor any spectator had misgiving of the result. Ere nightfall, the king's ships would return, convoying the lately defying ships of the foe, captive and abased.

Away they went down the river and out of sight. *They did come once again.* The sun clomb the cloudless sky. The meridian was reached, the anxious spectators still waited. Noon passed, then a single boom; another, then a roar came rolling up the lake, striking the wooded shores, lifting and rolling over the forest, swelling up the river, and spreading in waves over the level shores. The forts at Malden and farther Detroit heard the voices of their own guns. What a start that first gun gave them all! More than did the heavy broadsides later. Then came the fainter notes of the enemy's reply. The battle had joined, and raged, then a lull with single guns. The battle was over! No. A burst of guns, then quiet. Two hours since the first—sure it was over now. Somehow after the ships disappeared down the river, and were out of sight, misgiving stole traitorously into the hearts of the waiters, watchers, and prayers at Malden. Shots came again, singly, increasing, became indistinguishable; then

16

bursts upon bursts like awful peals of thunder! Louder and louder; overtopping, swallowing the memory of the earlier tumult. *All* the guns of *all* the ships, more than one hundred cannon in continous concert. *This was the battle* at close quarters! What man could survive it? What ship float under it? Briton and American madly bent on mutual destruction. Surely, Barclay had laid his foe close aboard, was breaking his line as taught by the great admiral. The cloud of battle rose on the south eastern horizon, spread and pyred upward. The lake was obscured as the southern breeze wafted the sulphurous cloud northward. Ten or fifteen minutes of this awful tumult, then silence as from heaven fell over the lake. That was the battle—past their conception of its possible din. How had it gone? Oh, how had it gone? Who had thought this question could arise? They had underrated this young American lieutenant. They had counted Dudley as exceptional. This Perry was the superior of Dudley. Surely—"Barclay of Trafalgar," as they were fond of calling the old hero, had been fairly matched. The American had fought all his ships, all his guns, all his men, to their utmost. Had he submitted? God, what a question!

The battle was really over, all the glasses from all the heights saw no further signs, nor heard further note of it.

Light craft were down in the lake—the "Edith" with others, to observe, gather up the news. Indians were on the lower shore. Mid afternoon—nothing. Later, a sail, then another arose. Their lookout returning? No. They were war vessels. The van of their victorious fleet returning! Joy! Joy! Soon two more appeared. How is this? Victors would come together. They must be their craft of observation, only they had but three.

While these queries were pending, the two stern-most opened fire on those nearest. Were these the Americans fleeing? They would not come that way. These nearer returned the fire. Not many shots, and the affair between them was over. The two in pursuit approached the pursued who made no effort to escape. The ships neared, were in a group, then all headed down the lake! God of heaven! This was not victory! These fleeing were their ships, crippled past escape or defence,—were captured, lost!

The fleet was lost, Detroit, Malden, Canada West—all!

What a night of despair for the British shore.

CHAPTER XX.

TECUMSEH and his warriors, as claimed, may have seen the battle, and the sailing of the ships the next morning into American waters. The lookout sails stole back to Malden in the night. It was certainly known on the morning of the 11th, that the united fleets sailed into Perry's Bay, and Tecumseh demanded of Proctor the meaning of this movement, whenever he learned it.

"My ships have whipped the American," he replied. "Of course they are much damaged. They will all be here in a few days."

Tecumseh was unbelieving. He saw signs of flight. The eyes of his chiefs were acute. They shared their leader's opinion of Proctor. They believed his ships were lost; that the Americans would now be upon them. "We will fight them when they come. In the woods, if they march; when, and where they land, if they come in the big canoes. We will not retreat,"—was the result of their consultations.

Tecumseh saw the valuable and heavy property sent up the river. He demanded the meaning of it. Proctor said he was sending it up the Thames for safety. The chief would not be trifled with. He demanded a council. Proctor was compelled to assent. All the chiefs were present. Elliott was to interpret. In his speeches

Tecumseh always used his native tongue.   When all were seated, he arose and delivered the well-known speech or phillipic part of the history of the war.*

The English, though simple and dignified, reads tamely. The chief arose in his native costume, the simple hunting shirt and leggings; fixed his eye upon the general, and never removed it.   His look and mobile face, his flashing eye, graceful, rapid, vehement gesture, and tones of voice, quite advised Proctor of its biting qualities, its sarcastic irony, and contemptuous spirit.   He did not wish to hear an oral translation of it.   Elliott secured it by a method of his own.

Proctor had the tact to say when it was ended, that it was of such importance that Colonel Elliott would deliver him a written copy, which he wished to lay before their father, Mr. Grayson, who as they knew represented their Canadian father, Governor Prevost, and that by him his answer should be returned the next day.

This was satisfactory because the chief had unchanged confidence in Grayson, undiminished regard for Edith. The only thing in her he ever disapproved, was her treatment of Dudley—American though he was.

Mr. Grayson delivered Proctor's reply in the first person.   It was in fact his, and translated paragraph by paragraph as delivered.

" My brothers will hear me," he began.   " I have considered the chief's words, which are weighty.   I will not say he labors under mistakes.   The same things appear differently to different men.   I will not now speak of the past.   To-day is too important to be wasted on yesterday. General Proctor has to depend on Governor Prevost.   If

---

* See Drake's " Tecumseh."

he has failed in his word to you, his Canada father did not furnish the means.

"Listen, that we may hear and know how we are situated to-day, so that we may act wisely and all together. We have lost all our ships. The Americans, contrary to our expectations, captured them. Brave men do not sit and cry for a lost battle. Let the women do that. The wise chief sees how he can repair the loss, save himself from more loss.

"What is wisest for us now to do? We can bemoan, we can find fault, we can reproach. These do not help us. They help the Americans. Our scouts say General Harrison has 15,000 soldiers at Sandusky. Let us suppose he has half that many. That gives him nearly five to our one. He has all the ships to bring them here. Can we meet him when he lands, under the muzzles of all his great guns? Were Brock here, would he attempt that? Our great guns went in our ships. The Americans will now bring them to fight us. Our forts without their guns could not destroy his ships. nor have we enough left to defend them with.

"Let my brothers hear me.

"Could we beat the Americans back, how can we live here?

"We are very short of provisions now. We have no corn, no wheat. Winter is upon us. Your warriors and women are without blankets, our soldiers without clothes.

"We can bring no more from Long Point. Everything now must come ·from Burlington Heights, 200 miles through the woods. When they reach the Thames, they might now be captured before they reach us.

"Would it not be wiser for us to all go on to the

Thames, where we would meet our supplies and so be sure of them?

"Let my brothers listen. Where can we best fight the American? Here, where he can come with all his ships, all his soldiers, all his big guns? If he had to follow us on to the Thames, he must leave part of his ships, men, and guns, here. The farther he had to go, the fewer soldiers could he bring to fight us with.

"We will not go beyond his reach. Is it not wise to go so far, that he will be obliged to fight us with an army, that we can be very certain of beating? Then he must turn and run from us and we pursue him.

"If for these reasons it is wise to take up a new position on the upper Thames, where our remaining guns can be carried, where our gunboats can go, where a fort might be built, and where but a part of the American army could follow us, it would be wise to go at once, and have everything in readiness to meet the Americans.

"We will destroy the fort at Detroit; ruin and make useless all the fortifications at Malden, so the Americans shall find only wreck and ruin. We will take off every horse, all the means which would help him in his war against us, leaving only food for those who do not go with us.

"Colonel Elliott has made all my words plain in your ears. My brothers will ponder them wisely and General Tecumseh will render an answer to General Proctor, when it shall please him."

"Will my father go with the army to the Thames?" asked Tecumseh.

"So long as my brother and the chiefs and their warriors remain with General Proctor, I shall go with them."

"My father has spoken well," said the chief, and there was a general assent on the part of the assembled chiefs.

Tecumseh met Proctor the next day, and assented to the plan of a new position on the upper Thames. The chief imposed the sole condition, that at such point as he should select, subject so far as the ground was concerned to the approval of the general, they should give the Americans battle. With this Proctor expressed himself content.

Meantime the Indians were to pass over to the Canada side, and be subsisted by McKee, Proctor promising a supply of blankets and food—a promise the sorely tried general knew was beyond the hope of present keeping.

American officers and writers agreed with Tecumseh that Proctor's true course was the heroic one, assault Harrison at his landing. They allege that his personal fear inspired his action. Whatever were his faults as a general, or infirmities of character as a man, whoever examines the straits in which he found himself will be satisfied that his weakness was not shown so much in his resolution to retreat as the mode and time of conducting it.

It is clear that he did not expect to be pursued up the Thames. It is equally clear if he was, he never intended to turn and give battle. What he ultimately intended for his allies is less certain. Probably retain them till he was safe and then leave them to shift for themselves. He would hardly break openly with Tecumseh. It is said he pretended to the chief in this conference that he expected to find reinforcements on the Thames, where he intended to build a strong fort.

Measures for the evacuation were now actively entered upon. Such an effective demolition of the fortifications, navy yard and public works, was made, as precludes the idea that Proctor expected to return to their occupancy. So cleanly he picked up the horses that on the arrival of the horseless Americans but one sorry beast could be found for the weary generals, and this Harrison assigned to the venerable Governor Shelby, of Kings Mountain fame. Leisurely—criminally so, if he expected pursuit, Proctor sent off his valuables. Many of the loyal citizens wanted to go; in short a vast amount of unmilitary material and men accompanied him which could but embarrass him, should prompt action become necessary.

Finally the army took up its march. The Indians, warriors and women were on the move—the easiest mobilized of any force.

Proctor's rear guard did not leave Malden till September 28, and then it was almost an escape.

Harrison was at that hour landing four miles below.

Colonel Johnson with his famous Kentucky legion of mounted infantry was at Camp Meigs. When the fleet and transports reached the Maumee, he marched to Detroit, keeping abreast of the transports up the river, bringing joy to Frenchtown, and sending a thrill to Detroit from which fell Proctor's fetters of odious martial law. The American flag was raised over the dismantled fort, on his arrival.

Harrison landed on the low shore covered by sand ridges. Beyond these he expected to find the embattled Britons flanked by their allies. His advance found an empty plain. The approach to deserted and dismantled Malden betrayed its condition.

With his staff and a guard, Harrison pushed forward near the town. Instead of an army he was met by a small party of ladies apparently seeking an interview with the commander.   Seeing the enemy, they paused, waiting to be approached.   Harrison, attended by young General Cass, went forward to learn their wishes.

Lovely Mrs. Gordon was with them, whom the general had met at Fort Stephenson.   She took a little step forward and stood distressed, hardly daring to look up.

"Mrs. Gordon!"   cried the general, lifting his plumed hat and smiling graciously.   "What do you wish?   You have but to name it if it depends on me."

She hesitated, reddened, turned pale, tears in her eyes. "How can I say it!   How "—she broke down.

Harrison advanced, took her hand.   "Be composed, I pray you.   You have no cause for alarm at my presence. You, your friends and people, shall remain as free and receive as full protection in all possible ways as if under your own flag."

"Oh, I knew it, I knew it!   It was that we came to ask."

"Those whose pleasure it is to protect you, have been called by duty elsewhere ; we will see that want of safety is not added to your other troubles.   I may not hope my presence will give you pleasure.   I will make it as little painful as possible.   This say from me to all your people. I will issue a general order which will allay apprehension, I trust."

"Thanks! thanks, General!   Had I—had we selected an enemy to rule us, it would have been General Harrison."   She said it very well.   The general bowed.

"These are ladies of Malden.   You have so kindly · anticipated our errand that we can only thank you," she added, now her usual self.   They all murmured thanks.

"I can have but a word now, Mrs. Gordon.   I shall send round to inquire after your husband."

"Thanks, General." And the ladies turned back to discuss the general, as women would under any circumstances.

Harrison had taken in the whole situation, or he had not lingered there in the first hour, in the enemy's country.

CHAPTER XXI.

FLIGHT.

WHEN the Gordons returned from Sandusky, everything at Malden was alarm and expectation. There were abundant opportunities for meetings and long talks between the restored friends. Mary had her husband, who had passed the period of anxiety with his wounds to one of tender care, and for whom time alone was needed for full recovery. His position was to her one of exceptional advantage; he was exempt for the present from the peril of battle, yet the poor fellow was beginning to chafe at this enforced inaction during this time of din and preparation for coming conflict, which would involve all arms.

Edith was a person of scarcely less interest to her friend. She now for the first time had a tender appreciative woman of her own race, to whom she could confide her heart's history. Mary was a woman of a sensitive, proud nature, not yet abased, as some are, by the intimate association which marriage permits with a coarser fibred man. She understood and appreciated Edith's motives, the action of her mind, the elusive play of her maiden instincts, so unappreciable by the average man. She had more than her letter contained to tell of Dudley. Their intimacy was a source of exquisite satisfaction to Edith, who looked upon Mary as an expert in the ways of the hearts and loves of men, from her position as a lover and her two months' experience as a bride.

There was no time or material of which plans could be constructed to advance the tender interests of the exceptional lovers, in the presence of this horrid war. They were in hostile camps, about to send forth their soldiers to battle.

Then came the awful fight on the lake, followed by the certainty of Harrison's approach, the terror of his coming, the hurry, disgrace, and mortal depression incident to the escape from him. Escape it was in the eyes of these women.

The gay, high-hearted Anita was a source of hope and spirit through the darkness of these days. She hoped Edith would remain at Malden, with her friends the Gordons. She was conscious of occupying a position on her own account. She had several times met the young Red-Wing from the distant Rock River, beyond Lake Michigan. It was thought, too, that the defection of young Little-Turtle was on her account. Whether it was or not, he had returned to his village beyond the Wabash on the Eell River.

Edith had no choice save to accompany her father, who saw if the war on the lake was adverse, that retreat or surrender was inevitable for them. She had an interview with Tecumseh. He had made up his mind: He was firm, resolved, doing all in his power, but oppressed with the gloom which is not a stranger to men of the highest endowments. He expressed concern for her, spoke of Dudley, his own personal obligation to him, and his purpose to spare him in battle, if in his power. Edith expressed a doubt of there being a battle. The chief said there would be, and he himself should not survive it.	Edith was shocked by his gloomy view of his own fate, and combated it.	She made little impression on him.	He spoke of his niece with tenderness and concern.	His brother, the prophet, was present, and he attended the girls from the chief's quarters on their return. He said his brother looked forward to the Thames expedition as the close of his career.	That the prospect for his people filled him with gloom.	Anita rallied him in a brave, high-hearted way, as she had not dared to in the presence of her greater uncle, and spoke words of cheer and hope for him.

Her example was not lost on Edith.	This was the province of a woman in the day of darkness.	She, too, had shared the common depression.	She was anxious for her father, for Dudley; she had not thought that Tecumseh could be slain, though impressed by his words and manner.	She saw Anita was not, and she now rekindled her own spirit from that of her sister.

She returned to her father's quarters quite in a glow of revived hope and enthusiasm.	She visited Mrs. Proctor, whom she found strong and brave, and for the last two or three days ere they departed with the advance, she became a source of courage and cheerfulness, of hope, to the many whom she met.	The effect upon herself was inevitably to restore to her own heart and spirit, not their old enthusiasms, their old illusions, but their old poise, firmness, strength, purpose, and much of the hope, the devotion, of the spring, when they sailed to the conquest of Camp Meigs, now so long ago.

Cheerily covering from her eyes the ruin about her, she took her seat with Anita in the carriage, with one of Mrs. Proctor's children, and started on the journey for the Thames.	Her father had become a member of the general's staff for the present, and the daughters, a part of Mrs. Proctor's family, for the time. These young women, exceptionally endowed, yet differing in gifts and accomplishments, as in race, their lives and fates involved in the great problem of the nations, rode almost gayly forth to the approaching solution of them, in the fiery alembic of battle. The sky was bright, the sun effulgent, the air rich with the sensuousness of ripening autumn.

They gave themselves to the influences of the day, not dreaming of the forms crystallizing just beyond their horizon, awaiting their approach.

Let us in advance see something of the scenes of the final catastrophies of our history. The mouth of the Thames is thirty miles due east from Detroit, the river comes from an easterly direction, emptying into Lake St. Clair. In its lower course it is a deep, sinuous, sluggish stream, then navigable for light draft vessels, seventy or eighty miles. In 1813 the easternmost settlement was the Indian Moravian town, of quite an hundred dwellings, standing pleasantly on an eminence on the north bank, a place to be often mentioned. It was about thirty-two or thirty-three miles from the mouth of the Thames. Two or three points along the river are to be borne in mind. One is Dalson's, sixteen miles from Lake St. Clair, on the north side, the first eminence that breaks the level, and near the present town of Chatham.

There Dalson had made a small opening, and four miles below Dalson's, on the south side, was Drake's farm. At this point the character of the stream changes from a broad, sluggish river to one much narrower, more rapid, and walled in by higher banks; and the face of the country assumes an undulating form. Ascending from Dalson's, four miles on the north bank was Bowles' farm.

Still above, and at the foot of the first rapids, was a creek entering from the south, on which was Arnold's mill. Eleven miles further takes us to a point on the north bank, two or three miles from the Moravian town, of great importance in this narrative.

Returning to the mouth of the river, it may be said that ten or twelve miles of its lower course was through a rich alluvion formed by the Thames and tributaries, won from Lake St. Clair, of the usual character of such deposits; and for several miles, the surface was a treeless prairie.

With the rise of the surface to the older formation, began one of the noblest forests of the continent, consisting largely of the now nearly extinct black walnut, then in its perfection, and nowhere, save exceptionally, did the trees attain such size and height as here. Very many were from four to six feet in diameter, at the usual height of being cut to fell, and it was not remarkable to find one springing round and straight, 90, 100 and 120 feet, to the lower limbs. Grand columns, and crowned with noble tops, huge branches, reaching symmetrically out, like those of the finest elms, or the largest and most perfect hickory. Trees of this species and size command breadth of space. They cannot grow near each other, as do the largest pines and some other conifers, though, like the pine, little or nothing grows beneath their shade, save springing children of their own planting, while the ground is usually firm. After a breadth of this timber other varieties of the trees of the temperate zone appear, and the walnut is the exception.

It may be remembered that from the Moravian town eastward to Burlington Heights, a distance of 170 miles, the country was covered by the primitive forest.

Riding forth, Edith was at the first little inclined to talk. Anita usually took her cue, if not her mood, from her, and left her to her own thoughts. Edith's, as often in these later days, turned to her sister with growing concern.

She had fancied, as older persons have, that an Indian girl, by education and training, might become in a few years much like herself. She was wholly unaware of the indestructibility of human nature, and that radical changes require generations under favoring conditions.

She had planned a joint career : their mission would be the civilization and education of some of the finer and nobler natives. The scheme included nothing of the tenderest and most intimate relations with the other sex— marriage—such an alternative had never been presented to her mind save with Home, and that she ever turned from. Her recent experience had given her more accurate ideas of herself, and sharpened her thoughts and observations of the nature and possibilities of Anita. She was coming to appreciate her for what she was, and would remain,—a true daughter of the wood and wild plains, of forest stream and lonely lake, the child of unknown centuries of wandering barbarism. Her future was a matter of the greatest anxiety, daily more pressing. Even before the war she had many times noticed a wistful look in the child's eyes, token of virgin longings for barbarian life.

With the arming of the painted warriors mid the women and papooses, there was a re-awakening of the girl's untamable nature. She greatly enjoyed the adventure, and wild life, at Camp Meigs ; and now it was plain to Edith, that the child's only regrets at going upon this new quest, were wholly on her sister's account. She naïvely admitted she preferred to be a captive with her sister to the Americans, where the captivity would not be so very irksome.

"And where the gallant and handsome Red-Wing might swoop down and carry you off. The 'Young Chief' as you call him, if he ever wishes as you dream, would never think of a bride in the midst of a campaign. My little sister, taller than I am, may as well turn her fancy to her own affairs. I admit I am a little anxious about her, with all these brave young chiefs caracolling round on their gayly pranked ponies," was the substance of Edith's speech in reply.

"Anita can wait. Indian girl see Americans come, all his horsemen; Anita heard of them; they surround the soldiers, take them all, war over them. It won't be long. Young chief come then," looking weirdly from the sides of her eyes, as at a vision beyond the horizon.

"Anita! What are you saying?" half laughing, yet a little disturbed.

"Won't be long. Indian girl wait;" laughing at the effect of her conceit on Edith.

"Child, you are a half witch. Please don't try that on me now."

Then the child laughed in her old happy way, leaning forward to adjust something, and bringing into relief the rounding lines of her graceful form. Oh, dear, what hope of reclaiming the average Indian, if this gifted daughter of a great and gifted family, was permitted to relapse. Was it a question of permitting? She remembered how fearlessly and how perfectly Anita rode and managed a spirited horse in the south side woods. She felt a sad certainty that she was equal to mounting another, and riding away with her people, if her heart was with a chosen one. What if one *should* ask her to ride away with him ? She left it unanswered.

Edith had escaped from the seat of many months of painful anxieties, trials and labors, to this wide country, with a sense of relief. She threw from her the past, she would not scan the possible future, she dwelt upon her sister—a very sister to be loved, cherished, yet still to half fear, as full of wild strength and power, with the nature and will to devote herself with the touching unreserve of a woman. She finally cast this from her thought.

Along that belt of the continent the season had reached its balancing pause, when ripest summer was changing to deepening autumn, preceding decay, the stripping of the forests of foliage and fruit. The nights were frosty, the days full of softened loveliness ere the faint reflex of summer called the " Indian Summer " was reached. There was nothing now for her hands to do, nothing for her active feet. Her mind was weary of her past. She would be a spectator of what might occur. She could not be an actor. She would be in the open outdoor, as dear to her as to Anita, in the autumn woods, with their color and fragrance.

The first day's moderate journey was restful to mind and body ; it carried them nearly to Lake St. Clair. The second to Dalson's ; the third to the Moravian town, where preparations were made for their party, and where they would remain till the army approached. Easterly from the lake, they took the road on the north bank of the Thames, up which the gunboats and light craft had transported the guns and material, stores, and heavy baggage, carrying many of the inhabitants, fleeing the dreaded Americans and *their* savage allies. Very leisurely this was performed. For obvious reasons this north bank would be the route of the retiring army. It was not called retreat, certainly not an escape. The officers euphuistically spoke of it as falling back to a stronger position on the Thames, nearer their base, really an advance upon their supplies.

Turning eastward along the low banked river, across the rich prairie, they came to the scattering walnuts, immense trunks, wide tops, not so tall as forest trees in the open, with no struggle for air and light, have less height.   Then clumps and detached groves, then the continuous forest. The sight of this succession—procession—of grand trees, any one of many of which would be a wonder in a wood of ordinary trees, filled Edith, who was a tree worshipper, with an ecstasy of amazement. Tall, grand, huge columns, supporting a dome of far up arches of foliage, of brown and golden tints, with solitary huge nuts of yellow tinted green, lying here and there on the clean, bare ground—mile upon mile of these, with here and there a maple, a smooth barked beech, a huge tulip tree, or a competing hickory.

" It reminds you of the lovely woods on the Black River, of two years ago," said the equally pleased Anita.

" It is impossible to forget that time, and those beautiful woods. These do not remind me of them, nor this country and river, though both improve. The sunshine and air are like that time, and I like the fragrance of these ripe walnut leaves."

" And, Edith, may I tell you what I think—as you cast your eyes up these big tall trees, that there were then eyes that went up with yours just a little way, and instantly came down to your face—they couldn't help it— and rested there, till yours came down and looked into them. Oh, I felt the charm that was working between you two. My sister dreams of the Black River;" turning away with a decided little motion of her head, as to say—"Don't tell me."

"And my sister—does she dream of Rock River Valley?"

"My sister knows very well one cannot dream of what one has never seen," was the naïve answer.

Then they talked of the possible long, long journey—Anita shook her head at the idea, entertaining it only conversationally—the journey through the interminable forest. It was happiness to be in the woods. No thing disconnected with the charm of young hearts was such a pleasant theme for talk, and she indulged it to any extent. She said, Tecumseh, Tecumapease, Black-Hawk, Red-Wing, would never go beyond Moravian town, and Edith saw her heart was with them. Both girls, as much as they loved a journey through a forest, secretly drew back from this. Each may have been conscious of the reason.

Edith's spirit was alway under the influence of a profound religious sentiment, which never left her in darkness uncheered, nor in light and joy permitted her exultant spirit to forget the spring and source of happiness. Alike in depression and exaltation her heart turned in humility for light and strength, or in gratitude and thankfulness. She had escaped the gloomy clouds and darkening storm. She was in the lovely woods. Her spirit was in the sunshine; to her in an unaccountable way, it would extend its wings and soar exultantly; the sun would have been too radiant, too joyous, streaming through the stained woods, but for this restraining presence, which brooded in sweet serenity over her, filling her heart with trust and worship.

They reached Moravian town on one of the last days of September; a small neat dwelling was assigned to the girls and a maid, with one or two natives as attendants, only a step from a larger, selected as the temporary residence of Mrs. Proctor, her children, nurses, and servants. The village was a lovely place, surrounded by cultivated fields, walled in by the not remote forest, with the Thames, here a beautiful river, deep, with a considerable current, flowing between high banks on its southern side.

Here Edith was to have some days of serene, restful, religious calm, a renewal of strength, courage, power of endurance. Four or five days, then alarm, battle, blood, loss of all, the seeming end of all.

CHAPTER XXII.

FOR two or three days General Proctor's arrival had been expected, anxiously looked for by wife and children. Toward the evening of the 4th of October, he drove into the village with a single aid, young McLain, a Canadian, attended by an orderly, and they flew to embrace him. He came for a day's rest, the inspiration of their presence, love, and religious trust. The strong, calm wife saw in the worn face, the weary look, the fret and chafe of a spirit easily irritated and put from its poise. Strong, confident, when borne on by the tide of success, its ebb left him helplessly aground. His nature was ignoble, not cruel, not wholly cowardly. When Elliott challenged him for what passed between them at the council of war, ere he abandoned the siege of Camp Meigs, he promptly accepted, and it was only by the united efforts of his officers that a meeting was prevented. He was now simply in a position to which he was unequal. Had he been, the position might not have been precipitated. His wife had long since seen his defects of nature and character. As they appeared, she bravely faced them, and with strength, tact, and prudence, did much to hide them, and save him from the mischiefs they might cause, giving him of her higher nature. Much she had done. She received him now almost a ruin. After caresses by his children, whom he rudely pushed aside, she withdrew him to herself for communion. The unexpected—that baffling demon of human calculation—always ambushing the way of mortals, had leaped upon and overwhelmed him.

He had not expected to be pursued. Who could have supposed an enemy destitute of means of transportation would try to follow him by land? Had any other general attempted pursuit he would have made his approach by water. This he could have eluded, or at the true point turn upon and crush. He was followed by land and water. Seemingly the entire combined fleet and army of the enemy were hard after him. He had that very morning turned at bay, posted Tecumseh to hold him in check. The chief had done that in a half-hearted way. A battle might be avoided. He might be compelled to fight the next day. He would soon know. His soldiers were already worn and exhausted with their packs and heavy loads—on half rations. The enemy, light and free marched two miles to their one. Who could have expected such energy? What had the Americans to hope for, by rushing after him, away from their base, into those interminable wilds? So he ran on, enlarging, repeating, reiterating, weakly and querulously railing at fortune, at the unfortunate Barclay, the untowardness of happenings he did nothing to prevent, and the enterprise of an enemy he affected to despise.

Instead of treating him with the contempt he deserved the large souled woman drew his unheroic head to her own heroic bosom, soothed his chafed spirit, fed the shrivelled sources of courage, and awoke something of the dogged pluck seldom absent from the least favored native of the island of his birth.

At a little supper the general met Edith and Anita. The manner of Miss Grayson had greatly changed since she met him two hours before. The lovely, pensive nun-like maiden was now the aroused, high-spirited, heroic woman, erect, with flashing eyes and firm aspect. A woman to inspire men to heroic endeavor—lead them, if need be. Anita's face and eyes had the half wild, eager flush of expectant battle. An hour with those three women and Proctor was a hero. Then he retired for greatly needed rest. A little past midnight came another aid with a guard. He brought a summons to battle.

Colonel Warburton had set the soldiers in array, face to the foe, a short three miles below, and General Tecumseh had posted his warriors. They awaited the general day, and the enemy.

Edith caught the word and arose, strong, brave and confident, as did Mrs. Proctor. She would let the children sleep. It was best for the father. To part with them on the eve of battle might shake his nerves; a little time was required to get his carriage ready.

"By George!" he said, looking into the eyes of the firm, calm Edith, glowing with her awakened spirit. "I wish Warburton, and Home, and all the boys were here, to light up from your eyes; you have spirit enough for a dozen."

"You don't need it, General," she said, with a glance at the noble wife. "Take my spirit for the soldiers, who are to stand in the line, receive and give the wounds." Her voice was low, but it had the timbre of battle.

"By George, I will! They shall hear those words."

Then he was called, and went out without leave-taking. The air had changed, was chill and raw, with a north wind soughing through the trees. He emerged into the black, unbroken night, calm and brave. The chill wind smote him as from an open tomb. He looked up for the calm, assuring stars in vain. The sky was dark. He was one to be moved by things from without. A chill which he could not resist, ran through his veins ; a rigor laid its hand on his spirit. His aid there awaited him.

Anita had meantime approached the young officer, well known to her. She placed a small parcel in his hand, and whispered :

"Give this to Red-Wing; say—Anita," and vanished. It contained the mate of the gift from Dudley.

The two officers entered the carriage and were driven away, followed by the orderly, leading the general's favorite charger, which had been for some days at the Indian village.

CHAPTER XXIII.

ANITA'S GIFT.

THE instances of record are rare where an army with time to start and means of removal, was brought unwillingly to battle by an enemy pursuing on the line of retreat. Proctor had this in mind. His ill star ordered his case to be an exception to the rule.

He had seven to eight hundred well trained soldiers, what there was left of the militia, and a small body of well mounted provincial cavalry, and he had at least a thousand horses.

Tecumseh commanded about fifteen hundred warriors, the best trained, the flower of more than twice that number who followed the British standard in July before. These in Indian warfare were fairly a match for two thousand soldiers.

Whoever would now attempt a clear detailed narrative of the once famous retreat of Proctor, and pursuit by Harrison, will be troubled to find the means; not from scarcity of material so much as from the contrariety of statement.

All the persons named in my opening chapters, and most of those who came into the current of my narrative later, were present at the impending catastrophe, or in the immediate neighborhood of its scene.

That occurred past noon of the 5th of October (not

early in the morning), on the north side of the Thames, some three miles west of Moravian town, and about thirteen east of Dalson's. The retreat was along the north bank. The pursuit along the south until near noon of the 4th.

At Drake's farm the American vessels and gunboats, commanded by Perry, were left, and he became an aid to General Harrison. Above that point, at Arnold's mill, at the foot of the rapids, the river was fordable for horses, and here Harrison, with the aid of Colonel Johnson's horses, crossed his army in the forenoon of the 4th, and pursued in the direct track of the enemy.

We must turn back and gather up a few details in the order of time, to place everything within the easy grasp of the reader who may care to know.

Proctor, as stated, had not dreamed of pursuit by land. He made his first considerable halt at Dalson's. To this point he destroyed no bridge, on either side of the Thames, though there were several, otherwise impassable tributary streams.

At Dalson's he became aware of land pursuit, and sent out parties to break down the bridges. This action advised his enemy that he knew he was pursued.

Tecumseh, who understood the intrepid character of his old enemy, Harrison, expected this pursuit, and himself discovered it. With the flash of battle in his eyes, he sought Proctor, to select the ground and prepare for the impending conflict. At last he was to meet this foe in something like a fair battle ; for nothing had he so longed since Tippecanoe. He reminded Proctor of his promise and demanded its fulfilment. To this the general readily assented. They selected Gregory's Creek, a little beyond Dalson's, near Chatham ; an unfordable stream, which with other favorable conditions was said to be the strongest position for their force on that side of the river. Proctor was entirely satisfied with it, and he declared,

"Here will I defeat the Americans, or leave my bones on this ground."

"My father makes my heart glad, "replied the chief. "When I look at these two streams, I see the Tippecanoe running into the Wabash," he added, a little sadly, as the past flashed back on his mind.*

Away he hurried to place his warriors in array. Away went Proctor to put his immediate command on *the march*, continuing his retreat. Then he commenced the destruction of the bridges, the burning and abandonment of his vessels, ordnance, and property, never taken from Malden had he expected pursuit or intended to fight a pitched battle.

He expected Tecumseh would fight with his old skill and gallantry, and hold the enemy until he could escape with his soldiers. The chief saw he was betrayed. He would not fall into this trap. He lost a few warriors, drew skilfully off, and retired also.

With his angry chiefs he then sought Proctor, and to his face denounced his treachery and cowardice. Grayson was present. Walk-in-the-Water denounced him for his speech in the council at Malden as a piece of intended deception, and reminded him of his promises on the Huron, every one of which had been . broken. He announced his intention of going with his warriors over to the Americans, saying Harrison had never told them lies. His personal following was sixty effective braves.

Proctor called on Tecumseh to arrest and punish the Wyandot. The chief told him his own conduct released

---

*Drake's " Life of Tecumseh."

his brother from all obligation to remain, and further follow him to disgrace and ruin. He and his warriors might go in peace, and they went.

From this interview, Proctor pushed forward to meet his family at Moravian Town, as related, leaving Warburton in command.

It is asserted by Canadians and Englishmen that from the abandoned position Warburton marched all night, was met at daylight by Proctor, who halted the fatigued soldiers, placed them in array, and that they fought early in the morning, with no food save the scraps and crusts in their haversacks; and thus convicting their officers of incompetency, to excuse the want of their native pluck, shown by the men of the 41st, during that day.

The position of the British and their allies was selected with skill, and the forces posted at leisure while Harrison was miles away. At that point the bank of the river is high; the current deep and rapid. Parallel with the bank, and three hundred yards distant, was the south margin of a cedar swamp of considerable breadth, of yielding surface, much of it under water and extending down the river for two or three miles. At 200 yards from the river was an intervening narrow swamp of considerable length, and thirty or forty yards' wide, passable, but obstructing, which ran to a point eastward. Here the regulars were drawn up in two lines, with several yards interval, and in open order, the left resting on the river, their right on the large swamp. The artillery was on the left, to sweep the river road. The cavalry were posted in the rear. The line crossed the lower end of the narrow swamp, and was interrupted by it, no men standing in it. The ground otherwise, and for miles along the river, was covered with the open wood described, free from underbrush save in the smaller swamp, and with nothing to embarrass the enemy's approach. Though there was ample time and implements at hand, no abatis, none of the means of defence resorted to on both sides by infantry, in our later war, seem to have occurred to the British, though having many years experience in the American forests.

Tecumseh posted his warriors along the margin of the swamp, skilfully for such troops, forming a slightly obtuse angle with the British right, and his own left. This position would effectively protect the right of the regulars, if attacked, as it must be, by the enemy. He had in his line about fifteen hundred warriors. His post was on his own left, where the fiercest struggle would be. He knew Proctor was absent, did not expect or care for his presence.

Warburton knew a battle was inevitable. He sought with the concurrence of the chief, the best ground; when he found it, he made his dispositions, sent for his general, and awaited the enemy's advance. He constructed no defensive works, placed no skirmish line in advance, no picket or outpost of any kind. He seems to have used no means to detect his enemy's approach. Proctor on his arrival made no change. His station was in the rear of the point of the small swamp mentioned.

Learning the arrival of General Proctor, Tecumseh, the magnanimous çhief, waited on him, and greeted him in his grave way, cordially. His own presence, full of high courage, confidence, and the will and purpose to conquer, was a tonic to the general and his officers; dignified, yet alert, every fibre showing him a great leader, on the eve of battle. Their interview was brief and satisfactory. Proctor told the chief he was there to keep his word of yesterday.

"My brother sees my soldiers with their faces toward the Americans," he added. "I stand or fall here with them. When my brother hears the voices of my great guns, that will tell him to attack."

"My brother's words are good. They make my heart glad," replied the chief, and he returned to his own troops.

Much was expected from this powerful attack of Tecumseh upon the enemy's left flank. On his return he passed through the British right, was recognized and cheered by the soldiers, their only demonstration of this kind heard that day.

McLain accompanied him to execute the mission of Anita. In a group of youths, one of whom was Tecumseh's son, at a look of the chief, a tall, slender, handsome young chief arrayed in full war colors, otherwise reduced to battle costume, bearing the native insignia of command, stepped forward. As he approached, Tecumseh said : "Red-Wing," with a gesture toward the officer, and proceeded on his way down his line.

McLain had seldom seen so fine a specimen of the young brave as he who now advanced to meet him. He produced the little parcel of pink silk and extended it to the chief, with the single word—"Ah-ni-tah," in the native accent.

The youth's eyes flashed with pleasure. He received it eagerly, opened the envelope, took from it the quaintly wrought trinket, gazed at it with a proud and happy smile, rather grim under his war-paint. He removed a small-jewel from one of his ears, and replaced it with the maiden's gift. The other he gave the officer, speaking softly the very magic name " Ah-ni-tah." In the youth's presence McLain enveloped it carefully in paper, deposited it in a small pocket-book, with an assuring motion of the head that it should be faithfully delivered. Red-Wing noted everything approvingly, uttering soft gutterals, which the envoy translated— "good-good." The chief then turned back, covering Anita's gift tenderly with his hand, moving away from his observing companions, as if it was too precious and sacred for their profaning eyes.

Tecumseh went down his line, giving last orders, instructions, encouragements, and exhortations. His sagacious mind had pretty accurately grasped the ultimate fortune of his people, whatever might be the result of the impending battle. On his return to his post he called his principal chiefs around him, and addressed them as follows :

" Brother warriors ! We are about to enter into a battle from which I shall never come out. My body will remain on the battle-field."

He then unbuckled his sword, placed it in the hands of one he greatly trusted, and said : " When my son becomes a noted warrior, and able to wield it, give him this sword." He then laid aside his general's coat and insignia of army rank, leaving himself standing in simple hunting shirt, leggings and moccasins, without paint or ornament. In addition to his native weapons, rifle, tomahawk and knife, he wore in a belt a brace of beautifully mounted pistols, of that time. Thus dressed and armed, he assumed his place a little in advance of his line, to await the signal gun, which was never fired.*

---

* Drake's "Life of Tecumseh."

18

CHAPTER XXIV.

HARRISON did not linger at Malden. He had little hope of overtaking Proctor. His thorough demolition of property showed that he did not intend to fight for a chance of resuming possession of the dismantled position. He sent forward the ships and light draft vessels, left General McArthur and a strong force at Detroit, and another general at Sandwich, with a force. Here he learned that Proctor had halted at Dalson's, and taking about 3500 of all arms, he pushed hard after him. Notwithstanding Armstrong would raise a force of regulars exclusively, with the exception of 150 of that branch of the service, his troops were militia, with the training received at home.

It included Colonel R. M. Johnson's famous regiment of mounted infantry, 1200 strong; 200 were called spies, armed with rifles, always in advance. The rest had rifles or muskets, a weapon as effective for the average man on horseback. Each man owned the horse he rode. They had been in service a year or more, and man and horse were trained to effective service in the woods and wild forays of the border. The arrival of this body at Detroit enabled Harrison to secure mounts for his field officers. He had with him also the famous Black-Hoof, the greatest of the Wyandots, who in his youth fought Braddock, as he had since everywhere fought the Americans, until now. Black-Hoof had under him 150 Wyandots and Seneca warriors at Sandwich. Harrison stripped his soldiers to the lightest marching form, their arms and ammunition, and they made twenty-seven miles the first day; at Baptist Creek, near the mouth of the Thames, a deep, troublesome stream, crossed by Proctor, he found the bridge untouched, a most encouraging sign of the confidence and carelessness of the British officers. He left a strong guard there. He turned up the south side of the river for the best of reasons.

At Dalson's he knew he should overtake Proctor. He knew very soon also that the Englishmen knew of his pursuit. He pushed Johnson forward with a party to secure the bridges. Tecumseh's stand did not delay him long. At Chatham he had an interview with Walk-in-the-Water, who wanted to join him. He curtly told him to go back to Detroit and in the meantime keep clear of his army.

The chief found his old friend Black-Hoof more sympathetic. Their warriors were brothers, cousins, friends, and he received him and a third or so of his band, which for the day did not come to Harrison's or Dudley's notice.

The Americans came upon abandoned vessels, burning stores and bridges, which he had to fight for, from this point. The distance was not great, nor the time long. He left his own vessels at Drake's, and crossed the river at Arnold's, as stated, a little before noon of this, the 5th day of October. After crossing, they came upon the last bivouac of the enemy, where their fires were still burning.

Johnson dashed forward and captured a wagoner who told him the British army in line of battle, awaited them a half mile in advance.

At last, the account of blood between Kentucky and

Proctor for Frenchtown, and Fort Miami, would be adjusted. The American made a rapid disposition of his force for immediate action. A selected body of infantry were to advance, and charge the British line, supported by Johnson's mounted men, which still held the advance. The regulars, 120 strong, were to carry the artillery. Black-Hoof's Indians were to steal up under the bank of the river, gain the British rear, raise the war-whoop and attack, to create in the minds of the soldiers the impression that their Indians had turned against them. Shelby and Desha's brigades were to be opposed to Tecumseh. With this plan the army advanced, John-son's mounted men still in the lead, divided in two columns, the right under Colonel R. M. Johnson's brother, Lieu-tenant-Colonel James Johnson, and the left led by the colonel. The movement was along the road near the bank.

Meantime Carter, who had been ordered by Dudley to scout ahead, discovered not only the position of the British, but their formation, the Indian line of battle, and the post of Tecumseh in his own line. On his way back he met Major Dudley and Major Wood of the engineers, who had hurried forward to ascertain the exact position of the enemy. He told them everything they could have ascertained, and they turned back to inform the general. Carter accompanied them part of the way, and described the small swamp in front of Proctor's line, and in answer to Dudley, said, the ground otherwise was open and free from fallen timber and underbrush. Dudley said the way to deal with the British was to send Johnson to ride through and over them. That regulars in this order, accustomed to touch at the shoulders, would present but a feeble resistance. Wood was so impressed that he said he should bring it to General Harrison's notice, which he did on the conclusion of their report.

"Dudley says Johnson's mounted men would make short work of them. I confess, General, I am greatly struck by it."

"Is that your idea, Major?" asked Harrison of Dudley.

"Most decidedly," said the young officer. "When he passes their second line, he will deploy right and left, wheel and deliver his fire."

The eyes of Harrison flashed from one to the other. "It is a novel idea," he said.

"The position to be assailed is novel. They will be surprised and can really offer no resistance if the heads of the column can be held steady—as they certainly will be. The guides are picked men," was Dudley's reply.

"I will do it, Major Dudley; order Colonel Johnson to charge the enemy in his front," he said crisply.

"I have your permission to lead, or accompany, General?"

"Go," said the general.

Dudley had secured a fine mount from the Kentuckians, and was instantly in his saddle.

"I am not certain as I should have permitted him to go," said the general, reflectively. "He is in the mood to be reckless, and has been ever since the Meigs days."

"The plan was his; let him see to its execution. No man handles soldiers better," said Wood in answer.

"Reckless! Good Lord, a man must have his chance!" said Perry, smiling at the idea of reckoning the danger.

None knew better than the general that the tug of war would be with Tecumseh. His thought was to first dispose of Proctor and his soldiers and then attack the

Indians.   His plan for the Indians was admirable.   The veteran Shelby, and Desha, were placed in position to engage and hold them, so that Johnson's flank would be free.   Then they should be developed and overwhelmed in turn, by all his force.

Colonel Johnson's mounted men stood as stated in two equal columns.   Lieutenant Colonel James split his column into four, of two files each, his spies in advance, himself seconded by Major Payne; the left column under Colonel R. M. consisted of two, of four files each, the right led by himself, the left by Dudley, each at the head of the spies.

On approaching the enemy, it was found that Colonel James would require quite all the space between the small swamp and river to give him the needed room for action.

"Let us charge the Indians!" called Colonel R. M. to Dudley.

"Agreed!" was the response.   He had already explained to the colonel the personal position of Tecumseh. He would still have answered as he did, notwithstanding he graduated second of his class.   His general understood his mood perfectly.

"We will drive straight on Tecumseh," called the colonel.

"Agreed!" answered back the major again.

This was the final crisis.   No personal considerations could then be taken account of.   Tecumseh must also take his chance.

As the head of the colonel's column wheeled to the left—"Look out!" shouted Carter.   "Look out, Major! 'E can pass the little swamp.   'E can't charge in't the big un, an git out again!"

If heard he was unheeded. The horses would take them speedily into battle anyway. What did a Kentuckian care for Indians in the woods! The heads deflected to the left. They passed the small swamp without serious delay, gained the hard ground the other side. The bugle sounded and away they went.

Colonel James had less distance to go than had his brother, to the point of impact. We will charge with him.

Has the reader ever heard an elk, a buffalo, a wild bullock, leaping and plunging over hard ground? He has certainly heard a horse run, and knows he can be heard at a considerable distance. Let him fancy twelve hundred of the large bony Kentucky horses,—her lime-rock makes everything large and bony,—weighing ten, twelve, or thirteen hundred pounds, each bearing a man averaging 160, going at full speed yet held in a body, and he may form some conception of the smiting roar of the charging Kentuckians. A cavalry charge is effective from mere weight and velocity, without, as with, arms.

When the heads of Colonel James' columns burst on the eyes of the startled British,—who could then understand the cause of the mighty uproar, as if it were the simultaneous crashing and falling of the forest itself—a heavy volley greeted the advancing Kentuckians. The leading horses recoiled, an instant's wavering was overcome, and six hundred practised throats gave forth the warwhoop, and on they plunged over the level ground, among the wide apart trees, with the sweep and roar of a low down storm cloud kissing the earth with thunder. The seventy-five intervening yards were devoured as by a hurricane. *" River Raisin !" " River Raisin !" " French-*

town !" " Frenchtown !" they shouted, with eyes aflame, and faces aglow.

Sir Colin Campbell, with his slender thread of red, repulsed a rushing cavalry charge at Alma. But what could any men do four feet apart, against these wild riding Kentuckians, away here in the woods? Whoever heard of such a way of attack before? Through and over the first line of dodging, thrusting soldiers they ran, never pausing still shouting their vengeful cry, flashing in a torrent across the intervening space, taking the ineffective rattle-fire of the second line, sending the thunder of their coming, the swell and roar of their shouts and plunging steeds to the not far off Proctor. They passed this line and wheeling, two columns to the right, two to the left, riding along the rear of what once was a military formation, brushing aside the captains and lieutenants as wooden toys, they turned and emptied their six hundred rifles and muskets among the now mixed, broken, and lost soldiers, retaining no rudiment of order. The power of defence, resistance, as a body, was at an end. These assailing men were not raw volunteers, but trained men and horses. The instant the fire was delivered, the horse became a statue, his rider could as well recharge his gun on his back as on the ground, and now save the rattling of their arms, while this was simultaneously performed, no sound from them was heard. An instant—the smallest fraction of a minute—and they were ready. Each man would sight a man now. That bit of time crystallized the Englishmen's sense of their helpless condition.

"We surrender!" shouted some of the officers along the broken lines, and down went the useless muskets, simultaneously, and up went the depressed muzzles of the Kentuckians, ere a trigger was drawn. Not a man fired.

Not thus fared Colonel R. M.'s column. We saw them successfully pass the small swamp, re-form, and dash forward through the open, a counterpart of the charge of their comrades, and at nearly the same time. Passing within sight of the infantry of Desha and Shelby, advancing to attack and hold the Indians in check, who remained silent, awaiting the expected signal gun from Proctor. On they went, north-easterly, plunging in the supposed direction of Tecumseh's post. Then they gave voice, whooping and yelling like madmen; they approached the margin of the swamp,—no Indian answering yell, no warriors in sight. All at once from the low margin of green below them, a volley as nearly as Indians ever so fire, close, withering, running west along their line, and then their yell, wild, fierce, prolonged, startlingly cadenced, the *real* thing in tone and effect, inimitable by white men save in exceptional instances. The soul of wildness, savage hate and fury, it was yet with something plaintive, coming from the Indian heart. The forlorn advance of spies was for an instant withered by the fire. The colonel on the right went down at the first shots, receiving four wounds. Major Dudley on the left went down also, his horse receiving a missile.

The Indian fire and yell brought Desha and Shelby hurrying into battle. Dudley was on his feet instantly. "Halt! Dismount!" he shouted. The trumpeter, unhurt, sent it sharply stabbing through the thickening confusion. Everything was revealed to him amid the shots, the yells, that filled the forest. The horses turned back, the riders cool, alert, expert woodsmen, and in Indian tactics stole forward with their loaded guns, covered by the old trees, firing at the lower lying Indians only when they were seen.

The Indian position, just within the margin of an impassable morass, whose greenery veiled them and which would have been fatal to regular soldiers, was to them a source of strength. They would be overshot, the bayonet could not reach them. If the fire became too heavy and scorching, they could retire through the swamp itself, as so many lightly leaping foxes, whom the enemy could not follow.

A half minute of confusion, of wheeling, and retiring the unridden horses, and the battle equalized itself along the swamp's irregular margin. These splendid forest rangers of the dark and bloody ground, who in boyhood defended their tree-sheltered cabins, with their mothers and elder sisters, against savage foray, while the fathers and older brothers were away on an expedition to raise the siege of leaguered fort, or defending themselves in lightly built stockades, were at home here, with their rifles, in the woods, the hated painted Indian confronting them, and the appalling long drawn yells only quickened their blood. They were born and reared to this form of war.

Already the battle with Proctor was over. Already Desha and Shelby's infantry had joined battle down the line on their left. Better armed and as skilled as the average Indian, and well posted, though pitted against their best, under the eye and voice of their greatest leader, and more numerous at this point, the battle here raged at short range with fury for fifteen or twenty minutes. There was no general rush of the Indians. There were many individual hand to hand duels. The natives did their best execution here, and were severely punished.

As was their wont their fallen were snatched away mysteriously, many of them. Heavily assaulted, sustaining the weight of the American army save those of the mounted who attacked the British, the battle was against the Indians, comparatively invisible and inaccessible though they were.

On his right front, as he struggled to his feet, Dudley heard a clear ringing, far reaching voice, in the tone and accent of command. He had heard the same voice in the same accents in the wood on the British bank of the Maumee. Whoever had heard it would never mistake it. The voice of Tecumseh, steadily maintaining his war where the battle raged the fiercest. Several times it reached him, while the battle was yet uncertain. Then it ceased.

He heard it no more. The battle at that point grew faint, subsided almost suddenly, along Dudley's immediate front. The Indians melted away, stole out of the unavailing struggle. A moment before the green margin was full of yells, gunshots, stirring, leaping, flashing, disappearing painted forms, plunging forward to snatch a scalp and vanishing, perhaps shot down. Then they ceased, were not, faded like phantoms, and silence fell where late they fought. To the left the battle continued, and thither the dismounted Kentuckians drifted, or turned back to look after their horses, support a wounded comrade, or have a hurt looked to by the surgeon. The hospital was a settler's house below. Some of the surgeons were on the river's bank of the battle-field, near the post of Harrison and his staff. Thither many were carried in the first instance. Very soon the scene of the severest passages of the battle was left vacant and silent. None but the dead, and apparently but a single one of the living combatants, remained upon it.

CHAPTER XXV.

DUDLEY lingered there alone. His purpose was to ascertain, if possible, the fate of the great chief, who had so singularly influenced, and once or twice controlled, his own fortunes for the time. He was impressed that when the battle was at its fiercest, Tecumseh had fallen, and that something like a panic had come upon his immediate followers, who at once ceased their efforts. If this was the solution of the sudden subsidence of their efforts, they may have left his body on the field. He moved toward the point where he last heard his war cry, just in advance of the swamp's margin, where the trees stood thick.

"'E's furder this way," called Carter to him, who unnoticed had stolen near, motioning with his hand to Dudley's right.

"He? Who? Tecumseh?"

"'E's done fer," said Carter sadly.

"Killed?"

"Dyin'," was the laconic reply.

A few yards farther, and just below the upper margin of the declivity, and a little back, as if withdrawn from the notice of his followers, Tecumseh had fallen.

"It is too pesky bad," Carter said, sadly, pointing to him where he lay.

Dudley found him ghastly and silent. Sadly he bent

over him.   He had been wounded in front, the blood still stealing from the hurt.   His eyes were open, with signs of fading consciousness in the face.   The gaze was far away.   The fire of battle had faded from the dimming half-closed orbs, over which the invisible shadow was darkening.

He noticed Dudley, a smile played about the pale lips. The youth wore his restored gift that day.   He placed it in the fading vision of the dying chief.   Tecumseh roused a little with a movement of his brow, a turn of the eyes as if toward the swamp.

"Your warriors—you would have me call them?"   A smile almost of joy was the answer.

"Stand here by him," said Dudley to Carter.   "Let nothing disturb him."   He picked up a lost gun rod, attached his white handkerchief to its screw end, and started to pentrate the high ferns and greenery of the swamp. As he did so, Carter raised a low, peculiar note, which rising and increasing was prolonged.   It was instantly answered from the near distance.

"There they air," said the old hunter.   A few steps and Dudley gained a bit of hard land running into the swamp's depths.   Here he waved his little flag of peace, and almost instantly his name—"Dudley"—was spoken from his right and near.   He saw no one, but answered, "I am Dudley."   The greenery parted, two or three painted forms appeared but a few yards distant.   One of them he recognized as one of the young warriors whom he met the day of his escape from Detroit.   They were both there.

"I am Dudley," he repeated.   "I will give Tecumseh to his children," turning as if to go back.

He was understood.   The youths stepped forward, accompanied by a tall handsome young chief, and one or two older warriors. Evidently not the whole of their party. As they approached Dudley, one of the youths, touching the tall young warrior, said—" Red-Wing," a name then new to him. Silently he conducted them back, pushed aside the high fronds, disclosing the prone form, and Carter standing over it, sadly leaning on his rifle, not more than three yards distant.

They were prepared for the sight. Prepared to bear hence the mighty form. Mutely the sad warriors stole to his side, bent over him. He seemed to know them even then, and a look—it may have been Dudley's fancy—of satisfaction stole over the placid face.

Two other slain warriors lay near the chief. One was of the noblest stature and finest form, cinctured about the loin, from which the trunk and limbs downward were showily clothed in the weeds of a native dandy ; painted from the girdle upward in war colors, otherwise unclothed. The warriors with scarce a look turned from this to the third, whom Dudley now learned was his benefactor Wasegoboah. They lingered tenderly about it, and then turned to the great chief. He was raised with care, and blankets passed under him. As they were about to bear him hence, Dudley placed the decoration of the Queen on his breast, with his fingers he tenderly pressed down the now useless lids, and bent reverently over the regal brow, never more kingly than now, pressed it with his hand, and the dead chief was borne away.

Within a minute, one of the youths, with a band of warriors, returned, and in the same way carried the remains of his brother-in-law, who fought and fell by his side.

They did not return for the third, which was left to be claimed, disputed about, and I fear disfigured, by those who believed it to be the body of the great Shawanoe who fell the fourth of an hour after his reputed slayer, Johnson, had tottered to the rear, supported by a friend, to seek a surgeon for his wounds.

The warriors did not return. The two Americans stood looking sadly in their direction for a half minute, and turned away.

" It is too pesky bad," repeated the old hunter. Had he ever heard of Walter Scott he might have quoted his grim Moss-trooping knight :

> " I'd give the lands of Delorain,
> Dark Musgrove were alive again."

They moved over the ground, torn and trampled by the plunging, halting, wheeling horses, with the bodies of four or five of their late riders, stark and dead, prone as they fell, and here and there a horse, one of which was Dudley's own. The smoke and vapors of the battle hung low in the damp air of the woods, through which came the warm rays of the declining sun, and which to Dudley's ears seemed still haunted with the [dying echoes of the shots, shouts and yells of battle.

He at once took his way with rapid strides to the station of his general, who stood receiving the hasty verbal reports of the different commanders. Ere he gained his presence he met an orderly in search of him. Rumor had in some way reached his chief that he was missing. Men contradicted the first statement that he was slain, as he had been seen and heard at the closing of the battle about him.

CHAPTER XXVI.

THE MESSENGER TO EDITH.

HE found his general animated, yet calm and business-like, as if receiving unusually numerous morning reports, gathering information, verbally given, answering questions, issuing orders with the cool clear-headed dispatch for which he was distinguished—an accurate man of affairs, the details of which were never left to accident. As he approached he was greeted with a gratified look and pleasant smile. He gestured the youth to a group of British officers a little apart, saying, "A gentleman has a matter of importance to you, personally. Take time for it." Warburton, with three or four officers, had made formal submission, were permitted to retain their swords, and were awaiting the leisure of the victor, for any directions he might give them.

Dudley knew him, advanced and gave him his hand as if nothing special had occurred.

"You know Mr. Edward Grayson, Major Dudley?' said Warburton.

"Yes. What of him?"—a little startled.

"The casualties of battle reached him. He is danger-ously wounded."

"Wounded! Was *he* under fire?"

"It would seem so. He was in our rear, not far from General Proctor's position. They retired early. Your, or our Indians—ours lately, I fear—gained our rear.

The fight with us was over. Grayson was approached and deliberately shot down, by Walk-in-the-Water, we think."

"Walk-in-the-Water! We met him yesterday. He wanted to join us. General Harrison refused to take him and told him to keep clear of us."

"We are certain it was he. He had a grudge against Mr. Grayson, the most upright and honorable officer."

" Did the Indian escape ? "

"There was no one to deal with him. What can you do with an Indian, with the warwhoop in his ears! The unfortunate man asks for you, is importunate to see you."

"Take me to him at once, Colonel—if I may ask it."

On the way to him—"His daughter is with Mrs. Proctor, at the Moravian town," said McLain, to whom the colonel had introduced him.

"Gracious Father! These two, Edith, and her father! He dying, perhaps! The British army destroyed, captured." Brokenly these things came to the young man's mind.

" Our surgeon says the wound is mortal," said McLain. " He may not rally from the shock."

. Under an old tree, on a camp mattress, they found him. Way was made for the American officer at his side. The youth knelt by the fallen man's couch, took his hand in both his own, and bent over his face. The dying man's eyes lighted, a slight assuring pressure met the clasping hand.

"Cliffton Dudley, son of Philip," murmured Mr. Grayson.

19

"What would you from me?" tenderly and greatly moved.

"Edith?" with an anxious look into the eyes near his own.

"What of her?" asked the young officer.

The answer was a mute appealing look, which the youth understood.

"I told her how I regarded her," he said in reply to it.

An exquisite smile came into the wan face, about the lips and eyes.

"You are her all, lover, husband, father, kindred," he murmured, closing his eyes, as if he was naught. From the shut lids tears were now distilling. For a half minute the bystanders thought he had closed them finally. The surgeon placed a little brandy at his lips, raising his head. He sipped it, opened them, his thought still of his daughter.

"Bring her here, or take me to her," he said, a little revived.

"I will bring her at once," said the youth rising.

A curious spectacle to the British officers who knew the dying man, his prejudice, bitterness toward the Americans, here now receiving this officer of the enemy. They knew his name, something of the rumored romance of his attachment to Edith, whose name they caught from the father's lips, and enough of his words to imply that she was to be committed, at this last, to his protection— to become his bride, perhaps.

There was a hurried consultation, a litter was brought, the mattress carefully lifted upon it, some of the British soldiers called as bearers. McLain took charge of the cortege which was soon on its way to the Indian village.

A horse was led to Dudley, which he mounted and set forward to prepare the daughter to receive her dying father. They to thus meet, who parted last on that night, on the banks of the dark swift Maumee. He, the scorned lover, now commissioned to bear this message to her who scorned him, unknowing of her love as he was.

The ladies at Moravian town were thoroughly awakened by the call that summoned General Proctor to battle. No more thought of rest for them or of retirement. The hours of darkness brooded prolongingly to them. The rough north clouds, tinged with winter, that breathed upon the departing general, disappeared with the night, and the sun arose cheeringly and with good omen, as it seemed to the three women.

Edith and Anita had the impression that the armies were encamped, confronting each other, and with the light would join battle. The elevation on which the town was built was for the region considerable ; its slope was gentle toward the west. Below them the primitive forest beyond the cleared fields—not wide, in that direction—stood unbrokenly, to the river's bank, as continuously on the southern bank. Nothing could be seen save the grand innocent woods.

Anita, with the wild heroic blood of her race quickened by the certainty that her people were in ambush near, awaiting the enemy's coming, to attack, moved lithely and nervously about, her hand toying with her father's dagger which she wore, her splendid eyes flashing, her thin nostrils distended, with the eager expectancy of the hour, every fibre of her exquisite form quivering, every sense alert.

Edith, externally calm, her face colorless—the blood

had gone back from the surface to fortify the citadel. She knew she must passively wait. The mouth was firmly set, her long, dark, nearly straight brows almost meeting, were low, like a resolved woman, who had many approaches to her heart to guard. She could not do, and must endure passively, the severest test of strength, power, will, which would find relief, as vigor, in action.

The sun clomb slowly toward the zenith. The wild serene peace of the forest was unbroken. Life there flowed in its undisturbed channels. What did it mean? In the final hour did the Americans hesitate—had they turned back? Where was Dudley? Did he think of her, now? Did he know he was near her? Two armies,— bloody battle were between them. Her heart was beseeching Heaven to guard him, the more as she had, seemed to—to—no matter. He had no mother, sister, to ask God to guard him. In some vague way, as her thought would linger with him, the impression of impending evil to her seemed to gather about him. If he was to be stricken, let her but see and tell him all her heart while he would yet know. Tecumseh, notwithstanding his impressions of not surviving, she felt would pass through untouched. She knew there was no reason for this impression that did not as well apply to Cliffton. Her father, as in personal peril, did not occur to her. He was not armed, would not be exposed, save as a surgeon, a chaplain might be.

At high noon the forest still seemed a solitude. She noted the time—one! two! three! Then the indistinct sounds of tumult; low down thunder, like the smothered roar of millions of pigeons getting on wings from the ground and beating the air together. She had never heard anything like it. Was that the battle? Then shouting, a volley of musketry, a wild, great continuous tide of human voices, with a roar, which then diminished and still the woods were full of it. Then another wild shout, and the answering yell of 1500 Indian warriors. They had joined battle—this was their war. When this struck the ears of the Indian girl she sprang into the air, with her brandished dagger in her hand, and in her woman's high, clear, far-reaching voice, answered, echoed it back. This cry she knew. It was the battle-cry of her people, her blood and kindred, striking the hated American, avenging a century of wrong.

Edith sprang to her, yet could hardly control her, in this first firing of her wild blood.

This, the warwhoop, was followed by the Indian volleys, the replying Kentuckians, the heavy and nearly simultaneous musketry of Desha's and Shelby's men. A continuous rattle and then the firing died away. Silence, and while yet the tumult was audible to them came the sound of beating hoofs, up the near road—the sound of many horses. Two horsemen, riding madly, dashed up the swell, then more, half a hundred, as if escaping. On they came—the two in advance, in the livery of the Prince Regent, not drawing rein, bending forward over their horses, flashed past, blasting Edith's sight. Their followers hard after.

She recognized them—the two. She threw up her arms in a frenzy of amazement! Proctor and Home—fleeing! A British general fleeing the enemy, running away from battle, where his soldiers yet faced the foe. Craven! dastard! coward! "Oh, my father! my father!" she called wildly, sinking down and covering her face with her hands, in an agony of shame and anguish. For the time she saw and heard no more save an indistinct beating, as of the feet of running horses. Later, Anita told her of the pursuers, who captured a body of running foot soldiers, with whom a few horsemen were halted. The rest dashed forward, gained the summit, and disappeared in hot pursuit.

Tecumseh, then, had made the real fight; the British general had escaped, was the reading by the girls of what they saw. Edith's hope now was that the noble matron had been spared the spectacle of the fleeing man, as oblivious of wife and children as of soldiers and honor. When she turned her eyes again down the river she saw a single horseman, at a rapid, springy gallop, riding up the road. An American officer, she thought, from his dark uniform. He came up, drew rein, and she recognized him.

"Blessed Father! Cliffton Dudley! What brings him? How can I meet him?" were her mental exclamations. "Anita! meet—detain him, for an instant!" she said to her sister, and hurried into their small dwelling.

"Dudley!" cried the still greatly excited Indian girl, approaching him as he alit, withholding her hands. "It is all over!" she cried, her eyes flashing in his face.

"All over, my poor dear Anita," his voice as his look very sad.

"Poor Anita! What has happened? Tell me the worst."

"The British soldiers are prisoners."

"Oh, I don't care for them! Tecumseh? The warriors?" eagerly.

"They fought like tigers, till long after the soldiers threw down their scarcely used guns—then they withdrew."

"All? all? My uncle—Tecumseh? tell me of him."

"He was badly hurt. His son and cousin and the young Red-Wing—the chief and his warriors, helped him away."

"You saw it, you know it?"

"I helped them."

Now tears relieved her. She held both her hands to him, which he took tenderly in his, looking sadly in her face.

"You came to see my sister?" raising her eyes again to his. "You love Edith?" in a solemn voice.

"As I love life, honor."

"Then you must carry her away this time. She has gone in. I will show you." She conducted him through the open outer door to an inner room. When he entered this, she closed the door, leaving the two alone, and ran out to meet some returning Moravians, who had seen something of the battle. She did not return for many long hours.

Edith arose from her seat, with outward calm, her face very pale, and advanced to meet her visitor, to whom she extended her hand, her eyes just meeting his, and drooping under them. He took the extended hand in both his, as assuring her of the greatest consideration. She was the first to speak—must speak.

"Oh, Cliffton, what a time! You know I must be humiliated, crushed, and you come to see it, to triumph in it."

"Triumph! You still think so meanly of me? I am still less to you than your worst enemy."

"Oh, Cliffton! You do not, you cannot think that. You do know, you must know, your own true heart must tell you. You are dear to me, more to me than all friends, King, his cause, my father—I had almost said," now trembling, breaking into sobs and sinking into a seat.

He knelt by her side, placed one hand on her waist, with the other drew her head down upon his shoulder.

" Dearest, most precious of earth and heaven,—you know my whole heart, my life, are yours, to be devoted to you."

At the word dearest, she stayed her emotion to hear. What woman would not, a speech thus begun. As it was ended, a hand came up, clasped the one that timidly touched her waist, and pressing, drew it about her, as if that was the arm's proper place. There was nothing more to tell. Her words had told all. This priceless act compensated all.

For a half minute the youth could not speak. There was another more precious office for lips. They were not to be thus blessed till after many hours.

" I come from your father," he said, at length, oppressed with the message he bore.

" My father !" springing to her feet, turning to him. He arose, still retaining the willingly captured hand. " My father ! from my father ? What of him ? I had a dread. You were more in my mind. It was for you as so exposed," speaking with frank courage.

He placed his disengaged hand about her waist.

" Why don't you tell me, Cliffton ? Is he hurt, slain ? "

" Not slain, but he is hurt. The fortune of a widely scattered battle."

" Oh,—Oh ! take me to him at once, I pray ! " strong when an appeal came for action, though for such a cause.

" I am having him brought to you. You will be brave and strong. Be patient for a little. He will soon be here. He sent me to you, as if it was my right to come. We will now think only of him."

"Let us go and meet him," she said, leading towards the door. "It was your right to come to me. No need now to think, to speak, of ourselves. Surely we are each other's now and alway. Nations may war, they shall not separate us again," and their hands joined.

"Never—never again!" was his response.

"Our—my father's awful mistake was to involve these unknowing ones in our cause and its ruin. Oh, if he can be spared to help repair it to them."

"Be brave, Edith."

"Oh, I know what that means," she said, yet moving firmly and rapidly, cherishing the arm that supported her, because its pressure gave her such comfort, not because its support was needed.

To the innocent Moravians, the Americans were objects of a superstitious terror. They fled, and hid from the passage of the tempest of them—the large, bony Kentuckians, on their strong, rough, tall horses. Dudley, the handsome, brave, sad looking young officer, was of different form, but one of the dreaded Americans. They were surprised to see him stop in their village, and in front of Mrs. Proctor's house; more surprised to see Anita fly to him so cordially. They now drew near, then she led him to the beautiful English lady's house and left him there. Very soon she came out with him. They saw him pass his arm about her waist—and she seemed to like it! They were lovers! And the innocent things did not greatly wonder at that, if once they had met. And then they walked down the road, toward the place of battle, she with one hand in his, his other arm keeping its place, and they followed—the amazed young girls and children, while the elders stood staring after them wondering what it meant.

CHAPTER XXVII.

THE FOREST PRINCESS.

AH–NI–TAH started with a purpose, heroic for a woman of even her spirit. Her cousins, who had as yet won no names for themselves, and would now each be known by the name of his slain father, had the night before made their way to Moravian town, sought out and had an interview with her, bringing messages from Tecumseh and Wasegoboah, telling her of the doings of the day and the expectations of their morrow. She knew in a general way where they would encamp this night.

She had attached a young Moravian girl to her service, for the few days of her remaining, and who with all the women of the village regarded her as a very superior being, and especially as like them she was a Christian. She called her, and together they walked down the road toward the battle-field. She had been reared with her people, lived with them all her life until within the last three years, when with their consent she became the adopted sister of Edith, by whom she had been known and taught in childhood. She was an expert in the native sign language and knowledge of the forest. On the way, her companion described the passes of the long and comparatively narrow swamp, well known and often used by the villagers to gain the open wood north of it. It was her purpose to visit the Indian camp. The returned Moravians knew of the death of her great kins-

man, and though the words and manner of Dudley left
her in no doubt of his fate, their report was decisive.
She must be there to mourn, as a daughter, with the bereaved family, and take her place in the general lamentation at his interment which she knew would take place
ere the next dawn. Her place was with her sorely
straitened, defeated, and destitute people, in this awful
visitation. She may have been conscious of another
motive, which she put by as well as she could. She knew
the preferences of the gallant young Sac chief. He had
sent her a tender, half sad message by the young Tecumseh, as he would now be called, to which she had made a
light, half coquettish reply. It was the memory of this
that induced in part the decided act of her token by
young McLain. Child of nature that she was, at the
moment, on the eve of battle, she was equal to the act,
had she heard no word from him. Skilled in the ways of
the heart, from her intuition, and careful study of her
sister's affair, she had no doubt of her supreme place in
the young chief's regard; and she had no hesitation in
letting him see in that hour, that her thought was of him.

A fourth of the way to the American position they met
the slowly moving litter of the wounded man. It was
set down, and she had some touching words with him,
told him her errand, had his whispered blessing, kissed
his cold hand, leaving her tears upon it. As she was
about to go forward, McLain told her of the delivery of
her trinket to the young chief, the disposition he made
of it, and placed his gift in her hand. What an exquisite
thrill, as she clasped it closely in her slim, taper fingers
and palm, shot along her nerves—so new and so delicious.

Day dying was yielding to shadow in the mysterious
depth of the old wood, as the girls approached the now

peaceful scene of the late conflict.   Evidently victors and captives had encamped on the ground occupied by the Americans, along the river, at the commencement of the battle.   The many sounds of a great camp, as the gleams of its fires, met the ears and eyes of the alert Anita.   She had an especial object for a closer inspection of the camp. She left her companion, and under cover of forest trees, stole near and moved along the eastern border of their camp, until she satisfied herself by intelligent observation, that they certainly would not move that night. Armed with her dagger, lithe and noiseless, she was near enough to hear their careless words more than once. As she made the nearest approach, there came the thought—a fierce, momentary, passionate desire, to lead a thousand warriors in a wild, swift rush upon them that night.   She shook her hand in a menace at them, silently laughed the next instant, at her childish passion, and turned back to her patiently waiting maid and companion.

She placed a coin in her hand and received from her the large, long blanket she wore, capote fashion, over her head, as was the custom of the native women ; and with a low spoken message to Edith and Dudley, she dismissed her, and stood looking after her retiring form until it was hidden by the trees in the now fast growing night.

Alone, she replaced her weapon, opened the paper parcel containing Red-Wing's gift, which she now saw for the first time since it came to her hand.   It proved what she would have hoped for, one of his own ear jewels.   A flat, plain, wide ring or rim of gold, containing a fiery red stone.   She had seen it and its fellow in his ears and knew they were greatly admired.   She pressed it to her lips, her slight but rounded bosom, examined it in the fading light, and placed it in her small ear, robbed for his sake that morning. Then she made a warm little cup of her hand, and prisoned and pressed it with low, sweetly murmured words, directing it to stay there, and cling to her ear like a dear, precious jewel that it was, and may the blessed Saviour keep and bless it forever.

She then opened out the coarse blanket, gayly worked with beads and red yarn, on a ground of now not pure white, with a red border. She coquettishly threw it over her shoulders, drawing it up over her head, and adjusted it deftly to her form. It was not wanted for her walk, and folding, she laid it on her arm, and then in her light half-barbaric costume, short skirt of rich cloth, hose, moccasins, close bodice of gay color, her sash over one shoulder, sustaining a small reticule in which was her feathered scarlet cap, her belt having her dagger, her head dressed only in its wavy, glossy, black hair, with merely a red ribbon to confine it, she addressed herself to her heroic adventure of passing the swamp alone in the darkness, to find the camp of her stricken country-men. The night had already darkened the forest, but no thought of personal fear approached her.

There was, as stated, a way along a narrow strip of continuous hard land, to find which was her first care. The camp of her friends must be on the hard land on the other side, a considerable distance below, where the swamp, deepest and widest, lay broad and impassable to the American, unless this way was betrayed to him. She knew the roar and tumult of the battle must have frightened the predaceous beasts out of their covers in the swamp for the time, and sent them cowering miles away. Instructed by the Moravian girl, who had pointed out to her an immense tulip tree which marked the southern terminus of the pass, she had little trouble in finding it. Faint signs of the trail along its summit were easily traced by her sensitive moccasined feet, and fleetly and noiselessly she skipped along. Once she was attracted by the fragrance of a late blooming wild rose, found in the swamp; she paused to secure it and then resumed her flight. Nearly two miles over this carried her to the higher land of the north side. Confirmed night was now in the gloomy forest. The approach of the uprising moon was discoverable through the tree tops and very soon the northern bank would be lit up by it.

She knew sentinels would be posted at or near this point. As she walked along she practised to herself the various signal notes and calls in use among her people, to indicate presence or a wish to communicate, under similar conditions. They would know this pass, though its southern connection was in the rear of the English position.

Keen eyes were upon the child ere she gained the high ground. Not many yards had she gone from its margin toward its low lying summit, ere she was aware of a human presence. She paused, withdrew a white kerchief from her satchel, and waved it about her head, when a warrior advanced noiselessly from a tree near her. He had read by her movements and form, her race, sex, and youth.

"Whither goes my little daughter in the night, alone?" he asked, in a low voice, in a dialect she understood, as he came near where she paused.

"I seek the camp to weep with the mourning women," was her reply, in accents sad, as the full force of the purpose of her mission was brought by her own words to her apprehension.

"She knows of the anger of the Great Spirit toward his children?" he asked.

"I do. It is very black. What is the name of my father who keeps watch here?"

"Standing-Bear; and there are others. Did my little daughter see the camp of the Long-Knives?"

"I was near their fires to see. They will not move to-night."

"How does she know that?"

"They were scattered. Their guns laid by. They are weary; their horses were lying on the ground."

"My child's eyes are sharp for a little (young) woman."

"I am the daughter of warriors. I come from the English peace chief." A little proudly these words were said.

"Standing-Bear is glad to hear her words."

"Where shall I find the camp?"

He pointed north-westerly with his hand. "Keep near the swamp, a half hour's fast walk, my daughter, will see the camp fires from the higher ground."

"Who shall I meet?"

"Red-Wing is the first."

"Red-Wing?"

"The young Sac chief. Light and gay, pleasant spoken."

"Light—gay, my father says?"

"He fought like an old warrior to-day, and brought off the bodies of Tecumseh and his brother."

"Wasegoboah? Is Wasegoboah slain?"

"Yes, by Tecumseh's side."

The maiden remained silent an instant. This was news to her. A great loss, but now swallowed up in the greatest! She now opened her blanket, drew it about her form, and up over her head, so as to conceal her slender proportions. The act and its motive were approved by the warrior.

"My young daughter is prudent. She need not fear."

"She does not," was her answer.

As she moved away the warm blood went in surges over face and neck. She drew the blanket well over her, confining it with her hand across the lower part of her face, exposing little save her eyes. Without leave-taking she moved forward. When distant many yards, the girl assumed the manner and carriage of her sister, careless of the sounds caused by her feet.

For her the forest was no longer dark and empty. Red-Wing and her shy girl love lit up and glorified it. She was not a Caucasian maiden, troubled how she should or could meet her lover, who had spoken only by a token, and that in response to one from herself. She had no thought, save a half fear that he might not see or hear her. For the rest, if he did, she took no thought. Now she bethought her of her real character, a stealthy moving Indian girl, and fell into its form, walking noiselessly over the leaf-strewn ground, making no more sound than the leaping white-footed mouse of the wood. As she went, warm with feeling and consciousness, she twittered to herself the notes of the small, dark-plumaged oriole, interspersed with the peeps of the little hylode, the trill of a bluebird, and then a low breathed whip-poor-will or two.

"What singing bird goes here?" was softly breathed near her, in a musical voice not to be mistaken.

The hot blood in its upward leap almost raised her from the ground, as the tall, lithe, young chief stood by her side unseen, till he spoke.

She recoiled a step. It was her rôle to be surprised; nature and art united to make it perfect.

"No singing bird," in a feigned, small voice, drawing her hiding drapery more closely over her face, while her head drooped forward. "A girl going to weep with the maidens," she added.

"May I not see my young sister's face? The night hides it sufficiently," he said, now advancing nearer her.

"Standing-Bear told me about a young chief," she said, shrinking from him. "Are you he?"

"What did he say of Red-Wing—the grim old growler?"

"That he was light and gay, and pleasant spoken. Young girls should avoid such."

"Oh, he did! My little sister does not know Red-Wing. She is alone in the great woods, and has far to go," in a tender, pitying tone. He stepped aside and asked, "May Red-Wing know who she is?" most respectfully.

His voice and manner touched the girl's heart exquisitely.

"She came from the Moravians," she said.

"She knows Ah-ni-tah?" eagerly.

"Very well; she came from her."

"She did?" excitedly. "Tell me of her," drawing nearer.

"Why should I; you not wear her jewel?"

"Don't I?" lowering his head for inspection, the paint washed from his face. "See if I don't. Tell Ah-ni-tah."

20

She put up her hands and placed them simultaneously ever his ears. In the right hung her gift. The act released the blanket which slid from her to the ground, and the princess stood revealed to the young chief's eyes.

"Ah-ni-tah!" in a glad voice. He clasped the slender waist with his arms, lifted her from the ground to himself. For one moment she abandoned herself to him wholly. Then her form became rigid in his embrace.

"Unhand me!" she commanded in an imperious voice; "the daughters of the Shawanoe are not to be taken thus."

"You sent me your jewel," in a tender, beseeching voice.

"You make me regret it, though you were going to battle."

"You wear mine," he urged. It gleamed on his eyes from her ear. She placed her hand on her dagger. He saw it flash as it leaped upward the full length of her arm for a blow.

"I will free myself," in a voice not to be mistaken, she cried.

He released her, stepped a yard back from her; put the silken sash from over his breast where it hung from his shoulder, placed his hand over his heart to show her where it was, and withdrew it with a little gesture. "Strike!" he said in a proud, sad voice. "The horses of the Kentuckians turned aside from me; their rifles flashed in my eyes, their bullets shunned my breast. Ah-ni-tah does not love Red-Wing. He would die."

The girl drooped, she dropped her nerveless hands, the dagger fell to the ground. She sprang forward, threw her hands on the young chief's shoulders, her head fell upon his breast with a sob, her cheek resting against the heart offered to her dagger. A half minute and she lifted her face, her eyes raining tears, in a mute appeal. The tender eyes of her lover met hers, his arms went again about the slender, yielded waist; his lips were placed upon her mouth. The light wind wafted the leaves aside, a shaft of moon rays shot through the opening to witness this forest betrothal.

A half minute and then the young chief—"I may ask you of your uncle the Prophet, and your aunt, when their tears are dry?" he asked.

"I will be your true wife; gather wood, build your fire, cook your corn and venison, when you come from the hunt," answered the maiden, with the meekness and self-abnegation of the Indian woman.

"It shall not be said that the daughter of Cheeseekau, of Tecumseh, the wife of Red-Wing, is a drudge," he replied. "I will be as the proudest white man when he receives a bride."

"Anita is not an English girl. She is an Indian woman. Her husband a warrior, a chief. He must be served as chiefs and warriors are," she answered, proudly, for him.

Red-Wing caught the gleam of the knife where it fell. He stooped, picked it up and returned it to its sheath under the girdle which cinctured the girl's waist.

"You must not take another step alone," he said.

"Red-Wing will not leave his post to go with a girl; that were a shame to a man," she said.

"Then you must remain with me till our spies return," he replied.

"You forget, my uncle and aunt have not given me. To remain alone, a girl with a young warrior, in the woods, is shame to a woman," was her reply to this. "I go; Red-Wing goes with me in my heart," placing her hand on her bosom. "You stay; Anita stands by your side, her hand in yours," she said.

They stood, two simple children, holding each other by the hand, loath to part. A sound caught the ears of both.

"Hist! they come," said the chief, turning in the direction of Anita's approach. Very soon Standing-Bear and his co-sentinel, with three scouts returning from their inspection of the American camp, drew near. They confirmed Anita's report. Nothing was to be feared from the enemy that night.

The mere presence alone of the Indian girl at that lonely place, was not cause of surprise. When Red-Wing announced her name, the warriors betrayed a good deal of interest. They are less stoical among themselves than in the presence of those of European descent. She was a born chieftainess of the highest rank, and as such to be honored. Standing-Bear, leaving Red-Wing as by right of rank to attend the high-born maiden, arrayed the party for its return, with a front and rear rank, leaving the young pair to walk between them, thus covered. It was in a way understood that the young chief was a favored suitor, but this had nothing to do with the consideration extended to the daughter of lost Cheeseekau. They passed down the swamp's margin, gathering the watch as they went. Then turning to their right they went over a swell, a ridge of land, and came upon the margin of a small stream along which on both sides was the camp of the main body.

Before the arrival of Anita and her attendants, the interment of Wasegoboah and two or three minor chiefs and such of the private warriors as had been recovered, was accomplished by their kindred and friends.

That of Tecumseh, a matter of international importance, was by solemn council of the head chiefs, appointed for the hour when the now full moon should attain meridian. The grave had been already excavated with reference to an opening in the tree tops, so that its rays should fall on the head and face of the *imperator* of the tribes, placed in state over the opening in the earth to be lowered to final rest, when the beams of the distant orb should signal the time.

Adjacent, on the fallen chief's left, was the circle of mourning matrons, the conspicuous elderly women, and such of the younger of his immediate personal following as he had distinguished by acts of kindness, or who were of his household, seated abjectly on the earth with their heads bowed. These from time to time sat up and united in a melancholy wail, which rising with the first in place was joined in by the one on her right, taken up by her neighbor, until it circled round swollen by all the voices into a dirge loud and peculiar, and dying away as it began, with an effect upon the ear of a listener singularly expressive of woe.

Red-Wing conducted Anita to this weird circle of lamentation, at the point occupied by the widow and sister of the fallen chief, between whom she took her place as an equal mourner. An intimation of her presence went swiftly around the band, producing a sense of relief that now the circle was complete. She at once joined in the vocal manifestations of the general woe, so aptly expressive of her personal sorrow for her own loss, and that of her family, and of the divided and broken Shawanoe nation to which they belonged.

Long the young chief lingered near her, catching and
following her low sweet voice, which filled his breast with
longing to carry her away to some blessed retreat of his
far off lovely land, and soothe and assuage her sorrow.
He remembered that his own place was with the younger
chiefs and warriors, and finally, reluctantly, he stole away
to find and occupy it.   There his romantic adventure of
the night was already known, which, with his exploits of
the day, united to make him the hero of this disastrous
expedition.

CHAPTER XXVIII.

THE moon gained the zenith and threw her silver urn full of light down, deluging and lighting the grand face of the mighty dead. Born, living, and ruling in the wan twilight of barbarism, whose broken bands of children with saddened faces were turning away for a final exit, already vanishing phantoms of a past, what place and surroundings, what light more fitting for his obsequies !

Around him the inner circle of the elder chiefs, the wise men, distinguished by valor, prudence,—qualities best esteemed,—were sitting with bowed heads in silence. Back of them the less conspicuous middle aged, with still an outer circle of the young men and youths, beyond which were the rabble of boys and children, the weak minded, and such as failed to fill the common requirements upon the male' savage. All silent, sad, struck each as his nature was, by the common blow.

At the thus Heaven-designated hour, Laulewasikaw, the surviving brother, who, as prophet was called Tenskautawa, slowly arose, under the weight of the public and personal grief which oppressed him.

Injustice has alway been done this chief. That he was early sincere in the needed reformation of his own life, and his now wholly unsuccessful efforts to reform the lives of his nation and race, cannot be doubted. That he acted much under the influence of Tecumseh, and was to some extent the victim of his own delusion, can admit of no question. His enmity to the Americans won their enduring hatred, while his failure at Tippecanoe discredited him with his own race.

He was a man of ability, an orator, a politician, a logician, persuasive, not a warrior, nor in any way a leader in war. It was his office to speak first.

"Fathers and brothers : The face of the Great Spirit is not turned from his children in sorrow. It is upon them black with anger and wrath! He took away the heart of our British father this day, that his hand might fall the heavier on his red children. He lies there," extending his long arm and slender hand to the prostrate form. "He·lies there, because we are unworthy of him. Whoever this night praises him, condemns himself. Tenskautawa mourns in silence. His voice is lost in grief for the wrongs, the sins, the sorrows of his people." He then slowly drew his robe over his head and face, and sank into his seat. His closing words were received with groans of responsive anguish.

Then Osh-aw-ah-nah, the Chippewa, Tecumseh's commander of the right in the battle of the now past day, arose : "We are little children," he said, "wandering in the woods. Lo! the sun falls from the middle of the sky, and goes out. Who shall light up a new day for the little children? Who shall lead them from the woods?" He sat down amid groans and sobs.

Then arose Black-Hawk and said, with solemnity : "Black-Hawk echoes the words of his brothers."

Round-head arose: "Round-head mourns with the nations. Eldest brother, eldest of all men, of all women."

His voice broke with irrepressible sorrow. His huge frame convulsed with emotions of anguish.

Sobs were heard from all the outer circles.

So one after another they arose, the orators speaking some words. Some remained silent. Many had but a word. More arose and made a gesture expressive of grief. The last exclaimed, "We mourn father, mother, husband, wife, children, nation, all, all lost!"

Then followed a full minute of utter silence, when a way was opened for the matrons to make their last offerings to the great chief. Slowly and solemnly the sobbing women entered the sacred inner circle. The widow as first and nearest in place, paused by her husband's side, and said: "Tecumseh's wife mourns the truest husband, father of her son," and laid a chaplet of woven autumn leaves upon his breast.

His sister was the next. "Tecumapease lays this spray of cypress green, on the heart of her great brother. Brother of all stricken, mourning women. Leader of the wronged nations." The voice of the twice bereaved woman was clear and strong, with a tone of sadness but also of pride.

Now approached the child of Cheeseekau, drooping and sore hearted. She paused and let fall the blanket from her right shoulder, leaving her bare arm free in the moonbeams. She stood a moment and in a low, sweet voice spoke: "Ah-ni-tah, lonely child of lost Cheeseekau, lays this last rose on the head of her uncle. Summer held it for this." As she spoke, she bent over the form, and performed the act with touching grace and tenderness. She arose, and as if suddenly inspired, she threw up both hands, thus giving her slender form to full view, and exclaimed in a clear, loud, far-reaching voice. "Tecumseh, lifter up of the hearts of the nations,—mighty carrier of the tribes in his arms,—great to govern, great to lead in war, never conquered in battle, farewell!"

Anita's words were received as inspired by a higher power. As she threw up her arms, her tall form lifting itself above her ordinary height, and sent out her clear, ringing voice, she seemed a priestess touched to speak. The whole multitude, the circles, the innermost, all arose to their feet, they stood a few seconds after her voice ceased, and then in absolute silence sank back to their places. Earth and nature said farewell to the dead chief, in the voice of the Great Spirit, by this his favored child. The tribes arose as they recognized it.

The procession of matrons paused, and stood until the multitude sank to the ground and then moved forward.

The next was a very ancient woman, in snow-white hair, left to flow and shimmer in the night as it would. It now caught the moonlight, and throwing it off seemed to double its light, forming a faint silvery halo about her head. Pausing, in broken accents she said:

"Hunter for sonless mothers, bringer of food to child-less fathers, comforter of the old and lonely, this I offer!" laying daintily prepared food by the chief's hand.

Another cried: "He rescued my husband from the fire kindled by the Mingos."

"He gave his horse to bear my wounded son from the battle and led the enemy away from his trail," said the next.

So one after another bore testimony, telling of some act of kindness, generosity, or some deed of devotion, by the hand of the fallen chief.

When the matrons departed, came the youths, bearing the food and water. Although pagan that he was, Tecumseh had taught that these contributions were silly rites. The Sacs, the Chippewas, the Sioux, would have placed his weapons and slain horse in the grave by him. His family and friends would not permit it. When all was done, the grand form was lowered to the couch made for it, and hidden from human vision. Large timbers were placed about and over it, the earth packed and rammed hard and firm, the whole reduced to the original level, and dead leaves strewn over it as before, while the displaced surplus earth was carefully removed as of all the buryings.

Then the chiefs and principal mourners bathed their hands and faces in the limpid stream, and in form partook of food, and to the eye resumed their wonted air of composure. When all was done, the moon was westering.

There was yet another and a different rite to be performed, no less important to the immediate parties.

On an open space at the head of the chief's hidden grave stood Red-Wing, with his uncle, Black-Hawk, and supported by the western chiefs in a body. A group of their matrons and maidens were in the near distance. To those in the foreground came the Prophet, leading Anita, accompanied by her aunts, and followed by her cousins, while Round-head and the chiefs of the Ohio and Wabash tribes, with their wives and daughters, came upon the ground from another direction. When the principal parties were thus in presence of each other, the Prophet led his niece forward, her head and face to the eyes covered, in front of the expectant young Sac chief. He said :

“ We here in this presence give our daughter, child of lost Cheeseekau, to Red-Wing, nephew of Black-Hawk, to be his wife—this let our brothers witness all. See it our sisters all."

Red-Wing took a single step forward, extended his hand and received Anita's hand from her uncle, who then lifted and spread abroad his hands, with upturned face, seeming in silence to invoke the grace of the Great Spirit upon the heads and union of the lovers.

Red-Wing turned and presented his bride to his uncle. She bent her head, he laid his hands upon it, and then taking her by the hand presented her to each of the chiefs in turn, when she was passed into the more effusive arms of the matrons and maidens. Very soon a chosen number of these last led her away for some rite of their own, while the bridegroom was taken possession of by the young men. The Prophet explained that in their present fortunes, the death of the child's English father, it was deemed best to place her under the protection of a husband.

Later the girls returned to find Red-Wing, with his favorite white pony dappled with black spots, gayly tricked, and a charger, also five or six of his immediate friends, holding each his horse, who were to be the escort, awaiting the readiness of the bride, to set out on her return to Moravian town. She was to remain with her adopted sister, under the protection of her American friends, until the present darkness resting upon the affairs of the nations, friends of both parties, should dissipate.

Anita soon appeared, was placed in the saddle, her limbs arrayed for horseback, in gayly decked garments given her by the Chippewa chief's daughter. She was soon ready, her bridegroom chief gallantly mounted by her side, their escort in place, when two or three of the leading chiefs who were in council in the earlier part of the night, approached her.

"My daughter knows the straits of her people?" said their spokesman to her.

"I do. My heart bleeds for them. Anita's marriage does not draw her eyes from the distress of her sisters and their children. So far away and so little food."

"My daughter is wise. What counsels she? Old men ask her."

"Make peace with General Harrison. It will be easy. The Americans are tired of the war. I know one nearest General Harrison, the lover of my English sister. Tecumseh knew and loved him. He saved Tecumseh's life in battle. They will fill the hungry mouths of my sisters and their children. My English sister, Edith, will buy bread for them. Go to General Harrison in the morning. You will be safe with him. This is the only course."

Sadly and effectively this slender young girl, so suddenly called to leadership by the divine gift dwelling in her family, spoke these words.

"My daughter says wise words," were the responses of her auditors, who now turned away to the council, called to a final decision of their immediate course.

Then the cavalcade moved away through the old wood to return the strangely wedded bride to her stricken household.

They skirted along the northern margin of the swamp, which terminated a little east of the town, passing around this, as portions of the pass across it were not without difficulty, even to Indian horses. Red-Wing dismissed his escort at the margin of the wood, not remote from the village, then unable to decide whether he would be safe from capture, or would return to camp.

With his bride he entered the town in the gray of the chill morning. He set her down near her own door. Her maid, her companion of the evening before, was abroad gathering fuel. She admitted her, and conducted the handsome young chief, who so gallantly rode out of the forest with her mistress, to a place where for the time, he and his horses would be secure until Anita should receive Dudley's protection for him.

CHAPTER XXIX

AS surgery was then understood and practised, Mr. Grayson's wound was necessarily fatal and within a day or two. He was subjected to no needless torture. No medical edict was needed to assure his daughter of his hopeless condition. To her this was certain, as attended by Dudley she met the procession bearing him to her presence. As she approached, the litter halted. When the eyes of the stricken father and stricken daughter met, each saw that the other knew the hour of final separation was at hand. To Edith it was in a way the end of the order of all things. For her he had always existed, as a part of it, an important part of providence. She had never thought of what would be when he ceased. Suddenly, with no premonition save a formless dread, that seemed to attach itself to another, the greater share of her world was dissolving, and in some way she was called to survive it.

The instances were rare where a father and daughter had been so much to each other as these, whose ways were to part. For her at the instant the whole world seemed about to pass away. A gleam, a smile of his eyes, restored her to the consciousness of the actual conditions. She with the fragmentary world were to remain. Great anguish has no fitting means of expression beyond that of the lesser.   When she took the arm of her silent lover and turned back, following the stricken form, so inexpressibly dear was it, now sole stay, comfort, and rest, she could not forbear pressing it, clingingly, equally blessed in giving its support.

Soon after gaining Edith's temporary residence came the surgeons of both armies, the chaplains of both generals.   The first found their work useless, the second their work done.

Dudley was temporarily relieved at headquarters, had authority to parole and make use of any of the prisoners who might be willing to be of service.   More than could be useful tendered themselves to him.

It had been anticipated by the surgeons that Mr. Grayson might die on the return of day, instead of which he seemed to rally in the night, and perhaps had the methods of later years been applied, he might have recovered.   With a reawakening of strength, his mind was called into activity.   It seemed to have gained vantage-ground, where, in a backward survey, the things puzzling and incoherent when they occurred, fell into perspective and their relations revealed.   Devout and fervent, he accepted the prevalent notions of such minds of that day, that the affairs of men were ordered and supervised not by any broad and comprehensive scheme, but from day to day as exigencies arose, by the immediate hand of God directly, and that while men were the direct and unavoidable instruments of accomplishing moral purposes, they might themselves be punished for the parts they thus performed.

He had a clear apprehension of the supposed source of his present injury, and his mind busied itself with it, in its relations with other things and events.

"To me," he said, "it matters little whether my death is caused by a stray shot of the combatants, or was sped by the hand of an intended assassin. For each man the earth was in effect created on the day of his birth. For him it is dissolved in the hour of his death. An accident dissolves it, as certainly as a purposed slayer; the casualty is the murderer. A man might prefer to reach his end by natural causes. Are not all causes of death natural causes? Mine most so, if it comes from the hand of one employed by me to slay others. There is little profit in this speculation."

He remained silent for a little space. "In that event it is a curious instance of a man's unconscious agency in his own destruction. You remember the Huron?" to Dudley. "Of course you do. You saw this Indian there, know why I was there. Its pretence was to secure soldiers for England; it was to employ the benighted creature to meet and murder me here, on the remote banks of this river. No matter—no matter, Edith, child, let me follow it out. I must think the main purpose—the larger was God's purpose. I was merely his instrument. For me it was not a right thing to do probably,—not that it is quite certain,—so while doing God's work, I am punished individually for doing it.

His mind lingered on this as if satisfied with its logic at the last, and then it took up another strand of the complex web of human association. "How curiously runs the thread of man's life—at least so it seems to the man himself, when he disentangles it from other threads, from the sum of human life and association, sets himself apart as I may now, and traces the influence of others —of events on his individual life and fortune—becomes himself a principal figure in the drama of his own life—

a part of the great ceaseless drama which to history never begins or ends. The men, the events, which controlled his life and destiny, are to be withdrawn from the broad current of history, and so arranged that their influence on him is brought into clear light, everything else to become background and chorus as in Greek tragedy. Spectators will find the piece dull."

He closed his eyes, seemingly to give time for the mental segregation of which he spoke, to take place. " I, the smallest atom in a great contest, would serve my king. Well, it turns out that King George, the Prince Regent, President Madison, their councils, parliaments, and congresses were really but conspirators against poor small me. The old rebellion, the minor plots of all the years since; your father, Philip Dudley," to Cliffton ;—" You, my child," to Edith ;—" our meeting you," to Dudley. " How clear in this colorless light, all these now lie in my mind's grasp; ending as all tragedies must, in death."

The voice was low, clear, exquisitely sad, as if the spirit had passed from its shattered tenement and lingered an instant for a hasty retrospect ere final departure.

Edith was kneeling by his couch, resting in part upon the knees of Dudley. The voice, its summing up, the pictures and reminiscences of her past, with the pathos of the present, united to renew the flow of her tears beyond her control.

" My poor, poor child," said the suffering man, placing his hand on her head. " That was the pagan in me. Pagans are pessimists, you know—things work for evil and not good. God overrules our evil, though we suffer for its commission. See ! See ! We work each for himself, yet altogether on the lines of God's great enterprises, unknowingly doing his work while intending to do our own. We are used to punish others, yet in so doing commit sins for which in time we suffer. What a strange, inexplicable scheme, simple and clear if we could attain God's view of it. We do not know the real quality of our own work, or whether important or ignoble. Are there really any important and trivial things? Are they not after all of the same size? Well, let us not worry these last sands away. God 'knows. It is really all his work, and for the grand come out he is responsible."

Then came a longer pause. He had not yet said what was in his mind to these two.

"There must have been wrong between Philip Dudley and myself. Not on his part—mine, by my not knowing. I may have been in fault for not knowing. I thought he plotted my destruction. He really saved my life' at the expense of his own honor. As it then looked to me, he plundered me to enrich himself. He really rescued and saved my estate for me, using his own money for that purpose. When it was all revealed to me it was too late to rectify anything to him. I learned of this child of his, this Cliffton; I could not find him. When we did find him he repeated his father's benefaction. I did not even then see how much I needed to suffer to expiate wrong, partly from blindness. I don't know the extent of my sin. I had to be re-educated. Clear as his father once stood in my love, lovely as this youth stood in my presence, when it came to me that he had been educated in the school of the hated republic, to command its soldiers, wore its uniform as an officer in the rebel army—they were still rebels to me—I would have given the world had you two not met. He wore a blue coat!

"It was not in nature, in God's holy law, that you two should meet and not love. And I would sacrifice this love to the color of a coat, a sentiment of clothes and buttons! A shadow, as it now seems. I deserved—I needed punishment, nothing less than this. I've lived to see a British general flee like a coward from the Americans, from his army, his honor, and on British soil. I am punished. All these things so far as you, my child, are concerned—"

"O father! I pray you, I implore you—"

"Only a little more, my child. The compensation— the come out of all this—the end of my drama, is your love, happiness. You are to be followed by others, springing from you, reared by you, in a new, fresh land, not yet polluted, scarcely stained by the crimes of the old. Our older mistakes, sins, have worked out this fruition in God's way. You two—especially Cliffton—have been sorely tried. The world for me is dissolving, only to be renewed and glorified for you."

He closed his eyes and remained silent for a minute, and without opening them said, "I understand, Cliffton, that you know nothing whatever of the early life—the old time relations between your father and myself."

"Nothing whatever. I know little of his early life, but don't, I beseech you, exhaust your remaining strength in recounting this history to me."

"Within a few months, since the Maumee days, he wrote out a complete history—much of it not before known to me. It was done at my request, so—so that if anything happened, I could show it to you, or send it to you," said Edith to Dudley; and turning to her father, "Shall I get it and read it to him, Papa?"

"Do, my child, writing it was the only pleasant thing of this wretched, wretched summer."

The child produced and read it, which with explanations and incidental talk occupied much time, with occasional interruptions of the two hospital nurses in attendance. An abstract of portions of it will bring some details within the reader's apprehension.

It is to be understood, that the Dudleys and Graysons were of the oldest colonial families of Boston. The boys of the same age, and diverse temperaments which complemented each other. Almost more than brothers from boyhood, not being brothers were more careful of each other's feelings; were school- and class-mates; Were almost as one in sentiment, until the growing differences which drove the colonies to separation from the Crown.

From the first, the Graysons were pronounced Loyalists, and Edward was soon the leader of the young Tories. It was to be gathered that he was proud, indomitable, intolerant. His friend frank, generous, gay, and high-spirited. He was also imaginative and incapable of giving pain; in heart and soul a patriot, which he dissembled from regard for his friend. A rupture came early, forced by the unaccommodating temper of the Loyalist. They parted, never to meet save as foes. Tears, anguish, on Dudley's part; scorn, anger, contempt, on Grayson's. The separation preceded the formal revolt of the colonies; was as radical and incurable. Grayson became so obnoxious that he was with others proscribed, and shipped out of the colony. Later he was by name included in the Massachusetts Act of Confiscation, that denounced death for a second voluntary return to the state. He came a second time for his bride and her proscribed family. He was arrested, tried and condemned. His former friend was a lover of his affianced, and he believed that Dudley caused his arrest. He escaped by

unlooked-for means. His promised bride and her family
were placed in his reach, and he thus accomplished the
object of his visit. Years of war followed. After it was
over, Grayson learned that Dudley became the purchaser
at the sale of his confiscated estates; very considerable
for that time. Grayson was unfortunate in his family.
The loss of his wife, and all but the youngest of his children, sent him abroad for a prolonged residence. He
from the first enjoyed the confidence of the Crown officers, was employed in important positions, was liberally
paid, and fortunate in his investments.

　Years elapsed. The bitterness of his personal wrongs
lost something of its pungency, though his hatreds had
lost little of their strength. Finally, in London, he was
overwhelmed by the receipt of a package transmitted
through the American Embassy. It contained sterling
bills, for the proceeds of the confiscated family estates,
of which he was now sole heir, recently re-sold, with an
itemized statement of costs and disbursements. The
property had been held, until peace and renewed pros-
perity enchanced its value tenfold.

Stranger yet, he also received in authenticated form,
a statement of the real facts of his arrest and escape, as
well as of the escape of his wife and her family. Dudley
had no knowledge of his arrest, until after it was accomplished. He planned and executed his escape, and
placed his intended wife in his arms. He became suspected of complicity in this affair, and resigned his
major's commission in the Massachusetts troops, made
his way to Washington's headquarters, and enlisted as
a private. He was soon commissioned, his ability, dashing courage, fine person and address carrying him
forward.

The paper also contained a statement of Grayson's return to America. The attainder remained in force against him, in Boston, and he dared not visit his native town. He learned that Dudley was dead, as was his wife; that he left a son with his wife's family, in New York. Her family *name* his agent did not learn. He caused search to be made for the child, but got no trace of it, for the reason as he supposed when he wrote his sketch, that the child was known by the mother's family name, and not by his father's.

Then followed a statement of his fortune. He had set apart a liberal provision for his adopted daughter Anita, and divided the bulk between Edith and Cliffton. There was added to this supplemental matter a recapitulation of the events set out in the opening chapters of this history.

The reading greatly affected all three. Dudley was the most moved. He said he had always felt that something had been kept from him, by his mother's family, as to his father. He knew there was something connecting him with the daughter of a Loyalist, which brought a cloud upon him, and that he became alienated from Boston. All these early trials came upon his father when he was twenty-six, his own age. His father, as he understood, was reputed wealthy, but that he had lost his entire property and lost caste with his wife's family in consequence, as he supposed. This was explained to him now. The Clifftons were Scotch, and thrifty, but he himself was supposed to have inherited his father's weakness—a lack of appreciation of money values.

"A royal weakness of the once almost royal Dudleys of that glorious Elizabethan age," said Mr. Grayson. "In compensation for his and your loss, in the wise economy of God, this gold also comes to your hand, with at least honest usury."

"I wish I had ten thousand dollars now," said the young man thoughtfully.

"For what?" asked Edith.

"To buy food for Tecumseh's poor Indians."

"My royal Dudley!" cried the girl joyfully, clasping and kissing his hand.

"You see I cannot be trusted with gold," he said to her father.

"You shall have your way," was the reply. "I do not like your name Cliffton so well as Dudley," he added.

"O I do! I called him Cliff the second day I saw him," said Edith. "O what a day that was! Our day of young love, that we did not know," said Edith in a sad ecstacy.

"You blessed Edith! Yet how awfully I was punished for *thinking* that you loved me," was Cliffton's reply.

"Not that, Cliff, but for assuming that *unasked* I had confessed it. Some time I want to talk all that over with you."

"What precious things your maiden lips will tell each other of your virgin hearts. Poor boy! You" (to Edith) "wasted a kiss on his hand, when his unkissed lips were so near," said the father, almost vivaciously.

"Well, his lips have not yet had a chance," said the girl in a regretful small voice. Then coloring, she exclaimed, "Surely! surely! we cannot think—O father, we forget you in these light words."

"Let me have it to tell your mother that I saw her daughter and Philip Dudley's son join their lips in a true lover's kiss," he said, with touching solemnity.

She arose to her feet as did her lover. He bent to her,

proffering his lips. She shyly lifted her red mouth to them. A sob, a gush of tears, were inevitable. An arm went up around his neck, and for a moment bliss banished all else from the child's heart. Then she stood, sustained by his arm, her head resting on his shoulder, when came again her father's voice speaking in weakness.

"Time and strength pass ; one, a more important thing, I must report to all the departed, the rite which makes you two one."

Edith had not thought of this as an immediate thing, and heard his words with a half scared look.

"Surely you can trust me," said Dudley, assuringly to her.

"I do, I do trust you ; it shall be as our father wishes," she said in a very low voice.

The night passed. With the next day came Anita, that sorely tried child whose strength and elasticity of form and spirit arose with fresh vigor to the demands upon her. This stricken household, the dearest and most sheltered home her strange life of wandering had ever known, was as dear to her heart as if born of it ; this for the time was her place. Her marriage though hastily entered into was not lightly assumed. To her the new relation was solemnly made, with self-devotion as entire and unreserved as the heart and nature •of one as gifted and exalted as was hers, are capable of. She was one never to be sunk and lost in another's life and being, but herself to be and remain a centre attracting others.

For the time her adopted sister and father had claims paramount to this nearest and dearest one, whom she gayly put by for the time, feeling the tonic of his presence near her. She did not forget or neglect the needs of her sorely pressed kindred. She knew her English father, as she called him, had made the amplest provision for her, and if he lived he would exert himself to the utmost for them. If he died, Edith and herself would in like manner care for them, and she had the most entire confidence in Dudley.

These things were in her thoughts as she rode through the moonlit old wood, and emerged from it in the chill gray of the morning. She should hasten to Dudley for her husband. Her husband! she, Anita, had a husband! What a property! She should tell her romance to Edith at the first possible instant. What a solace, joy it was, buried in the silent depths of her nature, amid the darkness and blood that rested upon and flowed over her kindred and her families of both races.

Edith was struck with the sweet, subdued radiance that seemed to illuminate the child's face child no longer, as she had before discovered, save in the mode of speech she and her father indulged in from habit. The chance to tell Edith of the happenings beyond the gloomy swamp, occurred on her entering the house. Dudley, as she wished, was present. Both had lost the faculty of surprise. At the first Edith was shocked. Another tie was dissolved. All were loosened by the blow which prostrated her father. Dudley thought Anita's marriage the most natural thing in an orderly course of events. He requested the pleased girl to bring in her chief. Distressed, distracted as Edith was, she knew he was no common man. The handsome young barbarian's form was not strange to her eyes; and was an ample excuse, if not a justification, for her sister's act. It was her going away, going back to barbarism, that was the blow.

Dudley gladly gave him assurance of safety in presence of the American army, whose lines were a little later extended to embrace the town, for police purposes. He placed in his hand a written pass which would protect him from annoyance, and give him the rights of a privileged visitor.

CHAPTER XXX.

ABOUT ten that forenoon General Harrison, Commodore Perry, General Cass, Colonel Warburton, Major McLain, and one or two others, on Dudley's invitation, were in attendance. Mr. Grayson wished to see the American commanders, and Dudley conducted them to him. He said to them that he felt a wish to see men who had rendered such service to their country. Harrison, with the sympathy and kindness of his nature, expressed his profound regret for his misfortune, assured him he was more pained by this incident than by any other casualty of the affair. Grayson inquired the condition of Barclay, and Perry was able to report him as doing well. Mr. Grayson was especially interested in the frank, modest, rather shy young sailor.

The bride was then conducted to her father's side, followed by Anita, and her stately young chief; also by the noble form of a veiled lady. The British chaplain was present in canonicals, and rendered the beautiful marriage service of his church. The dying man gave away the bride.

No one of the party had ever before witnessed nuptials so impressively celebrated; no one had witnessed them under similar circumstances, probably. Dudley led his bride apart and presented the American guests. General

Harrison said he approached her as a veritable heroine of romance, for once realized in actual life, something of which he knew from the hero himself. From his heart he congratulated Dudley, who was worthy of his rare fortune. He really felt for once to congratulate a bride. He only hoped she would not withdraw her husband from his side.

"General Harrison," she said, with touching sweetness, "I know now how perilous the place by your side is. I have no wish to withdraw him from it. I am an American. My mother was one; always felt herself an exile from the land of her birth. It will be my home. I hope to be worthy of it, and of him," raising her eyes to her husband's face, with tears in them. Not in a continuous speech as here set down were these words spoken, nor do I report all this conversation.

Edith then spoke for the unfortunate Indians; she was certain they would sue for peace, and she hoped to be permitted to buy food for them.

"My dear Mrs. Dudley, if anything could prove my friend's rare fortune in winning you, it is this thought that at this hour," glancing toward her father's couch, "you should plead for these unfortunate people. I am very glad to assure you they are now my friends, and ample food is on its way to their camp."

"Oh, father!" cried the gratified girl, turning back to him, "do you hear his words?" which she repeated to him.

"Tell General Harrison he has brought the greatest possible solace to a dying man," he said. "It does much to reconcile me to our changed fortunes."

Then Red-Wing and Anita were presented to the American general, Anita as the adopted daughter of Mr. Gray-

son and niece of Tecumseh.   He received them with the
utmost kindness.   Anita made Red-Wing say, that had he
known General Harrison, he might not have joined in the
war against him—a free rendering of his words.   For
herself, she said, she had learned much of him, and was
sorry he and her uncle were ever enemies.

The general was a thorough student of Indians.   He
was greatly struck by this daughter of the race.   She had
been moved to tears by his kindness to her people.   He
was glad to give her assurances of his care for them, and
many warm words for her personal well-being.   He should
return at once to Detroit, where he hoped to meet her
and her husband, who might rely on his good offices.
Then with leave-taking the general and his officers returned to his camp.

Red-Wing was greatly impressed by Edith's marriage
ceremony.   Anita translated its liturgy.   He expressed
an ardent wish to be married by the same service.   He
thought that Anita, educated, and an English woman by
adoption, and a Christian by conversion, should be married as would an English maiden be—as her sister had
been.   Anita was charmed with the idea, and very much
by his thoughtfulness for her.   Edith and Dudley were
consulted and cordially concurred.   The chaplain on
consideration thought it proper, and consented to offi-
ciate.   At two that afternoon the tender and impressive
service was repeated in Mr. Grayson's presence, and
these high born children of forest and plain were wed
and blessed as the Christian church unites in marriage.
In reply—who gives this woman? the dying man nodded in
reponse.

It was one of his last intelligent answers.   His room
was then declared sacred from further things of earth;

save his nurses, the American chaplain of his own church, the noiseless footed brides, and Dudley, no one invaded its sanctuary.

As the ensuing night was yielding the earth to the arms of another day, when the stars were recalling their rays, with their returning beams his spirit departed, and at the sunfall what remained was for the time committed to the keeping of the earth, on thel ovely bank of the Thames, near the resting-place of the Moravians.

The army, its prisoners, spoil, and trophies started the day before on its return to Detroit. Among the things of interest taken was a small brass three-pounder, worn and battered, bearing the royal arrow of Britain, with the date 1775. On it was inscribed " Taken at Saratoga, October 17, 1777," to which had been added " Retaken at Detroit, August 16, 1812," now to be supplemented with—" Recaptured at the Thames, October 5, 1813."

The Indians also moved in the afternoon of the same day. With them went proud and happy Red-Wing, the only man of the British force, white or red, who had occasion to be glad that he saw the Thames.

The fine little Ariel with her four short 12's and gallant commander, Packet, which with the other light vessels worked up the river, after the battle, was left with space for Major Dudley and his party, who got on board on the morning of the eighth. With a clear sky of serene blue, sparkling sunshine, and crisp air, they swept down past the battle-field, along the now silent banks of the Thames, which so lately bore the fleeing and pursuing foes in the panoply of war.

Warburton and many of the English officers were of the party, the colonel having charge of his absent general's wife and family. The Indian bride, piquant, alert, subdued by the misfortunes of her family and race, yet feeling the play of the abundant energies stored in her form, which she had been taught to hold in the subjection of the daughters of the highest civilization, her heart full of her gallant chief, and conscious of the added dignity which all women feel from marriage, her thought was of her bridegroom as he disappeared from her in the twilight of her marriage day, riding away to join his band, mounted on his strong, active charger, and attended by her own gayly decked pony, her husband's gift. She was now on her way to meet him, and enter upon her new, and in all other respects, her oldest life ; moving gracefully about, with the air of a newly wedded princess, married according to the ritual of an ancient Christian church. This greatly pleased her, as she reflected that she was married by the same ceremony and observances as was her sister.

Was she a Christian in the sense that Edith was? Hardly, as we estimate children of a thousand years of Christian civilization; not at all in the sense of a radical change in the wild nature of a savage. A slip of that wild tree, planted in no matter what Christian soil, or with what care pruned and cut, will grow up with the essential nature of its parent tree. An hundred years, with careful tending it and its offspring, would be essential to transform that. A savage bud on a Christian stock is not Christian. A Christian slip in the heathen trunk cannot change the stock and root. Anita identified the Great Spirit with the English God, which was much, showing the wide kindred of all the races. Jesus, whose life and mission were of the deepest and tenderest interest, and for whose death she shed tears of passionate sorrow, was, nevertheless, not so much her Redeemer, save as she became English by her adoption. He did not come to her native people. The other race rejected and slew him. That was matter between them and him. The Indians had nothing to do with it, never heard of it for thousands of years. Had he come to them they certainly had not tortured and slain him. She was certain she was Christian, as much as an Indian may be. She was sad at the thought of her near separation from Edith. Her sister did not now need her; she had this, her own young chief; she, Anita, would be but a hindrance. She was born to a different life, and her dark eyes went westward, seeming to traverse the forest, the wide blue lake to the free plains, and their wilder, freer life beneath the sundown skies, beyond her present horizon. She would carry with her what was her own, gained from civilization. She would have many things to teach the women of her new people and her husband. Her sons would be chiefs, her daughters wives of warriors. They should be told of all the life, the exquisite pathos of the death of Jesus, and so become better, truer, and tenderer.

She looked up into the still, warm sky, the gold, bright earth, the mass of bronze and buff, the soft rich brown of the still apparelled trees. She noted that the waterfowl was still at home in the river and reedy margins of St. Clair. There was plenty of time for the journey across sandy Michigan, and round the swampy end of the lake to her far away new home. There would be bright, happy days under all the shadows ere she departed. Her sister was never so dear, so beautiful as now. She turned from the lovely outside world to note the tender loveliness of her face. Her beauty had gained in ripened, softened sweetness, gained from the suffering of these latest days of the past months, and now, secure in her love were to be days of serene rest, under his eyes, his arms ever near her. She was with her all the night after her father's remains had been consigned to earth; had been near her all the morning, was now only just out of the reach of their voices, Dudley's and hers, as they remained near each other on the ship. Hers was the love, the devotion of the tamed, wild thing, for her whose hand, voice, and will had wrought the charm, the willing slavery. Dudley was the only man of Edith's race she could have loved. She felt with a true woman's instinct, that he of right was the chosen of her sister, and it cost her nothing to guide her strong liking into its truer channels. He was a dear, precious brother, and she never before quite comprehended what the love of a sister was. She loved him for Edith's sake also. He was now Edith's husband, and so her brother of right. She was almost as blessed in Edith's happiness as in the wild flavor of her own. It was because Edith was happy that she would abandon herself to her own. Was Edith alone, she would have remained near her.

Edith caught some words of the group of captive officers near, that this was one of Perry's ships, and she felt a moment's curiosity. Dudley conducted the two girls, attended by the courteous Packet, over the taut, well-appointed schooner, and the officer explained her position in the battle, marks of which her timbers bore. Dudley fancied that the naval battle was not an attractive subject to Edith, and managed to make her excursion over the vessel occupy no great time. He led the girls to pleasant seats on the sunny side of the ship, where, when his slight duties permitted, he lingered. The histories of the young ladies were known to those

about them, as well as the latest events of their lives;
and they were the objects of great interest during the
voyage, though for the most part left to the society of
each other, and the care of the fortunate Dudley. Edith
was at the first not inclined to talk. For Dudley to be
near, see her, feel her presence, were for him all sufficient. He had more words with Anita than with her,
during the early hours of the voyage. Edith had
inherited an introspective tendency of mind from her
father. Her experience for these many months had
developed it to a mental habit. She was entering upon
a new existence. The boundary line separating it from
the old was traceable under her eye. She saw herself a
maiden of the mediæval ages, set apart, dedicated to a
cause by religious enthusiasm and superstitions, a phan-
tom cause. She now saw the things of that past frayed
and faded; they had become ghostly, and what were left
were buried in her father's grave, himself a victim of the
illusion; she, now standing in the kindling light of new
life, in a new world, glorified by perfect love, the world
of wifely duty and observance. She hardly identified
herself with the high, cold maiden before the Ohio mission. Of all that past, the experience of the last two
years which created her new world, left nothing but a
memory. Two years ago she would not greatly have
cared to survive her father, and it would have become
her duty to devote herself to his memory, as to the cause
for which he trained her. She looked into the river
whose tide bore her returnlessly away, like the tide of
life, flowing ever onward. These waters would never
return to their native springs. Did the fountain hidden
in the earth mourn their departure? She was wafted
away. It was the law of life. Her father fell asleep on

the banks of life's great river, and she and her chosen
were swept onward. It was God's law. All were within
his arms. By and by they all would drift to the land
and find the lost awaiting them there. She would not be
sad ; another took sunshine or shadow from her. She
wanted to see that lovely face light up with its old smile,
break into its old mirthful expression.

Not on this first day could she wholly pass from the
life of yesterday. She saw herself coming out of its
shadow, and wondered what manner of person she now
was. She turned to her lover bridegroom of two days,
and saw he was still uncertain of his position toward her,
only sought to be near her.

"Your thought is with the past. It is due that it
should be," he said tenderly.

"Be patient, Cliffton," placing her hand in his in the
twilight gathering about them. "Though it seems treason to my father's memory, I shall be all smiles again.
I shall be so entirely blessed and happy in your love that
I cannot long look sad if I try. Be patient a little with
me."

"Be patient ! why think how little of your voice I have
heard, how rarely I have ever touched your hand. I can
count the times. Was ever a man so blessed who had so
little acquaintance with the one, in a way compelled to
wed, so—"

"Compelled? no, no, Cliff, don't say that. No girl's
heart was ever more entirely given than mine, my will,
my pleasure, were to be wedded."

"Bless you! bless you! and yet—and yet—may I say
it? I am so much a stranger I hardly dare approach you
to take your hand. I was not permitted to woo you, as

I so gladly would. You don't know me—the bad, the coarse in me, and I am in—well, a half fear of you."

" In fear of me ? how strangely that sounds ! "

" I have not in these later years been where I could see, know, and associate with ladies; I don't know them. Now, my fear is that in some unknown way I may wound the subtle sense of delicacy that is part of woman's nature, the sensitive net-work that surrounds her, and I may lose in your estimation."

" I wonder if a man ever made such a confession before ? I am sure we may trust each other." And in the deepened twilight many low voiced words were spoken.

" And do you know, Cliff," she later said, " I am afraid there must be some hurt—a sore place in you—I want to search it out, and heal it. Tell me now if such there is, that I may explain it, charm it away now, when you love me most, hope most from me."

Gayly the young bridegroom passed his hands over his breast, his head, and limbs, laughing. " I declare ! a few days ago I was sore all through, but do you know at the touch of your hand, at the sound of your voice, saying that I was more than all, dearest of all to you, it was like the touch, the voice, of the priceless One, forgiving sin and making whole." The voice was light and gay when it began. It had a *tremolo* when it ceased.

There was a half minute of silence, the stir of the deepest emotion, then she said—" We shall have all the past—*our* past reconstructed and lived over. A woman's life is in the heart, the heart and love of her husband. There must be nothing left to spring up out of our past. Black River is all sweet and precious. The Huron, the Maumee—well, in the near future there is nothing in my heart, in my thought, that I will not gladly have you know. I want you to know—know it all."

They had passed the lower sluggish, sinuous Thames. St. Clair was found still agitated by the tempest of yesterday, a historic storm. Here the saucy little schooner spread more canvas, and went flying across her southern margin, and down the Detroit. She did not stop at the little town of the Strait. Her destiny was Malden.

CHAPTER XXXI.

ANITA'S LEAVE-TAKING.

THE sympathetic Mrs. Gordon heard of her friend's marriage, the one ray of joy in the blackness that closed over Canada West. She expected her return very soon, though the day was uncertain. With such means as she had, she arranged her bridal chamber. In the smaller hours, the weary and overtaxed sisters came and shared it.

The next morning as Anita pulled aside the heavy curtain which darkened a window, and looked out to the well advanced day, her eyes fell on the statuesque form of her wedded lover, tall and slender, sashed and feathered, posing in unconscious grace in a place commanding a view of the house where she was lodged, with his gaze on another part of it—eager, as she saw by the flash of his eyes. He knew the ship had arrived, and hurried to the house, where for an hour ere day broke, his eyes had bored the darker walls that imprisoned her from him. He had not now long to wait ere she went forth to greet him and bless his eyes with the sight of her. Two or three words she had with him, and she conducted him within the house—the Grayson residence.

As they were entering it, Anita saw old Carter standing near the doorway, whom she had not met since the night of their adventure on the Maumee, though she knew he accompanied Dudley to the Thames, and was present at the death of Tecumseh. She now ran to him and greeted him effusively.

Red-Wing and he recognized each other, in the grim way of warrior and scout. Anita told him who Red-Wing was, and of their marriage, which, though interesting, he heard with silence and composure.

"I'se a lookin fur Major Dudley. I's tole I might fine 'im round 'ere," he said finally.

"Well, he should be here. I do not know where he is. The truth is, Mr. Carter, there are two very bad young men who should be here, and they were both missing; one belongs to Edith, and the other to me. I have captured mine you see," laughing and showing her teeth at her best.

"Yis, 'h'es got the best on't though," a little grimly. 'The idee that such a gal should marry an Ingin!' was in his mind. "Is Miss Grayson in 'ere?" he asked.

"Mrs. Dudley you mean, Mr. Carter."

"Yis; I'se glad to heer o' that. I knowed purty well 'ow that ud be, ever sin that air time on Black River."

"Oh, so did I; we are glad we helped, ain't we, Mr. Carter?"

"I done w'at I could," said the old man.

"I know you did; and she is grateful and loves you for it. And she will want you to live with them. She is here and will be very glad to see you. We talked of you yesterday."

"Wal, ef she's 'ere, the major ain't fur off," was his answer.

"No 'e ain't!" said the major himself in Carter's manner, and just then near enough to hear his words, now laughing in his old way. He greeted Anita warmly, asked about Edith, shook the young chief's hand with great cordiality, passed his hand within Carter's arm, and spite of his reluctance took him inside.

Edith arose from dreamless, restoring sleep. Anita had left her side. Her first thought was of her bride-groom lover. She knew he was not remote from her. She thought of her father, with regret for herself rather than for him. Then she turned for brief thanks, grati-tude, and prayer for grace, as her custom was. The articles for her toilet were arranged the night before. Her hands were deft in arraying her form, her heart full of love, her eyes full of liquid sensibility. She heard *his* voice, his musical laugh, as she was taking a hasty satisfied survey of herself. She turned, ran down, and electrified him, surrounded as he was, with a kiss, fairly bestowed. The grace thus rendered electrified the admiring chief also. He murmured something to which the laughing Anita replied.

"What does he say?" asked Edith, her face full of color.

"That I was married like an English girl, and should do as English brides do," she answered, in a tone show-ing that she thought his remark was just.

"Well, he is right. I am sure you may let us see you render him his dues."

The laughing Anita turned to the young chief and kissed his lips shyly and demurely. He received it with a look of appreciation and thankfulness, placing his arm about her waist, as Dudley had done.

Mrs. Gordon entered in time to witness the morning rites.

"Well, I declare!" she cried. "If boys ever deserved

it they do. Poor fellows!" laughing. And then gravely,—

"Oh, these have been sad times for all our nuptials. Let us think we have all wisely done our duty. A time for rest has come, no matter how, to us all. The fault was not ours. Let us pray that peace may come ere the spring comes again."

She had an unique breakfast party that morning. Carter was fully determined to be excused.

"I raly seldom or *ever eat* ennything myself," he was desperate enough to say. But Edith, who had taken an immense liking to him, declared that henceforth he was to be a part of her household, quite won him to an embarrassed acquiescence in her wish. Red-Wing, the forest born gentleman, cool and collected, was quite equal to his new surroundings, quick and alert, with Anita by his side. Lieutenant Gordon also made his appearance at the table.

Some things may be disposed of finally, and a little space and quiet found for my hastily wed Anglo-American lovers to cultivate each other's acquaintance, and prepare for the inevitable. Art may not require it, I trust my readers will.

There was joy in Detroit, in Michigan, in all the wide North-west. Slow as were the currents of intelligence, news, this was so good, so precious, so like a message of mercy down out of heaven, that it took wings and blew itself "in every eye." Evil tidings, slander, malignant lies, never propagated themselves with greater celerity. In a geographical way the North-west was isolated. That which is now a centre and seat of power of the Republic, was then a dim outline, cut off by mountains and wide sweeps of wilderness. The lakes, instead of being a highway to and along its northern borders were desert wastes of water, hindrances to intercourse. For all this vast region, the war was over. It was to rage for fifteen months along the lower border, the Atlantic coast, in the south-west and on the ocean. Harrison had conquered a real peace for Michigan, Ohio, Kentucky, Indiana, and Illinois.

Young General Cass was appointed by Harrison civil and military governor of Michigan, and retained his brigade to maintain his dignity and authority, and commence a brilliant career in the civil service, which was only to miss the highest place in the republic.

The "Ariel" reached Malden after midnight of the eighth. Two days later, she started down the lake carrying Mrs. Proctor, her children and servants, the paroled officers, Colonel Warburton and his subordinates. Mrs. Gordon and her husband, now able to travel, also sailed in her. A sad parting it was to the tender friends, and as each anticipated, a final one. Each had her young husband and no parting from another could be inconsolable. Another awaited Edith, a sorer trial.

Detroit, the region around both sides of the river, was full of Indians, without clothes, without food, abject. Harrison treated them with the kindest consideration. No effort was made to secure undue advantages and cessions of land from them. All he required was peace, a return to their villages, and a cultivation of good-will toward their white neighbors. He was told of the magnanimous conduct of Tecumseh toward the unfortunate inhabitants of Frenchtown, which he fully appreciated. He had a personal interview with the Prophet, which gave him a more favorable impression of his character.

On the morning of the tenth, Round-head, Walk-in-the-Water, and their Wyandots, left for the Sandusky, Black-Hoof and his bands undertaking to see them safely home.

Harrison saw the uselessness of attempting to deal with Walk-in the-Water, for slaying Mr. Grayson. The chief was not in his service, nor in any way answerable to him. The act occurred in the territory of a foreign power. It was a time of war, and although the British had laid down their arms, the battle was raging on their right. He refused to see the chief or permit him to appear in the general council.

The Miamis, with Rouceville and the warriors beyond the Wabash, started for home in the afternoon of the same day. With these went Jim Blue-Jacket, and all except the Sioux, the remote Chippewas, the Sacs, and Foxes, who were to move the morning of the second day later. Their journey was three or four times the distance of any of the others, their preparation more extensive and elaborate.

With them would go Anita and Red-Wing. They had remained guests of Dudley and Edith. Everything that could be done—that their means of transportation enabled them to carry for the journey, for use when the young wife should reach her husband's lodge, was furnished. Remittances in the future were also provided for.

General Harrison treated the chiefs of the remoter nations with distinguished consideration, made them presents, and ample provision for their return. Colonel Ball, with 250 of his dragoons, would attend them to Fort Dearborn, with part of a regiment of infantry who would repair and for the time occupy that post. Dudley presented Red-Wing a finely caparisoned horse, pistols, and all complete.

Half the afternoon of the last day the daughter of lost Cheeseekau went about silent, a little nervous, with a peculiar light in her eyes. Edith two or three times caught those almost wonderful eyes, wide and large some said for her face, fixed upon her with an expression of sadness that disappeared in a sweet little smile, and then she would turn away. She who had made a study of the girl, knew her thought was of their last moment on to-morrow. She was her old self the next morning. She made her appearance arrayed for her journey.

The Indian army, their lodge poles and covers, all the movables of a body or rather bodies of travelling natives, with their horses and dogs, their women and children, moved early on their westward returnless journey.

Anita and her husband would be accompanied by Edith and Dudley, the first few miles, and they sent their horses over to the American side the night before. The morning was cloudless, the sky and earth lit up with a softened splendor of light and warm color.

Anita on horseback was an unique, an ideal figure, and never more striking than when she sat her gayly caparisoned pony this morning. Her scarlet hat, with its war eagle feathers, her closely draped upper person, rounded and quite perfected, branching to exquisitely formed shoulders over which she permitted her glossy black hair to fall unbound, her short skirt, and perfectly formed lower limbs from the knee down, shown in bright closely fitting garments, with her slender moccasined feet lightly touching the stirrups,—not needed for one trained as she had been,—a silken sash worn over her right shoulder with her ivory hilted dagger,—altogether a figure to ride at the head of a squadron of the wild horsemen of the plains, toward which her way led.

Edith in her civilized draping was scarcely less striking; mounted on a taller horse, which equalized her seeming height, the two contrasted, and each helped the advantages of the other. The brides rode in advance, followed by their husbands. Red-Wing, in the gay trappings of a young chief, on his return with his bride, was in excellent spirits. If there was in his finely wrought nature anywhere now a tint of sadness or regret, it was sympathetic for the hidden sorrow of his wife. For the present the eyes and thought of each of these fortunate youths was filled with the form just before him, which was every half minute flashing back eyes and face to gladden him with the light of her beauty.

Rare and rarely blessed young men, permitted to follow these so tenderly attached young women to the near final parting, where each shall receive his own from the arms of the other! Is there a more blessed privilege of love than its right of consoling the loved?

The girls wisely had, as they thought, their real parting the night before, said their final words, taking last embraces, shed their tears and then turned each to the eager arms of her husband. They were to ride forth to the parting of the ways this morning, and were to wave each other good-by kisses, gayly, from the hand, and so they rode out, and were gay and bright, talked and laughed, let the morning have the music of their voices as if no fountain of tears could exist in either of the light soft swaying forms. The young men shared their moods. They had little to say to each other, and had to call the aid of Anita to say that little. Neither was essential to the other. Red-Wing had complemented Dudley's present, by the gift of his war horse, with its trappings. The young man was not yet a full master of all the horse's wild ways, and found some employment in his mere movement and in humoring himself to them.

At length Anita became silent, with her eyes looking forward. She spoke not a word. Edith said two or three little things, essayed to sing parts of two or three little airs, and then amused herself with cutting the bright autumn leaves within reach of her whip, as she passed. They had ridden an hour, over the level plain, along the dry sandy trail, the rear of the ever receding western fac' ing column in sight.

At length, upon the margin of a shallow little spring run which crossed the track, the Indian girl drew her rein, sprang from her saddle, and turned back to Dudley. The eyes of the expectant young men were upon her, and both stepped to the ground, the chief leading his horse forward. As she approached him Dudley received her in his arms, she threw hers about his neck, pressed her lips upon each cheek, ran back, took Edith from her saddle and pressed her with a passionate cry of pain to her heart—again and again, with sobs and cries of anguish she pressed her—kissing lips, and cheeks, and brow, and eyes. For a minute or two there was an utter abandonment to sorrow. Then suddenly controlling herself, she placed the overcome woman in the arms of the waiting Dudley, turned, vaulted into her saddle, cast her face down into her hands, with a sharp call to her horse, which leaping the stream, flew with her after the disappearing rear guard. Red-Wing had to put his mettled steed to full speed ere he overtook, and gathered up her abandoned rein. The child never raised her face, nor threw a glance backward; nor did Edith cast a look after

her vanishing form.   Holding her gently, the eyes of
Dudley followed that, until streaming hair and dancing
plume were lost in a turn of the trail.

This was the leave-taking of the Shawanoe's daughter.
In the coming years did Dudley and Edith visit her
beyond the Great Lake?   We know they did.

CHAPTER XXXII.

EDITH was entirely overcome by the passionate outburst of Anita's grief, which took her by surprise. She had not correctly estimated the strength of the band which united them nor the pain of breaking it, until it was torn asunder in this last moment by her sister. Perhaps this was requisite to a true apprehension of the real position the child, unconsciously to her, occupied in her heart. Dudley purposely retained her in his arms until the space within vision had lost the voiceless form. When the obtruding forest hid it, he tenderly conducted her back to a little recess in the small trees bordering the trail, led her horse to her side, placed her in the saddle, and mounting his own they moved on their return home.

"Oh, Cliffton, your wife is such a poor weak child, her heart has been so broken and torn. How would she have lived through it all were it not for you? How can I ever sufficiently thank God for you?"

"She has been so tried. Never a precious girl so much so," he said with a caress. "What she calls her weakness is her noblest woman's strength. It seems I fell in love with a high, proud heroine. There came to my arms a tender, loving woman."

These words were said as she would have had them. A look of tender gratitude through her tears was his

23

reward.   A little later her eyes cast downward, she said, "I shall deserve these words."   Then raising them to his face she went on, "Do you remember when you made that strange speech to me, on the "Ariel," I told you that whatever you said, whatever you did, would be wisest— best?"

They rode silently and slowly for many minutes, her thoughts turning to—pursuing—her flying sister.   His, as his eyes filled, with her.   Then she trusted her voice to speak of the lost one.

"There never was—never will be such another.   The utmost possibilities of her race, were her wonderful family. She found a new side of me and struck her roots and tendrils all through me, and when she tore herself—" Her voice broke and her head went down— "And there was that exquisite flavor of the woods in all she did, in all her ways."   She raised her head, and let her vision sweep off over the tops of the scattered wide branched oaks, seeing nothing, but trying to call in her thoughts, which were yet too nearly akin to feeling.   "I had such funny notions of being set apart when she came to us, and as the strong elements of her nature made themselves felt, she should be set apart too.   Lovers—husbands —were not to be thought of.   I think she understood me better than I did, so free and natural had been her life and dreams, which girls' thoughts often are.   The study of me, my position toward you, led her to think of lovers of her own, if a girl needs leading in that direction before a lover comes.   There were a score of young chiefs about her all the last year," looking off.   "Then came this young prince from under our sundown, and— well, she is gone."   These last words cost her an effort, but she said them.   "It is best for her, best for her race,

She will be a great woman, an uncrowned queen, ruling in wisdom and prudence. Tecumapease is a great woman; Anita will be greater. She is educated, knows something of the world, of the modern nations, has a wider outlook."

Then she told of her family, the early loss of the father, the mother, a wise woman—of Cheeseekau, his tutelage of Tecumseh, the tragedy of his early death, by which he gained the lone title—"The Lost." Then passing to Tecumseh she told the incident of his speech to the chiefs, and the delivery of his sword on the margin of the swamp, and eve of the battle. She said in reply to his questions, that the wife of the chief was a very commonplace woman, and the son a youth of no promise. Resuming her talk of the incidents of the day of battle, learned from Anita, she said she knew of his own part at the death of Tecumseh.

And then she insisted he should tell her of his personal experience in the battle itself, which he did, giving her in modest, graphic words a fair account of himself.

As she looked at the slender, erect, lithe form, broad of shoulders, and pictured the now tender laughing eyes, flashing with battle ardor, riding at the head of the onrushing column of shouting Kentuckians, directly on the muzzles of Tecumseh's warriors, her face blanched, she hastily sketched her vision in words.

"Oh, what a wonder you escaped! God spared you in mercy to me. Tell me what you thought of in the minute or two, after passing the small swamp, before you received the fire?"

"Well, there was no clear thought—a wild rush, trampling horses, yelling men, a rush of feeling. We

were going for Tecumseh's warriors, would be upon them.
—that was about all."

"No fear of death—apprehension?"

"Oh, well, men have that, I suppose, above the average
brute, when he approaches a battle. It was all one with
us, when we were fairly under motion, the bugle *tanging*
in our ears."

"Did you think of nothing, remember nothing, see no
inner thing?"

"Oh," laughing, "one thing was always with me. I saw
the most beautiful, the most scornful face, wearing the expression of that tent scene," looking toward her, and
laughing.

"Oh, you did? Oh, Cliffton, is it true? Is it true?"

"It was always with me."

"And you thought—?" pausing.

"Well," laughing, "death was not to be avoided."

"Cliffton! It was not that which sent you to lead that
rushing column?"

"No. Had I known what I now know, I should have
gone all the same. I should have thought, perhaps Edith
will know I am not unworthy her love."

"And you did think—Oh, you did think—what?"
eagerly.

"Well, something, a little—perhaps she may hear that
he knew how to die as a soldier should."

"Oh, Cliffton! These words reveal all to me. I am
glad to know it—to know how much I owe you."

"It seemed a little grievous, then," he said, laughing
again in his old bright way. "I am glad it all happened
as it did. It brings out all the hidden things of your
nature—Oh, Lord! what a speech!" he said, interrupt-

ing himself. " I'm what Home once called me, I do believe," laughing again.

" Home ! what did he call you ? "

" A prig—he said ' a damn'd prig.' It was not intended for my ear, so I did not hear it—until now," laughing pleasantly.

" Well, never mind Home—go on, finish what you were going to say."

" Well, merely, that you were all the time nearer and dearer to me, for my having not read you truly at first."

" Did I never appear to you in another light ? "

" Oh, before *that time*, you were in the light of dear Black River days."

" When did you begin to love me, Cliff ? " in a delicious confidential voice.

" When I first saw you."

" Oh ! Oh ! when did you know you loved me, I mean ? "

" The very next day—before noon."

" Oh, you did ? Had you loved so much, you knew it right off ? "

" Oh, I had a boy's, a young man's fancies. I knew this was love, it was so different, so deep, so high, so stimulating to do and try to deserve."

She looked up in his eyes, as if she would gladly cast herself into his arms. She said—"Oh, Cliff ! This has been the saddest, dearest morning ! I am so glad to have had it—I am only learning something of you. I must learn some things now. Nobody knows anything of you but dear old Carter."

" I am glad to hear you call him ' dear old Carter '—I am so glad you want to keep him with us," he said.

" I do love him. I mean to keep him. I am going to

talk with him.   Then there is a little place I am going
to take you to, just as soon as General Harrison spares
you to me, and to yourself.   There, don't say a word."
Then raising her bridle hand, her trained horse dashed off
in a light, billowy gallop, emulated by the trained Indian
war horse.

CHAPTER XXXIII.

EDITH had more time on her hands than she cared to consume alone. Dudley was still very busy at headquarters, where for the time his chief could not dispense with his services, and Edith cultivated Carter, who, from shyness and diffidence, became communicative, under the skill and delicacy of her approaches. She found him a gentle, tender soul, with an unsunned nature, having a good deal of information upon the one absorbing object of interest to her. She led him to talk of her husband, the afternoon of Anita's departure, a subject of quite as much interest to him as to her.

"You see, Mr. Carter, I really do not know much of my husband; he don't talk of himself, and I don't know any one who knows him nearly so well as you do. You've been with him alone in his careless hours, as on the march and elsewhere."

"'E ain't much uv a hand to talk 'bout 'imself," said the old hunter, reflectively.

"No, and I don't yet have much of his time, and then he does not want to talk of himself, and I do not know what to ask him about."

"Wal, you jes start 'im on things we're you 'r consarned, an 'el talk fast eñuff."

"O—h! That will bring him out—will it?" greatly pleased.

"I never seen a young feller sick 'o talkin' 'bout 'is gal."

"Did you ever have a girl, Mr. Carter?"

"Who—me have a gal? Oh, I was allus in the woods, and kind o' shy like," he answered, grinning grimly.

"You take a good deal of interest though, in the likings of young men and women for each other?"

"Sartin, sartin. I allus wanted to see 'em true and git to have one anuther, uv course."

"Well, when did you fancy that Cliff and I liked each other?"

"The fust time I seen ye."

"Tell me about it—what you thought?"

"Wal, 'e was a helpin' yer pa up the side 'ill, an' you was a lookin up in 'is face like."

"Yes, I remember it very well. What was Cliff doing?"

"Wal, 'e was a lookin' down inter yourn, mosely. I didn't see 'im do much else long them air times."

"Well," laughing, "he did do a good deal of that I am very certain," the lovely color growing lovelier in her face.

"Thinks I to myself—thinks I, young woman, ef ye wants a young man, 'ere 'e is."

Edith laughed with genuine mirthfulness. "What a dear, funny old hunter! I wasn't thinking of wanting a young man at all, then. I was only so glad for his saving an old one—my father."

"Mebby so. 'E may a got inter yer 'art, without yer thinkin' on't a' tall. I ruther guess tho, ye thought on 'im purty soon—that's my idee."

"What makes you think so?"

"Ye asks questions, 'n I'll—an' I'll have to answer

'em well's I can. I'le bet 'e thought 'o you that night, by the way 'e looked at you."

" Did he say anything ? " asked the deeply interested girl.

" Mose fellers so reddy to laf is reddy to talk. 'E ain't one 'o them sort. Enny one could a tole w'at 'e thought."

" Well, I asked you what made you think I must have thought of him, as my lover ? "

" Wal, I spose a feller 'oo thought as much uv a gal as 'e did 'o you, would let 'er see it, an' know it, purty soon. An' enny gal would be glad to like 'im back, sartin shure."

Edith's laughter at this speech was delicious to hear. " What a dear, delightful, logical old hunter you are ! You are too funny for this world. So you think any girl would like Cliffton ? "

" Ef 'e liked her."

" Did you ever see him anywhere, where young ladies were present ? "

" No 'en I 'ardly ever seen a young lady."

" When did you first see him ? "

" 'Bout three year ago, or a leetle better. 'E was to Cleveland, fixin a block 'ouse. 'E was to my bruther's tavern there."

" That was three years ago—when next did you see him ? "

" Wal, my bruther Lorenzo 's a hunter, an' Major Dudley, 'e 's Captin then, wanted to hunt, 'n so 'twas 'greed on that 'e should cum the nex year, 'n 'e cum, so we fixed on Lorenzo's ole campin' place, you see, on Black River."

" So I am indebted to your brother after all, for meeting my husband !   How strange things so remote, should be the hinges of our fortunes ! "   She paused to think of it.   " Now let us come back," she said.   " You thought he loved me, and I should like him when I found it out —how is that ? "

" Wal, I dunno as findin' out has much hand in 't after all.   I think them as God means to jine, loves soon as they see's one anuther.   Them's my idees."

" And you think God meant to join us as husband and wife ? " much moved.

" I sartin do.   That 's wat 'e wus in the woods there fer, an' that 's wat you cum there fer—to see 'n be seen."

" Bless you—you dear old hunter !   So of course we were to love each other.   How would he know I was the one ? "

" Enny man would a trusted ye fust sight."

" Oh, you dear old man ! You believe in me. You shall love me as your child, be as my father, or a dear old uncle.   You will help me care for Cliffton—*our* Cliffton. You can be with him where I cannot go. I want to go back to the Black River days—'days of the shining river ' Anita called them. When you got back from Cleveland, what did you think ? "

" I was glad on 't."

" Glad of what ? "

" Wal, I thought a good deal o' you two—you see."

" Yes, well ? "

" I thought 'twas all right 'tween you ; I sartin did."

" You thought we had told each other—each knew the other's thoughts and feelings ? "

" Ye see I'd never seen a rale young gentleman 'an ·lady afore."

"Before they came to be in love with each other—is that it?"

"I 'spose I sposed they'd kiss one anuther—an'—an—"

"And that would be the end of it?" laughing.

"Wal, no—the beginnin' on't, mebbe."

"Oh," laughing almost immoderately.

"I mean they'd git married—that's w'at I meant."

"You dear, true-hearted old man! A young man and woman love, kiss, and get married?"

"Yis, w'y not?"

"And then more kisses?"

"Yis, I spect so," grinning funnily.

She now laughed with perfect abandon, and though he fancied the lovely creature was laughing at him, he rather liked to hear her, her mirth was so musical.

"Don't ye think that's the true way?" he ventured to ask.

"That is not Shakespeare's idea. He says the course of true love never does run smooth."

"Wal, I dunno nuthin' 'bout Shakespair. I guess true love 'l run smooth and fast if you'll let it. 'N if you'n Dudley 'd staid there with yer pa an that Ingin gal, in the woods, a week, alone—I'd like to know?" with considerable spirit.

The young wife burst into peals and shrieks of laughter, with a flash of color suffusing cheek and throat.

"O you dear, funny, direct old hunter! I must tell Cliff of that. You would have left us there?"

"I done all I could. I managed so 't 'e had to go on with ye."

"O—h, was that your work? Thank you! Thank you!"

"I kinder tho't ye'd hate t' part," looking her honestly in the eyes.

"It was time we parted according to you. But, you dear old man,—thought of things bad is as impossible to you as it was to us. Now, sometime I will tell you of the Huron and Fort Miami, when Cliffton and I have talked them over. He has cause to feel sore over some things that happened at each of those places. I don't want there should be a speck of misunderstanding left in his mind."

"Ye needn't feel consarned. 'E don't see enny specks in ye," said the moved old man.

"No, I know he don't now. I don't want to leave the germ of one. I want to ask one or two things that you know of that happened at your Camp Meigs."

"The major had a tough spell on't there," said Carter, reflectively.

"I am afraid he did. It was an awfully '*tough spell*' to me, but more blessed than sore, after all."

"I'm feáred 'twas all sore for 'im. Wat kin I tell ye?"

"I want to know how he knew I was at Fort Miami?"

"Wal, I spose Wasegoboah must 'a tole 'im somethin' 'bout 'oo ye was, and mebby his seein' ye and Red-Wing's wife to Detroit that air time may have gin 'im a notion—ye must ask 'im. Enny way he ast me ef I'd know ye, er know Nita. He depended on her, I suspec'. Ye see I'd been t' Detroit 'n had a suit o' close, and I'se down there the day afore 'n I seen the Ingin gal; wal I seen ye both, an' tole 'im. 'E said 'e meant ter try and see if he couldn't see ye."

"Did he tell you that?" a little eagerly.

"'E said, sez 'e, 'I mus tell 'er somethin'.' I sed, sez I, ''e might write it in a letter 'n I'd take it.' 'E sed, sez

’e, ‘No, a man as writes wa’t I wants to tell ’er, mus’ be a coward enny way.’ Them’s ’is words as I say em,” emphatically.

“Oh, Carter, you ain’t making this up?”

The old hunter looked surprised and hurt. “You kin ast ’im,” looking at her reproachfully.

“Oh, it seemed most too good. Go on, you dear old man.”

“Wal, I thought twas mose too pesky risky for ’im to go there, but ’e knowed bess. ’E wanted I should see Nita right off; wal, so nex mornin, ’e set me cross an ’e foun’ a squaw-blow, bout the fust o’ that spring, ’an ’e gin it to me to gin to Nita, ’n I did, ’n tole ’er wa’t ’e wanted, ’e ’d be there that same night. Wa’l, she wus tickeled enymose to death. You seen me there in the little gully there.”

“I saw you and can understand all about Anita,” greatly interested.

“She sed you’d be drefful glad to see ’im; an’ she’d meet us, jess up the holler, by the spring run, an’ take ’im in to ye, ’n I didn’t know, I sposed ye’d be glad t’ see ’im. Wal, we talked it over, ’n she gave me a scrap o’ paper, fer to han’ to ’im, and some cole meat an biskit for myself, ’n that night we went.”

Edith drew a long breath, as if some dark matter was finally made clear, and strangely enough, was profoundly interested in his dull narrative, in the broad elliptical vernacular of his native New England. She now knew that Cliffton acted from his own prompting, and not by any supposed word from her.

“Mr. Carter, I can’t tell you how much this pleases me. So he wanted to tell me something, very, very much?

It was too precious to be written, and sent to me. He must tell it himself. What do you suppose it was?"

"Wal, I spect it was suthin ye's most dyin' to hear."

"Indeed it was.   You brought him, and he did tell it, as a woman wants such a precious thing told, and—" · Her head went down with a little sob, as the scene came back to her. "Oh, it was a thing, a scene from a lovely romance, such as rarely happens," musingly, as to herself.

"Ye see, Miss Dudley, I reely thought ye wanted to see 'im enymose as much as 'e wanted t' see you—I sartin did."

"You had a right to think so.   I did want to see him, Mr. Carter, there was a misapprehension.   I was to blame, and I was not.   I fear I cannot make it clear to you ; perhaps not to him."

"Wal, I won't bleeve nuthin' bad o' you ennyway. The groun' where ye stand is richer fer ye'r stanin' on't, an' I cant begin to think so well on ye, as 'e does."

"Oh, you old flatterer ! what a way you have of saying things that a woman loves to hear."

"Wal, ye see I spose its all in me yit—all that a man has to say to wimin."

"All saved up for me?   And it never turned sour ? " laughing very pleasantly.

"One thing more—when he met you later—that night —you went back to Camp Meigs together; tell me all that he said, how he looked, if you could see him, and the tone of his voice," settling herself to hear a long story.

Carter, in his simple, direct way, told her in ample detail, bringing out the features of Dudley's depression in a striking way : so much so that the young wife was

greatly moved. It had many " Sez 'e to me, sez 'e," and
" Sez I to 'im, sez I," in it. She laughed over the wagers
made and won. Declared that he should demand pay-
ment.

"You had a great deal more confidence in me than
he did, Mr. Carter," she said. And later—" I want you
should do something for me, and for him too. I want
you should take a little boat I will give you and go down
the river, to Frenchtown, carry a letter from me to some
good friends there, and stay there till *we* come. You can
take your rifle, and hunt if you are lonesome ; it won't be
long."

"Sartin, sartin. I'll be glad to. And ye needn't be
in no hurray. I long to git inter the woods agin; the
Ingins must a killed and scart off purty much all the
game roun' there. No matter, the woods is all there."

And so that was arranged.

CHAPTER XXXIV.

ON the morning following this conversation, with rifle and supplies, Carter set out on his voyage down the Detroit, leaving the wedded lovers to the cultivation and revelation of their latent selves, each possibly astonished to find that a love seemingly so perfect was yet endowed with a capacity for augmentation. We know the wise woman had a purpose to explore the hidden, the sore places in the young husband's heart and memory, for hurts from her own hand.

On the evening after Carter's departure, Cliffton, by the merest accident of course, discovered a certain ribbon before mentioned, which, with a shy, half help he identified as his own, attached to Queen Charlotte's decoration, —so often shown the reader,—when he tossed it with scornful contempt to the feet of the girl, in the memorable tent scene. He regarded it with amazement. It will be remembered that later on that night, the oft transferred gift was restored to him by Tecumseh. Angry, and then indifferent to it, on his return to the fort, he put it by, without inspection, and never opened the parcel, until hurriedly on the morning of the last fateful battle, and when again restored by Anita, on the morning of her return with her bridegroom to Moravian town, his heart and thought were too full of the engrossing things of that day to note the difference of color and texture of ribbons.

This was the hour of perfect fulness, yet capable of receiving more. He produced the trinket, and compared the attachments—the first that Edith knew of his re-possession of the bauble.

"Oh, Edith!" he cried, "you retained and wore this for my love, even then?"

"Yes, Cliffton," both much moved.

"And this?" holding up the ribbon still attached to the trinket.

"I tied it in, myself, hoping it would tell you of Edith and her love. Had it failed to reach you, that night, Anita would have carried it to you in your walled camp."

What he did just then, not having words, was to kneel by the low camp-stool where she sat, and place his arms about her. Then in due course followed all of the interview of the Maumee, that romantic episode of the war, the sequent act of our little drama, now recalled, explained and forever disposed of as a possible source of future disquiet. Edith then told of the rumor of his death, and the anguish of an hour which seemed an eternity of suffering to her.

Holding the recovered gift of the German princess, she said :

"I am so glad Anita restored this. What curious things it has done, and misdone ; poor, unconscious thing. I shall now cherish it for Tecumseh's sake."

"And I, mainly for its message of love, now just delivered," said Cliffton. "How stupid and blind a man can be! You suffered more in an hour than I in my lifetime," he added.

They were, in talk, on the backward journey over the old road, and soon reached the full banked Huron. What a theme that was, and so fully talked up! When Cliffton

24

told her that had he met her for leave-taking, he should
have declared his love, even in the presence of her father,
she opened her eyes in surprise.

"What if I had?" he asked.

"Oh, I don't know." Then she told him of her talk
with Carter, some parts with a little increase of color, and
recurring to his question, repeated :

"Oh, I don't know. That first flash of the Huron was
a revelation of my heart to me. We should part.
When I got back the next night and found you had
gone, I was very wretched. Had you told me, I think
my father would then have assented to an engagement,"
closing her eyes to let all the possibilities present themselves to the inner vision.

The paradise of the Indian summer was in its decline
and yet had gained in charmed and melancholy beauty.
It would take parts of two days to reach river Raisin.
They started the next morning. The first few miles were
in a way abandoned to the emulous horses—a little over-
spirited from the two days idleness. Edith was exhilarated. Her presence, the crisp air, sunshine, the half-
wild leap of the wholly wild Indian trained horse, lent
wings to the spirit of Cliffton. When the steeds subsided
to a more ordinary travelling gait, he from choice
remained silent, giving himself to a seeming study of
the flexile grace of Edith's form, and the ever varying
expression of her face, which seemed to catch even added
light from his eyes.

"Why do you look at me so this morning, Cliffton?"
she asked.

"Look at you so—do I not alway? If it pleases you
less to look *so* at you, I must look at you some other
way."

"No, no. I love to have you. I feel exalted when your eyes praise me. I feel—I *feel* beautiful," dropping her eyes in quickened sensibility.

"Then you shall live ever with a consciousness of beauty," said the confident man.

"Cliffton, you will spoil me with praise."

"My tongue seldom, my eyes ever. You ask me a question and almost reprove my true answer," he said.

"Then I will enjoy your eyes in silence. Let me think there is some inner goodness, and fancy you see it in my face. That is not a bit a nice speech," after a pause, laughing and coloring.

"Truth must know it is true, and that truth is beautiful. Oh, I think it was a lovely speech."

"Praise me only with your eyes, Cliffton ; your words are much like a flatterer's."

"I am more than content, Edith, I do not want to talk. I like to hear your voice—only don't talk wisely, as you are apt to do ; talk idly—a mere murmur of words, that I may laugh with you at them."

"You have not answered my question," looking from the margins of her wide eyes. "Why you looked *so* at me ? "

"Because—because since your words of last night, I see more in your face ; so I look *more so*." And then they laughed as children at a wit which none but children see. The wedded girl had still a purpose. She sobered down. Her mood was his.

"I wish you felt like talking some. There are so many things I want to know, which no one can tell me but you."

"As what—Edith? I'm sure you can get anything I know—or half know, by asking."

"Tell me of your father."

"My father?" The voice fell a little, and some of the vivacity went out of his countenance.

"Is he a sad theme, Cliffton?"

"No, not sad—so much—I've learned so much that throws light on what I never understood—it came so late." What he said fully confirmed her father's statement. He never made his home in Boston after the final escape of Mr. Grayson. Cliff's mother was the youngest daughter of the wealthy Scotch house of Cliffton of New York. His father was well toward forty at marriage. Cliff, the sole child, losing his mother in infancy was cared for by her elder maiden sister Lucy. "Dear, dear Aunt Lucy." Colonel Dudley died when the son was ten years of age, having lost his fortune—supposed to be considerable. Cliff was by his mother's family thought to share the open handed nature of his father, and trusted with but a narrow allowance for his mother's portion, one-third of which he would receive at twenty five, and the residue five and ten years later. Many questions were asked and answered. Aunt Lucy was brought out in high relief, as was Boston.

Edith was thoughtful and tender.

"Do you remember my father's idea, that all the events of all these years, large and small, were but the shaping hands, conspiring to make or mar our fortunes—to produce, lead, direct us to each other? And so it can be easily made to seem. Oh, dear! All that has happened, the pain, suffering, loss—the long years of war and blood even, which have so strangely wrought to this end—I am sad and humiliated. Oh, weak and impotent conclusion!"

"That is too depressing," answered the youth, a little under the influence of the sombre spell their talk had worked up. "We, our fortunes, lives, even, are but the most trifling incidents thrown off by the march of great events and the forces impelling them. When you sink their importance to the mere causes of us and ours, striking things in a small way are the seeming result. It was by noticing these seeming events and their play with men that the old Greeks took and perfected the idea of their drama. Always the work of the gods, blind, relentless forces—their drama and its 'unities' never possible in human life."

"My father said his idea was from the pagan in him—you remember," she added.

"It is too depressing," he replied. "Let us run away from it." Laying a hand lightly on her rein, and signalling the horses, away they went at nearly full speed, over the hard level road through the forest, whose trees seemed to whirl and fly the other way. A third of a mile was thus passed, when the horses were checked, and held in, the Indian merely blowing out a long breath, while the civilized horse was a little longer in regaining his ordinary respiration. During the race the eager boy and girl looked into each other's faces with laughter-flashing eyes. When they drew rein—

"Oh, that was glorious!" exclaimed she, when the excited animal spirits burst forth in peals of laughter, meaningless save to say they rejoiced in their escape from depression.

"Well, I shall see Aunt Lucy the first of anybody," was Edith's first declaration.

"She's more romantic than dear old Carter," said the still laughing man. "She'll spend more wonders, and tears, and 'did you evers,' over you and our story, than living woman ever shed before!"

In the afternoon of the second day out, they drew near the little town. It had not yet occurred to Dudley to ask the particular reason, if any, which moved Edith to visit it. His trained eye ran over the ground, stockade, and surroundings, and he made some observation which betrayed a want of information of the battles of which it was the scene, and she corrected him in a way showing her perfect familiarity with details. To a look of surprise she said,—

"I was not at the last battle, I was very near here immediately after—the same day."

Then she told the story of her alarm at Malden, her presentiment, half vision of him dying in the snow. Spite of her, she was much affected by the recital. He heard her with astonishment, paused, turned his horse, and sat facing her, greatly moved, till her clear, rapid recital was ended, and then resumed the way, silent for a minute.

"Oh, Edith! and that was away back, before Camp Meigs!"

Much was said of it by this moved man. Finally, "What have you brought me here for? Was it to tell me this precious thing of your love and devotion? What else is there? I begin to feel abused," laughing again.

"Well, I have some friends living here. I wanted to see them; I wanted to draw you away; I wanted to show them *my husband.*" She was not yet used to the last two words, and spoke them with a sweet bashfulness, very charming.

"Oh, you did?" in a small honeyed voice.

"Of course; any girl would. They've heard of you, and will be glad to see you," running her eye over his well worn undress uniform.

" You ought to be in full epaulets, and feathers—perhaps."

He laughed. "You know except in Cass's staff, there ain't a good coat in the army."

Light soon came to him. Children, one or two women were abroad, as if on the watch. As they passed the first house, all the inmates came out, and very soon along the one street, in advance of them, until before they reached the bridge, quite all the population were at large, eager, respectful, yet seeing Edith only, saluting her, running forward to salute her, touch her hand, her habit, her horse.

Dudley at the earliest manifestation saw he was on the eve of important discovery.

"Oh, Carter is here," he said at first. "What has he been saying, I wonder?" The happy Edith only laughed. " Ah, this is none of his work." And then as he saw she was *the one* object of interest—" By George ! I believe *I'm* showing *my wife !*" he said, " only I have nothing to do with it," he added later.

They reached the bridge, attended by all the population of that side, and passed it to find all on the south side awaiting them. They made their way slowly, to the late headquarters of the once general of the North-western Army, where they alit, surrounded by the pleased and happy villagers. On the bridge, Dudley saw a man he knew, whom he beckoned to him, and from whom he learned the cause of this ovation to his bride. When he removed her from the saddle she saw he knew.

"Are you glad, Cliffton?" in a low voice.

His answer was to raise and press with his lips the hand he held, in silence. All saw the act, its grace, many then knew the cause of this homage. Many glances of but half approval had been cast at him. What man could be fit mate for the peerless Edith? As he now arose from this tribute, so tall, gallant and manly, they were content with him.

As the lovely, tearful, blushing, smiling girl, now by his side, turned to them and said "My husband," exclamations of approval, admiration— "What a lovely pair!" came to them from all parts of the two or three hundreds of gratified people. Then they were conducted to their quarters, the best the little town could furnish.

Carter returned from his hunt at sundown, bringing the venison of a fine "spike horned buck." He reported large game scarce, but the woods were there, and Edith announced her intention for a ramble in them the next day. Cliff expressed a wish to make an excursion down the river the next morning, to which Edith assented. She divined his purpose—to find Wasegoboah's boat. Poor Cliff!

"Mr. Carter will row," she said, and then noting a flitting shadow pass over Dudley's face— "He will be as glad and proud to go as a boy of ten. Not the least restraint upon us, and as silent as a child, to whom speech has not yet been sent." That settled it.

The next was one of the last serene mornings of the waning season. The sun lost his rays in the lower atmosphere, through which he showed but a dim disk. Carter, with the boat ready for its burden, by the little quay, awaited the approach of the favored ones. As might be expected, the man was too absorbed by his companion to more than note that the little birch was one of the smaller and most exquisite in model and finish, which would once have challenged his wonder and admiration. He placed Edith in the bow, and when Carter had taken his place as boatman, carefully disposed of himself midships—quite filling the dainty, yet in Carter's hands, perfectly safe little shallop. The prow is turned down stream. We have misgiving. Will it ever turn back? In fancy we follow along the sandy shore. A little burst of exclamation from Cliff, and laughter on Edith's part, and we know he has discovered the secret and identity of the boat. We know he will hear the glad, happy girl's story of it, and tell her his own. As we move along, catching their glad voices and mirthful notes, anticipating their future, the boat approaches a wooded bend of the river. We may go no further. Its gayly decorated prow, Edith Cliffton, Carter, pass it, and are forever lost to our eyes. Eagerly we bend forward. A faint echo of laughter ending in a sigh, as do all echoes of things past, and silence and solitude, never again to be broken, are upon us.

Have I a reader who stands with me, gazing down the vanishing stream with regret for our loss, we may turn again to the idyl of the autumn woods on the banks of that stream, called in the soft tongue of Anita, " River of the Shining Water."·

FINIS.

SUPPLEMENTAL.

TECUMSEH.

PUCKISHINWAY, Tecumseh's father, was a chief of renown, and his mother, Methoataskee, was an extraordinary woman, of the Shawanoe Turtle Tribe. The family all had fine persons, and unusual mental endowments. Losing his father, Tecumseh was reared by his eldest brother, Cheeseekau, who spared no pains to form an exceptional and extraordinary character. The statement of Grayson to General Brock, as in my text, of his teaching, is strictly true in fact, as are most of the remarkable things there set forth. The brothers were both slain in battle; both had presentiments of their fate. The speech given as that of the younger on the eve of battle, is authentic, as is his more famous speech to Proctor.

Various translations have been made of the name Tecumseh, or more properly Tecumtha. Drake renders it the Shooting Star. Another the Flying Tiger, and still another, Wild Cat that leaps. It marks the eminence of Tecumseh, that an otherwise not remarkable man was elected to the Vice-Presidency of the United States on the popular delusion that he slew the chief at the battle of the Thames. Colonel Johnson never claimed this for himself. It is incontestable that he fell, and was helped away at the commencement of the battle, which continued with great fury till Tecumseh was slain fifteen or twenty minutes later. His fall caused a panic.

The disposition of his remains was, and may still be a matter of dispute. Upon that mainly turned the fortune of his supposed slayer, an important factor in the politica fates of men, later. The Indian supposed to be slain by Colonel Johnson was found on the field next morning. There were but two men in the American army who knew Tecumseh; General Harrison, and Anthony Shane, an adopted Shawanoe, a life-long friend of Tecumseh (whose statements are accepted as to much of his life). Both saw this dead Indian and failed to identify him. He is shown by Drake, Tecumseh's biographer, to have been slain by a private, who removed much of his gorgeous finery. Harrison did not mention the fall of Tecumseh, in his dispatch of the battle, which was made a point against him later. Black Hawk, who served under Tecumseh, and fought near him, gave an account of his burial in 1832, which took place in the rear of the swamp some five miles from where he fell, the night following.

As known, the Indians always carry off their dead. They were engaged in this, passing the swamp the night after the battle; and none but the most fatuous will doubt that the body of their greatest chief, was the first to be secured by them. Wasegoboah fell by his side, and was also cared for. His wife was the great chief's sister, Tecumapease, in her way as remarkable as her brother. The spring of 1814, she with Tecumseh's widow and son, visited Quebec; and were treated with much distinction by the English. The Prince Regent sent the young Tecumseh a sword. He and his mother were commonplace Indians, and I discover no trace of them, nor of the Prophet, after he left Detroit in the Autumn of 1813.

Tecumapease also disappeared at the same time. A commanding woman, she doubtless after the way of her sex, under the hardships of savage life, finished her career in the shadow of the diminishing forest, deepened by the misfortunes of her family.

THE FALL OF DETROIT.

Dr. WILLIAM EUSTIS of Massachusetts, who had served as a surgeon of the army through the Revolution, was secretary of war, when war was declared. He yielded to Major Armstrong, author of the famous Newberg letters, in January, 1813. One of the acts of the new secretary was to bring General Hull to trial for the result of his campaign.

Among the consequences of the fifteen months war of the North-west, were three military trials of three commanders.

General Hull was charged with treason, cowardice, and gross neglect of duty, with several specifications under each; they were signed by A. J. Dallas, Judge Advocate. The court was made up of officers in the regular service, of which Major-General Henry Dearborn was president. It consisted in addition, of Brigadier-General Bloomfield, Colonels Little, Irvin, Fenwick, and Bogardus, Lieutenant-Colonels House, William Scott, Stewart, Conner, Davis, and Livingston.

The Army Judge Advocate was Philip S. Parker. He was assisted by Martin Van-Buren, who was the first of the three Presidents who had to do with the war of the North-west.

The court convened at Albany, January 3, 1814, and set almost continuously till March 28, following.

General Hull was aided by Robert Tillotson, and C. D. Colden, Esquires, and later by the famous Harrison Gray

Otis. I have always understood that the remarkable summing up, read by General Hull, his final defence, was Mr. Otis' work. He was a pronounced Federalist, a member of the Hartford Convention, a man of great power, witty, sarcastic, eloquent, pathetic. His defence would make a book of three hundred pages. He hated Madison, the war, and all on that side, and he spared nobody. McArthur and Cass appeared in their new uniforms of Brigadier-Generals of regulars. Many of the militia officers had been so transformed, and used as witnesses by the government. They were handled in a vein of mingled irony, sarcasm and ridicule. Never was there a successful campaign so fruitful of promotions as this of disaster and disgrace.

Mr. Van Buren was permitted an oral reply. A report of it was promised for publication of the trial. Mr. Van Buren may not have cared to be bound up with Mr. Otis, able as it undoubtedly was.

In its conclusions, the court found the hapless general guilty of the second and third charges, and sentenced him to be shot to death. It refused to take jurisdiction of the first—the charge of treason. On the record is this indorsement,—

" April 25, 1814.

"The sentence of the Court is approved, and the execution of it remitted.

(Signed) "James Madison."

No trial before that time, not even that of Burr for treason before Chief Justice Marshall, at Richmond, nor perhaps has any since, so moved the people of the entire republic as did this trial of Hull.

Many years later the unfortunate general published an

elaborate vindication of himself, which in the minds of the few thoughtful readers, removed the stains from his character. Perhaps nothing could redeem his conduct. At a still later day, General Cass said, that "the errors and misfortunes of the general were wholly due to imbecility." His unhappy son, who served as his aid at Detroit, was killed, while gallantly fighting, in one of the later battles of the Niagara frontier.

COMMODORE BARCLAY.

THE loss of a British fleet in what had been in fact until it occurred British water, no matter what were the odds, called for a rigid investigation, and the old man was put on trial before a naval court.

I quote two paragraphs from Coffin's Chronicle of the War in Canada —his reference to it, written by the son of a refugee.

"Barclay was the type of a British sailor. He had served under Nelson. He was noted for personal courage, and for that moral courage which at the call of duty defies despair. He was one of those old sea-dogs who lose their hold only in death. He expected more from human nature than could be found in any other nature than his own. Defeat disturbed a nature which death could not daunt. His dispatch on this occasion (his account of the battle) did not do justice by the brave men who stood by him so truly. (The men recruited from the Canadian Lake Marine are here meant.)

"Some months afterward (after the battle) he tottered before a court-martial like a Roman trophy, nothing but helmet and hauberk. He had lost an arm at Trafalgar, the other was rendered useless by a grape-shot through the shoulder. He was further weakened by several severe flesh wounds. Little wonder that men not given to such weakness shed tears at the spectacle. Little wonder that the president of the court, in returning his sword, told him in a voice tremulous with emotion, that the conduct of himself and his men had been most honorable to themselves and to their country."

Cooper, certainly a high authority, in commenting upon the battle, says this of the seamen reflected upon by the grim old commodore— " The history of this continent is filled with the instances in which men of that character have gained battles which went to increase the renown of the mother country, without obtaining credit for it. The hardy frontier men of the American lakes are as able to endure fatigue, as ready to engage, and as constant in battle as the seamen of any marine in the world. They merely require good leaders, and these the English appear to have possessed in Captain Barclay and his associates."

GENERAL PROCTOR.

The moment General Proctor saw the wild Kentuckians dash through his red lines, he seems to have lost his head and heart both. He was quite the first to escape. So quick was the pursuit he was obliged to abandon his carriage, which contained his papers, among which was found the famous speech of Tecumseh. It is supposed he saved this criminating, contemptuous philippic, to show his officers what he had to endure from the Shawanoe.

Some 250 of all arms got away from the field. The pursuit of Major Payne of Johnson's regiment, and

Colonel Todd of Harrison's staff, cut off and captured some sixty of them. The rest, after great suffering, reached Burlington Heights, at the head of Ontario.

Proctor, true to the mendacity of his nature, in his report of the loss of his army, accused his soldiers, the men of the 41st, with want of good conduct in the presence of the enemy, in consequence of which General Prevost censured them in a general order.

Proctor returned to England, where something of the real facts from Warburton and others came to be known, and he was tried on charges of cowardice and negligence in conducting his retreat.

To the disgust of the British army, he was acquitted of the first charge, convicted of the second, and suspended, with loss of pay, and was reprimanded.

The Prince Regent censured him severely in a general order, and the court also for acquitting him, and directed that the order be read at the head of every regiment of the British army, the world over, and it was.

GENERAL HARRISON.

It should perhaps be remembered that General Harrison, immediately after adjusting matters on his western border, hurried with his available force to the Niagara frontier.

For some reason never made public, Armstrong was his enemy, and purposely treated him with so many slights and indignities that he offered his resignation in the May following, which the secretary, in the absence of the President, at once accepted, against the protest of those who knew of the offer, and in disregard of the usage of the department.

Whoever makes himself familiar with the history of Harrison, and the personnel of his army, citizens of Ohio, Kentucky, and Indiana, including one or two of the regular army, will be surprised to learn the number of great and conspicuous men found in its ranks. Two of the future presidents* of the republic, while a third became the public prosecutor of the unhappy general, the surrenderer of Detroit; one vice-president, many senators, a great many representatives in Congress; several foreign ministers; governors of states and territories ; judges, national and state, with quite innumerable members of state legislatures. In the later years, to have served with Harrison against Tecumseh and Proctor, was in Kentucky, Ohio, Indiana, Michigan and Illinois, an honor only second to service in the war of the Revolution.

---

*Capt. Zachary Taylor defended Ft. Harrison.

25